"*Renunciation* is a stimulating and thought-provoking novel that exposes the reader to a wide range of religious and philosophical ideas. These ideas are unfolded through the relationship of two brothers. Will converts to Bhakti Dharma, a new religion, in 1971 while Peter becomes a religious scholar. They take different, and at times painfully divergent, paths as they each struggle to understand faith. The novel captures the spiritual quest of that decade."

—TRIPP RYDER
President
Midwest Independent Booksellers Association

"The story moves the reader to consider renunciation as both a letting go—and a letting in. Like nature, religion abhors a vacuum, and the space renunciation hallows and hollows out easily fills with something else: despair, blind devotion, violence, and possibly even hope."

—MARTHA E. STORTZ
Bernhard M. Christensen Professor for Religion and Vocation
Augsburg College

Renunciation

Renunciation

A Novel

JOHN D. BARBOUR

RESOURCE *Publications* · Eugene, Oregon

RENUNCIATION
A Novel

Resource Publications
An Imprint of Wipf and Stock Publishers
199 W. 8th Ave., Suite 3
Eugene, OR 97401

www.wipfandstock.com

ISBN 13: 978-1-62032-845-3

Manufactured in the U.S.A.

To St. Olaf College
and the University of Chicago Divinity School,
where I learned as much about religion
as I have from my family.

Renunciation—is a piercing Virtue—
The letting go
A Presence—for an Expectation—
Not now—
The putting out of Eyes—
Just Sunrise—
Lest Day—
Day's Great Progenitor—
Outvie
Renunciation—is the Choosing
Against itself—
Itself to justify
Unto itself—
When larger function—
Make that appear—
Smaller—that Covered Vision—Here—

—Emily Dickinson, no. 745

Contents

Author's Note and Acknowledgments

Bhakti Dharma, the fictional new religious movement portrayed in this novel, is loosely based on 3HO, a group following Yogi Bhajan with which I was involved for several months in 1973. I was drawn to the yoga and communal living and left the group when I decided I did not want to become a full member. In depicting Bhakti Dharma, I have taken considerable liberties, blending characteristics that were even stronger in other religious groups that I have encountered and studied, such as ISKCON ("Hare Krishna") and groups devoted to a leader believed to be divine.

The characters in this novel draw from my own life and people I have known: family members, friends, and faculty and students at several educational institutions. I transformed these raw materials of experience into a story true only in imagination.

Some terms from other languages, such as *sanyasin* and *satsang,* are italicized only the first time they appear in the text, for they passed into the ordinary speech of devotees. I am deliberately inconsistent about this, for in certain contexts these words retain their foreignness.

I am especially grateful to Gary Deason and Graham Ojala-Barbour for extensive and challenging critique. Helpful insights and encouragement were also generously offered by David Barbour, Deane Barbour, Ian Barbour, Jere Chapman, Philip Deslippe, Alvin Handelman, Christie Hawkins, Randy Jennings, Meg Ojala, Reed Ojala-Barbour, Carol Rutz, and Douglas Schuurman.

One

Give It Up for God

L AKE SUPERIOR CAN BE as flat as glass, but when the north or east wind blows for a day or two, big waves build up and crash on the shore like the ocean surf. Always the water is cold, and my father said that out on the open lake it will kill a man overboard in fifteen minutes. In the summers we would swim off Park Point, a promontory several miles long sticking out from downtown Duluth towards Wisconsin with a sandy beach and dunes. On a hot afternoon the cold water was wonderful for a few seconds. The screaming was part of the fun.

One windy August day, it was too blustery to swim. Will and I charged the waves and then ran back up to the safety of the sand beach as the waves broke. I must have been about ten, and Will was eight. Our mother warned us several times to stay well back from the water. But my brother was always testing the limits, pushing to see how far he could go before he met resistance from his parents, the ocean, or whatever held him back. He needed to know where his will ended by smashing into something that he couldn't budge.

He ran down the shore alone away from Mom. There was a slight curve in the beach there, and the waves piled up, poured in, and funneled out at a different angle. A big wave caught Will, knocked him over, and dragged him out. It was what Dad called a rogue wave, the freaky big one that doesn't fit the pattern, perhaps started by a huge iron ore ship. I screamed and ran down the beach. I could see Will's skinny body pretty far out there, and I was afraid to go after him into the big waves and riptide. It was too rough, too cold, and I didn't know how to do a lifesaving rescue. There was no one else within a hundred yards. I heard a faint cry from

1

Will, but his head was turned towards the open lake, bobbing and drifting away. My mother came running. She was a weak swimmer who almost never went in the water, but she kicked off her sandals and was in the lake up to her thighs. Then, amazingly quickly, another wave pushed Will in and smacked him down in shallow water. He was on his hands and knees as the water rushed back, clutching and dragging him. Mom scooped him up and clawed her way up the beach before the next wave. Will had been in the water less than a minute, but his teeth were chattering, his head jerked to the left and right, and his wide eyes showed his terror. Mom wrapped him in a towel and hugged him back to warmth.

When Will had recovered, she told him how glad she was that he was all right, and how frightened. She reprimanded him a little. "You can't play with Lake Superior. You have to be more careful. I don't want you ever to do this again."

Will shook his head and said, "I know, Mom. I won't do it again." He screwed up his face and thought intently for a moment, searching for a fleeting intuition. "But if I always have to be careful, it's no fun. I can't be me if I always have to be safe."

Mom scrutinized his face. She didn't say anything. Will stuck his jaw out defiantly and looked at her as if daring her to argue with him. Mom nodded. She said, "Come on, Peter, come on, Will. It's time to go home."

We got in the car and headed back across the Canal lift bridge, up the steep hill, toward home. Will looked over his shoulder and whispered softly. "Big waves, deep water, carry me away." That was the first time I almost lost him.

I found out about Will's conversion ten years ago, at the end of the summer of 1971. I had been working as a counselor at a boys' camp, leading canoe trips into Canada's Quetico Park, so I had been out of touch with my family for almost three months. I went home to Duluth for a few days to see them before I would return to Carleton College for my senior year. While I was sitting at the kitchen table eating breakfast with my mother, she handed me a letter that she said Will had written six weeks earlier, in early July.

"Peter, something incredible has happened to Will," she said. "He's had a most unusual religious experience. I think his own words explain it better than I can."

Dear Mom and Dad,

I want to share this with you first. I have found God at last. When I was driving through New Mexico with Julie, we stopped at a religious festival we had heard about from her friends in California. There I found Yogi Bhakta. He found me. His message is love. It's the message of Christianity, the message Dad has preached all these years, but Yogi Bhakta, my teacher and guru, isn't just a preacher. He embodies love, incarnates God, is God. When we do yoga and meditate, we know the love inside us. We aren't just hearing about it or mouthing words. We don't have to make it happen in the world. We don't have to do anything. Getting out the vote won't save us. Electing a Democratic President to replace Nixon won't save us. Ending the war can't make us one with God. We already are divine, but we don't know it. That's why we have a war in Vietnam, that's why politics are so bitter and hopeless. Only devotion to God can save us. I'm scared and excited. I hope you can find God too.

Love,

Will

"Wow," I said. "I'm stunned. Who is this Yogi Bhakta guy?"

"I had never heard of him either," Mom replied. "Apparently he's from India originally. His name sounds Hindu, but your father says he's a Sikh. All I know about that group is that they come from India and wear turbans. Dad did some research and found out that bhakti means devotion to the divine. That's probably not his real name. He came to the United States a year or two ago and started a new religion. We don't know where he lives or if he has a place of worship. He isn't in the news like the Hare Krishna people. He mostly travels around the West talking to groups of believers. Some of them follow him in a bus."

"Sounds like the Grateful Dead," I said. Mom looked puzzled. "That's a rock band," I added.

"I don't know what to think," she mused. "Will is so sincere and idealistic, but lately he's been drifting. Now he sounds happy to have a direction, something he cares about. But this is foreign to everything he grew up with."

"What does Dad think?"

"He's pretty upset, but he's trying to be open-minded and supportive. He knows Will is not a child and makes his own choices. Any sort of pressure or control he thinks is coming from us makes him more determined and stubborn. We try not to be judgmental, but Philip is angry and agitated, way down deep. So much of this Yogi's message, at least Will's account of it, seems like a repudiation of everything your father has believed in, stood for, and given his life to."

"I'll say. But isn't it striking that Will also presents this Yogi as the fulfillment of Christianity? He found a religion that isn't just about preaching love, but practicing it. That sounds like Jesus condemning the Pharisees. And what about the idea of incarnation? He's one-upping the Christians by saying that if you really want a God made flesh, here's a living, breathing one."

"Yes," Mom reflected, "Will was always drawn to the figure of Jesus. I think maybe you weren't so much. I remember you loved the hymn 'Immortal, Invisible, God Only Wise.'"

"Yeah, but I have to admit that a totally transcendent God is pretty abstract. He doesn't give you a hug. So how did Dad react? I mean not just to the letter, but to Will? Have you guys seen him?"

"We've only seen him once since the letter. He came back home for just one night. He had followed the Yogi around till he ran out of money."

"That figures," I muttered. "And you gave him some money, right?"

"No, he doesn't want us to support him. He came home to ask us to sell all his possessions and send him the money. And also the trust fund your grandparents set up for his college tuition. Will wants to give all his money and property to the Yogi and join a band of his followers who live in Minneapolis. They live together in what they call an ashram, worshipping the Yogi and practicing their kind of religious devotion. He's not going back to St. Olaf."

"That doesn't surprise me," I said. The previous year while I was a junior at Carleton College, Will had been a first-year student at St. Olaf, the other liberal arts college in Northfield, Minnesota. We had seen each other often that year, usually meeting downtown for coffee or pizza. He said that he didn't care about his classes. When he barely made it through his first semester, the authorities put him on academic probation. It takes a determined effort to get thrown out of a private liberal arts college, but Will had accomplished this feat by skipping nearly all of his classes, not doing any written assignments, and ignoring repeated notes and phone calls from instructors and the Dean of Students. His mind was on other things, he said. He smoked a lot of pot and tried mescaline and acid. He had a tumultuous relationship with Annika, a strikingly beautiful girl from Milwaukee who tried to stop him from using drugs and finally broke up with him. After that Will referred to her bitterly as the Frigid Nordic Princess on her throne of ice. A good guitarist, Will spent most evenings and nights jamming with a couple of other guys in the basement of Ytterboe Hall. His fellow musicians must have convinced the Dean of Students that they would amend their academic performances the following year, but Will informed the Dean that he didn't see the point of college. "It's just jumping through other people's hoops," he told me.

Will did a lot of reading on his own in the hours between waking up about noon and his nightly jams. He liked talking about philosophy, but not the academic kind. He wanted to develop his own ideas about what he called the big picture. He read Hesse, Kerouac, Kafka, Aldous Huxley, and contemporary authors I hadn't heard of, Alan Watts and Baba Ram Dass. He dismissed as "details" and "a house of cards" the kind of technical precision and logical moves that you learn in a college philosophy class. After Will was expelled from St. Olaf during exam week in May, he immediately took to the open road. He headed west, hitchhiking, to stay with an old high school friend, Julie, who was going to college in Chico, California. That connection led to another road trip through the Southwest and to Yogi Bhakta.

"I don't think Will is ready for college," my mother went on. "I think he needs to find himself first. Grow up a little. Decide where he's going after college, so he's motivated."

"That's always helpful," I agreed, although I wasn't sure where I was going after college. "But I don't think it's going to happen any time soon. From what I saw this year, he doesn't really want to be in school. Religion is what's most important to him now, I guess. But it has to be different than yours and Dad's. Devotion to a guru is his own thing. What happened when Will came home?"

"Will and your father were each trying their hardest to be honest and open about their faith, and frustrated that the other saw it so differently. Philip is so distressed about the situation in Vietnam and what the war is doing to our country. And you know how much he cares about civil rights and the race question. He believes to the marrow of his bones that God cares about justice in this world. That's why your middle name is Amos. Righteousness isn't pie in the sky; it's about how we live today. He has said that in various ways in countless sermons. He can't listen calmly when Will says that divine love is a state of mind or a feeling. As Will talked, Philip started shaking his head, twitching his hands, breathing faster. He got up and paced around the living room, trying to choose his words care-fully, wanting not to get upset. Then he said, Yogi Bhakta may be a prophet or a teacher, I don't know. I do know that he is not God. Only God is God."

"How did Will react to that?"

"He burst out, How would you know? You haven't seen him. You didn't hear him. If Jesus came back today, you would probably turn away from him because he's not wearing sandals."

"Actually Yogi Bhakta probably does wear sandals," I joked, "if shoes are any evidence about divinity."

"Your father can't laugh about a question of ultimate devotion. The biblical prophets didn't mince words about idolatry. Philip has to say that anything besides God, no matter how good it is, is not ultimate."

"Yes, Dad has always seen himself as a biblical prophet," I said with a sigh.

"Is that a criticism?"

"No, not really," I responded. "I wish I had as much conviction. I admire his courage and wisdom, among other things. But it can be hard to live up to his standard, that's for sure. And not everybody can do it his way."

I poured another cup of coffee, and Mom and I sat in silence for a moment. I mused about my own religious orientation. The previous year I had declared a religion major at Carleton. I had originally been thinking of following in my father's footsteps to become a Lutheran pastor. But I had begun to think about graduate school, that is, studying religion in a PhD program. I couldn't imagine myself as a professor, but I liked being a student and the subject matter of religion. I was fascinated by charismatic figures like St. Francis, Luther, and Dorothy Day, and by the Church's turbulent history of corruption, hypocrisy, and intolerance leading to protest and reform. Christian worship, in the bland Lutheran services to which I was accustomed, usually left me bored, although I couldn't point to anything specific to which I objected. As I studied Christianity and, the previous semester, a course on world religions, I began to doubt that I had the dedication or zeal to be a preacher. I wasn't a prophetic voice like Dad and I wasn't the pastoral type either. What could I say to a grieving parishioner who had just lost a sister to cancer, a young couple wanting to get married, or a bunch of fidgety Sunday school kids? Studying crusades, monasteries, and the Puritan experiment in New England, on the other hand, was intriguing. It engaged my intellect and imagination while allow-ing me to not take sides. I didn't have to stick my neck out. I could criticize someone's theory or summarize the scholarly literature about a theological controversy without having to say what I think, much less what God wants Christians to believe. I could talk about ethical ideals without having to practice them. Maybe if I studied religion for a few years it would lead to something I couldn't quite picture yet. Will's conversion disrupted this comfortable, detached attitude to religion. It upset me, and I didn't understand why.

"I'll ask Dad about Will at supper tonight," I said. "I hope you're okay, though, Mom." I wondered how she was dealing with this startling event in Will's life. And about how my sister was reacting. "So what does Sophie think?"

"You should ask her. Me? I admit I'm worried about Will. He has been so depressed for the last year or two, and now this sudden impulse. He's volatile, unstable, and he has lost his quirky sense of humor. I haven't seen him laugh for ages. I hope that he finds his own path to God. I believe in his essential goodness and will love him no matter what happens. But it is hard not to feel rejected, shut out of his heart. I think he sees us as temptations."

"To what?"

"To turn away from God. He wants to convert us. When I explained why I couldn't believe that the Yogi is God, he got frustrated, then angry. He tried to describe what he had experienced in New Mexico up on that mountain in the desert. Suddenly he burst out, 'Get thee away, Satan!' and stormed out of the living room. He slammed the door on the way out. We just sat there, bewildered and hurt. I cried a little, and your father kept repeating, Satan? The devil?"

"That sounds pretty un-Asian," I said. "Do Sikhs believe in hell?"

Whether they do or not, Will's religious faith blended what he had believed as a child and what appealed to him about the new religious movement led by Yogi Bhakta.

The next day, same time, same place, I was reading the paper at breakfast. I saw Will's profile go past the window as he came to the back door. He walked into the kitchen with a grin.

"Hey, look who's here," I said. "Welcome home."

"Yeah, home. I guess so." He came over to me and gave me a hug. He was my height but thinner, and strong and wiry. He had long black hair and wore hiking boots, shorts, and a dark blue sweatshirt that said "Grand Marais" on it. He looked pretty good, energetic and glowing with a deep tan. "I heard you were going to be around for a few days before you go back to college. Thought I'd say hi and tell you what I found. I hitchhiked up I-35 from the Cities."

"I heard about Yogi Bhakta from Mom and Dad. He must be quite a guy, huh?"

"He's quite a guy. A heavenly guy, holy guy. You have to see and hear him to understand. He knows the way."

"The way where?"

Will raised his eyebrows in a way that suggested disapproval. "It doesn't go anywhere. It's the way to be here, living on this earth. Traveling light. Being free of worldly attachments and cares. That stuff doesn't matter. You have to give it up for God."

"That sounds like what Christian fundamentalists say."

"It's true, whoever says it. No pain, no gain. But Bhakti Dharma is very different from Christianity. This isn't about worshipping a man who lived two thousand years ago. It's about recognizing God now, today, this very minute. Can you do that? Do you even want to do that? It might change your life."

"Well," I said, momentarily taken aback, "I really don't know." I hesitated, recognizing my brother's familiar style. In chess, he was the aggressive one, going for checkmate, while I was cautious and tried to pick off his pieces one by one. Wearing an Indian robe or thumping a Bible, he would always be Will. I decided to argue with him. "A lot of people claim to be divine, and a lot of religions say that only they can bring me happiness. Why should I believe you or Yogi Bhakta?"

"If that is a serious question, you can easily find out why. You just know it when you find God. You have faith or you don't. You look at Yogi Bhakta and see how he lives, how he loves and inspires us to love. By your fruits you shall know them. Jesus says that, too. Actually, this new religion is a lot like Christianity. It's the fulfillment of what Christians have been trying to do ever since Christ left, but it's not just talk any more."

"Okay, maybe I'll come and see the Yogi sometime. Let me know when he's around and I'll check it out. It will at least be entertaining."

Will looked disappointed, whether because I was speaking lightly of his guru or because I didn't beg to see him immediately, before I finished my coffee. I needed some time to get used to this—both the weird religion and the evangelistic brother.

We heard footsteps, and Mom came in the kitchen with her hair still wet from the shower. "Will, welcome home! I didn't know you were coming. How wonderful to see you." She gave him a warm embrace and three kisses as he bent over her. Will often brought out the nurturing, caretaking side of older people, and not only my parents. They loved him even when he drove them crazy. Maybe especially then, and they could treat him as the prodigal son. I felt uncomfortable and wondered if I had received three kisses. I couldn't remember.

"I didn't know till today that I was coming home, Mom. I just decided to see you all one more time before I move into the ashram in south Minneapolis."

He explained that he would be living in a big house near Powderhorn Park with eight other devotees. They got up at four in the morning to practice yoga, meditation, and prayer. Everyone worked a job, either for money in the outside world or doing chores around the ashram. On several evenings a week they taught yoga to the public, presenting it as the first step towards a life of complete devotion to Yogi Bhakta. "It's the appetizer before the feast," Will said. He told us that yoga is not simply physical exercise but spiritual practice, a discipline and training of the body, mind, and imagination so we can better love God.

"I'd like to try that," said my mother.

"Me, too," I said. "I think my soul is getting flabby."

"It does get that way," Will said quickly. "And the body influences the soul. Thinking about desires all the time, for money or sex or food, that is not the way. It's like trying to play guitar with your toes. Or like trying to make music with your brain alone. You can't be religious with just your spirit."

"I think your metaphors are mixed up," Mom said, "but I know what you mean. Everything is connected."

That night the five of us had dinner outside on the patio. It was a lovely evening, with a cool breeze keeping the bugs away and that late August twilight that you wish would last forever. My father had come home from his office at the church at about six and grilled some chicken, and there was a vegetarian pasta dish for Will. When Dad said grace, he added an editorial. "Heavenly Father, we ask you to be with us as we try to be reconciled with those from whom we are estranged." He paused and cleared his throat. "Amen."

Sophie was back from her summer job scooping ice cream down by the lift bridge. She told us about her adventures on a bike journey in July. I described my canoe trips. Then, with dinner finished, my father pushed his chair back, folded his arms on his chest, and asked Will about his new faith.

"What I can't understand," he said, "is how you can be drawn to a faith tradition that seems to have so little concern for social justice. You always cared about people less fortunate than yourself. You went on church youth projects and to that Quaker work camp in Kentucky. Will all that idealism and compassion still find a place in your life?"

Will frowned and said, "I'm still an idealist, and I have a lot of compassion. But I'm looking for God, not a social service agency. I've been hurting a lot since high school. Sometimes I ache because all the things my old friends care about seem so empty to me, so hollow. Monday night football. A Mustang convertible. Cold beer and hot babes. I haven't had anything to give myself to until now. Finally I've found purpose and direction."

"That's okay," I half-heartedly acquiesced. "But the thing that bothers me is the idolatry of Yogi Bhakta. It is dangerous for any religious leader to be worshipped, because then there is no room for other points of view or doubts about the faith. Yogi Bhakta may be an inspiring guy, full of charisma or wisdom, but he's still a human being."

"I just don't know," Dad mused. "Whether to argue with you, Will, and try to use reason. Or should I just listen, hold back my reaction, and let you come to your senses? I'm confident that you will eventually see the light and realize the limitations of this cult."

Will's body tensed and his brow furrowed.

"That is an incredibly condescending thing to say," he said in a strained voice, with his jaw clenched. "Do I treat your religion as a phase you're passing through?"

My father winced and paused. He realized that he had been insensitive, even insulting.

"What's a cult?" Sophie interjected.

Rather than apologize, Dad looked over at me and asked, "Can you answer that, Peter?" He slumped in his chair and looked at his plate.

"Hmmm. I don't know the dictionary definition, but I think of a cult as a small group of religious people who stick together and think outsiders are evil. They tend to be fanatical in their devotion to their version of the truth and to their leader. They think he's God."

"Isn't Christianity like that?" my sister asked.

Dad frowned. "There are all kinds of Christians, Sophie. Some of them are closed off to the world. I don't think Lutherans are like that. Our enemies are not on the outside, but inside: fear, guilt, and despair."

"But Sophie has a point," I said, doodling with my fork a little cross in some leftover barbecue sauce. "The earliest Christians were pretty much of a cult, at least in the eyes of others. The Romans thought Christians were nuts, and arrogant, too, because they wouldn't acknowledge other people's gods. What's a cult is in the eye of the beholder. It's a negative word for a new religion that the old established ones view as kooky. They also see it as a threat, because the cult is competition. These new Asian religions like Hare Krishna, and some of the Christian ones, too, the fundies and the end of the world people, steal away the sons and daughters of the churches and synagogues when we leave home."

Will had been sitting at the table silently while this discussion went on. He looked angry, with his eyes glaring and his fists clenched in his lap. He spoke slowly, as if working out something that puzzled him. "I can't believe you people are my family. I've just had the most powerful experience of my life, and you sit there analyzing it and trying to talk me out of it. Comparing it to other things like we were talking about T. V. shows or which magazine to subscribe to. Do you hear what I'm saying? This is your chance to find God."

There was a long awkward silence. Dad bit his lower lip while Mom looked anxiously at Will, twisting her cloth napkin.

"I don't know anything about Yogi Bhakta or his religion," Sophie burst out. "I just don't like it when people fight about God. Now Dad and Will are mad at each other. Next thing you know, they'll be yelling like they did a month ago. They each want to make the other one think just like him. Is that love? Why can't we get along without trying to convert each other and having to believe the same thing? Sometimes I want to forget about God. I want a religion that brings people together. If it doesn't, let's dump the whole thing."

My father looked crestfallen. After a moment he said softly, "I'm justly rebuked, Sophie. I don't always practice what I preach. I'm sure it's my failures that are partly responsible for Will's attraction to another faith."

I liked that about Dad, that he could accept responsibility or blame himself rather than getting defensive or exploding when criticized. He did tend to carry the sins of the world on his own shoulders, for better and for worse. He was often angry with Richard Nixon, corrupt political institutions, or the complacency of his congregation, but he was quick to include himself as part of the problem. While his sermons upset many of the earnest, stolid folk in his congregation, he wasn't a pompous or self-righteous person. If anything, his danger was the opposite tendency: he saw so much moral complexity that he confused people looking for a simple answer or clear direction. His awareness of mixed motives and moral ambiguity was profound, and he credited this sensibility to the influence of Reinhold Niebuhr. It was a difficult legacy for his children to understand and live out. We had a lot of idealism and plenty of scruples, a combination that can produce paralysis. In different ways all three of us, Will and Sophie and I, carried a religious inheritance that we sometimes wanted to cast off. Yet in other ways we each wanted to take another part of our parents' religious worldview and translate it into our own terms.

Until recently, Sophie's religious beliefs had been an enigma to me. She didn't like to talk about religion. She had grown up a dutiful daughter of the Reverend and Mrs. George, Philip and Hope, attending the usual youth activities in the church, but she was developing an increasingly sharp critical side. The previous spring she had decided to go to the University of Minnesota a year hence, ignoring Dad's encouragement to go to a Lutheran college. Sometimes a parent's gentle suggestions, even a raised eyebrow, are harder to defy than a firm laying down of the law. But Sophie had made up her mind.

Sophie cared about people, about their well being in all its aspects. She explained her desire to go to the U by saying, "I don't know my major but I know I want to help people." At a big university, she could get technical training to qualify as a social worker, nurse, or psychologist. Now, as we sat over the dinner dishes in the dusk, she defined her view of religion with newfound clarity. "If Christianity can be an ally in my work, I'll take as much of it as I can use and leave the rest. If Christianity, Yogi Bhakta, or any other notion of God creates conflicts and estrangement between people, I don't want anything to do with it. I would rather ditch religion than reject people for the sake of some doctrine or moral ideal demanded in the name of faith. Better to forget religion and its horrible goodness and stick to what is human."

Sophie's outburst ended that conversation. Mom gazed at her with surprise. My mother is a rather small and gentle person, and Sophie a vigorous volleyball player, bold in manner and emphatic in her opinions about many things. My father nodded thoughtfully, trying to understand how his three children could be so different from each other, and their spiritual orientations so different from his own version of Christian faith. I noticed how gray the hair at his temples was getting, although it was jet black on top. He wasn't old or young, but at some middle aged turning point. He didn't wear glasses yet, and his sharp green eyes looked deep into Sophie. She nodded her head once decisively, stood up, and began to clear the table.

Sophie probably hadn't known what she thought about religion until that dinner argument sparked her reaction. Will's conversion was a decisive event not only for him, but for everyone in the family. It fractured our assumption that we were on the same page religiously. His fervent response to Yogi Bhakta's message was a catalyst that precipitated changes in a family solution that had been suspended or frozen for many years. We would all have to leave behind the idea that we were a happy family united by the same Christian faith. Now what we had in common was a myth we each thought that we had left behind. Two myths, rather: the Christian one and the family one. Yet the stories we grow up with have a way of living on and getting told in new ways.

I went to see some old high school buddies that evening, after making plans to see Will the next day. But when I woke up late in the morning, he was gone, and so was Dad.

They had made a snap decision to take an overnight trip up the North Shore of Lake Superior. Dad had canceled an appointment and planned to be home by noon the next day. He and Will would hike, camp at Split Rock Lighthouse, and observe the stars. I was a little surprised that they didn't invite me to go with them, but Dad knew I had a lot of errands to do before I returned to college. And maybe he wanted to be with just Will.

Astronomy was their thing to do together. About a decade earlier, my father purchased a telescope, a beautiful instrument that he ordered from Germany. It was covered with maroon leather and had little tattoo-like engravings of the planets on the leather. The telescope was mounted on a substantial tripod and looked ancient, like something Galileo could have used. Will got very interested in astronomy at that time, and this passion immediately became a bond between him and my father. After one of their early trips, Will announced proudly that they had seen the moons of Jupiter, "four of them, lined up like shish kabobs on a stick." They talked about the constellations fondly as if they were old friends who had moods and eccentric habits.

Dad would smile proudly, pleased to see Will so enthusiastic about his avocation, one that he had shared with his own father. For Dad, astronomy was connected with his religious sensibility; he spoke of "the handiwork of God" and "the architecture of the heavens." He didn't view the constellations as a logical proof of the existence of a divine Maker, but they evoked his awe and reverence for the mystery of Creation. Sophie and I never caught the astronomy bug, but for years, Will and Dad headed off to dark places to view an eclipse, meteor shower, the Milky Way, or another celestial sight. They especially loved the cliffs and hills above Lake Superior, with their unobstructed views of the horizon and distance from the light pollution of Duluth and Two Harbors. Now Dad had persuaded Will to go on another stargazing expedition, no doubt hoping that their shared love of the heavens would allow them to stay connected even if they disagreed about how to get to Heaven.

The next day, Dad returned home alone in mid-morning. He looked defeated, limp, and tired. I had been running errands, doing laundry, and packing. Mom and I stood in the kitchen listening to him report on the ill-fated trip. They had seemed to be having such a good time, he said sheepishly. They made a vegetarian chili at their campsite and Will meditated for an hour. When it was dark, they set up the telescope on the top of the cliff near the lighthouse. It was a calm evening, with only a faint westerly breeze blowing from the land, so the wave action was slight and it was strangely quiet. With a new moon, conditions were ideal for seeing constellations and the Milky Way. They observed Draco the Dragon, the scorpion, the Great and Little Bear, and other celestial chums. Under bright stars, they crawled into the tent and fell asleep.

"Will woke up at first light," Dad said. "I heard a zipper buzz and Will rustling around, and then his footsteps went off towards the cliff. I was immediately alert. It had clouded up and the air was misty. I crawled out of the tent, got dressed, and noticed that Will had taken the telescope. There wasn't much use for it in those conditions. As I came out of the woods, I saw Will sitting close to the cliff, meditating. I didn't want to disturb him, but I didn't see the telescope. I was puzzled. I walked over to him to see what was going on, where he had put it. I looked all around. I asked him, 'Will, where's our scope?' He didn't answer. I just stood there, wondering. Then he lifted his arm and pointed far away, towards the east and a sliver of pink and red below the clouds. I looked out, and then down at the waves.

"Oh, no, Will. You threw it in Lake Superior? Are you crazy? Why?"

Will calmly put his hands in prayer position, against his chest. He bowed to the east, got up slowly, and said, "I didn't want it in my life any more. It holds me back. It's an attachment. I'm not a kid anymore, Dad. I can't play our old games again."

"But why did you destroy it? Why not leave it for others to enjoy? Like me, for example?"

"It was really my telescope, wasn't it? No one else uses it."

"I would use it. It's valuable. And for me it has sentimental value. We saw the moons of Jupiter on your tenth birthday."

My father paused at this point of his story and slumped into a kitchen chair. All his energy seemed to drain away. My mother put her hand gently on his and said, "Then what happened, Philip?"

"Will said again, I'm not a kid any more. Then it was like a shutter came down. Will went into himself. He wouldn't talk to me any more. I sat down and waited, not knowing what else to do. After a few minutes, he got up from his meditation pose and walked back to the tent. He threw on his coat. He hadn't brought much else with him except the clothes on his back. The camping gear was our family equipment. He said to me, 'I'm going, Dad. I've got to move on.' He started walking toward the park entrance and I followed him, asking what was wrong. He was icy cold and determined. I begged him to talk to me. But he just looked back once and said, 'No, Dad. Leave me alone.' I went back to the campsite and packed up. When I drove out of the park, he was gone. He must have hitchhiked through Duluth and headed back to the ashram. I guess he's not stopping here."

Both of my parents were upset by this turn of events. And this, even more than concern about Will, disturbed me. No, it pissed me off. He was always dominating their emotional lives, making them worry, giving them grief. For the next two days, until I left for college, a dark cloud settled over the house. They pretended it wasn't there, and that they cared about what my friends were up to or what academic courses I would enroll in. They really did care, I'm sure. But I could see their anxious preoccupation in my father's knotted forehead and the tiny lines of tension around the outside of Mom's eyes. They were wondering whether it was their fault that Will had left so suddenly, as if in revulsion against his childhood home.

"If only he would have given me a chance to talk to him," my father muttered to himself the next morning as he left the house for his office at the church. And at dinner that night, he said, "Maybe I should have apologized. Would that have made a difference?"

"Apologize for what?" I asked.

I hated to see this self-recrimination as they took upon themselves responsibility for everything painful or difficult in Will's life, including his moods and impulses. I said, "I think whatever Will is going through is going to happen regardless of what you two say or do. You have to let go of Will and of the illusion of control."

"Let go?" my mother wondered. "Of my child? Of my responsibility and my love for him? Peter, wait until you have a son or daughter. Then you will understand."

"Do you know the Beatles' song called 'Let it Be'? It has simple lyrics but a profound message. Sometimes you have to give up your need to do something and trust in God or the universe."

"The grace of doing nothing," said my father. "I remember an essay about that by my teacher, the other Niebuhr brother. There's a lot of wisdom in that idea. But letting go can also be a cop-out, dodging one's duty, lazy avoidance. That's what I'm wrestling with right now. What is my responsibility? How do I go on loving Will when he seems not to want us in his life? Before I leave God to do the rest, what is my part?"

"I don't know," I said. "I have no idea."

We sat for a minute in silence. Then my mother spoke quietly. "Will was also letting go of something when he destroyed the telescope. It's like he was blinding himself, or one kind of vision." She closed her eyes for a moment, and then went on. "I don't know, either, Philip, what my part is. But I think you put our challenge nicely. We must figure out what we need to do and trust God to do the rest. That's what it means to let it be."

The next day I left home, catching a ride to Northfield with a friend who was also returning to college.

Yogi Bhakta wanted his followers to give up a lot for God. I found out later that he sometimes posed difficult tests for individuals hesitating to make a commitment. He asked certain prospective members of his group to donate all their possessions and wealth to the movement. This was an expectation for anyone who called himself a *sanyasin* (renunciate), although not a duty strictly imposed on ordinary members. Yogi Bhakta presented dramatic challenges to particular people, for instance asking them to make a vow. He told certain couples that they were well suited and should consent to an arranged marriage. He commanded some of his followers to adopt a specific vocation or move to an ashram in a distant city. Yogi Bhakta interrupted individuals' plans and directed them to arrange their lives according to his instructions. His demands were often posed publicly in a dramatic proclamation that put a person on the spot. The challenge was sometimes refused, and a vacillating hanger-on slunk off elsewhere. But for those people who responded affirmatively to the guru's challenges, the test usually made their commitment firm and long lasting. Several times over the next few years, Will told me of sanyasins who had entered the movement in response to the Yogi's version of a targeted altar call.

I was at first puzzled as to why a guru would make it difficult to join his movement. A striking example of this was the Sikh garb adopted by hard-core believers. The white turban, dagger, and uncut hair and beard visibly marked off the members of Bhakti Dharma in American society. As I later began to see parallels to the early Christians I was studying, I realized that costly demands can strengthen a religious group in several ways. Strict rules of observance clearly demarcate a group and separate its members from ordinary society. Some people don't want to fit in with the rest of the world. The Yogi's demands for a distinct identity and genuine sacrifice eliminated lackadaisical seekers who were just curious or looking for good vibes. A demand for renunciation increased a believer's commitment to the movement, releasing the rush of energy and enthusiasm necessary to make a leap of faith. Those who were willing to sacrifice their old life found themselves in the movement's inner circle, surrounded by other true believers who praised their resolution. They were rewarded with feelings of shared love and belonging to an intimate community just as they were finding it difficult to maintain old friendships and interests. It was like being accepted into a new and ideal family that was free of the faults of the family that they had just rejected. They called each other brother and sister and obeyed a paternal figure who was always right.

Self-sacrifice wasn't an obstacle for some people; it was a huge part of the appeal. Most converts to a new religious movement had either a secular background or grew up in a liberal church or synagogue. These people wanted to make a commitment that cost them something, not just to show up for worship once a week. They didn't want easy. Cult members were like the early Christians who turned away from established Roman practices of piety to give their lives as martyrs for a persecuted fringe movement. Later, after Constantine adopted Christianity as the official religion of the Roman Empire in the fourth century, the Church became entangled with the economic and political powers of the day. Then a few hardy souls headed out to the desert to live as hermits and monks, leaving it all behind. The people in my generation who accepted Yogi Bhakta's demands resemble those early Christians, tapping into the spiritual energy released when they denied themselves the usual pleasures and satisfactions offered by their society. Rather than flowing out to drugs, sex, rock and roll, and material acquisitions, a convert's desires turned inwards, to an ideal of how he ought to be, and to God and a guru.

During the year after Will's conversion I read two magazine articles about Yogi Bhakta, one by a disgruntled former member of his movement and one by a reporter in Los Angeles. The writer of the anti-cult essay was bitter about the sacrifices she had made. She had given Bhakti Dharma her inheritance of several hundred thousand dollars and worked in their community garden for more than a year until she "came to her senses." She received no wages and developed an iron deficiency that left her weak. She had lost eighteen pounds, stopped menstruating, and often felt dizzy. She fled her ashram and now asserted that her desire for service had been manipulated and her trust abused. In striking contrast, the article by the Los Angeles journalist quoted several Bhakti Dharma members who claimed that their acts of self-sacrifice, including working to exhaustion in a community garden, were expressions of gratitude and devotion. "We do it for Yogi Bhakta," said one interviewee. "It's a sacrifice I'm glad to make. Why would I want to be part of a religion that doesn't demand everything that I have to give?"

Will gave all he had to God. Was this self-transcendence or self-destruction? For a decade that mystery has gripped me. Now, as I try to understand how and why my brother died, that's what I most want to know.

Two

Losing the Past

I DIDN'T SEE MUCH of Will during my senior year at Carleton. I was excited about my academic work, and that autumn I decided to go to graduate school in religious studies. Christian history interested me, as well as literature, psychology, and Buddhism. Bradley Scott, a professor who had gone to the University of Chicago, recommended it as a place that encouraged interdisciplinary studies and comparative religions. It was the home of the great Romanian scholar Mircea Eliade, who founded the field of History of Religions, and it also had a strong tradition of liberal Christian theology. I could study widely for a year or two, get a masters degree, and decide how to focus my studies for doctoral work. I applied to Chicago and several other schools, mailing off my materials during Christmas vacation.

That autumn, Will was still riding his conversion high. He telephoned twice in September, hoping that I would see the light. Both times he gave me a little sermon about the Yogi's amazing spiritual powers and invited me to go to California to see him as soon as possible. We could leave the next day. When I was non-committal and jocular, he abruptly hung up. It was not a subject he could take lightly.

Will cut off his old Duluth and St. Olaf friendships, and he didn't see Mom and Dad until Christmas. He told them that he had twice hitch-hiked west to see and hear Yogi Bhakta at something called a Celebration of Divine Love, a long weekend of yoga, *satsang* (teaching and discussion), chanting, and meditation. He also visited a number of ashrams that autumn, hitchhiking to the East Coast and spending a week or two in Philadelphia, Syracuse, and Boston. He must have been checking out those places, trying to decide whether to make a commitment to join an ashram there. The ashrams welcomed Will for a while, but something happened in each place that made him move on. If he had to make a deeper commitment in order to stay, he wasn't ready to do that.

I was at home with Sophie and my folks for a few days before Christmas. Will had told my mother on the telephone that he would visit at some point, but he gave no definite commitment. I could tell from my parents' distracted manner that they were watching for him. When Dad was in the living room, supposedly reading a book or making notes for a sermon, I would find him gazing out the front window at the drifting snow. Mom rushed to answer the telephone and looked disappointed when she found out who it was. Her eyebrows dropped, she exhaled slowly, and her tone of voice fell slightly. Christmas is a hectic time in a minister's home, so my parents weren't at a loss for ways to stay busy. Still, there was a sense of anxious waiting, even foreboding, as we neared our first Christmas since Will had become involved with Bhakti Dharma.

On December 23, Will appeared in the early afternoon, having gotten a ride with the brother of a woman in the Minneapolis ashram. He was wearing blue jeans, several cotton sweatshirts, Red Wing hunting boots, and a battered army surplus overcoat. He had on a lot of layers, but he didn't look ready for winter. Will was less exuberant than he had been in the summer, and was brooding and preoccupied. We sat in the living room for half an hour as he told us about his situation. He had been on the move for several months and planned to join the Minneapolis ashram on New Year's Day. He would accept the rules of ashram discipline and work on community chores until he found a paying job. He thought it would be good for him to live in one place and have some structure in his day. "I've got a lot of new energy I need to focus," he added. With one leg resting on the other knee, he nervously twisted his bootlaces around his fingers and spoke without much expression or emotion. After reporting his plan, he said he wanted to perform devotions to Yogi Bhakta. He went upstairs to his bedroom, closed the door, and we heard nothing for the rest of the afternoon except for when he chanted over and over a four-syllable mantra: Sa Ta Na Ma.

When supper was ready, Mom asked me to call Will. I knocked on his door. After a few seconds I heard, "Yes, I'm here." I opened the door and saw him in the lotus position, meditating in front of a candle, a picture of Yogi Bhakta, and a dish with three pennies in it. On the floor beside him was a pile of beads. He stood up and said, "I'm ready," and we went downstairs. He seemed to be avoiding eye contact.

Sophie gave Will a big hug. "I'm glad to see you, brother, it's been too long." Will didn't respond with words, but he looked in her eyes and smiled.

Mom had made a vegetarian stew to accommodate Will's diet, with cornbread and a salad. Dad said a simple grace and we began eating. There was tension in the air as we cast about for a conversational gambit that would be neither painful nor trivial. I had the feeling that my academic interests and Sophie's whirl of activities were part of a lesser, material world that was not important to Will. They seemed insignificant even to me at that moment. Everyone praised the food lavishly. Dad described the freezing over of Lake Superior at an unusually early date and the effect that this had on shipping and dockworkers in the port. Sophie was excited about a friend's birthday party on New Year's Eve. Will listened and nodded, but he was aloof, thinking of something far away. He was with us physically, but not present; he seemed to be still meditating, his eyes a little glazed. When I asked him whether he knew what kind of work he would do in the ashram, he said that he didn't know and would be glad to do whatever was needed. Mom asked him about his yoga practice, but he didn't say much. "I'm working on it. It's pretty intense." It was an awkward, halting conversation. We sat around the table for our "after dinner fifteen," as Dad called it, the minimum number of minutes of verbal interaction that showed we were communing, not just eating. Then Will pushed back his chair, leaving his arms straight out, holding the edge of the dining table. He said quietly, "I've got to head back to the ashram. I wish I could stay longer."

"Now?" My mother looked alarmed. "Will, it must be twenty below zero with the wind chill. Can't you wait until tomorrow?"

"No, I must be going. The ashram is my true family now, my spiritual family where I feel loved."

"Can't you stay through Christmas Eve? It's such a wonderful service, with the candles and Dad leading us through the liturgy."

"No, I'm clear about what I need to do. The ashram is where I want to celebrate God coming into the world. We're going to have a special *puja* or worship offering. Could one of you drive me over to highway 35, and I'll hitch a ride back to the Cities?"

Everyone hesitated. Dad said tentatively, "Do you think that's a good idea in these conditions?"

"I'm going, one way or the other."

Mom and Dad were speechless, still, their eyes shifting between Will and the dishes on the table. They didn't want to beg him to stay, and they could hardly bear to see him leave. It was a foolish decision to depart in this dangerous Arctic weather, but it was obvious that Will would not change his mind.

"I'll take him," I said gruffly.

Will grabbed his bag, which he had not unpacked, gave Mom and Dad a hug, and headed outside without a word. There were tears in my mother's eyes. I put on my coat and boots and grimly walked out to our ancient Volvo station wagon, struggling to contain my rage.

As soon as we had turned the corner and were out of sight of the house, I lashed out at him. "God damn it, Will. Can't you think of anyone beside yourself? You are one selfish asshole, you know that? Can't you see how much what you are doing hurts Mom and Dad? To come here for a few hours and then leave before Christmas, telling them there is no love here."

"I didn't say that, Peter. I just said I want to be with my people at the ashram. That's my spiritual family now. That's who I choose to be with. I won't be manipulated by guilt. Why are you so upset, anyway?"

"You are a real prick, I think, a monster of egotism. All your spiritual talk is bullshit. You romanticize an ideal family because you are utterly incapable of appreciating the one you have. You talk about love, love, capital L love, but you can't do the one thing that would express love to your own parents. Have a goddamned Merry Christmas with your elves and Indian Santa."

We drove in silence through deserted streets piled high with snow, down from our middle class neighborhood on the hill, through a commercial district and a working class residential area, and we came to the entrance ramp to the freeway. It was about eight o'clock and there wasn't much traffic. "Call home if you can't hitch a ride," I said to Will as he shouldered his bag and stepped out of the car. He was strangely composed, not looking at me, his jaw clenched. He got half way out of the car and turned back to me.

"Thanks for the ride, Peter. Good luck with your final semester. I'll pray for you, brother."

"Yeah, right. Groove on, baby. I hope you get enlightened. So long, kid."

He closed the door and I drove home. Still agitated, I rejoined the family as they finished washing the dishes. I felt heaviness in my chest and throat, a weight of unspoken sadness, and again a surge of anger when I saw my mother staring vacantly at a clock on the wall.

I'm not a very angry person; at least I don't often express my irritations or resentments. I take after my father that way. For him, anger is an "unproductive" emotion and a selfish demand. He is the child of missionaries to Africa who believed that anger is not a permissible feeling and usually a sin. I can't remember Dad losing his temper at a person. His only expressions of anger are directed at situations of social injustice. In the 1960s he was agitated about racism and the Vietnam War, and he fumed about his congregation's indifference to poverty on nearby Indian reservations or dangerous conditions in the taconite mines. But even in those cases, he would catch himself and say, "I'm not angry at individuals, but frustrated at the situation. I don't label people as sinners, but I must criticize acts or conditions that violate God's will for humanity." Dad had renounced the right to get angry.

Although I fought my impulse to express it, I was seething at Will that Christmas vacation. Above all, I blamed him for hurting my parents. He was morally wrong, a bad son, while I was taking care of them, wanting to protect them from his selfish, irresponsible behavior. The day before I left Duluth, however, something happened to complicate and confuse my high-minded outrage.

Sophie had been unusually solicitous of our parents, offering to help around the house and suggesting a game of cribbage or scrabble. She didn't really like games very much, and I knew that she was trying to give Mom and Dad the feeling that, yes, we really are a loving family, even if Will isn't with us now. I thought, She is being the perfect daughter. Sophie is doing this for them to make up for Will. In spite of her good intentions, I felt mad at her, too. My chest got hot and I wanted to yell, "This is bogus, false, phony. Your niceness isn't real, Sophie, it's bullshit."

After I returned to Carleton, I kept thinking about why I felt so angry with Sophie as well as Will. Only now do I realize what my sister triggered in me. My anger was genuine but it was also phony. I thought of it as righteous indignation, an ethical reaction on behalf of Mom and Dad. Yet there was something fishy about it, like Sophie's theatrical eagerness to play a boring game rather than go out with her friends. She was well meaning and compassionate, however, while I was just pissed off and confused about what I really felt. They were qualitatively different forms of bullshit.

My way of getting angry is like my father's: it has to be on behalf of someone else. Suppressed anger erupts when we can find a pretext outside ourselves, such as a person who has been harmed or an unjust situation.

Then bottled up fury comes out as moral indignation and harsh judgment. Then I can feel virtuous, like Jesus with a whip driving the moneylenders from the Temple. It was a relief to be able to blame Will for hurting my folks.

My family's Christian disavowal of anger created some big gaps in self-knowledge, an inherited blind spot. Now I recognize how furious I was at Will for dominating my parents' attention and changing the terms of our relationship. Something else was involved, too. Will's choice of a religious path evoked in me painful feelings of ambivalence about my decision to pursue an academic vocation. I, too, believed I was going to have to renounce something. I resented Will for having religious faith when I thought I would have to leave mine behind.

It was difficult to get reliable information about Yogi Bhakta or his outfit, Bhakti Dharma. The name of this religious organization is roughly translated as the truth and way of life (literally, "path") of devotion. It also suggests the teachings of Yogi Bhakta. For several years my main source of information was my brother, who was full of fervid enthusiasm but often sketchy about mere facts. I found a few magazine articles about Yogi Bhakta by two ex-members, but they were quite biased. Most helpful was a graduate student of anthropology at the University of Chicago who was researching new religions inspired by Asian traditions. I had lunch with this man, Samuel Nielsen, several times in the Divinity School coffee shop in the basement of Swift Hall. Sam had spent a year doing fieldwork on Bhakti Dharma and other cults and had gone to India to trace Yogi Bhakta's early life. Apparently the authority of an Indian guru does not rest on biographical accuracy about his life before his spiritual leadership. Sam had to sort through a lot of ambiguous rumor, hagiographical legend, and hostile criticism. Drawing from Sam's research, the journalistic accounts, and my own conversations with Will and other cult members, I can reconstruct the guru's career up to 1971, when Will became one of his followers.

Yogi Bhakta was born in 1925 in the Punjab region of northern India. Originally named Ustaad Singh Talib, he came from a well to do Sikh family of civil servants and pursued a university education to prepare him for a career in a government department. He began to work in the Indian Ministry of Education soon after the partition of India and Pakistan in 1947, and was responsible for maintaining standards in high schools in the

Delhi area. In the 1950s he studied and worshiped with several religious groups, and by 1960 he was teaching his own unique blend of spiritual practices.

The Punjab is a region where Hindu, Muslim, and Sikh traditions mingle and influence each other. Many eclectic and syncretistic movements have claimed to integrate the best of these traditions or to express their common core. Central in most of these new cults is the tradition of bhakti, from the Sanskrit word that means devotion to God. For these groups, dedicated service of a particular deity is the best way to realize permanent union with the divine. Many Hindu cults worship Vishnu in his incarnations, especially Krishna and Rama. Hindu bhakti traditions engage in extended communal chanting of the names of God, and visual images of God are bathed or symbolically "fed." A Bengali tradition of Krishna worship inspired a missionary movement to the West, The International Society for Krishna Consciousness (ISKCON), popularly known as Hare Krishna. Their leader, A. C. Bhaktivedanta Swami Prabhupada, arrived in New York City in 1965. His followers glorified God with song, dance, and offerings of food and other gifts, expressing their passionate devotion to the divine with tears and laughter.

Other traditions of devotion, such as Sikh ones that influenced Yogi Bhakta, praise the transcendent God "without attributes" and bless his Name, especially in song. Yogi Bhakta carried on the Sikh emphasis on sound as a preferred way of knowing and praising God, teaching poetry, music, and chanting. Eventually a disciple who practices bhakti should experience a transformed consciousness, recognize God's presence everywhere, and adore God fervently with all the senses, heart, and mind.

Yogi Bhakta resembled Hafiz, Kabir, Rumi, Nanak, and other mystics and poets who drew from the rich expressions of bhakti in several religions to create a personal synthesis. He had personal magnetism and charisma that made people want to be near him, follow his instructions, and devote their lives to worshipping him. He started out in Delhi in the late 1950s, teaching his followers that the old religions were tearing India apart and had become obstacles to the peace and love that God wished for humankind. This message took root in a few hundred Muslims, Sikhs, and Hindus who had been displaced by the Partition and were anxious about India's future.

The eclectic nature of Yogi Bhakta's message and his effort to include so much within his movement was controversial. He taught kundalini yoga, which many Sikhs mistrusted as a form of Hinduism. He asked his followers to dress in white cotton tunics and turbans and to grow a beard, a Sikh appearance that limited his appeal to others. In his first years as a spiritual leader, his devotees practiced a form of ecstatic circle dancing resembling Sufi rituals, raising the ire of Hindus and other Indians who thought that Muslims should emigrate to their own country, Pakistan, and take their practices with them. Yogi Bhakta's attempt to foster peace and reconciliation among India's quarreling religions made him a target of conservatives in all the traditions from which he drew. Preaching harmony and good will, he infuriated just about everyone he did not convert. The movement received threats of violence and in 1967 several of his followers were brutally beaten by mobs.

At the same time that he became a trigger for conflict among Indians, Yogi Bhakta began to attract the notice and devotion of Westerners. Backpackers on their way to or from Nepal, hippies recovering from excessive drug use, and a few musicians and wealthy patrons of Ayurvedic health resorts were drawn to the Yogi's intriguing blend of yoga, meditation, spiritual teaching, and emphasis on love and world peace. They came to adore this man who taught them profound spiritual truths and seemed to incarnate divine love and elicit a passionate devotion that had been dormant in them. In March 1969, a bomb threat forced the evacuation of one of his public presentations in Mumbai, deeply disturbing Yogi Bhakta. Attending this event was a wealthy couple from Santa Barbara, and they persuaded the Yogi to come to California for the summer and offer an intensive yoga retreat. They paid his travel expenses, arranged the logistical details of the retreat, and advertised it. Accompanied by his wife, two children, and three trusted disciples, Yogi Bhakta arrived in Los Angeles in June 1969.

After teaching two month-long yoga retreats, Yogi Bhakta shifted his focus, in the first of several transformations of his message and organization. He had a remarkable capacity to reinvent himself and adapt his movement to a new environment. He realized that his message resonated particularly well with two overlapping groups of young Americans: college students, especially those unsatisfied with conventional career goals, and people taking psychedelic drugs. To students losing interest in academic achievement, Yogi Bhakta said, In my movement you can learn what is truly important, and your knowledge will serve other people. To the hippies and druggies, he proclaimed, I can blow your mind with a high that lasts. I will give you knowledge beyond ordinary consciousness. Let me show you a better way than drugs to know ecstasy and bliss. Try it and see.

Most of the recruits to Bhakti Dharma were double dropouts: they had lost faith in the traditional American dream and embraced an alternative youth culture, and then wearied of the gratifications offered by the counterculture.

Like other gurus who found ready disciples in the late 1960s and 70s, Yogi Bhakta fed a hunger for spiritual experience that Christian churches did not satisfy. Young people wanted to have faith in something, but they could only do so if they had what they considered to be an authentic personal experience. When they meditated, did yoga, and chanted together, they felt in touch with the divine. Or that the divine was within them. Yogi Bhakta did not worry about precise theological distinctions, and his varied statements about God and himself appealed to different types of religious personality and need. In the beginning there was no need for theological hair-splitting or criteria of orthodoxy.

Gurus, swamis, and yogis tapped into a widespread feeling of disillusionment with American politics at that historical moment. Many events contributed to the feeling that political action was not going to change the problems at the heart of American life. A lot of people in my generation were frustrated by the seemingly endless war in Vietnam and disappointed when Richard Nixon was elected in 1968 and 1972. We were shocked by the assassinations of Martin Luther King, Jr. and Robert Kennedy, and we sensed that the hopeful promise of the early 1960s was not going to be realized, for instance when civil rights legislation did not end racism. Some young Americans invested their wavering hopes in a small religious community, believing that its way of life would demonstrate to the larger society how people could live together for a higher purpose than individual gain or pleasure. Peace and love could be more than individual feelings; they could shape the common life of a group of people committed to a spiritual ideal. They would start small, in a face-to-face community, and the effects would ripple outwards and eventually transform the larger society. That ideal motivated college dropouts to put on Hare Krishna's orange robes, join a rural commune of Jesus people, or sell flowers in traffic to earn money for the Reverend Sun Myung Moon.

During the 1970s, Yogi Bhakta spent most of his time in residences attached to places of worship in Oakland and Los Angeles and at a mountain retreat in Colorado. He selected his most able disciples to teach yoga and start ashrams in major urban centers and near large state universities. Bhakti Dharma ashrams sprouted in the Midwest in Chicago, Minneapolis, Madison, Ann Arbor, and Bloomington, Indiana, as well as big cities on the east and west coasts. According to Sam, the Chicago anthropology student, most of the fifty or sixty ashrams in the mid-1970s had about a dozen residents, usually single adults but also married couples and a few children. Each ashram had a lead teacher and director. Some of these leaders called themselves sanyasins, the Indian term for those who, usually at an elderly age, renounce family, possessions, and their earlier life in order to devote themselves to God. This role is foreign to Sikh tradition in India, which affirms the role of householder and does not support a celibate order of priests. Yet Yogi Bhakta sometimes referred to his lead teachers as sanyasins, even when they were quite young or married. He wanted his followers to renounce the world, but he was realistic and flexible about how much each individual was expected to give up. This made for inconsistencies and confusion. The conflict between the ideal of self-sacrifice and the practical needs of an organized community would later disrupt the Bhakti Dharma movement and shape Will's destiny.

Also living in each ashram were devotees who had not yet made a vow to join the group but were considering doing so, or just learning about yoga and meditation, or experimenting with a communal lifestyle for a period of time. All ashram members practiced *sadhana*, an early morning session of yoga, rituals, and devotions, and participated in public sessions of yoga instruction several evenings a week. Unlike the Hare Krishna movement, Bhakti Dharma did not proselytize for new members, but rather waited for sincere inquirers to make a fuller commitment to the movement. Thousands of people practiced yoga for a few evenings and moved on to other things. Hundreds lived in an ashram for a few months before drifting away to another cult or back to their former life. And for a few people, powerful experiences of kundalini yoga, meditative trance, or surging love for Yogi Bhakta persuaded them to devote their lives to this guru and his teachings. This was what had happened to Will in New Mexico during the summer festival. He felt immediately that he had to give his whole life to the man who seemed to embody God's love and elicit from him longings that he had never known. Yogi Bhakta evoked a newfound depth of commitment in my brother, and now Will wanted to find a way of life that would sustain and express his gratitude, joy, and desire to give himself away.

Yogi Bhakta demanded a lot, both in terms of disciplined practice and what he asked devotees to give up. It was quite a shock to the typical American college student or drug-addled hippy to arise at four in the morning for yoga, eat a vegetarian diet, and practice celibacy before marriage. Yogi Bhakta discouraged television, sports, popular music, and other frivolous pursuits. Yet for those who joined Bhakti Dharma, the strict discipline was a large part of the movement's appeal; it gave their lives a focus and intensity they lacked when they could do whatever they wanted, yet had no goal beyond the next momentary gratification. Yogi Bhakta promised his devotees a future for which they were glad to lose their pasts. Giving up the past, however, is not something that can be done at once, like quitting smoking. It is a choice that needs to be reenacted in a believer's life again and again like a ritual.

In March of 1972, a few months before I graduated from college, I received a telephone call from my father. He invited me to join him and Mom at a public forum on new religious movements in Minneapolis. Dad had been contacted by a member of a group called the Cult Exposure Network, who had heard that a Lutheran minister in Duluth had a son who was involved with an Indian religious group. The announced purpose of the meeting was to educate the public about the dangers of cults and to share resources and provide support for the families of cult members. Mom and Dad were going to find out more about this organization and wondered whether I wanted to go. They could detour through Northfield and pick me up on their way to the meeting.

The forum was held on a Tuesday evening in a bland chain hotel on Highway 494, the ring road around the Twin Cities. An anemic meeting room held about a hundred chairs facing a table with three speakers. The room was about half full, and most of the audience looked about fifty, no doubt the parents of young people in fringe religious groups. A heavy-set, gray haired man in a black suit named Henry Parker chaired the meeting. He said he was a professional psychologist and had placed "PhD" after his name in the publicity for the event.

Parker began by asserting that this was not an anti-religious meeting. Rather, it was an organized effort to protect true religion. There is a very simple distinction between true religion and a cult, he argued. "Religion is based on free choice. A cult practices mind control. The young people in cults have been brainwashed. They have been coerced in ways that resemble the brainwashing techniques done to American prisoners of war captured by the Chinese during the Korean War, brave soldiers who, under torture, adopted Communism. The stories that you will hear this evening will prove that cults can take away a person's freedom and make him accept what he would never believe if he were in his right mind. After the testimony of two ex-cult members, let's talk about what we can do to rescue our young people."

The first speaker, Wilfred, was a guy my age with a pronounced Southern accent and a quiet, intense, manner. He had been a member of Reverend Sun Myung Moon's Unification Church for two years. During that period he said he was "a zombie, a robot," blindly following orders from Church leaders. "Looking for a different future, I lost my past." Absolute faith and complete obedience were the highest virtues in this group, Wilfred asserted. The Church supported him at a time when he felt utterly alone and hopeless. He spoke with bitterness of the way his longing for love and community had been exploited by promises of perfect harmony and bliss in a "heavenly marriage." The Unification Church assigned him a bride and a wedding date. His turning point came when, the day before a mass wedding, he rebelled against marrying a complete stranger. Without telling anyone in the Church, he packed his bags and moved back to his parents' home in Mobile. He was so ashamed of having wasted two years and so furious at the Church for abusing his trust that he had spent the past year working to expose its frauds. "I found my purpose," he said, "at least for the time being, in thwarting the purposes of the Unification Church. I don't want others to go through the hell I have endured."

The second speaker, a lively redhead named Jessica, had been a member of the Hare Krishna movement, the International Society for Krishna Consciousness. She asserted that her brain had been chemically altered by this group's practices. A Spartan diet of rice and carrots left her weak with hunger. She had spent up to fourteen hours a day selling flowers on the street and proselytizing, at the same time engaging in early-morning and evening devotions. Exhaustion and prolonged sleep deprivation caused auditory hallucinations, so that she thought that she could hear the voices of Hindu saints and gods speaking through ordinary people she met. Sleep deprivation, she added, was one of the main techniques used by Communist interrogators attempting to reeducate prisoners. She also claimed that Hare Krishna's practice of rhythmic, repetitive chanting of mantras for up to two hours was a form of hypnotism. "I couldn't think straight, see clearly, or know what I was feeling," she said. "I thought I was in an ecstatic, mystical state of union with God. I heard chanting all the time in my head, like a radio I couldn't turn off. I didn't know what was going on."

Jessica's exit from the Hare Krishna group had come about through a kidnapping and forced "deprogramming" organized by her family just a few months earlier. One evening, when she was returning to the ashram where she lived in Madison, a van pulled up and three athletic men forced her in. "I tried to scratch their eyes out," she said, "I was that desperate to stay in my illusory dream world." She spent the next four days with a man and woman who were mental health professionals specializing in adolescent disorders. Jessica was vague about exactly what her deprogramming involved, saying only that it was "not pleasant but convincing" and a form of "tough love." She was grateful to have been rescued. "It's pretty ironic," she concluded, "but I saw the light when I became an apostate. The truth set me free, and I renounced my religious loyalty." Her voice wavering, Jessica explained that she was still in transition. "Right now I have no religious beliefs. Perhaps I will go back to my synagogue some day, I don't know. But whether I turn to Judaism or another religion or no religion, I will never again give up my identity or my freedom. There are already so many threats to independence, like mass advertising, government surveillance, and jobs that turn you into a robot. We don't need religions that take away your conscience."

"Thank-you, Jessica," said Henry Parker, and quickly added, "I want to make clear again that the Cult Exposure Network does not think that all religions do that, but only cults. Some of our biggest supporters are Christian churches that are concerned about these invasive movements taking over our land."

Parker concluded by explaining what his organization proposed to do about the menace of cults. First was a publicity campaign that would educate Americans by exposing the "mind-numbing" practices of cults. He asked for financial contributions toward that effort. "We have found that the media are eager to help us publicize the threats," he asserted. Second, the Cult Exposure Network was involved in several legal cases in which ex-members sued a cult for compensation for emotional damages suffered as a result of coercive techniques. The apostates claimed that they were owed actual and punitive damages for being forced to join a cult, held against their will, and prevented from pursuing educational or vocational goals that they had been seeking when they were deceived by false promises. The ultimate goal of these legal actions was to force the cults into bankruptcy and dissolution, sparing young Americans from "the gruesome ordeal of mind control." Third, Parker stated that the Network did not itself engage in deprogramming activities, which he admitted were highly controversial and being challenged in several current legal cases. "We do not organize or advocate deprogramming. But if you have a son or daughter who has been deprived of the use of reason by a cult, we can get you in touch with people who can help you. It is expensive, but we are talking here about the fate of people we love." Parker opened up the forum to questions and discussion.

It was hard to read the audience. Most of us were confused, I think. We were concerned about a friend or family member who had done something inexplicable, "gone off the deep end" as one young man described his sister. Yet there was something disconcerting about the brainwashing metaphor, because the individuals we knew had freely chosen to join a cult. Will was not a zombie, even if his eyes were a little glazed sometimes. Even more unsettling was the way in which the coercive techniques of deprogramming seemed to mimic the very thing they were intended to remedy. I had read a newspaper account of a woman who escaped from a deprogramming session. She described sleep deprivation, prolonged mean cop/nice cop interrogations, and emotional manipulation by playing on her guilt and shame about rejecting her family, friends, and career plans.

I realized, a few hours too late to have said so in the meeting, that there was also a contradiction between the claim that members of cults were brainwashed and the first speaker's description of how he had made his own decision to defect from the church. If a cult devotee was a zombie or hypnotized, a forced intervention was necessary to break the trance and restore sanity. But many people like Wilfred seemed quite capable of changing their religious convictions. And Jessica's successful deprogramming was fraught with paradoxes. Was she forced to become free? I wish that I had been quick enough to press Parker on this issue. The fact that he was able to stir up the audience, and his savvy with the media, show that America's worries about cults reflect underlying anxieties about threats to personal freedom. Controversies about fringe religious groups reveal as much about the rest of us as about the cults themselves.

During the forum, members of the audience shared alarmed anecdotes about relatives in various cults, including The Divine Light Mission, practitioners of Transcendental Meditation, the Children of God, and some groups I had never heard of. One elderly gentleman wondered whether his granddaughter's Pentecostal Church was a cult. "She speaks in tongues. I went to hear them and she was shaking and babbling. If that's not out of her mind, what is? But they're Christians, too. By golly, I don't know what to make of it. And what about the Mormons? They seem pretty strange to me, but there are millions of them and they've been around for a while. Are they a cult?"

At this point my father raised his hand. He stood up and spoke slowly and deliberately. "The previous speaker's remarks focus a question that has been bothering me. I don't know what a cult is. But that uncertainty is itself significant. Mr. Parker, you stated that religion is based on conscious and intentional choice, while a cult is based on coercion. That's a white or black, either/or distinction. But I see many shades of gray. Think first about the variety of groups we are calling cults. Some are based on Hindu ideas and some on Christianity, like Pentecostal traditions. Millennial groups think the end of the world is coming soon. Some Asian-influenced groups require communal living in an ashram, while the appeal of other movements, like the Unification Church, seems to depend on the ideal of a traditional marriage and family. Some cults do meditation or chanting and some worship pretty much like my Lutheran congregation, with prayers and hymns and a sermon. We have to notice important differences among these folks, as well as how similar they are to religions we know better."

My father, the preacher, looked calmly around the room, appealing to these stolid Midwesterners to use their common sense. "When you get right down to it, can you really say that any of these new religions is all that different from the old ones? Take this question of freedom. I freely choose to believe in God as known in Jesus Christ. I'm not brainwashed, I don't think. But I can't make myself not believe. I don't have the lever to budge myself away from unshakeable convictions about who made the world and how it's put together. Now another fellow might look at me and say I'm not free, but a captive of an ideology. I'm not opposing everything that your network is doing, because we all need to be more aware of these new religions. But I would want to be pretty darn careful before I try to deprogram my son or take his Yogi to court."

A number of heads nodded appreciatively. Parker looked to his two sidekicks and raised his eyebrows hopefully. Jessica leaned forward intently. "I can't explain how freedom and unfreedom are tangled up in religious devotion. Maybe a philosopher could do that. I only know that I wasn't free when I was with the Hare Krishna people and now I am free. Cults are dangerous. People get lost in them for years. I know individuals who have suffered sexual or emotional abuse. Who knows what the long-term damages might be? That's what is at stake for me. I care about people who are still in limbo, and I want to give them back their freedom. Won't you help me do that?"

The meeting had gone on for two hours, and after Jessica's appeal, Parker decided to call it a night. He thanked us for coming and handed out a little brochure with contact information. They were having a meeting in La Crosse in two weeks, and one in Des Moines in April. Donations were welcome.

As my parents drove me back to Northfield, we compared our reactions. "Hope, what do you think about the anti-cult people?" my father asked her.

"I have mixed feelings," she said. "I sympathize with Wilfred and Jessica. I know they mean well. But I could never support this deprogramming business. And I can't really see Will as brainwashed, hypnotized, or crazy. He made a choice and will live with the consequences. I don't think my best response is a negative one of opposition. He isn't a victim. We need to honor Will's choices and affirm positively our own beliefs. In time we will all see more clearly, and the truth will make us free."

"I agree," said my father. "I don't know if we will ever be completely free, whatever that means. But I sure can't liberate somebody by locking him up with an interrogator. That sounds like the Grand Inquisitor or the Maoist thought police."

"The thing that strikes me," I said as we drove up the Second Street hill and approached the college, "is how anxious we all are about being free. These cults make everybody upset and defensive because they make us aware of how when we are religious we are bound, taken over, coerced. In relation to God or cosmic forces, we seem so small, weak, and dependent. What is our freedom in the hands of the Almighty? It's a human delusion, a little sand castle we've built on the beach by Lake Superior."

"Amen," laughed my father. "I like your metaphor, Peter. What a family of sermon-givers we all are." We drove the last block in silence. Then, as we pulled up to the curb in front of my dormitory, Dad said, "Here's one more sermon. Only when you understand the limitations of human freedom can you be truly free. It's hard to explain, it's a paradox of Christian faith, but it's true. You let go of a very limited ideal of freedom in order to embrace something much larger and more significant. You let the big rollers coming off of Gitchigumi wash over your sand castle. When you ride those waves you are taken far, far away."

"Hmm, I'll have to think about that some more, Dad. It was good to be with you, folks. See you again in June for my graduation." I gave them each a hug and skipped up the steps into the dorm. I had work I had to do, chose to do.

After I graduated from Carleton, I lived in St. Paul in a house full of college buddies. Also living there was Maiko, a Japanese American woman who had just graduated from Macalester College, with whom I fell in love just before I moved to Chicago. She joined me in Hyde Park two long years later. During that summer of 1972, I worked in the Hungry Mind bookstore, mostly unloading boxes and cleaning up the place. In the evenings I sat on the porch talking with Maiko or we walked or biked along the Mississippi River. On Sunday afternoons we lay curled together like spoons on her single mattress, gazing at the curtains fluttering in the breeze.

I was only a few miles from Will's ashram in south Minneapolis, but I didn't see him that whole summer. We each kept a wary distance. I was angry and frustrated, but I didn't feel like working things out. The hell with him, I thought. Will didn't communicate much with my parents or Sophie, either, except for one weekend in July when he visited. I wondered why he went home at all when he was so negative about it, but he must have needed to stay connected. Or he had to reenact the scene of departing from it.

Shortly before I left for Chicago in September, I went home to say good-bye. I was sitting in the dining room after breakfast, reading about George McGovern's fading hopes to win the Presidential election. One newspaper branded him the candidate of "amnesty, abortion, and acid," and his vice presidential running mate, Thomas Eagleton, withdrew when it was disclosed that he had received electroshock treatments. When Mom joined me, I asked her about the first presidential race I remembered, the 1960 race between Kennedy and Nixon. I recalled my parents discussing Kennedy's being a Catholic, and whether that would compromise his loyalty to the United States. I knew Catholic kids in my school classes, and I didn't understand why this was an issue. That was the first dinner-table discussion of religion and politics that I remember. At ten, I couldn't understand exactly what Mom and Dad thought, but I saw that this was an important, even urgent issue for them.

"It's interesting that you remember that discussion," she said. "Childhood memories are so important, and in so many ways. They can provide solace when life is full of suffering." She looked sad, and I asked her if something was bothering her. She hesitated, and then told me that when Will was home in July, he asked to see his "box of treasures." This was a brown cardboard box full of childhood essays and school papers. Mom had stored a collection of each of her children's written work at the back of the closet in my parents' bedroom. If ever there were a fire, it was these boxes that she would first try to salvage, together with a box of family photographs. She treasured her children's written words as if they were sacred scripture.

Mom had an apprehensive feeling when Will asked for these precious documents. She took the box out of the closet and handed it to Will, who carried it upstairs. That morning she heard him leafing through the papers, and several times he laughed out loud.

During the afternoon she was awakened from a nap by the smell of smoke. She jumped up in alarm and realized that the smoke came from outside the house. Looking out the window, she saw Will by the old stone fireplace in our backyard, where we sometimes cooked marshmallows or warmed ourselves on a cool evening. Will had built a fire with sticks and was feeding his childhood papers into the flames. Mom ran downstairs and into the yard. She yanked the brown box away from Will, holding it away from him, her body sheltering the papers. "Neither of us said a word," she told me. "We both knew what this act meant. We listened to the hot wood crackling, watched the paper blacken and disappear. After a minute, Will looked at me and said, 'They're my papers, Mom.'

"In that box there was a drawing of a porcupine that Will had made when he was eight and we camped at the end of the Gunflint Trail. The porcupine was sniffing around our garbage, and Will wanted to share our scraps with it. There was a note that he wrote to Sophie when he was about eleven and she was nine. He promised never again to tease her because of her pigtails or any other thing—unless she had it coming and deserved to be teased! In the box of treasures was a paper that Will wrote for a junior high science class, an essay about the Amazon rainforest proposing that a Minnesota canoe would be the best way to explore the swampy wetlands and flooded jungle. And a high school English essay typed on blue paper that went deep into Hamlet's loneliness. I stood there with the box in my arms as if I were cradling a baby. I would have fought tooth and nail against anyone who tried to take it away from me."

Mom paused as she remembered and deliberated. She was far away, deciding something or recalling an intention. I asked her whether she had saved the papers.

"I realized that Will was going to let me decide. He wasn't going to fight me for them, argue, or even say any more to me. He sat on the bench as I stood there, watching the flames die down. Then I handed him the box. 'Thanks, Mom,' he said, and he put the whole box on top of the fire. I gasped and struck my chest hard. I longed to reach into the fire and save those irreplaceable treasures. Only the box is on fire, I thought, I can still save the letters. A minute later, I remembered that some of the letters he wrote from summer camp were in bundles; maybe the ones on the inside were still readable. Will stirred the flames and ashes with a stick, and then it was too late. I turned away without a word and went for a long walk, down to the lakeshore.

"I sat on a big stone thinking about why Will wanted to destroy everything about his past. I looked at the waves for a long time. I decided that whatever was good about the past would be preserved in memory, both his and mine. I know he suffered growing up and was lonely, but he must have some memories of old and happy times, too. From the ashes he will take what he wants or needs, and so will I."

I told my mother that I thought she had done something almost heroic. Will would have allowed her to save the box. Whose papers were they, really? Mom had carefully preserved, sorted, and stored them. Will's childhood doesn't belong only to him. As I talked to her, I felt a familiar surge of anger at Will, and it struck me that this act of arson was an aggressive, destructive blow. He knew what those papers meant to Mom. He had held her over the flames, too, roasting like Joan of Arc. It was a sadistic act.

"You didn't have to give those things up to the fire," I said. "You didn't have to make that sacrifice."

She looked at me with great seriousness. I was agitated and she was calm. "I was not trying to be a martyr, Peter. I was trying to honor Will's intention to become a new person. It is not easy to love your child when he seems to be rejecting everything about his childhood, family, and home. Will had a religious conversion, but it is not complete. Maybe he is stuck halfway to a new place, a new self. If he wants to destroy the traces of his former identity, I can't stop him. I will even hand him the matches, so long as what he destroys is not his soul."

I gazed at my mother in wonder, and my anger ebbed. How different she is from me, I thought, and how much like Will. I would never burn the mementos from my past, nor would I, as a parent, allow my child to do so. I would snatch them from the flames and hide them for decades, hoping that my child would someday gratefully pore over them, amazed that he had written those words. I would drag the past into the future, even if it were covered with ashes.

Three

Gravity Is Strong

I MAY HAVE MADE Will sound like a self-righteous jerk. He definitely had moments of jerkdom, but he was also one of the wittiest and funniest people I've known. His humor was not the joke telling kind, but situational, and not knee slapping hilarious, but wry. One aspect of his quirky sensibility was an iconoclastic view of authority that deflated the pretensions of a teacher, camp counselor, or Dad in the pulpit. Rather than being elated to expose someone's fallibility, Will seemed amused by the human flaw, the old Adam, lurking in attempts at virtue, rationality, or piety. Pointing this out was like a game of peek-a-boo a teenager could play. There was a period when he was going through confirmation class when he delighted in probing why our church didn't practice what it preached. Will pressed Dad on why Lutherans don't follow every admonition of Our Lord by prohibiting divorce, giving away our coats and cloaks, and, so as not to worry about the morrow, forgoing insurance. He was fascinated by the Reverend's convolutions as he tried to explain the moral limitations of human nature and his congregation.

Will included himself in the circle of well-meaning folks who couldn't overcome themselves. Once, when Dad was beating himself up for not being able to forgive a parishioner who persistently criticized his sermons, Will said with a grin, "Welcome to the club, Dad. Pastors are people, too." My father looked at Will for a few seconds, his jaw hanging down. Then he laughed, shook his head, and said "Ouch. But thanks." Will looked pleased and added, "You can be the club's treasurer. I'm the President." Being a sinner was companionable, in contrast to attempts at saintliness.

When he was about eight or nine, Will had a fight about something with Mom and Dad. Furious, he decided that he would build a rocket to send them to the moon. He would banish the evil tyrants and live an un-inhibited life of Riley, playing by his own rules or none at all. He sat in the dining room in pajamas all one rainy afternoon, drawing plans for the rocket on large sheets of paper. He included play compartments where his parents could recline in ease and watch television if they behaved, and he designed a punishment chamber where they would be sent if they were bad. When Mom asked him what would happen in the punishment chamber, Will said that for hours on end she would have to listen to Dad give sermons! This brought howls of laughter from each of them, and they were soon discussing together what kind of furniture to put in the rocket and whether a loyal dog could accompany them on their journey through space. Finally Will decided that he wanted to go in the rocket, too, so long as he was the commander. His attacks on authority figures or respectable institutions, which began in anger at a restraint on him, often turned into good-humored jokes shared, if possible, with the object of his criticism.

A lot of Will's jokes were self-deprecating. He did not pretend to be smart or a good little boy, but instead played the fool, clown, or lost sheep that couldn't get with the program. Will seemed to be amused that he was more interested in a comic book in school than a dull assignment. "My brain gets jumpy when people are so serious," he claimed, "it wants to be goofy." Once he was supposed to be playing left field in a third grade baseball game. He got distracted by butterflies and wandered off. When the teacher retrieved and reprimanded him, Will said that he wasn't much good at catching fly balls, but he could catch flies and butterflies. He asked the teacher whether he could use a butterfly net to snag baseballs, which would be a lot easier and allow him to have fun with insects at the same time that he did his onerous duty in left field. He didn't mind making himself the butt of jokes and he never mocked or teased other kids.

Silly memories, but sweet. One of the saddest things about Will's conversion was that his playful humor disappeared. He could not laugh at anything related to Yogi Bhakta or his organization, and his cracks about other religions or the beliefs of ordinary Americans took on a bitter, sarcas-tic, and scoffing tone. Nor could he poke fun at himself any more, because he was so deadly earnest about his project of spiritual self-improvement. Humor was one of the impure qualities of the world that he tried to slough off on his way to becoming one with the divine. Those who knew and loved Will remembered his impish grin, and were sad and concerned. If you met Will for the first time during his most fanatical phase, you would just think he was crazy and back off from his intense preaching of the Way, the Truth, and the Light.

Will went through a very dark time after the initial excitement of his conversion faded. His crash was more than just a letdown or anticlimax; it almost cost him his life.

In the spring of 1972, the war in Vietnam was winding down, but bombing raids on North Vietnam continued and American troops killed and died. Although members of Bhakti Dharma were not supposed to engage in political demonstrations, or even care much about what the news showed about the state of the world, you could hardly avoid it. Will got interested and then upset about what our country was doing to "pacify" that faraway Asian country. He started buying newspapers and watching television coverage of the war, sometimes in laundromats or other public places. He would be late for the ashram's community supper because he wanted to hear Walter Cronkite tell the news. Without telling anyone, he decided to take action. The leader of his community, Alex, was surprised to receive a phone call from the St. Paul Police Department, asking for someone to take custody of Mr. William George, who had been arrested for disorderly conduct. When Alex went to get Will, he put together the story from what two cops said and Will's version of the incident.

Will had seated himself in front of the Minnesota State Capital. It was a bright April day at noon. He was wearing a green army jacket, stocking cap, blue jeans, and running shoes. He had a gallon of gasoline, and after sitting in meditation pose for a few minutes with the can in front of him, he poured some of the gas over himself. He had made a little sign that said, "I am Vietnamese. Torch me." His outstretched hand held a cigarette lighter that he offered to passersby. He immediately attracted a crowd of tourists, office workers and businessmen on their lunch break, and others enjoying the fine weather. When the first cop got there, only a few minutes after Will's antiwar protest began, Will was pleading with his audience, "Come on. Please do it. I want to die for your sins." A couple of young men in uniform took offence, and one of them grabbed the lighter and taunted Will, "You really want me to? Or are you just bullshitting us?" He circled Will, playing with the crowd, trying to steal the show. Will sat expectantly, waiting. The heckler asked the audience, "Should I do it?" At this point a cop intervened, took the lighter, and dispersed the crowd. "C'mon, buddy," he said to Will, "you can't do this. Don't be a jerk. I'm taking you in. You need a shower."

A squad car was quickly on the scene, and several officers escorted Will to the nearest station and booked him. They took his gasoline-soaked clothes, cleaned him up, and gave him a jail uniform. They were uncertain about whether to make it a criminal case or treat the near-suicide as mental illness. When Will gave the name of the ashram's leader as his closest next-of-kin, the police decided to release him in Alex's care. They took his story and said he would probably have to appear in court before long. "So don't leave town. You'll be hearing from us."

Will didn't say much on the way to the ashram, but when they got there he said, "Someone has to do something to stop the war. To make people think. Someone must take responsibility."

Alex tried to get Will to see that this kind of act was not the Way, for many reasons. It was caring too much about politics. He told Will that the path to peace is not political, but spiritual, a peaceful way.

"Yes, yes, I know that," said Will. "But for me this was a spiritual action. I would give up my life for others. They deserve to live more than me."

"But you would have destroyed your life," said Alex. "Yogi Bhakta would never allow an act of self-destruction, no matter how worthy or noble your aspiration."

Will said that if he had been burned to death it would not have been self-destruction, but purification. "What is there to lose but ego?" he asked. Several times he muttered to himself, "the wages of sin are death." Alex thought that Will saw self-immolation as a punishment for his desires. During meditation, Will was bothered by lust and "worldly passions." He had been deeply impressed during one of Yogi Bhakta's tape recorded lectures when his spiritual master described how the fires of true devotion burn up all the attachments, desires, and resentments that make humans miserable. "Let it all go," the guru said. "Let it become smoke. Who needs it any more?" Yogi Bhakta often used metaphors of purgation or purification by heat or fire to interpret the effect of kundalini yoga. "It's like a sauna or steam bath for the unconscious, eliminating the poisons."

Alex and other devotees tried to reason with Will, telling him that he had misunderstood the Yogi and that suicide was inconsistent with his steady affirmation of life's goodness. Will may or may not have been persuaded, but he became silent and refused to discuss his action. The ashram leaders did not encourage Will to get psychological help, but rather to avoid news media and listen attentively to the positive meaning of Yogi Bhakta's teachings.

The day after Will's arrest, the St. Paul Pioneer Press had a tiny paragraph about it, tucked away in a long article about congressional debates about the war. It said: "Near the state capital yesterday, an antiwar protester threatened to take his own life if the United States did not immediately cease its military activities in Vietnam. Police arrested the man without incident."

After my first year of graduate school in Chicago, during the summer of 1973, I lived in south Minneapolis with Maiko. She was going to summer school at the University of Minnesota. I waited on tables in an Indian restaurant a few nights a week, finished two incomplete papers from my spring courses, and studied German to prepare for a language exam in the Divinity School. Will lived just a few blocks away, on the other side of Powderhorn Park, in the Bhakti Dharma ashram. He had lost a lot of weight since I last saw him more than a year earlier. He said that he craved sugar and his bones and teeth ached at night. Yet he refused to go to a doctor. He asserted that it was God's will for him to suffer and he should not think about his physical condition.

I ran into Will on the street in our Minneapolis neighborhood several times during that summer. More than once he would not speak to me or avoided me. One evening he was sitting in Powderhorn Park, watching the world go by. I was walking to a store and stopped to sit down next to him. We sat together silently for a few minutes, as I tried to decide whether or not it was a comfortable silence. Suddenly he jumped up and ran away from me. Another time we went swimming together at the Lake Harriet beach. He didn't come back to shore, but swam all the way across the lake, which I thought was a little dangerous. I jumped on my bicycle and met him on the other side. An hour later, Will emerged from the water, lay down in the grass, and fell asleep. When he woke up, he sat in meditation position for at least an hour, while amused passersby stared and children laughed and joked about him. Will's unpredictable, spontaneous behavior sometimes made me feel uptight, mechanical, and rigid, unable to go along with his whim. Being with him could also be fun, and he got me to do things I would never do by myself. Yet even sitting with him in silence that evening in the park, I felt vaguely alarmed, as if we were playing near a cliff.

I talked to my mother about my concern for Will's physical health. She spoke of his deep need to be punished and forgiven for some mysterious reason. "He says he doesn't like the language of sin and atonement," she said, "but that's what it sounds like to me. It reminds me of Luther's feeling of unworthiness before God." She saw Will's intense self-criticism as a profound religious experience, yet she also worried that it went too far and was dangerous, even self-destructive. "Would it be such a sin to see a doctor, for heaven's sake?"

It was hard to sort out how much Will's suffering was caused by psychological wounds and how much it reflected a deep experience of human finitude and guilt. It's too simple to just say he was crazy. Yet I think that my family's attempt to discern religious meaning in his situation blinded us to the coming crisis. We saw as spiritual insight what in hindsight seems obstinate and compulsive behavior and symptoms of deep disturbance. A psychiatrist would say that Will sent several obvious cries for help to his family. Yet Will deflected my parents' expressions of concern and refused to seek medical help. That summer I had several nightmares after I had seen him and sometimes awoke with feelings of unfocused dread. Once I dreamed that Will had died and I woke up shaking.

In late July, my father phoned to tell me that Will was in a hospital in south Minneapolis. He had tried to take his life three times. There had been a birthday celebration for Yogi Bhakta in Eau Claire, Wisconsin, and in the middle of it, Will declared that he had to go to India at once. He wanted to go to the Golden Temple in Amritsar, Punjab, the most sacred spiritual place for Sikhs. He thought that this pilgrimage would reveal to him whether or not he should become a Sikh, a decision he was wrestling with. The Wisconsin State Police picked him up running down Interstate 94, and he spent a night in jail. The next day he left jail with fellow Bhakti Dharma members. Near the University of Minnesota, he ran away from them and tried to drown himself in the Mississippi River. When they took him back to the ashram he talked about jumping off the Washington Avenue Bridge, where the poet John Berryman committed suicide. He tried to drink a bottle of iodine "to put out the fire," he said, but his roommate stopped him. Finally the ashram members admitted that his illness was more than they could handle. No amount of kundalini yoga was going to burn off these impurities. They took him to the hospital, which admitted him to a unit for adolescents and young adults with psychological disturbances.

My parents drove down from Duluth to see him several times while he was in a thirty-day treatment program. They stayed in a hotel and found out as much as they could about Will's condition in the days leading up to the suicide attempts.

I went to visit Will in the hospital three times. The first time, he said that he didn't want to see me. The attendant said that they had to honor that request, so I left. As I was getting into my car on the street just outside the entrance, I heard a shout. "Yahoo! Jail break!" Will sprinted out the hospital door and down the street, followed by three attendants. They caught him and, one on each arm and one following, walked him back to the hospital. Will smiled proudly like a king with his entourage. He looked happy, glancing up at the sun and turning his head to catch its rays. I wondered whether he had been trying to catch up with me, and whether my visit had prompted his escape attempt. After this incident, the staff isolated him from his family for a week.

The second time I went to see him, he allowed me to visit but didn't want to talk. "Don't feel rejected," he said, "but I'm beyond words."

"How about if we meditate together?" I asked.

"Back to back. Yes."

So we sat, back-to-back, and meditated for a while. It was a little uncomfortable and weird, but I felt close to him for the first time since he joined Bhakti Dharma. When one of our spines shifted a little, the other one would adapt his posture. As I was leaving, Will put his hand on my shoulder and said, "The wages of sin are frenzy and death. Almost dying was both selfishness and punishment."

At a loss for words, I shook my head, turned away, and left the hospital.

In addition to the Vietnam War protest the previous year, my father heard about several incidents earlier that summer that showed Will's desire to overcome egotism, as well as his scruples of conscience about the slightest hint of vanity. Several members of the ashram, including Alex and Will's roommate Gary, described incidents when Will's self-denial veered crazily towards violence. Once he stopped playing his guitar and smashed it irreparably. Gary thought that this action expressed Will's wish not to have material possessions and his not wanting to be proud of playing so well.

Will had strikingly beautiful long dark hair. The previous April, while he was home visiting our parents, he shaved his head, including his eyebrows. He had run into an old girl friend from high school that afternoon, he said, and he didn't want to ever see her again. Mom thought that he cut off his hair to avoid any occasion for vanity. Sikhs are supposed to grow out their hair, so this act violated one of the main requirements for a fuller commitment to Bhakti Dharma. When she asked Will about this, he said, "I'm not yet worthy to be a full member of Bhakti Dharma."

In his paradoxical struggle with himself, my brother was trying to stifle his will, yet every effort strengthened it. His will was at once his energy and his enemy. His desire for self-transcendence was a striving for reverence and commitment, and also a battle against egoism, against himself. In the doomed struggle against his desires, every victory made his will even more powerful.

My father learned about an incident that makes the suicide attempts more comprehensible. The Minneapolis ashram had discussed death several times during the previous week. Ted, a member of the Bhakti Dharma group in Milwaukee, had recently drowned while swimming in Lake Michigan. Because this man had once lived in the Minneapolis ashram, most of the group went to his funeral. Alex gave a little sermon in which he referred to the group's response to Ted's death as a positive experience. He thought Will may have misconstrued his remarks as saying death was a good thing for the group. In the hospital, when describing how he tried to kill himself, Will said, "I almost drowned like Ted." Perhaps he hoped that his death would create a beautiful experience for others. Alex said that in a tape recorded satsang, Yogi Bhakta had spoken of how the eternal lives on after death, and Will took this to mean that the body does not matter.

Will's friends in the ashram knew he was not in his right mind when he said that his body was burning up and that he was unworthy to live. Although they should have sought medical expertise more promptly than they did, they tried to reason with him and to help him see himself more positively. Alex said that when he told Will that there is good inside each of us, my brother seemed to snap out of a dark mood. Will asked him, "Will you assign me some service to do—a real service?" Alex replied, "The most important service now is to take care of yourself and to eat well." In response, Will hugged him. Later, brooding, he said eating was "a worldly thing to do." Gary responded, "Try meditating while you're eating, and perhaps you will feel better." Will's Bhakti Dharma friends challenged his obsessions as inconsistent with Yogi Bhakta's teaching.

Renunciation

Will's frugal diet must have affected his severe physical symptoms and disorientation. He had lost twenty pounds during the previous several months, and the hospital physician reported that blood tests revealed liver damage. Will's precarious mental state was exacerbated by, if not the direct result of, the medical condition caused by his Spartan regimen. He had chosen a vegetarian diet several years before he encountered Yogi Bhakta for ethical reasons focusing on world famine and ecological concerns. In the ashram he began to cut back on what he ate; he denied his body's needs and chose to suffer. As is sometimes the case with anorexia, his conscience became preoccupied with denying his body and relentlessly demanded self-mortification. Will's dietary scruples, and for that matter this whole period of mental instability, reflected many causes, including his medical condition, a probable vitamin deficiency, religious ideals misapplied, and a character drawn to self-denial.

I don't think that there is anything peculiarly dangerous or unhealthy about Bhakti Dharma's values or practices. Every form of piety has the potential to become dangerous self-mortification, as the believer's conscience becomes severe and accusing. I had begun to see, as a budding scholar of early Church history, how Christians have found meaning in suffering and advocated certain kinds of self-abnegation for a higher purpose. The saints used hair shirts, whips, and chains, as well as less dramatic forms of expiation and penance. Suffering Christians have justified their passivity or acquiescence in their misery, and sometimes deliberately provoked martyrdom, by invoking the ethical ideal of imitating Christ's suffering. Bhakti Dharma and other new cults of the 1970s didn't invent high-minded self-punishment.

Will, like me, may have absorbed the family's negative attitude to anger. When Friedrich Nietzsche described the origins of guilt and asceticism in Western culture, he argued that if assertiveness and aggression cannot be expressed outwardly, they are turned inwards against oneself, in the final and most complex arena for the will to power. Will sought a decisive victory over egotism by trying to destroy its source. His struggle for a better self nearly killed him.

Close to the end of Will's month in the hospital, his psychotherapist invited me to a session with him. The three of us met in a room on the locked ward for young adults with serious mental health disorders. Will

46

was stable and subdued. He would be leaving the hospital in a few days. Dr. Pendle, a brisk, decisive, red-haired woman who was about forty, was trying to help Will understand whether his suicidal behavior was related to his family upbringing. She brought in each member of Will's family for an hour with her and Will. Dr. Pendle started by asking how Will and I each thought our father's work as a minister influenced our own religious orientation. I said that while I admired him greatly, his strong emphasis on social responsibility was sometimes a heavy burden, and that, in different ways, Will and I had each been drawn to other aspects of religion.

Will pointed at me and interjected, "Peter, you study religion. I *do* it."

I pondered this remark for a moment and said, "Yes. Well, I suppose that I intellectualize a lot. I analyze what other people say and do in relation to what they think is holy. On the other hand, there is an intellectual side to religion. You can search for God with the mind, too."

"All right," said Dr. Pendle, "so Peter emphasizes the rational, while Will told me he was searching for some kind of direct experience of God, and he found it in Yogi Bhakta's teachings. What about the Christian conscience, the ethical demands, that you each grew up with? It seems like an issue for both of you."

"I have a pretty strong sense of moral responsibility," I said, "but I don't do much about it. At least compared with my dad. I know I should be more involved in everything from antiwar protests to tutoring kids in my Chicago neighborhood."

"It sounds like you feel guilty that you don't do more," she said. "Will said a few days ago that he wants to serve other people and can't find a way." She looked at the top page on her clipboard and considered what to say. "In a long-term course of therapeutic treatment, I would wait for a patient to come to certain insights. But this isn't the ideal situation. We have you for thirty days, Will, while your parents' insurance covers you, and then you want to go back to the ashram. So I'm going to push some ideas that you may not agree with, but they may challenge you to think about your suicidal impulses in a different way. This session is about Will's mental health, Peter, but I think he may be able to understand himself better by seeing similarities to you, especially a harsh and demanding conscience. Will, can you describe again that insight you had two days ago, about the time when you were on the highway?"

Will had been staring intently at Dr. Pendle. Now he jumped a little and responded to her question with great animation.

"Yes, I think it is sort of like Peter's sense of moral inadequacy. It was during the week I tried to kill myself. I was out on a freeway in Wisconsin, thinking that I was going to go to the Golden Temple any way I could. I was running because I felt I was burning inside, and I wanted that energy to power me. I felt totally worthless, and running was the only thing left that I knew how to do. I ran until I saw Jesus in a farmer's garden, off to the side of the road. He was hanging on a cross, his hat hanging down, his limbs turning to straw. I walked into the garden and began to scream at him. I said, Do I have to die to be worthy? I was in despair because I thought I could never be good enough. But Jesus was silent. He didn't answer me. I was panting, sobbing, and I could taste blood. I was so close to dying, but I couldn't get there. Then I turned away from the scarecrow and ran back down the highway."

"And then the police picked you up, and your friends from the ashram came to get you. What was that like for you?" Dr. Pendle leaned closer to Will, trying to draw out a new thought or feeling.

"They took care of me. They were there for me. They said Yogi Bhakta doesn't want me to die."

"Yes," she said, "they were there for you. And in Bhakti Dharma you have the opportunity for real service to others, and for joy."

"Yeah, I do." Will nodded several times, and the nods became a steady rocking motion of his torso. "I do. For joy."

I asked, "Are you saying that Bhakti Dharma is a better religion than Christianity because it doesn't lay a guilt trip on us? I don't agree with that."

"Not necessarily," said Dr. Pendle. "I'm a psychologist, not a theologian. I don't know what's ultimately true. Probably every religion has positive features and potential dangers for various individual temperaments. I'm just trying to get Will to think about how to be involved in Bhakti Dharma in a way that is healthy, not suicidal."

"There is the question of truth," I said. "That has to come up sometime."

"Granted, Peter," she said. "But not today, not here. For now let's focus on what will keep Will sane and healthy. Is the most important thing in his life right now, this religion, going to do that?"

Will jerked and spoke up. "I do see Yogi Bhakta's message as a huge relief. He's always speaking of the goodness of each person as a reflection of God. There's no mention of sin, even though he sees all the insanity and suffering of our lives. And here's another thing I like. He's not always analyzing motives. The way we always dissect motives in our family is like picking at scabs. It undermines my confidence. Plus, how can you ever be sure of your motives anyway? When I was in high school I fasted to raise money for a hunger relief organization in Africa. I started questioning my motives. I wondered if I was just doing it to feel good about my own virtue. That whole experience of altruism and generosity was tarnished. I felt poisoned by my own conscience. It's crazy! I gave up doing good things because it made me feel guilty! But in Bhakti Dharma, I feel good about loving and serving Yogi Bhakta and his community. And rightly so. I want my generous and compassionate side to express itself without doubt."

"Then tell me this," said Dr. Pendle, leaning toward him. "If what you say is true, then why did you feel so negative about yourself that you tried to kill yourself?"

"It seems contradictory," said Will. He looked out the window at the sultry August day. The humidity was as thick as mist. "I don't know how to explain it. Maybe I didn't really leave Christianity behind when I joined Bhakti Dharma. I've been parroting Yogi Bhakta's ideas, but they haven't really sunk in. I'm still a Christian down deep, at least in the way that I suffer a guilty conscience. Maybe my real conversion has yet to take place. It's in the future, when the ideas I've absorbed and my experience of devotion to Yogi Bhakta totally transform my whole being. I've always felt like I have a negative destiny or bad karma. When I tried to end my life, I wasn't really throwing away anything of value. But I've suffered so much now that maybe I've paid off some kind of debt. Maybe there is another way for me."

I shifted uncomfortably in my chair. "I don't want to undermine that sense of hope for the future. But I don't feel that Will has described Christianity fairly. It's not just a guilt trip. There are many kinds of Christianity, and I want a different version than what he describes. And I don't think our parents can be blamed for what happened to him."

"These are complex issues, Peter," Dr. Pendle assured me. "You may be right. But, again, we can't go there today. Coming back to Will, I think his devotion to Yogi Bhakta might—I repeat, might—be a positive thing, depending on how he understands it."

"I want to be good," Will said slowly, almost whispering, and looking at the floor. "I want to serve something beyond myself. I want to do it out of love. Not because I'm afraid to be bad." He looked up hopefully.

"Hold that thought," said the doctor. "Let's start there next time, and ask what concrete actions and attitudes would express that intention."

Our fifty minutes had gone by quickly. I hadn't said much, but Dr. Pendle had prompted Will and me to think about religion in our family and in Bhakti Dharma. We stood up. I shook Dr. Pendle's hand and walked Will back to his room down the hall. I felt troubled by Will's remarks about the destructive legacy of Christian conscience. I felt defensive and wanted to argue that the tendencies he described were corruptions or distortions of Christian faith, not the real thing. But I couldn't say this, because I was aware of some tendencies in myself that were essentially the same, if less extreme, than what drove Will to attempt suicide. The second guessing of my motives, the feeling of never being able to do enough for others, the endless self-monitoring and judging. So I just said, "Thanks for inviting me, Will. Maybe we're not as different as I thought."

"Yeah, brother, I know. The ladder is the same."

"Ladder?" I looked at him quizzically.

He shrugged. "Wherever you are trying to climb to, you have to go up a rung at a time. You have to leave some stuff behind. And gravity is strong."

He was always the one with a new metaphor, and I was the one analyzing what it might mean. I put my hand on his shoulder and said, "Call me when you get out."

"I will," he said, smiling. But our calls missed each other. I didn't talk to him again until I was back in Chicago for the autumn term. It's hard to understand or forgive myself for not being there for him. I wasn't my brother's keeper.

For the next year, most of what I know about Will came through my parents, who were going through a lot of soul-searching. Will's involvement in Bhakti Dharma, his suicide attempts, and his angry rejection of the family caused a lot of turmoil for them, Sophie, and me. My family situation influenced my growing interest in Christian practices of self-denial. One evening I was listening to the radio as I washed the dishes. A program was describing a psychological syndrome called obsessive/compulsive disorder. The psychologist being interviewed said that only the name was new, and that one form this behavior took earlier in history was scrupulosity about moral behavior. It was a huge problem in monasteries, he asserted. Certain monks and nuns appeared to be unusually pious and self-denying, but their behavior became so excessive and fanatic that they had to be restrained from practices of discipline and self-punishment. The monasteries struggled with how to differentiate between genuine religious fervor and the kind of self-destructive behavior that we now call neurotic. So, concluded the psychologist, self-denial can be either virtuous or pathological.

Scholars of religion call these disciplinary practices asceticism. I mentioned to one of my professors that asceticism in early Christian history might be a good topic for a dissertation. Professor Krupat must have intuited that there was a personal source of my interest in this topic. He asked me why I was drawn to it. I knew that there was a connection between Will's trauma and my intellectual interests, but I didn't want to admit this to Krupat. It felt too private, irrational, and scary. I said, "I think there's a lot of disguised asceticism around still. I don't understand it, and studying history might help." Now I see that I was trying to put my family's conflicts into a larger context. Was there any wisdom to be gleaned from Christian history about how to distinguish masochism from the admirable willingness to suffer for a cause? What makes commitment to God lurch towards annihilation?

For my parents, Will's suffering brought great sadness and self-examination. They could not help feeling responsible and tried to do whatever they could to help him. Yet there was very little they could do against his wishes, and Will cut himself off. My parents' phone calls and letters to me during the 1970s showed their sustained effort to understand Will, to believe in his goodness even when he withdrew or rejected them, and to affirm the value of a religious journey that they could not share. Dad went to Bhakti Dharma presentations many times, bent his stiff joints into yoga postures, visited Will in ashrams in several cities, and accompanied him to a religious festival in Colorado in 1978. He showed me photographs of them rafting down the Colorado River and, wearing white tunics, standing in a large crowd gathered to hear Yogi Bhakta. Will's arm is around Dad's shoulder, and they are smiling, looking tan, relaxed, and intimate. I felt jealous, having spent most of that summer in Regenstein Library.

In October 1971, shortly after Will's conversion, Mom sent me a letter affirming both the value of her son's religious quest and the importance of critical questioning. "I find it important, though hard, to try not to think of his going to the ashram at this time as a 'stage,' but to respect it for what it is, and to pray for God's love and guidance in his life. But Philip formulated some valid questions about the movement's lack of wider social concerns and seeming claims to infallibility. We must keep on thinking and evaluating as well as experiencing."

In the autumn of 1973, Will tried to be a college student a second time, at the University. When he abruptly withdrew, Mom wrote to me. "There is clock-time and there is the development of a mind and a spirit. There is getting a job, and there is finding a vocation. Through all anxieties, I have deep certainty that Will cares most about love, and about what is true and what is good." Will had taught her a lot, she said, including "certain things I couldn't have learned from my other children—for example how I am tempted to worship the family."

Dad later gave me a copy he made of a letter he sent to Will about a year after his conversion. Here's the ending:

> I find much that I can affirm, both in Yogi Bhakta's teachings and in their effect on you. The concern for experience rather than abstract doctrines is wonderful. The effort for peace, harmony, and unity is something this sorry world needs a lot more of. I sense a peace and a purpose in your life that I hope will continue and deepen over the years. I really believe that God is at work in Yogi Bhakta's life, and partly thereby in yours. Perhaps God is especially present in the chanting, the community life, and your love of your leader. I don't think these things are as free from human interpretation as the Bhakti Dharma movement claims, however. I find all these things (well, I guess not the chanting), and more, in the Christian church. I disagree with Yogi Bhakta's implied claim to articulate the essence of all religions, and I would not want to lose the distinctive figure of Christ or his teachings. Because I have limited knowledge of Bhakti Dharma, I am reluctant to proclaim the gospel to a son who knows better than anyone else how far I fall short of practicing what I preach. I wish for each of us peace, love, and joy.

I would bet that in their face-to-face encounters, too, Dad spoke to Will like that, in complete, grammatically correct sentences, and trying to be fair and generous. My parents were always restrained, rational, and respectful, good candidates for the Lutheran version of sainthood.

It drove Will crazy. Once he covered his ears, slammed the door, and left the house. Another time he said to Dad, "You always have your position worked out. You have logical reasons for what you believe. I feel like I'm insane, because I struggle between belief and disbelief. I don't have God figured out. What I do know I can't prove."

A few months before the suicide attempts, Will invited his "mother and father of the physical plane" to join him "at the feet of the one person with love sufficient to establish peace in this world." In response, my mother wrote this letter:

> Dear Will,
>
> Thank you for having written. I know your dedication to God and honor your announced intention, founded on your experience of God in your life, to join Bhakti Dharma and become one of Yogi Bhakta's ministers. My love goes with you wherever your life leads. Even though it is what you want to give me, and have me give you, I cannot do as you ask and join you at the feet of Yogi Bhakta, because of other vows that my own experience has led me to make and still hold. But if ever there is a ceremony for your dedication that one's physical parents are invited to, I will come. With hope, faith, and love always,
>
> Your mother

From the summer of 1973, when he was released from the hospital, until he moved to Chicago late in 1975, Will's unsettled life posed another set of challenges for my parents. He had many menial jobs, but he didn't hold on to any of them for long and was sometimes short of money. He also had difficulty with the rules and regulations of ashram life and occasionally left for a week or a month. Several times he returned to Duluth to live at home, and then he wanted our parents to support him financially. He was serious about his religious practice and wished to spend most of his time meditating, chanting, and doing yoga. Mom and Dad tried to be supportive and also encouraged him to become more independent. Will must have felt frustrated and angry with himself as well as them as he searched fruitlessly for satisfying work.

Sophie told me about several vociferous arguments about financial matters such as the share of Will's expenses that he or his parents would each pay. Will accused them of trying to "own" and control him by asking him to purchase groceries, and Mom replied, "Don't be ridiculous. This is about refusing to treat you as a child." They insisted that if Will lived at home for more than a short visit, he had to find paying work or go to college. Sophie was amazed and appalled. "You should have seen them, Peter. They were arguing about whether Will had to pay for cinnamon and salt, or just things like bread and vegetables. Will wanted olive oil, and for them to pay for it. They argued about what kind of soy sauce to buy! Then Mom said, Even a monk has to work to eat. You can't expect others to support your religious practice without some conditions. You can give up your wealth, but you can't give up the requirements for being treated as an adult."

"What do you think, Sophie? How do you see this whole business?"

"Mom is right. I think Will has gone bonkers. I was sympathetic at first, but then came the suicide attempts. Now he's trying to figure out how to live in the world again, but he won't compromise. Me, I just want my normal brother back. His goofy jokes. I miss his guitar playing in the next room. This goes on and on."

When Will was deeply estranged from the rest of the family, our efforts to communicate were utterly futile or led to fights. With the best intentions, and in spite of endless attempts to understand, we were incomprehensible to each other. Yet we went on hitting our heads against a wall. Our best efforts to reach out, love each other, and seek common ground brought only pain and alienation. Will bounced back and forth between cutting himself off from the family and moments of regression when he seemed to want to be treated as a child. It was a long ordeal that made me think that I would never want to be a parent and be so vulnerable.

Four

Teach It, Not Preach It

SOPHIE STARTED CLASSES AT the University of Minnesota in September 1972, the same time that I began graduate school. After her first year in a dorm, she lived in a house of students in northeast Minneapolis, so she had more contact with Will than I did. A major in psychology, she, too, tried to understand Will through the lens of her studies. Unlike me, she also tried to support him and stay connected in any way she could. Even though Will limited his contacts with the family, both because of his own desire and under pressure from the ashram leaders, Sophie had a strong personality and was not easily deterred. She showed up occasionally at the ashram for yoga and satsang in the evenings, and she invited Will to the University campus to have ice cream, toss a Frisbee, or talk. Will seemed to need an outlet from the ashram, and he confided to Sophie his doubts and difficulties in committing himself to the beliefs and practices of Bhakti Dharma. One evening during the fall of 1974, Sophie told me on the telephone about our brother's latest struggles.

Will wanted to be a steady practitioner of yoga and a committed member of the ashram community. He was also a very independent person who bristled when any authority figure tried to control him. He complained that in the ashram he was being "hassled" by petty rules and regulations. Every action had to be done in a certain way. Yogi Bhakta had strong opinions about everything from how much spice to put in a particular recipe to the proper clothing for different activities. Although many of his prescriptions were put in the form of advice or health tips, the members of the ashram adopted every saying as of equal and absolute value. The leaders of the ashram, Alex and Marge, interpreted the practical implications of Yogi Bhakta's often-cryptic remarks and enforced his instructions about the proper way of life for his followers. Marge, the ashram housemother, was a vigilant watchdog who viewed violations of the rules as both threats to the one true faith and a personal affront. Will had many conflicts with her and grew irritable, telling Sophie that Marge was "the czar of zealotry and the Inquisitor of infractions."

Early mornings in the ashram were cold, and Will liked to wear warm socks while the group did yoga. But Yogi Bhakta insisted that yoga be practiced in bare feet, so that cosmic energy could flow in and out through the soles. Although Will conformed to this stipulation, he complained to Sophie that it was ridiculous. "I'm stuck thinking about my cold feet when I want to be burning with devotion to God. I'm pissed off at Marge while I listen to sermons about love." The devotees were supposed to align their beds along an east-west axis, but this arrangement made for an awkward placement of Will and his roommate in relation to the windows. When Marge insisted on the correct alignment, Will seethed.

Sophie was amused by the superstitions and quackery in the Yogi's assertions about healthy living. "Did you know," she asked me, "that married couples are supposed to make love only once a month, on the date of the full moon?"

"Hmm, I bet they really get into it," I laughed. "But what's the reason for that practice—something to do with women's cycles and fertility?"

"I have no idea. Even Will didn't know that. There is secret instruction for the married members. Another thing made Will laugh out loud. You are supposed to defecate from a squatting position on the toilet seat. Will told me a fascinating bit of information, with a hushed voice imitating Marge. Do you know one of the amazing things about Yogi Bhakta? He poops perfect round balls!"

I cracked up, then said in mock reverence, "I'm in awe. Sign me up. That would make my life complete."

Sophie snorted. "And then there's the food. You know how quirky Will is about how he cooks and what he eats. Everything has to be a certain way. I think that's one of the reasons he got involved in the first place, because Yogi Bhakta thinks that what you eat and how you eat it have a huge effect on the state of your soul. But in the ashram, everyone is supposed to eat the same way. He shouldn't cook for himself and he's not supposed to snack. He can't eat meat, which he doesn't want anyway. But he can't pick his menu or eat whenever he's hungry. He especially misses ice cream. It's not against the rules, but sugar is discouraged, and Marge gave him a stern lecture once when he brought a half-gallon of chocolate almond back to the ashram. Once in a while we have a cone on the lawn by the student union, and he practically inhales it, he slams it down so quickly. I told him gluttons will burn in hell, and he chuckled and said, Yeah, I know, but I'll eat my ice cream there fast, before it melts.

"Then he got bitter, describing how Marge gives spiritual reasons for her personal food preferences. She is hypersensitive to too much salt or not enough ginger. She's obsessed with how her body reacts to everything, and then she spiritualizes her quirks. She's worse than an honest glutton, because she doesn't see what's going on. Her regimen is a sneaky sensuality. And then she preaches to Will. When Marge denounces enslavement to the body's cravings, she's a hypocrite. One mustn't drink liquids at meals because this dilutes the digestive juices. Okay, said Will, maybe there is something in that. But then she rambles off her cosmic mumbo jumbo about ethers and auras. She's also into astrology and thinks that because Will's a Virgo that explains him. Will doesn't know how long he can suppress his critical side. He nods at her but he's thinking, this is bullshit.'"

"Boy, it really poured out of him like a confession, Sophie. It sounds like he needs to talk to someone outside Bhakti Dharma, and you are the only one he trusts. You are his reality check now because he doesn't want to interact with me or Mom and Dad. Do you challenge his devotion to the Yogi, encourage him, or what?"

"I try to keep things light. He's come a long way since the suicide attempts last summer, but he's still in a lot of inner turmoil, I think, with conflicts and doubts. Maybe some continuing depression, too, from what I read in my course on Abnormal Psych. Borderline personality, paranoia, and ten other things, too—they all seem to describe him, as well as me and everyone else I know. Except you, and you're compulsively normal."

"Thanks for the diagnosis, Doc, and how much do you charge an hour?"

"I'll send you the bill. Anyway, I think joking about religion a little is good for Will. He looks guilty or upset if he thinks I'm criticizing Yogi Bhakta, but now he can laugh at the ashram and its kookiness. And sometimes—I just remembered something—I think he can see his own religious desires from another perspective and imagine something better."

"What do you mean? You lost me."

"About a month ago we got together to play Frisbee. Then we sat in the sun in front of Northrup Auditorium, sweating and soaking up the rays. He was explaining to me why he had left the ashram for a month and tried to live at home with Mom and Dad, and why that didn't work out, either. Hassles there, too. When he went back to the ashram, Alex told him that the discipline involved in serious religious practice is a way to humble the ego. Living in a community is the biggest challenge to the fat, demanding self. It's harder to give up your own way than it is to give up money, food, or sex."

"That's why Christian monks take a vow of obedience, Sophie. I was studying their vows just last week. There was a little anecdote about one of the *abbas*, the desert fathers. One monk had gone off in solitude to cultivate his virtue and become closer to God. The head honcho abba saw this guy becoming proud, so he told him that it is far more difficult and demanding to have to live with other people, and that is where you learn patience, humility, and compassion. And to obey an elder—that is where the soul must subdue the self. I'm translating this into my terms."

"Yeah, that sounds like the Bhakti Dharma ideal of communal living," said Sophie. "Well, after listening to Alex, Will latched on to the idea that life in the ashram is a way to give up his will. He called it the final renunciation. He said, I thought when I gave myself to Yogi Bhakta I had overcome my selfishness. But now I see living in the ashram as another spiritual test and discipline. Putting up with Marge's insane theories and her need to control us will help me renounce my desires. The hassles will teach me to be patient and forgiving."

"That sounds pretty wise and saintly, I guess. But I can't imagine Will stuffing his own desires."

"He said that submission to a guru is not a one-time decision, but a lifelong effort that isn't easy or ever finished."

"Wow, our brother sounds just like a desert father."

"Yeah, but then I said something that really threw him for a loop. I asked, what's the big deal about renunciation? Why do you have to give up something to feel okay about yourself? How come religious people get so much pleasure from giving up stuff they think is evil, like getting drunk or gambling or swearing? Why not give up something that is really difficult, like prayer?"

"Give up prayer?"

"That was Will's reaction, too. He didn't get me for a while. Then he flopped back into the grass and looked up at the sky. He said to himself, Give up prayer? Give up what's most difficult? That would be my devotion to Yogi Bhakta. Could I give that up? What would I have left? Who would do the giving?"

"He was questioning his whole religious orientation," I said.

"I guess so. But it was a beautiful day, and I didn't feel like analyzing the motivations of monks. I said, C'mon, you holy nutcase, if you are so into giving things up, why don't you scrap your fussy diet and have a Coke with me? And he did, and then he pretended to be high on caffeine and sugar, or maybe he really was. We had a fun time together. That's what's going to make him better, in my opinion. Not a lecture on true religion."

"Well, of course," I said, a little miffed. "I wouldn't say all this to him. I'm just talking with you, trying to understand Will. Our little Jesus. You have to admit, this whole business is pretty interesting when you aren't in the middle of it. When you can view it from outside. The religion of Bhakti Dharma, the psychology of the people in it, and what it does to their families."

"Sure, it's interesting. In fact, I had the idea the other day that maybe my psych major could translate into a job as a family counselor some day. I can imagine myself talking to people about how their families both messed them up and empowered them."

"You'd be good at that, Sophie. Maybe your studies will help us understand our own family."

"I hope so," she responded. "The way Will is isn't just him, but because of the family he comes from. And maybe, too, my family situation gives me energy that motivates my work. Isn't that true for you, too, Peter?"

"Yes and no. There's a big gap between academic study and the life you live. They just aren't the same thing. I've heard it said, by the way, that psychotherapists can't do therapy with their own families, or even understand them. Maybe you have to abandon that hope. Still, there are a lot of connections between the life of the mind and the rest of life. Why would I want to study a subject, if not to understand my reality? But it's an indirect route that leads to what I want to know, in my experience. Reading the desert fathers, I find an old legend that suddenly throws a light on Bhakti Dharma. If I tried to study Will's attraction to his yogi directly, I think I would just be baffled. I can't see what's in front of me; I have to see it out of the corner of my eye. I wonder why that is."

"I don't know, Peter. You seem to need to distance yourself from your own life. Some day I'll charge you forty dollars an hour to talk about it. I won't even say anything. I'll just sit back in my leather chair like Dr. Freud and let your unconscious work things out."

"Oh yes, my silly sister, may we both find employment some day working through old family traumas and getting paid to sound knowledgeable about what we don't really understand."

"Sounds good, Pete. And may brother Will give up his foolish desire for renunciation and learn to accept and enjoy whatever good things life brings his way."

"Amen, Reverend. Here's to giving up giving up good things for God or other noble reasons."

Will always put principle above practicality, even if someone had to suffer for it. During the period of several years when we had little contact, I sometimes searched through old memories for clues to what made him commit his life to Yogi Bhakta and his movement. In July 1967, when I was seventeen and Will was fifteen, we took a canoe trip with my friend Zink and Will's buddy, Tony. Zink was also a Preacher's Kid, the son of a Methodist minister in Duluth. He was a tough, scrappy kid who smoked and got in fights after school. We left from Seagull Lake, on the Gunflint Trail, and went through Lakes Ogishkemuncee and Kekekabic, then north to the Canadian border that stretches along Knife Lake. We had spectacular weather and got along pretty well together most of the time. There was one simmering conflict, however, between Zink and Will. Zink was an avid fisherman, ready to spend an entire afternoon paddling in circles so he could troll the perfect shady pool. Tony and I didn't much care one way or the other; we liked to eat fish but didn't want to spend all day catching them, and we sure didn't want to have to clean them. Will, who had been a vegetarian since he was thirteen, was adamantly opposed to fishing. I wondered whether he and Zink could agree to disagree about the fish question.

As long as Zink didn't catch anything, the conflict remained at the level of banter. After we had set up camp, Zink would go off by himself in a canoe and come back empty-handed but cheerful. Sometimes during the day he would make a cast or two from the canoe. Twice he caught little ones five or six inches long. When he tore the hook out of its mouth and threw the fish back, Will would look the other way and mutter his disgust. Zink and Will were never in the same canoe. They got along well enough in camp, and they had a common lively interest in jazz. They both seemed to want to avoid a nasty dispute about fishing. Tony paddled with one of them, and I with the other, and we kept the peace.

The trouble started when Zink caught a fish. Not just any fish. After six days of nibbles and little things and broken lines, he caught a Northern that he claimed weighed twenty pounds. Will groaned when Zink clubbed it. It was too big to get into the canoe, so we towed it to our campsite. We didn't realize how humongous it was until we had to eat it. That night three of us ate a lot of greasy, bony fish and threw some away, forced down a little more for breakfast, and still half the fish remained.

By mid-morning, when we broke camp, it was already getting warm, and the fish wouldn't keep all day. What could we do with it? Zink was for burying it, and I couldn't see any alternative. But Will insisted that we bring it along and eat it for lunch or dinner. He said, "After murdering Leaper, the least you can do is to eat him. Otherwise your murdering him was completely wanton." Will had given the fish a name, Rapidleaper. He claimed the Indians always did this when they killed game. Our argument about what to do with the remains of the fish carcass became a discussion of Native American spirituality and the rights of creatures.

Zink was not about to haul along ten pounds of decomposing northern pike, much less eat it on Will's command. "Are you kidding? We have four portages today. It's hot. The damn fish is spoiled."

But Will insisted. He put Leaper in a plastic bag and placed it at his feet in his canoe. I had the misfortune to paddle stern with him that day. By noon the fish was getting slimy, and it smelled awful.

We came to our first portage. Zink caught a whiff of the fish. He frowned and spat. There was a campsite located just off the portage trail, with an outhouse back in the woods. It was an odd place for a campsite, but this was before the environmental regulations. Zink wanted to dispose of the fish remains in the outhouse.

Will was adamant. "Leaper comes with us. Okay, so don't eat him. We can still bury him. With respect, with words."

Zink was perplexed. There was no way he was going to carry this rotten fish, much less give it a funeral, but he could see that Will had made up his mind. It was not something he would debate, but a matter of principle. The four of us stood at the start of the portage, looking at the canoes, the portage, the roof of the outhouse through the trees, and down at Leaper. A few flies buzzed lazily around Leaper's plastic, see-through coffin. Zink kicked the ground irritably. It occurred to me that we were standing around like old men thinking their inconclusive thoughts, and this didn't happen often to teenagers. Tony tried to argue with Will that he was being a fool, and a dead fish doesn't deserve the kind of respect a human does.

"Tell that to the Ojibway," said Will.

Finally Zink said, "Okay, someone's got to do something." He picked up Leaper in his transparent casket and set off on the portage trail. The rest of us just watched. Was he going to bury the fish without a shovel? When he got to the fork in the trail, he headed for the campsite. We could just see him through the trees as he headed for the outhouse. Will's eyes narrowed, his body stiffened. We heard the outhouse door slam once, twice. Then Zink came back through the woods. He looked embarrassed and brazen at once, like a kid caught with his hand in the cookie jar. Will was furious, but there was nothing he could do now. He cursed, threw his hands in the air, shook his head, and stormed around the clearing. "Jesus. A whole damn fish you had to waste. Poor Rapidleaper. First you kill him and then you won't eat him and then you won't bury him. You threw him on a pile of shit! God damn it. You deserve to be half-eaten yourself and left to rot."

Will paced the clearing, muttering and exclaiming. Zink watched with a smirk on his face, as if enjoying the entertainment. He laughed scornfully and then got defensive and angry. He said Will was a fool, sentimental, and "a holier than thou, just like your old man." He claimed that he had the right to feed himself, and that if Tony and I ate fish, we were just as guilty as he was.

Tony and I had been innocent bystanders and passive spectators of this bizarre confrontation. Now we tried to defuse the fight. I told Will that Zink probably wouldn't hook anything else, and that if he caught anything too big to eat, Tony and I would make him throw it back. That didn't please either Will or Zink, but we had to get going. We had been stuck at that portage for way too long and it was past time for lunch. We shouldered the packs and canoes, carried them to the next lake, and loaded up.

Later that afternoon, after the last portage of the day, when Zink was loading his canoe, he discovered some damage. The reel for his fishing rod had gotten smashed, apparently when the pack to which it was lashed was set down against a rock. He turned abruptly to Will. "Did you carry this pack?"

Will looked straight at him and said, as if counting his words, "No. I did not carry that pack on this portage."

"How did the reel get broken?"

Will walked over to the pack and reel and carefully inspected them, then glanced at some nearby bushes as if someone might be hiding behind them. "It looks to me like the reel broke when it struck this rock."

"Thanks a lot, Sherlock. I can see that. I don't suppose you had anything to do with it."

Will's face was hard to read. Did he look guilty? Or was he only holding back his glee that the hated rod, the weapon that had dispatched Leaper, was destroyed? None of us could remember who had carried which Duluth pack over; we had six of them, all green and bulky monsters. I thought maybe I had, but wasn't sure. Whoever carried the pack might have dropped it too quickly when he set it down. On the other hand, Will may not have carried it, but broken the reel while the rest of us went back for the other packs and canoes. We never found out whether he did it.

Will thought about Zink's last remark for a minute, and then he said, "I didn't have much to do with what happened to your weapon of death. It was an act of God. Or the revenge taken by the ghost of Leaper."

"God! Hell!" Zink's eyes sharpened, and his jaw tightened. His expression looked a lot like Will's had three portages earlier, at the scene of the crime. The first crime. There was nothing Zink could do. We loaded the canoes a final time and headed across the lake towards an appealing island where we camped. It was getting late. We didn't talk as we set up the tents, got the fire going, and made stew. Will had a separate pot with no meat in his portion, which took extra work and cleanup. Zink mumbled and grumbled about that sometimes, even though it didn't affect him. But on this night he was silent.

No one mentioned fishing again, except once. As we were sitting around the fire the next evening, our last in the woods, Zink lamented the fact that he hadn't had a rod and reel to use in a bubbling brook we passed. Will said appreciatively, "That brook would have made a perfect home for Rapidleaper."

Tony glanced up at me from the other side of the fire. Did we have to go through this again? But no one spoke. We all gazed into the dying flames. A light breeze stirred the pines overhead. Tony said, "Feels like the wind's shifting to the east. It's clouding up. Could be rain tomorrow on our way out."

Later that night Zink and Will argued about Thelonious Monk. Will thought he was the greatest jazz pianist ever, but Zink thought his recordings were uneven. It was a nice safe dispute, one we all enjoyed.

***

Other memories of Will's past surfaced when Dad told me that Will had turned over his inheritance to Yogi Bhakta. Dad didn't allow Will to do this until he turned twenty-one, which happened in September 1973. That autumn he had several telephone exchanges with Will, trying to persuade him to wait a little longer before taking this irreversible step. But Will wanted to give everything to his guru as soon as possible.

As usual, I was home for Christmas that year, and one evening I had a long talk with my father in his study in the back of the house. My father was an orderly person; his books were arranged alphabetically, his church papers and sermon notes carefully filed and stacked. I was in a rocking chair and Dad had a creaky desk chair that tilted way back. He described what Will had said to him about giving away his inheritance.

"Will wants to be unencumbered, light, and free. The inheritance didn't feel like it was authentically his. He said I see only what he gives up, rather than the positive goal of being free. Will is a contemporary Thoreau, trying to live simply without a lot of stuff. Long before he got into Bhakti Dharma he was inspired by *Walden*, and he has never owned many possessions. Hope told me that several times in high school Will went through all his clothes and books and gave away most of them. I think it isn't only a matter of ethical principle for him. It is also an aesthetic choice, because there can be beauty in simplicity, as the Puritans knew, and the Quakers and Shakers. Less is more, and feeds the spirit."

My father leaned back in his chair, and it squeaked painfully. He gazed at a wall of theology books, lost in thought. I remembered that we were sitting here when he had told me, a few years earlier, that the trust fund set up by his parents (Sophie called them "the triple G's," for Grandfather and Grandmother George) would help pay my way through Carleton. I asked him where the family money originally came from. His ancestors were English and Scottish, and the wealthy ones were a pair of brothers who owned cotton mills in Manchester. This industry was based on cotton imported from the Sudan, so it was enmeshed in the colonialism of the British Empire as well as terrible working conditions and child labor practices during the industrial revolution. It must have been a substantial fortune if even this much of it remained after being spread out over many branches of the family over several generations. I decided that it is possible to recognize the moral ambiguity of inherited wealth and still try to do some good with it. I asked Dad whether Will felt guilty about his trust fund or saw it as tainted.

"I think so," he replied. "He said that having it made him feel that he owed the family something, and a sense of obligation might prevent him from doing what he really wanted. It was a golden chain. Giving his money to Yogi Bhakta is an act of worship and service. It was hard to argue with him without sounding like Ebenezer Scrooge or a money-grubbing capitalist. I felt like I would be telling him to be one of the people in the gospels who turn away from the Lord in order to attend to worldly matters. Jesus tells a man who wants to bury his father, Let the dead bury their dead. How can I tell my son to hoard his money rather than follow God? Still, I wish he wouldn't give up the trust fund, which might give him a precious opportunity some day, especially if he wants to return to college."

I remembered a time when Will and I were packing for a canoe trip. We wanted to fit all our gear into two small packs, so that one of us could double-pack them while the other one carried the canoe, in this way crossing each portage in a single trip. What started as a practical question of efficiency was soon a philosophical argument. Will advocated surviving with as little equipment as possible. The question we should ask, he said, is not "What do we need?" but "What can we get by without?" A good birch twig is as effective as a toothbrush. He didn't mind living on nothing but oatmeal for a few days, and said it would "clean us out." One flashlight would do for both of us. He argued about what we could get along without, while I made claims about what makes a wilderness trip comfortable and enjoyable. This running debate became our main focus of conversation as we paddled through Big Saganaga and Northern Light Lakes or sat by the fire. We each preached the gospel of simplicity and freedom from care, but disagreed about what that means in practice.

Dad's reference to Will's disdain for "stuff" reminded me of several incidents when Will had not taken care of other people's possessions. He was irritated when my parents wanted him to take responsibility for losing a friend's coat. Even more than most kids, I think, he left in his wake a trail of forgotten sweatshirts, sports equipment, hats, gloves, schoolbooks, and bicycles. Once he replied to a mild reprimand by asking Mom, "Why should I always worry about stuff when human relationships are most important? Aren't you always telling us that people are more important than things?"

You could hear the capital "T" when Will, echoing my parents, appealed to this principle. People are more important than Things. He invoked this idea to rationalize carelessness or irresponsibility. For him, being concerned about material objects was an idolatrous demand as evil as child sacrifice.

Once when we were about fifteen and thirteen, we were racing our bikes around our neighborhood in Duluth. Several times Will launched his bike off a curb and came down hard on the pavement, or he banged his rear tire as he pounded up a curb. I laboriously stopped, gently lifted my bicycle up or down the curb, and peddled on, steadily losing ground as he flew heedlessly down hills, streaked through intersections, and cut across corner yards. I felt overly cautious and fussy about my bike and my safety. When we got home, Will discovered that he had broken two or three spokes and dented a rim on the bike. He had to take it to a repair shop. I was gloating as I imagined lecturing him. Ha! You see what happens when you don't take care of your stuff. You have to spend even more time and energy repairing them, and now you won't have a bike for a few days. Who is really bogged down with stuff? So did this elder brother congratulate himself on his different way of trying to reach the same spiritual goal: being free from preoccupation with Things.

Many biblical stories depict rivalry between brothers: Cain and Abel, Ishmael and Isaac, Jacob and Esau, Joseph and his brothers, David's quarreling children, and Jesus' parable about the prodigal son and his resentful elder brother. Sibling rivalry and jealousy is a fundamental human reality in the Bible. When there is reconciliation between quarreling brothers, biblical characters sometimes recognize the hand of God. One of the most powerful passages in the Hebrew Bible for me is when Jacob encounters his brother Esau, whom he usurped as the inheritor of God's promises to Abraham and Isaac. Jacob expects hostility, perhaps even to die at his brother's hand. But Esau runs to meet him, embraces him, and the brothers weep. Jacob says, "Truly, to see your face is like seeing the face of God—since you have received me with such favor." As in the parable of the prodigal son, the future relationship of these quarreling brothers remains uncertain. The Genesis narrative holds the possibility of harmony between Jacob and Esau in tension with their ongoing rivalry. Immediately after the brothers' reunion, Jacob takes his clan in a different direction than what he has just promised Esau. The older brother had planned to kill Jacob when their father died, and perhaps Jacob realizes that too close proximity will lead to dangerous conflict. The story of Jacob and Esau tells the truth about the rivalry between brothers, possible moments of reconciliation, and their need to go their separate ways.

I went back to Duluth for Christmas in 1974. Will didn't come home that year. One day I caught up on a lot of errands, going to the dentist and getting my boots repaired. I drove down to the old business section of

Duluth. On my favorite block there was a boat shop that repaired sails and nautical hardware, a store that sold gear to bow and arrow hunters, and Walt's Shoe Repair. My mom had always patronized Walt's place because she said he had a good heart and donated to the camp scholarship funds she organized. Walt had also given a job to Will a year earlier, during my brother's second attempt to be a respectable citizen in Duluth.

When I went in, Walt was talking to a woman about the zipper on her sleeping bag. He had to take a phone call in the middle of their conversation. In the back of the store, two grizzled old-timers contemplated the goings-on. They never helped Walt, but he didn't seem to mind. He let them hang around most of the day and gave them a place to ruminate. Walt looked a little harassed today.

My turn. "Got time to fix these boots?"

"It'll take a while. I'm way behind since my help quit. Business is too good to do right. Can't keep up."

"I'd be much obliged. But I'm heading out of town right after New Year's."

"I can do that. New soles?"

"Yes. And the stitching is coming loose on the side of that one."

Walt put my name on a card, put it in one of the boots, and threw the pair into a pile of footwear: battered Red Wings, shiny Florsheims, mustard-yellow Sears work boots. Even a pair of sandals from someone with a lot of foresight or procrastination.

"Will do. But I sure could use some help." His eye fixed on me for a moment. "Hey, aren't you Will George's brother?"

"Yup. Peter." I had come into the shop several times in high school with Mom. Walt had a good eye for faces, if not for names. I asked, "Say, what was it like when he worked here?"

"Didn't pan out. Had to let him go. Nice kid, though."

"Yeah, he sure is. Well I'll be back on the Second, okay?"

"That should work. Do my best."

"Thanks." I left the shop and walked down Third Avenue. I bought some radio batteries and a baking dish from a hardware store, and looked at records in the Electric Fetus. For Sophie I bought Joni Mitchell's album, "Court and Spark," hoping that she didn't already own it. Half an hour later, about eleven, I passed the Paradise Café. It still looked like it had when I was a boy: dark, with a marble countertop, big soda glasses, and middle-aged waitresses. A nice homey place. Sniffing the aroma of coffee in the cold air, I went in for a cup.

I was going to sit by myself when I saw Walt at the counter. There was a lonely pickle on his sandwich plate; he must have been on an early lunch break.

"Hi again. Mind if I join you? I can see you're leaving soon."

"Suit yourself." Walt wasn't exactly encouraging. Maybe he felt awkward about me being Will's brother. I ordered some coffee and looked around. It was too early for the regular lunch crowd, still quiet. The plants in the window were tall and scraggly and had probably been there for decades.

"Nice place, the Paradise."

Walt sniffed, from a runny nose or indignation. Then he said, "There used to be half a dozen places like this around here. Now people drive out to the burger joints. It's a shame, the changes in this town. You can hardly find smoked whitefish or venison jerky anymore."

"This is the last decent café in this part of town, and aren't you just about the last shoe repairman? Times are changing, Walt."

"You're telling me. Listen, when I started there were seven shops in downtown Duluth that fixed shoes. The sixth one closed last year."

"Why is that, Walt? People still have to walk, and their shoes wear out."

"Lots of reasons. People throw away their shoes when they're down at the heels. They want something new and they want it fast. Folks drive out to McDonalds for coffee and they sit there admiring their new shoes."

I waited. "What other reasons?"

"People don't want to work. Nobody wants to be a shoe repairman anymore. The work is too hard for the pay."

I thought about that. It didn't fit Will's case. He didn't work for Walt to make quick or easy money. "Is that why Will left?"

"Didn't leave. I fired him the second time he showed up for work at eleven. I had told a couple of customers I'd have their shoes ready for them and I couldn't deliver. You can't run a business that way. So I let him go. He didn't take it too hard. Seemed like he was waiting for it to happen, like he knew it was coming sooner or later. Well, what did he expect when he waltzed in at eleven?"

"Was he any good?"

Walt sat up straight, excited. "Yes, dang it. It's a shame, because he was good with leather. A craftsman, even. He said he was a vegetarian, which is pretty strange around these parts. He said if you think of leather as skin, living tissue, you know what it can do and how to treat it. He was really good, when he was in the mood to work."

"I guess the Lord didn't happen to move his spirit those mornings. Or the Yogi." I had developed a habit of sarcastically disassociating myself from Will's religious activities. He might have tried to convert Walt, though it was hard to imagine.

"Yeah, he told me about that new religion of his. How he got into it and how he was a changed person afterwards."

"It was a conversion. Like Saul on the road to Damascus." In a tone of mock-heroic proclamation I said, "I have seen a great light."

"He said you study religion at some university, right?"

"Right," I said. "Know the enemy. I go to the University of Chicago."

"Why the enemy? I thought you were going to be a preacher, like your old man."

"Nope. I aim to teach it, not preach it. In a college, if I can get a job."

"Well, what are you going to teach about religion?"

"Oh, I don't know." I hated to explain my academic career. "I study all kinds of religions, like Buddhism and Judaism, the myths of ancient Greece and the *Bhagavad Gita*. That's a holy book in India. I compare all these religions and see how they're alike and different."

"Do you tell students which one is true?"

"True?" I didn't know where to begin responding to this question.

Walt took a last gulp of coffee. "Yeah. I mean, you want to be a professor. So what do you profess?"

"I don't know, Walt. If I get a job at a state school, I have to be neutral. The legislature wouldn't be too happy if they found out the Religion Department was indoctrinating the innocent youth of the state. I study early Christianity, but I don't really want to have to argue with fundamentalists. What I do is more like studying history or another culture. Like anthropology."

Walt reflected for a minute. I finished my coffee. We sat there, chewing our cud. I liked the pace of this; it changed how I thought. Then I said, "Besides, I don't think I could say which religion is true. They are all true, in their own ways."

Walt looked skeptical. "But you have to think one of them is more true, at least for yourself."

All religions are true, but some are truer than others, at least for me. Well, I thought that, too. I stared down into my coffee cup and slowly rotated it on the saucer.

Walt got up from the counter and put on his hat, then turned to give me one more chance to explain my studies, my beliefs, and the meaning of life. I stood up. "I don't know what to say, Walt. Truth is a hard thing to talk about. What makes a religion true? I just stick to the facts, and try to explain why they're like they are."

We paid and went out. Walt said cheerily, "Be seeing you, young man. Good luck with the truth." He went back to his clutter of shoes, while I headed to the car, the coffee starting to make my nerves tingle. I thought about a theology paper I had written that fall, comparing how Origen and Irenaeus understood sin. I hadn't wanted to say one of them was right, but simply to understand why they each thought what they did. Now I felt a little uneasy about that, as if my conscience was nagging me.

In *The Varieties of Religious Experience*, William James describes a kind of person who can never be converted. "Such inaptitude for religious faith may in some cases be intellectual in its origin. Their religious faculties may be checked in their natural tendency to expand, by beliefs about the world that are inhibitive, the pessimistic and materialistic beliefs, for example, within which so many good souls, who in former times would have freely indulged their religious propensities, find themselves nowadays, as it were, frozen; or the agnostic vetoes upon faith as something weak and shameful, under which so many of us today lie cowering, afraid to use our instincts. In many persons such inhibitions are never overcome." I think he was talking about himself. I have known other ambivalent scholars of religion who, like James, inwardly long for the spiritual experiences they study, even as they question their reality or worth. I'm one. Part of me envies Will's capacity for intense religious experience and ecstatic emotion, because I've thought that my more intellectual outlook and prudent temperament prevent me from knowing these things first-hand. And in college and graduate school I learned to be detached and skeptical as I analyzed what is really going on when people think they see or hear God. The scholarly method can become how the scholar sees the world.

Talking to Walt brought home to me that my academic study of religion was also a way to avoid risking a genuine commitment. As I slowly drove home on icy streets, I wondered whether my students, if I ever had any, would ask me about the truth. I hoped not. I'd be relieved to weasel out of that discussion.

Five

Chicago Blues

A GROUP OF FOUR of us, all PhD students in theology or Christian history, met on Thursday nights at Jimmy's Woodlawn Tap, a bar on Fifty-fifth Street. Jimmy's was a dark, noisy den of mostly male drinkers, usually with some connection to the University. The floors were sticky, the tobacco smoke thick, and a long crack ran across the huge mirror behind the bar. We would drink a couple of pitchers of beer and argue with each other about what had gone on in class that week. All of us were taking Professor Krupat's course on "Classics of Christian Literature" that term. One wet February evening we found ourselves provoked by that day's discussion of Augustine's *Confessions*. We had reached Augustine's description of how he and several friends had hoped to start an intellectuals' commune or monastery, pooling their possessions so that they could devote their lives to study. The plan fell apart because the men thought their wives and girlfriends would not agree to it. Their carefully made arrangements were discarded, wrote Augustine, and "once more we turned to our sighs and groans. Again we trod the wide, well-beaten tracks of the world."

Joe was a quiet, thoughtful Texan with a huge black beard. "You know," he said, "what Augustine says is not all that different from one of our challenges here in Chi-town. We want to live the life of the mind, but we have to pay the bills, and money drags us back to a world we would rather forget. But I think Augustine is passing the buck. He blames his concern for worldly things on his fiancée, but he's the one who won't give it up. He's as attached to his possessions as he is to sex when he says, 'Give me chastity, O Lord, but please, not yet!' These guys don't want to have to share their stuff, but they blame it on the women."

This triggered a response from Robin, a Unitarian from Maine with thin blond hair who was now in his ninth year at the Divinity School. "You know what? My wife has been totally supportive of my going to graduate school. She's working and raising our kid while I study. And go boozing with you guys. But it's hard for me not to feel guilty. We're living on a shoestring and I wish I could buy her a Cadillac."

"We give up a lot to be in graduate school," said Joe. "Not just money. I was a preacher in a fair-sized Baptist church in Dallas. I came north to go to this school because books written by two theology professors here blew me away. I sure do miss my home, though. My daddy thinks I'll get corrupted by the liberals up here, like you evil tempters. Here I am, thirty-four years old and feeling like a kid, taking my peanut butter sandwich to school every day. In Texas, people looked up to me as a minister of God. I'm making a huge sacrifice to study process theology, but I think it is the key to the future of Christian thought."

"How about you, Sam? What did you give up?"

"A career in the N. B. A. I coulda been a contender." Sam grinned. His athletic abilities were an ongoing joke among us, because in spite of mediocre athletic abilities, he loved all sports, especially basketball, with infectious enthusiasm. He was a Catholic from Rhode Island, a muscular, jocular redhead. Sam was one of the happiest people I've known, and probably the only graduate student who didn't make complaining his primary form of entertainment, competition, and solace.

"But seriously," he went on, "for a Catholic like me, this is not exactly doing penance. If it were a decade ago, before Vatican II opened things up, I'd be stuck in a Catholic seminary where I'd have to toe the line. Instead, I study with Protestants and a few Jews and atheists. I learn about Buddhism and consider Marx's criticism of the opiate of the masses. I'm in intellectual heaven. I've been liberated to think for myself. And I can play basketball every day and drink beer with you groovy guys. Where's the self-denial in my life?"

"What about you, Peter," asked Robin. "Answer your own question."

"Well, I don't know," I offered cautiously. These were the first words I said in response to almost every question, even when I knew the answer. Unlike my impetuous biblical namesake, I'm pretty cautious. If Jesus said jump in the water, I'd feel it with my toes and consider the alternatives. "I'm not giving up very much. I'm twenty-four years old and don't have debts from college. I'm single and Maiko helps pay the bills. I don't mind living like a student, at least for a few more years. When I was home at

Christmas, I met an old high school buddy who works in St. Paul selling bonds to rich lawyers and doctors. He asked me how I could stand it, writing papers and sitting in classes. He said it sounds to him like a grade school punishment, like staying for detention to write some stupid statement a thousand times. It must be hell, he said."

"He should have said purgatory," Sam snorted. "There's light at the end of the tunnel."

"Yeah," I said, "but for me it's not a tunnel. I *like* going to the library, reading, and writing papers. I'm free to come and go and choose my working hours. This isn't penance, it's satisfying. What seems like renunciation to a hip young stockbroker is fulfillment for me. I'd be bored to death buying and selling interest rates. That would be wearing a hair shirt."

"Isn't it strange?" asked Robin. "We take pleasure in giving up other people's pleasures. I would rather sit in the library reading Paul Tillich than gamble, get drunk, or lie on a beach in Hawaii. I feel sorry for the people for whom those things are the *summum bonum.*"

"Do you guys know Lionel?" Joe put his arms on the table and held his hands out and open for emphasis, as if he were giving something away. "Now there's a guy who truly makes a sacrifice to study here. He's in the field of History of Religions, but I had a class with him and got to know him a little. He lived in his car last spring. He's totally broke, lives on the street like a bum. In the summers he works on oilrigs to make as much money as he can, but sometimes it runs out. Lionel is in debt many thousands of dollars and his family doesn't support him. He studies primitive religion, the aborigines and African tribes and American Indians, because he thinks civilization has fucked us up."

"Lionel is a rare bird," Robin agreed. "He lives like a wandering monk without a community. He thinks he has to give up the comforts of the mainstream in order to live a spiritual life. He chooses a solitary path to God."

I said to my friends, "You see, he, too, thinks he's renouncing the world for a higher calling. He isn't just putting in a few difficult years, like every grad student of law or medicine or science has to do. Studying religion is a spiritual path for him. It's like what the early Christians were doing, what Augustine longed to do. For him the life of the mind is a way to get closer to God, and he rejects unworthy pastimes and inferior pleasures."

"I don't think so," Sam said. "All of us just do what we gotta do to get our meal ticket. It's the hazing to get into the fraternity. To be able to teach religion. All this talk about self-sacrifice is malarkey. You can't have everything."

Sam and Robin called it a night and headed home, and Joe and I drifted from the table over to the twenty-yard bar for one more beer. We talked about Professor Krupat's amusing way of conducting us absent-mindedly with his pipe, ridiculed a pretentious student who talked too much, and then I went back to my new obsession.

"Another similarity to monks strikes me. It's like we take a vow of obedience, at least with certain professors. You can disagree about some little matter, but you damn well better agree with them about the important stuff, like whether Barth was right or wrong. Or whether Tillich's notion of ultimate concern opens doors or is vacuous. You better learn to think like the boss if you want to finish your dissertation and get a job."

"Tell me about it," the bartender suddenly snapped. He looked like so many of the University's perpetual grad students: full-bearded, gaunt, pale, with huge, thick glasses, a nearsighted Raskolnikov. He had been rinsing glasses further down the bar, and now he paused with a dishrag, drying his hands. Overhearing our conversation had sparked some deep feelings in him.

"I'm an ABD in history. One day my advisor tells me I'm never going to make it here. He says that I can't theorize. It was like he pulled the plug and now I would die, but I had a last moment to observe and say goodbye. I got up, shook his hand, went to the bathroom, and threw up. I could have tried to find another advisor and start over on a new topic. Instead I said, fuck it, I'm through. Excuse me for putting in my two cents worth, and I don't mean anything personal. But all night long I listen to the bellyaching of graduate students, people just like I used to be. They moan and groan and carry the weight of the world. But you guys have an easy life. You generate your own problems, and then you think that you are suffering nobly for an idea. You bleed self-pity. Like the Grand Inquisitor, your suffering is a pose. I heard you talking about giving things up. Well, I gave up my dream of being a history professor in the little college I went to in Iowa. But your word renunciation is fancy Latin. Let's just stick to the facts. There's always a price to make a choice. So live with the consequences. Why be melodramatic about it?"

I felt a little sheepish, as if a false pretense had been exposed as a sham. "Yeah, I guess so. Every decision is for something and against something else. There's always a road not taken. I see your point."

The bartender raised his eyebrows and nodded. He moved down the long bar to serve a gang of rowdy undergrads who had just showed up. He would be a good professor, I thought.

"Maybe he's right," I muttered to Joe. "Maybe this whole idea of renunciation is bullshit. I was getting attached to it, but maybe I'll have to give it up."

"Are you trying to be paradoxical?" Joe asked, giving me an elbow in the ribs. He downed his dregs and said, "C'mon, let's get outta here." We shoved off and headed down Fifty-fifth Street towards our apartments, with the streetlights glinting on the slick road. I kicked a can into the gutter.

"You're right, I'm fascinated by the paradoxes of giving up and getting. I think I'm going to make this my research topic." Our conversation that night was the seed that grew into my dissertation on Christian asceticism.

I started to keep my eyes open for Lionel. I often saw him in the coffee shop and twice we shared a quick lunch. We talked mostly about preliterate tribal societies. Lionel viewed the Australian aborigines as an ideal society of wanderers who shared all things in common. "Owning property, staying in one place—that's what kills the soul," Lionel said, his eyes flashing with an intensity that startled me. "Being on the move keeps the spirit moving." Lionel was looking for a different way to live in the world. He admitted that his ideal was totally impractical in a modern society. Without a community that shared his vision of the right way to live, he would always be a loner. I remembered Robin's account of Lionel's hand-to-mouth existence, but I didn't ask him how he was getting by. He looked pretty rough around the edges, with a few permanent crumbs in his auburn beard and rumpled jeans worn for many days.

One day in April I was walking down Fifty-third Street, where the races and classes of Hyde Park mingle. Several fast food joints catered mostly to African Americans, most notably the Chicken Shack, with its neon sign of a man in a chef's hat with an axe chasing a squawking chicken. Ribs N Bibs had a huge iron stove in the back, from which clouds of greasy smoke belched forth at all hours. In one block could be found an expensive chocolate shop, a store that sold oriental fish, a health food outlet that hawked vitamin supplements and herbal concoctions of powdered trees from Africa, a pawn shop, and two high-interest loan and check-cashing operations that gave expensive money fast. Wedged into this interesting marketplace was "Valois See Your Food," a grungy cafeteria. You pointed to what you wanted, and Mr. Valois or his crony, Shakey, served it up, usually with a distinct "plop" sound as it hit your plate. It wasn't appetizing, but it was cheap and the servings were huge. Gravy drowned everything and you mopped it up with all the white bread you wanted. The clientele was primarily African American men, including several old guys who seemed to be lifers.

As I was passing in front of Valois See Your Food on a Saturday about noon, I looked in and saw Lionel putting away a pile of mashed potatoes and a couple of pork chops. He nodded and waved a hand, and I decided to say howdy. I joined him at his window table and said, "How's life?"

"Not too great right now," he said. "I have to move my car. Can you help me push it?"

Lionel had been sleeping in his car, moving every night, and when the battery went dead watchdog residents reported him. The police told him he couldn't leave his vehicle there, and a jumpstart didn't work. He wanted to push the car to a gas station and get a mechanic to look at it. An hour later, the two of us, helped by a passing jogger, were shoving his old station wagon slowly along Blackstone Avenue. The car was packed with books, clothes, and a rudimentary kitchen, including a camping stove and a big jug of water. We pushed the car into the lot and waited for the mechanic.

"How do you do this, Lionel?" I asked. "The cold, the danger of getting robbed, the lack of privacy. How do you get your academic work done?"

"Oh, I'll get by until June. I spend a lot of time in the library. Sometimes I crash with a friend, but I don't like to ask. People feel sorry for me, but I like the freedom and aloneness."

"You like solitude?"

"Yes," he admitted. "I would usually rather be by myself than have to talk to people. I mean, really, what is there to say? Most talk is wasted breath. It just fills up the open spaces. Emptiness is better. I've noticed that when I don't interact with people much, I am hungry to read. I devour books. And I want God, I want to be closer to God. When I'm with people that desire goes away."

"What about finding God in church, or with some group of people who feel as you do about the indigenous Australian people?"

Lionel smiled a wry, lopsided grin. "Do you know of any fellowship of aborigines in Chicago? If so, sign me up for coffee hour duty. But I don't think it's going to happen. In the meantime, I keep God alive in my own way."

"What do you mean? Does God depend on you?"

"I'm hesitant to use the word God, because what I mean is different from what Christians mean. But for lack of a better word, okay, God. Yes, God needs us to be open and receptive. I'm not aware of God in church. But when I'm in some other places, I sense a spirit."

From what he had read about Australian and other tribal peoples, for instance in Mircea Eliade's books about religion, Lionel was profoundly impressed by tribal peoples' sense of living in a sacred cosmos. It was paradoxical to find God by reading, he said, because he thought that "the religions of the book" had lost touch with an older, more direct mode of apprehending the divine. Literacy seemed to entail a spiritual cost. Yet it was through books that Lionel had access to that preliterate way of seeing the whole world as saturated with signs of the divine. Cosmic religion was a matter of seeing the qualities of the sacred in nature: in trees, rivers, mountains, and the stars. When he read anthropologists' transcripts of the Navajo creation myth, an African hunting story, or the "songline" of a no-madic Aborigine recounting legends associated with natural landmarks, Lionel felt transported to another way of being in the world.

"Sometimes," he went on, "when I put my book down, I look out at Lake Michigan or the barren landscape of North Dakota in August, and I see the world as a holy place full of messages. Possessive attachment to little bits of the world, like what I own or the place I live, wrecks that aware-ness. When I was in college I read a lot of things by Nikos Kazantzakis, and one of his ideas that grabbed me was that we have to save God. To do that, to keep the spark of longing alive, we have to abandon the comforts of mainstream, bourgeois life. That includes family, owning a home, and the security of having a defined role in society."

I was fascinated. This guy was rejecting ordinary American life because of a religious vision. Lionel was going to save God by studying the religions of tribal people and living like a street person. His solitude would make a space for God, or at least for his desire for God. Like the early Church's hermits and monks, Lionel was choosing to empty his life of trivial and distracting clutter. But he was an ascetic in a society that does not sanction this practice and thought he was crazy. And in Chicago!

"Lionel," I said, "you are either a saint or off your rocker. You remind me of my brother, although he wouldn't spend so much time reading about religion."

The mechanic came back and told us that the car needed a new starter. He could put it in on Monday for seventy bucks. Lionel sighed and said, "All right, do it." He loaded a briefcase full of books and stuffed a few clothes into a small backpack. I offered him the couch in my apartment, but he said he had already asked Robin for a place to stay and would go there tonight after working until midnight in Regenstein Library.

"If you need a place to crash, man, please feel free to stay with me and Maiko. Any time."

"Thanks for the offer, Peter." He looked at me out of the corner of his eye, shyly, as if embarrassed. "I may do that. But I have to be careful not to get too close. I have to keep an empty space."

Keeping an empty place is a different metaphor than inflicting pain on yourself or self-denial, but Lionel, too, was trying to let go of secondary matters in order to make possible an intense experience of a mysterious spiritual presence. I felt a twinge of jealousy and admiration for that way of life as I entered a small supermarket to stock up on provisions. I had carefully prepared a grocery list of everything I thought I needed.

In October 1975, my father called to ask whether I knew where Will was. No, I said, I hadn't talked to him for several months, since a phone call in July. Dad had called the Minneapolis ashram and talked with Marge and Alex. Marge was testy, hinted at a conflict, and said bitterly, "I hope you are happy now. You can have him back." Alex, more diplomatic and communicative, reported that Will had found ashram discipline to be too demanding. As he left, Will stated that he would find another ashram focused on the spirit, not the flesh. Alex was concerned because Will had not been heard from since he left two weeks earlier. "We wish him well, whatever path he takes from here." He and Dad agreed to exchange any information that either of them received from Will.

A couple of days later, Maiko and I were sitting at the kitchen table over supper, catching up. She had landed a position as understudy for the character Honey in Edward Albee's "Who's Afraid of Virginia Woolf?" It was a controversial casting, because Honey is described as a "petite blonde girl, rather plain." Maiko was only the first of those adjectives. She had to learn all the lines, but if the lead actress didn't get sick, Maiko would never go on stage. We talked about what it takes to break into the theater world: hard work, being available, a lucky break.

The doorbell rang, and there was Will, grinning from ear to ear. He had taken a bus down to Hyde Park from the Bhakti Dharma ashram on the north side of Chicago, where he now lived. The three of us sat around the table, Will drinking tea while Maiko and I finished our beers from supper. He looked better than the last time I had seen him, relaxed and ready to laugh at a joke. He was working on a beard and wore a Sikh turban and Western clothes.

"Looks like you're going through some changes," said Maiko. "You are different every time I see you. I like your bell bottoms."

"Yeah, I'm always changing, like a larva. I'm still waiting for my butterfly phase. It's gonna be gorgeous." He smiled and reached for his teacup. "Good stuff. Can I have some more, please?"

"So how did you come to leave the Minneapolis ashram?" I asked.

"I hit the wall with Marge. She was acting like the big sister I never had, thank God. I can deal with a little sister, but not Marge. It seemed like sibling rivalry between us. We were competing for something, I don't even know what. She was trying to be SuperSikh, and always policing my infractions of the rules. The final straw was one morning when I wanted to sleep late. I had stayed out until midnight to hear some folk music in a Seven Corners bar. I don't touch alcohol, but I wanted to hear old college buddies try to make it on a bigger stage. After a few hours of sleep that night I couldn't get my eyes open. Marge actually poured a glass of cold water on me, and I blew up and swore at her. Later, after breakfast, I muttered that Bhakti Dharma is supposed to be about devotion and trust. It's not a religion of works righteousness. That really pushed her buttons. She comes from a Catholic background, and she must have had this argument before. Don't be ridiculous, she said, Yogi Bhakta is crystal clear about the nature of our practice. Our path isn't just about having faith, it's about putting faith into action. We do that in a community, and someone has to be responsible for the ashram's well being. That's my role, and frankly, buster, you are not pulling your weight. There is faith, and there is the life of faith, and if you want the life then you better make some sacrifices of your own sweet will."

"Whoa, baby," I said, slapping my knee. "It's the faith and works question all over again, but Luther and the Pope are wearing turbans."

"Sort of. She has a point, I admit. But mixed up with the theology is a personality conflict. That Minneapolis ashram is a weird social system that reminds me of a messed up family. I feel like I'm trapped in the role of the black sheep or the screw-up little brother. I keep breaking rules I didn't know about or think are trivial. Everybody else in the family tries to please the parents, in this case Yogi Bhakta, by being a good, obedient child. It feels like they want me to play a certain role that the system needs. It reminds me in that way of my own family."

"Ouch," I said, and frowned.

Maiko leaned over to poke my ribs and said to Will, "Peter is kind of an uptight prig, isn't he?"

"Okay, okay," I said, grumpily, and yielded to Maiko's teasing. "Marge has been giving me tips. She wants me to keep an eye on you here and report back to her. But seriously, do you think things will be any different in the Chicago ashram? What's it like so far?"

"It is a completely different group of people and a much bigger community, three houses with twenty-five people. Jeff, the leader, is married to Susan, and they create a different vibe than the two celibate leaders in Minnesota, Alex and Marge. The other ashram residents seem happier, lighter somehow. I feel like I can make a fresh start. The bad memory of that suicide summer and my time in the hospital hung over me in the Twin Cities. I was always the guy who might off himself if you don't watch him. I was the fuck-up, the guy who has to break the rules to do his own thing. I'm sick of that role but they wouldn't give me a new one. Now I hope things will be different. I'm going to become a Sikh and take a Sikh name. I'm going to do good work. I want to be a productive member of the ashram community and a good example for Bhakti Dharma."

"Well, that's great," I said. "I'm glad you'll be near me, too. Maybe we can get together more than we have during these last few years."

Maiko added eagerly, "Most of the theaters where I go for auditions and to see plays are on the near north side. So I can see you sometimes, too."

"I'd like that," Will replied, warmly. Although he had only encountered Maiko twice during that summer I lived in Minneapolis, he was open with her. "I want to give my whole being to Yogi Bhakta. But I don't think I have to cut myself off from everybody to do that. It's been more than four years since I first encountered my guru. I've made some changes. I know I have to sacrifice some things, like going to a movie or a blues bar in the evening. I could sing the blues about giving up the blues, but I won't. I'm not giving up what's most important."

"Moderation in all things, including renunciation," I suggested. "That's the path for me."

Will paused thoughtfully. He picked up his half-empty teacup and swirled the brown water around the cup. "Moderation gets boring. Intensity is good. Empty the cup and fill it up again. There's a difference between wise balance and fear of the edges."

"What do you mean?" Maiko asked quickly. "What edges?"

Will looked at her seriously, soberly. The beer had made Maiko and me a little woozy, but Will was suddenly lucid and icy. "The edges of human experience. You can live being afraid of intensity, cautiously avoiding all danger. That kind of moderation is different from what Yogi Bhakta talks about, which is total commitment. It's more like throwing yourself off of a cliff. Then you fall into the arms of God."

Maiko looked irritated. "That sounds like suicide talk. I don't know where I am with you guys sometimes, with your philosophizing about religion and renunciation and jumping off cliffs. What do you really mean? Or are you just playing around with metaphors?"

Will frowned. "We play with ideas to see where they will take us. When I do that in the ashram, people wonder about me. I just meant, a minute ago, that religious faith is not for the cautious. It isn't moderation; it's risky and scary. You put the pedal to the metal. Say goodbye to some things. You can't have everything, but you can have the best thing. That's different from lukewarm, half-hearted moderation."

Maiko sighed, relieved, and leaned back in her chair. "Now I get you. Luckily there aren't any cliffs in Chicago anyway. This city is flat as a pancake. Thank God for the lake, which keeps it interesting."

Our talk turned to Lake Michigan beaches, Chicago neighborhoods, and the bus system. Will got hungry, and Maiko made him a sandwich. I drove him over to the Illinois Central train platform, where he caught a train going downtown to the bus that would take him north. He would be home in time to be in bed for a good night's sleep before yoga at four o'clock.

Although devotees of Yogi Bhakta were supposed to have a job or be in school, Will seemed to have a lot of time on his hands during that winter of 1976. He meditated for hours every day and did household chores around the ashram, sweeping, chopping vegetables, and washing laundry. He had several jobs for pay, but they didn't seem to last long. He had enough free time, especially in the afternoons, to wander around Chicago. He liked to meet new people and discuss religion and philosophy with them. He might have been a good Mormon missionary, going door to door with a friendly smile. I'm sure that Will did not get as much lively argument as he wanted within the ashram. I can imagine him trying to strike some intellectual sparks and getting the message that debating and speculating is not the way to express devotion. So he sought out strangers to tell about his faith in Yogi Bhakta and the message that ultimate bliss comes through yoga and fervent love.

He seemed particularly attracted to Chicago's African American neighborhoods. There were some dangerous areas near the university that I was careful to avoid. I stayed between Forty-seventh Street and the Midway unless I drove to the Loop or the North Side. I never went to the black neighborhoods, which I called "the ghetto," except to the blues bars run by Buddy Guy, Junior Wells, and the established bluesmen. Half a dozen of us would pile into a car, assuming there was safety in numbers, and park as close as we could to the bar.

Will ambled all over the city, including the Cabrini Green housing projects near the Loop. He liked the Maxwell Street Market, a flea market on the West Side where you could buy back the stereo that had been stolen from your apartment yesterday. Will strolled up and down the street, checking out the scene. When it was cold he warmed himself by a fire in a barrel, rubbing his hands with the bums. He told me about some of his encounters there. Apparently the old guys adopted him as an eccentric and amusing companion. Some of them tried to get him to walk with Jesus, and some of them asserted with lavish profanity that all religion was bullshit. They were not afraid to challenge him, and Will enjoyed these freewheeling conversations, which reminded me of late night bull sessions in college dormitories. Will liked the unpredictable mix of bantering, jousting, and earnest argument about religion. The respectable folk he encountered at his work situations avoided the topic of religion; they seemed embarrassed and changed the subject. Those people would rather talk about anything—serious or trivial, their sex lives, cars, or baseball—than what they believed about God. The street people, in contrast, were openly incredulous, joshing, or curious about Bhakti Dharma, and this was a relief to Will. He could start over, again and again, reliving anew his conversion to Yogi Bhakta's way.

Will had conflicts and tensions with other members of the Chicago ashram because of his lax observance of certain disciplines and his extreme self-punishment in other ways. Once his eating an ice cream cone on the steps in front of the ashram provoked a long community meeting devoted to "criticism and self-criticism." Will nodded to me and went on, "People would make up some sin to confess and then look at me like it was my turn. Finally I came clean."

He laughed as he told me about a similar exercise devoted to convincing him to eat breakfast. "I just can't seem to get it right," he said, suddenly serious. "I bounce from one extreme to the other and get bored by a safe routine. All these rules and regulations seem to kill my spirit. But I'm making a sincere effort to fit in."

To get away from these frictions, Will occasionally disappeared from the ashram for a day or two. He was often able to stay with the old African American guys whom he met on the streets. They let him sleep on the floor of a cheap hotel room or they paid for a bunk in the Salvation Army shelter. Once when he was about to be knifed, two old geezers intervened to protect him, calming down an irate drunk. A couple of times Will slept in Bughouse Square, the park in front of the Newberry Library, guarded by all-night drinkers. When I worried out loud about his safety in the dangerous parts of the city, he said, "The old guys look after me. They spread the word. They walk down the street with me and get me on the bus. They like me. And I like them."

I didn't have close black friends, and I was curious about how Will crossed what often seems to me an insurmountable racial barrier. I asked him if it was hard or easy to be friends with an African American. He looked at me with surprise and said, "It's whatever you make it."

I had had an upsetting incident in college a few years earlier. In a literature class at Carleton, we were reading Malcolm X's autobiography and discussing black-white relations. I was pretty timid in classroom discussions, and racial issues were not something I had strong opinions about. But for some reason that day I remarked: "I think you have to look past skin color to the character of a person. When I look at people, I don't see a black person or a yellow or white one. I just see a human being like me."

A hand shot up across the room. An African American woman with big glasses and a bright red shawl around her shoulders asserted, "Well, honey, if you don't see my skin color, then you don't see *me*. Because my skin is part of who I am."

I felt humiliated, as if I had uttered a racist remark. And I had been trying to show that I was *not* a racist! I sunk into my chair and the class discussion veered back to Malcolm's remarks about white liberals, but I couldn't pay attention because I was so embarrassed. That was the last time I said anything about race, even to friends.

Will had found a way to connect with a certain circle of black people. I never met any of them, except once when Will took me to the Maxwell Street market. One wizened fellow kept calling me "the reverend" when he found out I was going to the Divinity School, and another one teased me that I should evangelize my brother and "bring him home." The meeting ground for Will and these friendly gentlemen was religion. Instead of talking about race, they discussed whether Jesus or Yogi Bhakta had the scoop on God, or whether you could really "get religion" without gospel music. "If you want to get high on God, now that's the way to do it, man. You got to praise Him loud and long."

Smiling broadly, Will opened his arms as if to embrace his street buddy. "We do that too, brother. You ought to check us out."

There was another ingredient, I think, that drew them together. Will was a scrawny, wide-eyed kid who seemed innocent and naïve. He was wearing what looked like a towel wrapped around his head, not driving a BMW. He was different than the smart-ass University of Chicago students doing sociology studies or the tough working-class kids from Cicero. Will trusted and depended on the street people. On some level his tender soul pierced their hearts, and even when they gave him a hard time about his Indian god in pajamas, or asked him if to convert they would have to give up barbeque, their teasing was affectionate. Will evoked their compassionate and protective response. A homeless street person, too, wants to take care of someone.

Six

Gurus and Professors

D URING MY FIRST THREE years in Chicago, when I didn't have much contact with Will, I became keenly interested in new religious movements. I saw Hare Krishna members soliciting in O'Hare and Midway airports, read about the opulent lifestyles of Guru Maharaji and Bhagwan Shree Rajneesh, and heard sensationalistic media reports about swamis or charismatic Christian preachers found in bed with a follower or being sued for harshly punishing a disobedient child in his movement. I met several students at the University who had dabbled in Asian religious practices but backed off from a fuller commitment, usually because of the demand for submission to an authoritarian leader. The Unification Church, making a bid for academic respectability, sent one of its members to the Divinity School to study for his doctorate in theology. He earned his degree but somewhere in Swift Hall lost his faith in the Reverend Moon. New religious movements seemed to be everywhere, and I puzzled over why this was happening at this historical moment, what they had in common, and the motives of people who gave their lives to a little-known faith.

The new groups are very different from each other. Some of them are based on ancient Asian traditions, like Hare Krishna and Bhakti Dharma, although Yogi Bhakta's synthesis of several traditions is rejected by the religions he tried to harmonize. Some cults began as Christian offshoots, for instance the Children of God and the People's Temple, and later developed controversial practices or beliefs, especially regarding the divine or prophetic status of their leader. Neo-pagan movements such as Wicca, Druidry, and shamanistic groups turn to ritual, magic, the Goddess, or healing powers in the natural world. Flying saucer cults profess beliefs about extra-terrestrial beings that will bring humans a message from God or rescue a few lucky souls from the coming time of trial. The 1970s gave birth or rapid growth to personal development movements with religious dimensions such as Scientology and Transcendental Meditation. Some of these groups do not require demanding lifestyle changes, but they make claims that most Americans think are—well, kooky, like Maharishi's assertion that if one per cent of humans meditate at once, an era of world peace will be inaugurated. He also claimed that meditators are able to levitate. The only thing that this miscellaneous grab bag of religions has in common is that they seem weird to the average American. They demand a sacrifice of what nice folks think is common sense.

Some established churches were once heretical strains of Christianity, including Unitarians, who reject the Trinity, and Quakers, who believe in an Inner Light and dispense with the Church and its sacraments. Negative reactions to 1970s cults are similar to earlier hostility to Mormons, Seventh Day Adventists, Christian Scientists, Jehovah's Witnesses, and countless smaller groups that eventually died out or were absorbed by other churches.

One obvious contrast among the cults, or new religious movements (NRMs), as they came to be called by scholars, is whether or not their worldview is apocalyptic. It is usually groups related to Christianity that have an eschatological orientation and see salvation as rescue from an impending disaster or a violent final conflict. Yet even Bhakti Dharma picked up and transformed the American counterculture's myths about an Age of Aquarius, a dawning new era of spirituality, a nonviolent Apocalypse Lite. Neither Will nor I had any interest in or anxiety about the end of the world. Growing up in a mainline Lutheran church had made eschatology familiar but not attractive. We heard a reading from the Book of Revelation about once a year, but our father spoke of its spectacular symbols as representing God's ultimate victory over evil, not a secret code for predicting historical events.

Not the end of the world, but expanded consciousness—that's what Will wanted, and I did too, if I didn't have to sacrifice my intellect. Expanded to what? We would know when we got there. We wanted direct experience of God, not simply a list of theological doctrines to believe, not polite coffee-hour chatter after church. There had to be more possibilities than ordinary consciousness was aware of. Why did we think so? For my generation, the Road to God went through the Valley of Drugs. For almost every person I've met who was involved in a new religious movement derived from an Asian tradition, disciplined spiritual practice replaced an experimental search for bliss or intense vision by using psychedelic drugs. A popular role model was Richard Alpert, who took psychedelics as far as they would take him, turned to India and a spiritual path, and became the Baba Ram Dass of *Be Here Now*.

I smoked dope occasionally in college and twice took mescaline. There is more to reality than ordinary consciousness perceives, and drugs can open "the doors of perception," as Aldous Huxley's popular book is titled. I saw the vivid colors, heard the deeper music, and ate the delicious junk food, all with no long-term effects. One moment stands out. I asked my college girlfriend, Cheryl, to watch out for me one day I took mescaline. We came to a stoplight and stood there for a minute. The red and green lights changed as cars whizzed by. There was a connection between these events, but I couldn't understand what it was, or how to get across the street. Realizing this, Cheryl took my arm and said with an infinitely wise smile, Come on, let me help you cross. I was flooded with gratitude. At the end of the day, describing what happened to me, I wrote, "Trust. It all comes down to that."

For me drugs were only an occasional diversion from my real life in school. Will had taken LSD and used cocaine, and for a couple of years pot was a daily vitamin in his musician's lifestyle. His disillusionment and depression when the highs didn't last made him desperate for a more reliable route to the alternate reality he craved.

One Sunday afternoon in Northfield, during the long winter of the year he was at St. Olaf and I at Carleton, he called me up and wanted to meet for breakfast at the Ideal Café on Main Street. For me that meant waffles for supper. Will staggered in and slumped into the booth. He looked like he had been airlifted out of a war zone: his face was pale and sunken, his eyelids half closed, and his whole body seemed listless and weak as he propped himself into a corner of the booth. He had taken a heavy dose of LSD on Friday night, stayed awake all that night, and finally crashed late Saturday night, sleeping for fourteen hours. He had had intense and colorful visions, he said, but he couldn't remember them.

"Right," I said, "drugs can be so overwhelming that you can't find words or understand what's happening."

"I'm starting to think it's a dead-end trip. If I can't remember it, did it even happen? My mind leaves my body and goes somewhere else. I'm floating, soaring like an eagle. I don't care about anything. Everything falls away. A few weeks ago Annika broke up with me. She said people tripping think they are profound when they are just stupid. I can't concentrate to study. After that bust at Carleton, I'm sick of the paranoia about getting caught. And when I come back down from a trip, like today, my energy is zapped. I have to sit and stare into space for a day before I can even talk. I see somebody who is stoned, and all he can say is, Groovy! Or, Wow, man, that's intense! I imagine how Mom or Dad would see this deadhead stupidity. Drugs send me into a lonely place where there's nothing to say or do. I want to come back."

I listened to Will and tried to be sympathetic, but I agreed with his gloomy self-diagnosis and wished he would get his head straight. He might have to hit bottom first, I mused. Drugs can give a shock to your habitual vision and shake things up, but when they become a way of life you are lost. During the 1970s I met a lot of people who came to that conclusion, gave up drugs, and turned to a religion promising to sustain a vision of another reality. Or to focus one's vision on this reality, because everything that matters is right here, right now. "It's not stupid," said Yogi Bhakta, "you are stupid. See what is right in front of you and learn to appreciate it."

I wanted to do that, too, but I hadn't found a Way. I understood Will's desire for intensity, altered consciousness, and embodied spiritual practice. I did a little yoga in college, in a class that counted for academic credit for physical education. It was just exercise, but I knew that there was a philosophy and worldview behind the postures. One winter term in a class on Asian religions, I learned to meditate. The professor who taught Asian religions, Bradley Scott, brought a Thai monk to Carleton to teach the Vipassana style of meditation and a Japanese monk to instruct us in Zen meditation. We practiced every morning at six. In the frigid darkness I trudged over to the gym where we sat on cushions for an hour or two and then talked about what it was like. I didn't have any cosmic revelations or ascend to another sphere, but I liked the serene and lucid state of watchfulness that seemed to arise in me, at least for a few minutes, about half the time. The rest of the time either "monkey mind" sent my thoughts and feelings tumbling over each other in distracted, freewheeling succession, or else I judged myself harshly for not feeling something more profound. When I moved to Chicago, I meditated infrequently, once a week or so when I was too tired to work any more. It wasn't a way of life or a steady discipline that produced any noticeable change in me, and it didn't connect me to fellow practitioners. It was just a reminder that this could become an important part of my life if I put a little effort into it.

Yoga, meditation, being here now—all this made sense. What puzzled me about my contemporaries who joined cults was their desire for a guru or charismatic leader. I not only didn't feel that desire, I was suspicious of it, even hostile to it. In our frustrating conversations during the months after his conversion, Will tried to spark in me some enthusiasm for a spiritual guide. Maybe, he must have thought, if Peter admits this need hypothetically, then Yogi Bhakta will start to appeal to him. Soon after he moved to Chicago, I showed him around the University. As we sat on a bench near Regenstein Library on a cloudy November day, he returned to a fervent belief.

"You have to have a living spiritual guide," he asserted. "It's not enough to read ancient scriptures or go through prescribed rituals. Those can be empty actions."

"So can obeying an authority figure," I contended. "Why is it necessary to have a guru?"

"Because you surrender to a guru. You have to give your all, not just ninety-nine percent. It takes a leap of faith to make the guru the center of your life, and without that leap, there's no faith. But to do that gives you rewards beyond your wildest dreams. You discover a power of love you never knew was in you. It's not just that I love Yogi Bhakta. I also want to be the person who loves him. The guy who makes the center of his life devotion, not self-gratification."

"But how did you know Yogi Bhakta was the one? There are hundreds of people claiming to be God or to speak for him."

Will pointed at the library. "Some books that aren't in there have helped me. One is Carlos Castaneda's *The Teachings of Don Juan*. You should read it, because it shows how powerful a spiritual guide can be. Another one is *Be Here Now*. Baba Ram Dass says that when you are ready for a guru, the guru will appear. You will recognize him."

"How did you recognize Yogi Bhakta?"

"I was at the festival in New Mexico with Julie. We were on the side of a beautiful mountain and the air was thin and cold, purifying us. I was feeling lost and alone, because nothing in my life had meaning or purpose. Even my friendship with Julie was falling apart, because she was still heavy into drugs while I was on my way out. We were testing each other, arguing, judging. It's hard to believe all the pain I felt before I found Yogiji."

Will picked up some fallen leaves and threw them in the air, and the breeze scattered them. "Poof. All gone. Like the past." He laughed. "I was at the festival with hundreds of people who were doing yoga and listening to our teacher. Yogi Bhakta spoke about world peace and loving God in our brothers and sisters. I wanted to have that blissful feeling always, to hold on to it forever, to go on and on with this new energy. It was devotion to Yogi Bhakta that brought all of us there and united us. He did it. You can't worship an abstract God or a transcendent principle. That's just talk. You can only love a real person. If God is personal, then God must be known in a person. Doesn't Christianity say that, too? Well, this is the person who lets me know God here and now. He has deep black eyes, a big beard, and a crooked smile. He has a certain tone in his voice that gets to me. I recognize him. God is not going to call me any more clearly."

"Go on. Did he recognize you?"

"There was a moment one evening after satsang, when Yogiji had finished teaching and was receiving his followers' devotion. The sun was going down, and the light fell slanting on the stage, so half his face was light and half dark. We were exhausted from the yoga and the service, but so happy. He sat there smiling and blessing us. I approached him, bowed, and found I was crying. He looked into my eyes and said, Those are tears of joy. They are a blessing. Now you must rise up from being dead. You will raise the kundalini energy within. I didn't know what he meant, but I knew God was speaking to me through this man. I was trembling and sweating. I tasted salty tears. I was so grateful to Yogiji for giving me this joy. You know that line from Coleridge's 'Rime of the Ancient Mariner'? I was blessed and could bless. That's what it felt like, as if I had been given the biggest gift in the universe, and at the same time I was able to be the giver of the only thing that really matters, the blessing of life itself. I rejoiced to be alive."

"That is a beautiful story, Will. I sort of wish it could happen to me."

"It's not just a story. And it can happen to you, Peter. Why not? If you want it, why not? You are ready for the guru, man."

"You think so?" I asked. But I changed the subject to what he was going to do next, which he had very little conception of, beyond serving Yogi Bhakta. I have thought about Will's question a great deal since that afternoon. Why not me? It's partly a matter of temperament and partly a matter of theology, and maybe these things are linked. When he was a little boy, Will loved Jesus. He wanted to be like the man from Galilee and, my mother told me, he prayed fervently, Come, Lord Jesus, come! In contrast, I saw Jesus as a nice guy. A good role model, truly wise and compassionate. But not exactly God. For me, God had to be transcendent, far away, the Creator and Judge, but remote, up in the control tower at Command Central. My prayers were intellectual propositions or polite requests for moral improvement.

I always notice how somebody's particular notion of Jesus reflects his own point of view. Even when I was a boy, I wondered whether my father's social justice Jesus, the prophet who would have stood up for civil rights or protested an evil war, would have voted the Minnesota Democratic/Farmer/Labor ticket. Was this the real Jesus, or a man-made, Dad-made image? I always stop and think like that.

Since idolatry is a central idea for Protestants, we have to do a lot of renouncing of penultimate claims. Yet Protestants, too, can be idolaters, worshiping the Bible or their good buddy, Jesus. I'm suspicious not of Jesus, but of every specific idea of him. In college I was fascinated by Paul Tillich's "God Beyond God" and his critique of the ways in which humans make their finite interests into ultimate concerns. Because I always see the human side of religion, I can't make a whole-hearted faith commitment. A little voice tells me, *That's just your idea of God, not the real God.* I'm suspicious, skeptical, at times cynical, when I look at the naïve trust that religious people invest in an all too human, inevitably flawed leader like Yogi Bhakta. At least discovering the truth won't disillusion me, I've thought, because I have no illusions.

It was the same in relation to my teachers in college and graduate school. In the Divinity School I saw fellow students who reminded me of rock star groupies as they fawned on a popular professor. They took every one of that professor's classes and internalized his terminology, methodology, and attitude to religion. There was a famous French philosopher on the faculty, and a few students adopted his French accent for words that had an obvious English equivalent; they talked about "phenomenolo*gie*," the "hermeneut," and "structural*eees*m" with a straight face. These students truly valued the thought of the great man and they wanted a mentor, father figure, or infallible intellectual authority. But I would not be taken in. Although I was jealous of the close bond, sometimes evolving into friendship, which these students had with a Divinity School professor, I held myself aloof. I didn't go to office hours, hang around after class, or invite professors for coffee. I was afraid of being overwhelmed by these powerful minds. My intellectual self-confidence was shaky enough that I had to protect my independence from any dominating theory or personality. I was as distant and guarded with them as I was with God's self-proclaimed spokesmen on earth, the priests, prophets, and yogis. I had the guru blues, not wanting the guide I wanted.

When I put up a wall between myself and my teachers, and when I reject as idolatry any attempt to give God a human face, I must be missing something. But I guess I'm still not ready to discover my guru. He would ask too much.

During the winter of 1976, I tried to put together a proposal for my dissertation. I was officially in the field of History of Christianity and had done most of my coursework on the early history of the church. I was especially interested in the desert fathers and Augustine, whose experience became a model of conversion for later Christians. Why, I wondered, did Augustine believe that in order to become a Christian, he had to give up his teaching career and family? Why did he think he had to renounce all sexual relations? By the time of his dramatic conversion in Milan in 387 AD, he had been in a long-term relationship for almost a decade, fathered a son named Adeodatus, and gotten involved with another woman. Why did he feel that turning to God required rejecting everything about his previous life and condemning it as dominated by greed, lust, and ambition? In his *Confessions*, Augustine described the powerful appeal to him of the first monks, who withdrew to the Egyptian desert to live in simple communities, away from the vices of the late Roman Empire. For years Augustine longed to commit himself whole-heartedly to the Christian life, but he remained on the fringes, learning about it but not ready to make a full confession of faith until he could renounce his former life. He prayed for God to give him chastity, "but not quite yet."

People in Duluth did not struggle with demons or withdraw to the north woods to defeat the devil. No one I knew gave up anything for Jesus, except for one Catholic boy who swore off chocolate during Lent. Every day he put a Baby Ruth in a shoebox, and he ate as much of it as he could on Easter Sunday. Even the money I put in the offering plate as a boy was an addition to my weekly allowance. In the circle of liberal Protestants, Catholics, Jews, and agnostics in which I moved in Duluth, at Carleton, and in Chicago, one thing we would agree on was that Augustine's ideal of self-denial was perverse. It was a sign of buried self-hatred or a twisted attempt to placate an angry God. Good religion, we agreed, enhances human life, while bad religion distorts or denigrates it in the name of a spiritual otherworld. As I studied the history of Christianity, however, I began to see that in every variety there is usually some wisdom as well as potential craziness. Our era's version of mental health is not the only criterion for judging religion. Soon after my PhD exams and the discussion at Jimmy's

Woodlawn Tap, I decided that to study asceticism, that is, self-denial and self-discipline, would sustain my interest for the several years it would take me to research and write a dissertation. I would be motivated to stay with this topic, I thought, partly because it might help me understand Will's version of religious devotion.

My advisor, Professor Richard Thompson, was an academic superstar in his mid-fifties. He had made his reputation with several books that examined the corruption of the Roman church during the medieval period. Thompson was either an atheist or an agnostic who thought that any religious organization, be it church, synagogue, mosque, or temple, was at bottom a duplicitous means of wielding power. His intellectual heroes were Voltaire, Gibbon, Nietzsche, and Michel Foucault. Thompson viewed organized religion as an expression of the will to power of the priestly caste. He was disgusted by any hint of piety or devotion, including Protestant expressions, and he inevitably saw in them either hypocrisy or convenient self-deception. In several classes I heard him make scornful remarks about Christian practices, puncturing the confidence of students who were sympathetic to martyrs, saints, popes, or monks.

It was going to be a challenge to work with Thompson, because I was much more ambivalent about Christianity than he. To put it more positively, I thought that there might be some genuine value in the ascetic movements I proposed to study. Their rejection of their society's notions of a good life provides a needed corrective or alternative. When I went in to see Thompson, he put his feet up on his desk and sat back in his chair with his hands behind his head. He had a huge gray beard like Karl Marx's. He always wore a bow tie underneath it, so that occasionally, when he shook or turned his head, you saw a flash of red or blue peeping out behind the beard. Students joked about whether the color of that little strip poking through the hair symbolized something about his sexual condition that day.

After I sketched out my proposal, Thompson considered for a moment and narrowed his eyes. "It might work. You need to be a good hater to finish a dissertation. You should want to destroy something."

"I'm not sure that I want to destroy anything, Professor Thompson. At this point I just want to understand why early Christians thought that they had to deny their worldly needs when they converted."

"Well, I guarantee you that you will hate them by the time you are finished. There is nothing like several years of intense study and thinking for yourself to shatter whatever vestiges of faith have survived from your childhood." He scowled, then shot me a grin, as if to say he didn't mean this as a personal assault, but simply a friendly heads-up about what he had seen again and again. It might also have been a confession. Thompson never spoke about his early years, and no one seemed to know much about that period of his life.

We discussed several research strategies, which figures I might best focus on, different kinds of asceticism, and the procedure for submitting chapters of the dissertation. There was also the question of who the other readers would be. I was pretty sure I wanted Professor Zachary Krupat, the genial older man with whom I had taken courses on "Christian Classics" and Kierkegaard. I liked his literary angle, his avuncular willingness to be supportive in intangible ways, and his own deeply held Lutheran faith, about which he made no secret. In all of these ways, I thought, he would balance things out and soften Thompson's jagged edges. I would in some ways have preferred Krupat to be my advisor, but his expertise was primarily in the post-Reformation church, while Thompson's field included the earlier centuries in which I was interested.

"All right," said Thompson, "he can be one reader. We disagree about many things, and he won't challenge your biases. But he knows his stuff and I can live with him. What about the second reader?"

This was an awkward moment. I wanted to work not only on Christianity, but also on Buddhism, comparing how these two religions saw asceticism. Buddhism, too, had a strong monastic movement with a system of vows and disciplinary rules and regulations prescribing a certain form of life. For instance, one of the innumerable ordinances for monks prohibited sleeping on a raised or soft bed, and many orders forbade eating after the noon meal. I couldn't claim to be an expert on Buddhism without living in Asia for several years, learning Pali and Sanskrit, and a lot more study than I would have time for. But perhaps, I thought, I can learn enough about Buddhism to be able to teach an introductory course to undergraduates, thus adding another arrow to my quiver as I anticipated searching for a teaching job.

Thompson was dubious about this plan. He wondered whether I could learn enough about Buddhism to do a respectable job. "Think about it some more," he said. "If you can find an Asian Studies faculty member who will sign on, I'll go along with it. The obvious choice is Sakorn Premchit. I don't know if he's interested in asceticism, but he certainly knows about Buddhist monasticism all across Asia."

"I was thinking of taking a course or two with him to see how it goes. Maybe I won't be able to get a chapter on Buddhism out of this, but I'm interested and it will feed in somehow. And I must admit, I'm drawn to Buddhism. The meditation appeals to me."

"Ha!" snorted Thompson. "One religion isn't enough, you want another one? What's with you preachers' kids? You have to have something ready to grab on to even when you know you are losing your faith. You can't sleep at night without a new teddy bear. Well, you'll get over that, too, I predict. But it's no business of mine, you can believe the moon is made of blue cheese or sacrifice carrots at midnight, so long as it doesn't influence your academic work."

That pretty much wound things up. Thompson was strictly business; he didn't make small talk about the White Sox or ask about your psychological well-being. If you were anxious or half-hearted, you shouldn't be a student at the University of Chicago Divinity School. To succeed in graduate school, you had to go for the jugular. When he said this, in front of about fifty incoming students during orientation week, he held his hands up and made a circle as if they were around someone's neck. Then he squeezed his fingers together. It was an odd gesture, at once a brutal and dainty throttling of his victim. The jugular vein was not the target; Thompson's form of murder would not shed blood, but cut off the air. The distinguished professor continued advising us wide-eyed, somewhat alarmed new students. "If you waste your intellectual energy doubting yourself, getting depressed, or wondering if you are doing the right thing, you should go into some other line of work. We like a self-starter here, the kind of guy who sees the target and goes straight at it."

I thanked Thompson for his feedback and told him I'd get back to him sometime next term, when I had plotted the chapters of the dissertation and formulated a proposal for him to sign. Meanwhile, I would sound out Professor Premchit and decide whether to ask him or a more predictable choice in Christian history to be my second reader.

The next week I went to see Sakorn Premchit. His office was not in Swift Hall but the corridor that housed the Department of Asian Languages and Literatures. Like a lot of professors in the Divinity School, he had multiple appointments in various departments. Premchit was a young man, still in his late thirties. Originally from Thailand, he was a member of the royal family, a cousin of the king. Premchit had gone to Cambridge University in the early 1960s and spoke very precisely with a pronounced British accent. Already he had published several groundbreaking books on Buddhism. He was especially interested in the relationship between monks and the Thai state, and how Buddhism interacted with Asian political institutions. His knowledge of Buddhism was extensive, from the Theravada traditions of Southeast Asia and Sri Lanka to Tibetan Buddhism and Mahayana developments in China, Korea, and Japan, and from the days of the Buddha to recent events such as the return of Buddhism to India.

Premchit had thick-lensed glasses and was near-sighted; he seemed like a kindly and much older man, although he was only a dozen or so years my senior. He was shy and reclusive, unfailingly polite and thoughtful but not inclined to reveal much of his own point of view. Lionel, my vagabond friend, had taken several classes from him, and told me that Premchit insisted that a scholar should always keep his own views strictly out of sight. "Our business is to understand the tradition and pass along our knowledge to the next generation of students and scholars," he said. "We stand on the shoulders of the giants before us and build on their work. We are not interested in proselytizing, debunking, or other personal agendas. If that is what you want to do, you should become a minister. Or stand on a street corner like the Hare Krishna people. In a research university like this we have a precious opportunity and duty to be scholars."

I knocked on Premchit's door. He called out "Come in, please," and peeked out from behind a desk covered with piles of books and manuscripts. The floor, too, had books and papers everywhere, and he had to remove a stack of student papers to make room for me to sit on a chair. He apologized for the mess, chuckled mischievously, and said, "Sometimes I leave papers piled up to discourage idle chitchat. But today I'm happy to be of assistance. How may I help you?"

What a friendly fellow, I thought, liking his cordial and welcoming manner immediately. I briefly explained my project and asked if I could audit his Introduction to Buddhism class during the spring term.

"By all means, certainly. And if you become really interested in Buddhist monasticism you will have to go to Asia to experience it first hand. I suggest that Chiang Mai University would be a good place to see Buddhism on the ground. Of course, if you get serious about textual studies, or really any kind of Buddhist study, you will have to know Sanskrit and Pali."

"Thank you for the encouragement," I said. "I'll have to see how my ideas about asceticism develop. Perhaps I can't go into Buddhism enough to do respectable scholarship. But I want to learn about it anyway."

"If I might be so bold as to ask one intimate question," said Premchit. He put his fingers together as if he was making a church steeple. "Do you have a personal interest in this topic?"

I replied that I was interested in comparing ascetic practices in Christianity and another religious tradition for intellectual reasons, because I thought that knowing another religion would help me grasp the distinctiveness of Christian views. In addition, I admitted, I'm attracted to Buddhism personally. "I am drawn to the idea of not-self."

"Ah, you mean *anatta*."

"Yes, I think so. I like the idea that my self, my ego, or whatever it is that I think I am, is not real, or not important. But I'm having trouble fitting this together with my Christian background and my belief that human beings have souls, or are souls." I was surprised that I was telling him about my own religious questions, given what I knew about him.

Premchit threw out a few thoughts about no-self. "Anatta is literally no-self, a negation of the Atman that is so important in Hinduism and the Indian schools of thought to which Buddha reacted. Anatta is one of the three characteristics of all conditioned phenomena, along with *dukkha*, or suffering, and *anicca*, impermanence. All things arise and fall, come into being and pass away, including what I think of as my self. This is a central Buddhist idea. Perhaps you will experience what it means if you practice meditation diligently for many years. But then you won't write a dissertation. Be careful lest a personal search distort your studies."

I looked at him quizzically. Why is a personal motivation for studying religion a problem? What better incentive could I have?

Premchit saw my raised eyebrows and inquiring look and went on. "These days I meet many students who think that the study of religion is the same as the practice of religion. At Cambridge they never made that mistake. But in America everyone wants to be a bodhisattva. They wish to receive academic credit for becoming enlightened. Why just the other day, Tuesday, an undergraduate came to ask me to supervise his independent study. He wanted to go to Japan and wander from temple to temple until he experienced satori. His travel journal would be the evidence, and he said he was sure he would get an A. I said no. He argued. Again I said no. More nonsense. Finally I got so exasperated that I said to him, Go! Go to Japan! I truly hope that you become enlightened. Maybe you are a bodhisattva. I think that what you propose to do is a good thing. But not everything that is worth doing gets academic credit. Just go!"

Premchit was agitated, sitting on the edge of his chair and speaking quite loudly, as if I were the pesky undergraduate. I must have looked alarmed. He caught himself, laughed, and said, "I fear I'm going to whack you like a Zen roshi arousing a sleepy student! Ah, well, I, too, am subject to causes and conditions that brought me to this moment. Never fear, Mr. George, I will not interfere with your spiritual search. I only wish to impress upon you that personal motives, no matter how sincere, often cloud a scholar's vision. You must be exceedingly careful to know the difference between your own religious ideas and the objective, disinterested, and impersonal knowledge that comes from disciplined study. You must give up your wish to be enlightened or to find salvation in my classes if you want to succeed."

"I'll try to remember that, Professor," I said, standing up and smiling. He showed me to the door and we shook hands.

"I will see you in the spring term, then," he said. "Best wishes as you put together your dissertation proposal. You know, it's a bit like a detective novel. When I was in England I developed a fondness for British murder mysteries. You, too, have a lot of bits and pieces of evidence, stray intuitions, and vague ideas that you must work into a coherent intellectual theory. How you understand human nature determines a great deal. No one can really tell you how to do it; we professors can only tell you when you've gone astray. There is a political dimension of your work, involving strategy, alliances, and diplomacy. I hope you can put your instincts and interests together and 'solve the case'! The case of the vanishing self." His eyes were wide, and his hands made fists, then opened suddenly as if they held something that dissolved into air.

I liked the detective story analogy and Premchit as a person, and hoped I could work with him. I shouldered my book bag and walked outside into a late-winter sleet storm. It was five o'clock, and people were fleeing their offices, all of them huddling against the wind, looking down at the sidewalk. I walked home with a grin on my face, enjoying my uncertainty about the future, the not-knowing of a scholar following intuitions that might lead somewhere. As the headlights of passing cars came on and a fierce gust scattered hats and umbrellas, a Sherlock Holmes line came to mind. "Come, Watson, the game is afoot!"

For years Will had been urging me to hear Yogi Bhakta. The guru was often on the road, visiting ashrams and celebrating festivals, usually in Montana or Colorado. In June 1976, Will informed me that the Yogi would be coming to Chicago for a public talk and satsang (teaching) at a theatre on the North Side. Eager finally to see the Big Guy, I agreed to meet Will at the talk. I was apprehensive about the encounter. I hoped that Yogi Bhakta would somehow inspire and uplift me, but I also expected to be disappointed. I was determined not to be taken in by glib or evasive answers or a charming personality.

On an overcast Saturday morning I rode the El up to Belmont Avenue and walked west a few blocks to the Star Theater, a medium-sized place Bhakti Dharma had rented for the day. Will was in the lobby, talking enthusiastically with two other guys. They were describing the satsang Yogi Bhakta had given the previous night in Madison, which had attracted a lot of college students. I joined them, Will introduced us, and they told me that when the Yogi talked, the love was so thick you felt like you were swimming in honey.

"Hmm, I guess that's good," I mumbled evasively, and we went in. A buddy of Will's had saved us two seats up close, on the right side. The yogi kept us waiting almost an hour past the advertised starting time of ten o'clock. Maybe he was behind schedule or maybe he hoped for a better crowd, because the theater was only half full. Then again, he must have known as well as a rock star how to make an audience eager for him. The devotees chanted a different mantra every few minutes, led by a spiritual cheerleader with long blond hair tied up on top of her head and a purple headband holding it in place. She had a strained, expectant expression on her face and gazed up into space rather than at the audience. She is a beautiful woman, I thought, although her body was hidden under a baggy, shapeless Indian garment. Its drab khaki suggested a desire to avoid color, but then there was the striking pile of hair and the purple headband, like an abbreviated turban, a half step in the direction of Sikh identity. I asked Will if this was some kind of uniform for women, but he shook his head and shushed me and said, "Don't think of such things. That's not why we're here." Maybe not, I thought, but lustful thoughts come unbidden, even to the saints.

At last Yogi Bhakta strode in from the wings, accompanied by two disciples who helped arrange his seating. They probably acted as bodyguards, too, and it occurred to me that it wouldn't be hard to assassinate their leader. These two would gladly take the first two bullets and then

I could shoot Yogi Bhakta. I remembered the assassination of Malcolm X in the Apollo Theater in Harlem, and then wondered why my mind veered in this violent direction. Saccharine spiritual talk sometimes brings out a nasty streak in me, although I only express it in sarcastic words or thoughts. I didn't like feeling cynical, and steeled myself to be open, trying to give the guru a chance.

Yogi Bhakta was about fifty. His long beard was starting to turn gray. He had a lot of wrinkles and was thick and powerful, with a massive chest and shoulders. His legs seemed too short, so that he appeared top-heavy. He dressed in flowing Indian robes colored red, purple, and yellow. Yogi Bhakta removed his sandals to sit meditation-style on a little tuffet. His unusually large hands rested in his lap and sometimes made impressive sweeping gestures. He flashed a warm, welcoming grin, what a cynic would call a dirty old man leer. The audience went wild, cheering and clapping. Turning my head, I could see several men and women with their arms outstretched. A few uncomfortable looking people held back, cautiously observing the scene. Yogi Bhakta took all this in, continued to smile, and sat contentedly for several minutes, nodding and blessing individuals who caught his eye. He told one couple, "I can see that your marriage is as good as I said it would be." His accent was slightly British, like many Indians, and I wondered where he had been educated.

He raised his left hand, commanding silence, and immediately there was only the sound of air conditioning and the rustling of a few people swaying back and forth like Orthodox Jews. I realized I was holding my breath and slowly exhaled.

Yogi Bhakta tossed us a few pearls of wisdom. His teaching was a series of disconnected anecdotes and parables. Some of them were amusing, often gently poking fun at the way ordinary people pursue worldly attachments like money or status. For instance, a girl who thinks that having the right boyfriend will bring her happiness. He asked the crowd if they thought she would find it. Several women laughed and called back to him.

"She's going to have to learn the hard way."

"I've been down that road."

"She won't see the light till she's tired of the dark."

Yogi Bhakta said that in the yoga he teaches, physical exercises prepare you for something much more important. He claimed to know the Hindu, Sikh, and Jain scriptures and to interpret them correctly. Yet the intellectual path to God only goes halfway. It's the heart that tells you where you are going and gives you the energy to get there. Much of his teaching was negative: this approach won't do, that object of devotion will fail you, and a lot of prayers are just the ego begging for what will make it bigger. Finally the Yogi said that "the bottom line" (for he had absorbed a lot of American slang) is experience. There is an experience that is so convincing and fulfilling that you immediately realize it holds the answer to the question that you didn't even know you were asking.

What kind of experience? He referred several times to "the event of love." It wasn't clear to me whether he meant being loved or loving something—God, or one's true self, or Yogi Bhakta, or perhaps all of these at once. Everyone seemed to know what he was talking about except me. I had the momentary sensation of being crazy, or deficient in some sixth sense. I felt woozy swimming through all that love honey, and then I burst out of it. I decided that these people were in the grip of crowd psychology. They would be wise to question their blind devotion to this aging charlatan and his boilerplate mystic goulash. They might not be as happy, but they would at least be living in the real world. I felt detached from these believers, as if I were looking down from another plane.

The Yogi said a lot of other things during that satsang, but I'm not going to try to make more sense of it than it made to me. He seemed like a charming fellow who has learned some magic tricks and enjoys playing with his audience. Everyone knows it is all a game and plays along, sustaining the illusion. But no, I corrected myself; these people really believe that every word he speaks is God's truth.

There was a time for questions and answers. Yogi Bhakta made a few witty responses, and several times he simply flashed a big grin and waited. His eyebrows twitched and he nodded his head. Then the audience would laugh together good-naturedly at the foolish question. One query came from a nerdy-looking guy in a white shirt, short black hair, and a moustache.

"You say that intellect is not the way. What am I supposed to do, lose my mind?"

When Yogi Bhakta did his shtick with the grin and twitching eyebrows, the audience gave a knowing chuckle, as if responding to an old family joke. The guru didn't answer verbally, but gazed at the young man with a friendly smile. The questioner frowned, then smiled tentatively, as if pretending to get a joke.

Another questioner asked why devotees have to follow so many rules if they are holy and good people after the Event of Love. For instance, male and female devotees are supposed to stay apart unless there is a Bhakti

Dharma leader present. "Are you worried that they'll have sex or something? Is sex a bad thing?" This question came from a good-looking fellow with long brown hair and bib overalls. It was hard to imagine him signing up for a religion where he couldn't have sex.

Again Yogi flashed the knowing look to his followers, and as if on cue they made little groans of approval and sympathy. He said, "Sex between man and woman can be the Event of Love, and it can be the betrayal of love. Sex is your karma, your destiny. It will find a place in your life. But you can find a better way to God, if that is what you want. Kundalini yoga raises that energy to a higher sphere."

This seemed to satisfy everyone, even the handsome hippy, who nodded thoughtfully. He wanted to learn more about the better way, for I saw him on my way out, listening intently to two animated women in saris.

After about forty minutes of this interaction, Yogi Bhakta led us in a chant for several minutes, followed by a brief period of meditation. He abruptly stood up, thanked us for coming, and announced that there was much more to know than he could explain that morning. "But it doesn't really matter what I say. You have the experience or you don't. You understand it or you don't. It comes as an event, all at once. When you have tasted the honey, you will never go back to eating salt." If we wanted to know more, we could talk to his teaching assistants, the sanyasins, who would be in the lobby afterwards.

I didn't really want to be lectured to by some pimply kid from Oak Park who had dropped out of college. I felt agitated by the satsang, and wished that I could argue with Will or Yogi Bhakta and attack what seemed like phony bliss and pseudo-wisdom. I told Will I was heading home and asked whether he wanted to have lunch.

"No, Peter," he said. "Not today. The spirit is here, and this is one of the most important days in my life. I'm going to stay with my love family."

"What happens now?"

"We talk about Yogi's teaching. We share how we have known joy in yoga or service or chanting the divine name. We plan our next events to spread the word."

"Okay, I'll see you," I said. "I've got to get to the library and get some serious work done today." I headed back to the El that would take me downtown to a bus going south to Hyde Park. Maybe hearing devotees describe their experiences would clear up certain things for me. But what I really wanted was the Love Event, and it hadn't happened.

I felt irritated and kicked an abandoned shoe as hard as I could against a trash can. I was disappointed, just as I had expected to be. Musing as I rode the El, I decided that satsang wasn't much different from a lecture at the University of Chicago. It was just talk about religion, with some humor and silent spells thrown in. Yogi Bhakta was right, talking only gets you so far. The main thing that was different about his presentation was his ability to get mileage out of pregnant pauses. Professors don't do that trick. They don't silently acknowledge mystery and paradox.

I was surprised that I felt so disappointed, given my suspicious attitude to Yogi Bhakta. I had yearned for a transformative moment, an epiphany, and now I was depressed. Part of me wanted to know, How do I get the Event of Love? Is it something that I can choose or something that just happens? If I get it, will I stop asking questions and analyzing everything? I would have to press Will on these matters the next time I saw him. He was more interesting to me than either his guru or my professors.

Seven

Kundalini

For about a year Will worked in a natural foods restaurant run by Bhakti Dharma on Diversey Avenue. He washed dishes, waited on tables, and enjoyed interacting with customers. When she was on the north side of the city, Maiko often stopped at the restaurant for tea and a chat with Will. They liked to talk about the similarities between Maiko's work in theater and Will's job as a waiter. They were both providing a service by giving a performance, playing a role. He said he liked representing Bhakti Dharma to the public and having a script to follow. Maiko had been a waiter in St. Paul and was now working at a restaurant in Hyde Park, and they bonded over their common experience. "Just like being on stage," Maiko said, "the same role feels authentic one day and false the next. And waiting, hanging around, is a big part of both jobs."

Will now wore a turban and the distinctive Sikh steel bracelet and sported a respectable beard. He had a Sikh name, Premka, that he used with members of the ashram and sometimes with others. When he answered the phone, "Hi, this is Premka," I said, "Hi, Will." I couldn't get used to thinking of him as a different person.

During the summer of 1976, Will took on more responsibility within the organization, teaching yoga and giving brief spiritual talks in the evenings at the ashram. The next winter, he began to handle certain public relations chores for the Chicago ashram, which served as headquarters for the entire midwestern region of Bhakti Dharma, twenty-two ashrams between Denver and the East Coast. I was a little surprised that Will was entrusted with these public roles, given his unstable past. He was seen very differently in Chicago as compared with Minneapolis. He had been involved with Yogi Bhakta's group for five years and was one of the most experienced members. Individuals moved in and out of ashrams all the time, and Will's knowledge about the group's history made him a voice of continuity and authority. The rapid expansion of Bhakti Dharma in its early years required leadership, and people like Will were suddenly thrust into roles they hadn't imagined for themselves. Will's judgment was sometimes suspect, at least in my opinion, and perhaps he was too much a free spirit to lead an ashram or start a new mission in another city. Yet there was no doubting his passionate commitment to the movement once he moved to Chicago and embraced the Sikh identity. He was an inspiring advocate and exemplar of devotion to Yogi Bhakta. Will also had a lean, flexible body for demonstrating yoga postures, a deep and gentle voice, and he could think quickly in response to questions. Maiko said to me, "I'm surprised that you are surprised. It makes complete sense to me. Let's go do yoga some evening when he's teaching."

On a Friday evening in early August we drove to the ashram where teaching sessions were held. We removed our shoes and padded into a large white-carpeted room on the first floor that served as the yoga instruction room. Candles burned before an altar with a picture of Yogi Bhakta and several leather-bound books that were probably Sikh scriptures. Maiko and I sat down with a dozen other visitors and an equal number of Bhakti Dharma members wearing white cotton clothes. Will smiled and nodded as he came in and took his place in front of the group.

He led us through half an hour of kundalini practices, starting with *pranayama*, breathing exercises. Inhaling through the left nostril and exhaling through the right, and then the reverse, balances the body's energy, Will told us. The warming sun energy on the body's right side is put in harmony with the cooling moon energy on the left side. We repeated a mantra out loud, then silently, to concentrate the mind and fill us with awareness of God's presence in all the rhythms of life.

Then we did physical exercises. Kundalini is more vigorous than hatha yoga, which involves gentle breathing and stretching in static postures. Kundalini demands powerful effort and releases strong flows of energy that are supposed to quickly eliminate blocks and tensions in the body and mind. Many of these exercises are performed while doing "breath of fire," a rapid pumping of the diaphragm that expels air from the lungs and allows the inhalation to rush back in. Will informed us that this technique charges the body with "pranic energy" and "raises the kundalini." I was soon drenched with sweat, and regretted that I had eaten supper, which I imagined as a load of bricks rolling around inside a laundry washer.

These practices were almost more than I could stand. We lay on our backs and raised our legs for half a minute at a time to a foot off the ground, then two feet, a forty-five-degree angle, sixty degrees, and ninety, huffing and puffing like locomotives all the while. I made it through the ordeal, although the next morning I was so sore that I could hardly sit up in bed. Another exercise involved sitting with legs stretched wide, catching the toes, and bringing the head down to the floor, lower, lower. "Relax into the pain," Will instructed, and, sure enough, I felt muscles and joints release their tension. For a spine-twisting exercise, I rotated my torso left and right with my hands on the shoulders, again pumping my diaphragm like a bellows. I caught a glimpse of Maiko, her eyes closed, whirling, completely absorbed. I remembered that her name translates as "dancing girl." Then I was back in my own body, utterly focused on these new sensations.

After each exercise, we rested for a minute or two of deep relaxation. With our eyes closed, we were to notice and feel what was happening to our bodies. After the pain, it felt wonderful, reminding me of the first times I smoked marijuana. I was completely open-minded, observant, and fascinated by every nuance of sensation in deep muscles and on the surface of my skin. A prickle, a cool spot, or a muscle relaxing was full of deep pleasure and significance. "Feel your body as a part of the cosmos," came a familiar voice, that of Will, my teacher. "The universe is a harmonious organism, and you are part of it. God knows himself in you." To simply follow instructions, to do what I was told without having to decide what to do next or for how long, relaxed some inner tension of will that keeps my ordinary self on duty.

Will's voice was strong, relaxed, and soothing as he guided us into chanting and meditation. He told us to pay keen attention to how the chant's sound waves affected us. Each sound makes a particular part of the body vibrate, and the silent meditation with which we concluded shows the harmony of all sounds and the healthy wholeness of the body. He's right, I thought, this chanting makes things hum inside, and I'm mellow and alert.

Then it was time for a little homily and questions. Will said that yoga is a necessary discipline as well as enjoyable for its own sake. "It can also become just an ego trip," he went on. "Yoga is about empowering the self. Yet finally the self must be handed over to God. That is why the next turn on the path requires commitment to other people and a guru. And for us, the community is Bhakti Dharma and the guru is Yogi Bhakta."

I was startled by how quickly and directly Will moved to this altar call. Several of the outsiders fidgeted a little, no doubt trying to reconcile their enjoyment of yoga with mistrust of Will's promise that much more would be theirs with a fuller commitment.

A middle-aged woman next to me put up her hand. She had curly hair, a halting manner of speaking, and a troubled disposition. She frowned slightly and pursed her lips, as if she were sad and disappointed about something. She said to Will, "I've been coming here, off and on, for almost a year. I really like this place, the people, and the positive energy I feel here. But it seems like you guys are pushing the Sikh identity more and more. Is it a requirement? I just don't see the connection with kundalini yoga. Why should I become a Sikh? And what does that really mean?"

"To become a Sikh is a process that takes a long time," said Will. "The external markers are easiest to define, but they have a deeper meaning that grows on you. We adopt the so-called five 'k's, which are five Punjabi words that symbolize the markers of our identity: *kesh*, or unshorn hair; the *kara*, which is a steel bracelet that represents our bond to our guru; the *kirpan*, a small sword that symbolizes our commitment to struggle for our faith; the *kacch*, a pair of breeches that symbolize modesty; and the *kangha*, a comb that represents our graceful and orderly way of life. We wear turbans and say Sikh prayers. Women often take the name Kaur, meaning princess, and men adopt the name Singh, or lion. We learn Punjabi so that we can read the Guru Granth Sahib, the sacred scriptures. All of these outward signs express membership in our faith community."

"But to do these things would set me off from everybody else in America. I'm already estranged from my family; I don't want to lose my friends, too." The woman looked alarmed and painfully torn between two things she wanted.

"Yes, it is true that they look at us as weird." He glanced over at Maiko and me, winked, then looked at the questioner. "But so what? It's a small price to pay for identity and community. Be weird in their eyes. It's well worth it."

I was impressed by how gently and gracefully Will acknowledged the woman's concern but assured her that something more important was at stake, something beyond her horizon of vision. He wanted to help her sense it, even if she could not see it. Will had come a long way since his Minneapolis days, when he was too conflicted to commit himself to Bhakti Dharma. Now he projected calm confidence.

He waited patiently for other questions. Maiko raised her hand and asked, "What about women's roles? Does Yogi Bhakta see men and women as equal?"

"I wonder if one of the women from the ashram would talk about that?" Will raised his eyebrows and looked to his left at two white-clad women.

"Sure, I can speak about how I see it," said one of them. "I'm Prabhupati, and I used to be Debby. Yogi Bhakta holds that men and women are equal in value but not the same. A definite role is prescribed for women, that is correct. But I don't feel oppressed. I like knowing what is expected, what women should strive for, and the ideal of a committed marriage. I found life out there—in the outside world—to be demeaning and confusing. I felt overloaded with all the things I was supposed to do and be: smart and independent, but also sexy and needing a man. I had to please so many people who wanted a piece of me or all of me. I wanted to get straight A's in order to get a fancy job, and I wanted to be a Mom someday. I'd be like my own mother in a cozy suburban home, and at the same time I'd be a high-powered lawyer who hires a housecleaner and nanny. I would stay out past midnight partying and be up for church Sunday morning. These contradictory demands were too much. I was squeezed out. I had no soul separate from all the performances I was supposed to give. I've found that here in Bhakti Dharma I can let go of some of these expectations because Yogi Bhakta says that first and foremost I am a spiritual being with a destiny of my own. If I get that right, everything else flows from it. I can—"

Maiko interrupted abruptly. "But isn't it contradictory, that you need a guy to tell you all this? And are you going to marry somebody Yogi Bhakta picks for you?"

The other woman in white laughed merrily and said, "I did that. Yogiji arranged my marriage when he thought it was the right time for that to happen. I'm totally happy, although I admit that I was terrified beforehand. I am part of a love that does not depend on the fluctuations of attraction or my husband's moods. Or my own ups and downs."

The first woman, Prabhupati, added, "I don't know what will happen to me. I'll cross the next bridge when I come to it. I just know that I used to feel overwhelmed by confusing demands, and now I can enjoy my life as well as take care of other people. American culture is fragmented and stressful. When I trust Yogiji's wisdom, life becomes perfectly simple. My own needs and the needs of other people are in synch."

Will shifted his position, stretching a leg out and tucking it back in. "Gender roles are an etiquette and a science and there's a lot more to say. But maybe we should close now." He said a little prayer in what I took to be Punjabi and then translated. "Blessings and grace from God and from Yogi Bhakta. Who knows one, knows both." He invited us to stay for tea in the dining room.

We toddled into the other room, my legs wobbly from sitting in meditation pose. I received a steaming cup of ginger tea and stood with Maiko for a few minutes, listening to the two women members describe their roles in the ashram. In the mornings they cooked and cleaned, and in afternoons they made desserts at the restaurant. They had no long-term plans and were relieved not to be worrying about the future. Prabhupati was originally from Oregon and hoped to move back there. Yogi Bhakta had told her that the Chicago ashram needs a strong spiritual woman like her. "I didn't want to relocate, but I'm proud that he values my abilities," she said. "I have a good singing voice, given by God, and I often lead the women in chanting."

I sensed Maiko tense up, gathering herself to continue asking questions about women's roles. Just then Will came up to me and put a hand on my shoulder. "I'm glad you could be here," he said. We moved away from the three women.

"You're a good teacher, Will. You inspired me to push through my pain."

"That's what Yogi Bhakta does," he replied. "Sometimes people ask why we punish ourselves. Isn't it masochism? But learning to deal with pain is a big part of what religion is about, in my book. You learn endurance and courage, and you realize that you can do much more than you thought by drawing on spiritual energy in you that is raised up by Yogi Bhakta. Kundalini yoga is not about hating the body, but rather harnessing or yoking its energy to realize the spirit. Yoga means a yoke."

"Yes," I said, musing about pain. A little bit seems to contribute to pleasure, as in sexual tension or hot chili pepper. Too much becomes torture or masochism. How much is too much? When does the goal of overcoming pain lead to cultivating or inflicting it in pursuit of that state of exultation and triumph?

Breaking into these ruminations, Will asked me what I thought about the discussion.

"I was wondering," I responded, "whether you ever find yourself in an awkward position. Do you sometimes get a question that you don't want to answer, or you have to give official dogma that is not your own view?"

Will frowned. He thought for a moment and said, "No, I have absolutely no problem with representing the movement. Sometimes I don't completely understand or agree with everything Yogi Bhakta says, but I want to represent him accurately, not start my own religion." He looked away and said more softly, "Yogiji has recently asked to be informed of any teacher who expresses doubts or challenges central doctrines." In a subdued voice, almost a whisper, he muttered, "Jeff warned me about that one time."

Will stared out the window. In the dusk, through a parting of the curtains, headlights flicked past. Will scowled as he remembered Jeff's rebuke. He obviously did not want to talk about it.

Trying to let him off the hook, I said, "It's a difficult issue in every religion. How do you reconcile individual conscience with the need for orthodoxy? When you are an official spokesman, maybe you have to make some compromises."

Will looked startled and came back to his firm commitment. "I'm not selling out, if that's what you mean. I'm on board. If I don't understand something Yogi says, that's my limitation, but I'll get it tomorrow. It would be delusion to judge Yogi Bhakta's wisdom, or pick and choose only what appeals to me. I'm not sacrificing my conscience to be part of this way of life. My guru is my conscience." He stared at me defiantly.

"Okay, it's great that you feel that way," I said reassuringly. "Everything is in harmony." I realized that, far from challenging Will, I wanted to support his commitment to Bhakti Dharma. That was quite a change in me.

On the way back to Hyde Park, as we drove along Lake Shore Drive, I told Maiko that, in spite of Will's vehement assertion, I doubted that his conscience was always in harmony with Yogi Bhakta's deeply resonant voice. The Yogi makes powerful sound waves, his followers avow, but the small, silent voice of conscience also moves a person.

Kundalini yoga was the hook that drew the fish into Bhakti Dharma. I had nibbled and felt a tug, but I wouldn't swallow the bait. Maybe I needed a different hook, one that would reel in my mind. What is kundalini, anyway? Once when I asked Will, he responded, "Don't have preset ideas.

After you experience the kundalini rising, you will know. It happens and only later you understand."

Maybe we have experiences and understand them afterwards. But expectations and ideas make possible certain experiences. Nobody has been "born again" in all my Lutheran church-going career, but it happens all the time down the road in the Baptist revival meeting.

One September day I was sitting outside the Divinity School, drinking coffee with my friend Bill Mahachek, who studies Hinduism. Bill is a Californian agnostic who practiced yoga in India. He has brown wavy hair, an enigmatic Mona Lisa smile, and an athlete's grace. We played tennis and jogged together, discussing things of the spirit while the sweat flowed. Bill was writing a dissertation about Shiva, and he told me about the paradoxical way in which this god is represented as both a celibate ascetic and an erotic lover. "India knows these apparent opposites are connected," he said. "Sexual energy has to go somewhere. That's part of what the Tantric traditions are about. Tantra means 'loom' in Sanskrit. This loom weaves together *shakti*, female energy, with male energy, and it unites matter and spirit. The Tantric masters teach bodily practices that liberate the spirit. They raise the kundalini."

"Did you say kundalini?" I asked, coming out of a daze. "That's what my brother is into, kundalini yoga. But what is it? Is there a theory behind it? I don't know what he's talking about half the time."

"Not exactly a theory, but a world view," said Bill. "There is a fundamental human energy called *prana* that flows in channels in the body. In ordinary human life this energy is not in our conscious control, and it concentrates in *chakras*, or nodes. The lower centers are at the rectum, sex organs, and naval, and energy there is expressed in greed, lust, and striving for power. The central image of kundalini is a coiled power, rather like a serpent, that resides at the base of the spine. Kundalini yoga is based on the idea that this latent or potential energy can be raised up the spinal cord and united with the higher centers, the chakras at the heart, throat, brow, and top of the head. These points are associated with love, truth, wisdom, and consciousness of God."

Bill had read a lot about kundalini yoga when he was studying for one of his doctoral exams on Tantric traditions in Asia. He described dramatic accounts of spiritual awakening. "Practitioners speak of waves of euphoria flowing over them. They feel hot energy, like surges of electricity, streaking up their spine. Brilliant colors and mandalas appear inside their eyelids.

They are intensely happy and find superhuman energy and enthusiasm that they want to express in the world."

"All right," I said, "so we have this snaky power inside us, coiled up and taking a snooze. I can see why a land with cobras would go for this symbol of dangerous power. But if the divine force is within me, why do I need a guru? What's the connection of the yoga with my brother's teacher, Yogi Bhakta?"

"The guru awakens the kundalini force. And this brings a surge of love for the guru. The awakening of love is grace, because it is beyond your control and feels like the greatest gift you could possibly receive. Bhakti arrives unbidden, mysteriously. I met a devotee who was brushed by the silk robe worn by a swami passing by him. He had a spontaneous rush of energy and devotion. It's like falling in love, because it transforms your whole sense of reality and who you are. You discover a bottomless fountain of love within your heart. That fountain metaphor, too, expresses upsurging power that overcomes gravity. In India I met several people who swear it happened to them."

"I know one, too. And he's trying to wake up the serpent power in me."

"There is a lot more to say about Tantra," Bill said, "and a lot that can't be said, because certain esoteric traditions can only be revealed to a devoted practitioner by a guru. Some forms of Tantra involve drinking alcohol, eating meat, ritual sexual intercourse, or sitting with a corpse, reversing ordinary moral rules for Hindus and Buddhists. You can imagine how these attempts to transcend everyday dualisms appear to outsiders. And some gurus misuse their power. Tantra welcomes back all the parts of life that religious devotees think they have to give up to be religious. It's the return of the repressed."

That non-Indian phrase stuck in my mind. Thinking about Freud's notion, I realized that there was a huge part of Will's life that didn't make sense to me: his sexuality, or rather his celibacy. How could this handsome red-blooded guy, who had many girlfriends and sexual encounters before he joined Bhakti Dharma, embrace a life of celibacy? It didn't seem desirable to me; it didn't even seem possible. I would have to ask him about this the next time I saw him.

So I did, in a record store on Wabash Avenue, underneath the El tracks. We had walked down Michigan Avenue for several miles from the ashram. As we flipped through bins of records, I suddenly blurted out the question that had been bothering me. "Will, how can you give up sex?"

"I don't give it up, Peter. That energy is in me, it is me, a part of me anyway. Sex is part of kundalini power. But I can choose what to do with it. I choose to raise the kundalini. I'm looking for another kind of bliss, union with the Ultimate."

I sensed a sermon coming, and my mind glazed, impervious. We were standing by a bin of Bob Dylan records with several album covers mounted above them on the wall. Distracted, I looked at the way Dylan's face had transformed since he left Hibbing, Minnesota about fifteen years earlier. I gazed down at the cover of "The Times They Are a-Changin'," which Will was holding. Sometimes an image seems to confront or challenge you with a hidden meaning. Will was always finding significance in random events and coincidences. Following my gaze, he made a metaphor out of what was at hand. "Did Robert Zimmerman leave his past behind? He hated Minnesota and never went back. But he's still acting out his boyhood anger at the uptight conformity and hypocrisy. Some of that energy became music. So it is with sex. Some of its energy drives me, but purified and made holy in my love for my guru, Bhakti Dharma, God, and the world."

"But what about making love to a woman? Do you miss that? How can you swear it off? It's inhuman."

"Peter, you must study this choice all the time. Are you saying that all the Christian monks and saints who vowed to be celibate aren't human? How about your main man, Augustine? I want to be a sanyasin just like him. I want to give my utmost effort of devotion to God. And believe me, my spiritual life is intense. Partly because of what I give up."

He put the Dylan album back. "Come on, let's go," he said quietly, "this place is too public. I'll tell you a story." We went outside the store as a train thundered over us. We walked over to the Chicago Public Library and leaned against a wall in a spot where a sliver of waning October light slipped between the towering buildings.

"It's hard to admit this, Peter, and it might sound a little crazy. It's not easy to be celibate, but it helps me to remember something that happened when I was in Minneapolis. I got involved with a girl in the ashram. She was only seventeen and had run away from home. Her name was Aria, she was from Savannah, and her eyes made me tremble. One day in the ashram I'm sweeping the floor and she stops next to me. She puts her hand underneath my shirt and caresses my chest. Neither of us says a word. The next thing I remember, we are in her room on the third floor. We start to make love and tear off our clothes. And then I stop. I'm in bed with this luscious Georgia peach, about to enter her, I'm on my knees, and she moans, a long 'mmm.' I flash back to Yogi Bhakta leading us in chanting 'Om.' I feel a terrible stab in my chest and I freeze. I hear his voice, I see him, and I go limp. Aria says, 'Come on, go for it.' I tell her I can't do this. I sit there naked on her bed and cry. She sighs and says, 'It's all right. I shouldn't have tempted you.' Aria seemed a lot older than seventeen, and I felt like a little kid caught by his parents. It was utterly humiliating to have given in to temptation. It wasn't exactly impotence, because I just wasn't into it any more. I hated myself for being weak. Boy, did I kill myself in yoga practice for a few weeks after that. I converted a lot of karma into spiritual gold. Now I can accept what I did as a step on my path. I had to learn what I really need, what satisfies forever."

"So now you're beyond sexual desire?" I asked.

"Are you kidding? Look at that one there," he said, nodding at a striking woman striding by. Coming at us, her auburn hair spread out in the breeze as if on a pillow. She glanced curiously at Will, arched her eyebrows, and then her slinky blue dress sashayed down the street. Will and I looked at each other, gulped, and laughed. "It's not like I'm a block of ice or a stone statue. I still have lusts and it's hard to stay detached from women I find attractive. Plenty of them come to yoga classes. But I can make choices. Don't you read about this all the time in your research?"

"Augustine writes about how he can't control his dreams and shameful memories that still haunt him. It's a pretty startling confession, really, for a bishop in the Christian church to make publicly. Yet he affirms that God will help him keep his vow of celibacy."

"Maybe he knew about kundalini energy," Will laughed. "We have animal instincts and spiritual desires, and they aren't totally separate. It's not like you can choose one and reject the other. We are embodied spirits. We are flesh that wants to be animated, to dance to the tune of the soul. Like Dylan says, with one arm waving free, silhouetted by the sea. Celibacy doesn't change my basic human nature. It just alters the direction of my energy."

"Yes," I said, musing, "things are a lot more complicated than I realized. Tantric sex, kundalini energy, celibacy driven by eros. And maybe what we call lust is sometimes not just physical desire for a body, but also a longing to possess or merge with another person who offers you something that your soul needs. Maiko is that for me sometimes. She is an unobtainable, independent presence in the world that I want to keep and hang on to. It's also her mystery and her dancing spirit that draw me to touch her."

We stood in the shaft of sunlight for a long moment as the shadow of a looming building slowly engulfed us. I awoke from reverie and found Will staring at me intently. "Ready to go?" he asked, and we turned up Wabash towards the Chicago River and the North Side.

The mailman brought me a two-page mimeographed report called "Bhakti Dharma Midwest News and Events, number 1, December 1976." Will was responsible for producing this occasional regional newsletter of Yogi Bhakta's movement. Will had a new title, Communications Associate, and he told Maiko that he was the hands-on guy who wrote most of the articles, typed, and reproduced this report. Most of the national public relations were handled in California, but the Chicago newsletter fostered communications and coordination among the ashrams in the Midwest and publicized upcoming events. The News and Events also contained inspirational pieces and short essays on aspects of yoga, Sikh culture, and the Bhakti Dharma way of life. I recognized metaphors and ideas Will had expressed to me, although I suppose they were common currency and paraphrases of Yogi Bhakta's lessons. An essay called "Sacrifice to the Guru" asserted that there is no love without sacrifice, and no true sacrifice unless there is a living person to receive the sacrifice. In "Sadhana as the Ocean," the anonymous author described how difficult it is to arise at four for the spiritual discipline of morning yoga and worship. He compared this to throwing himself into a big ocean wave and finding that the turbulence floated him gently onto the beach. You have to throw yourself away, he said, but in the end you are safe. I thought of playing with Will in Lake Superior, where the waves weren't as warm and friendly as a gentle Hawaiian beach.

I paid close attention to the newsletter for the next few years, watching for hints about what Will was thinking and how Bhakti Dharma was evolving. The articles were invariably positive, even when I sensed a shadowy conflict or defensiveness underlying the good cheer. There was never mention of an ashram closing, a marriage dissolving, or a teacher leaving the organization. The Age of Aquarius was about to dawn, and followers of Bhakti Dharma would be world leaders. I suppose every religious organization is like this, but a steady diet of compulsive cheerfulness soon

wearies me. I wondered whether the relentless pressure for an upbeat public face ever made Will feel that he had to suppress the truth. Could he
describe unresolved controversies within Bhakti Dharma or evaluate the
pros and cons of various theological opinions? Once I asked him this, and
he replied that his work was public relations, not academic debate. His
role required him to overcome what Yogi Bhakta criticized as a peculiarly
American problem: negativity.

I chuckled and asked, "Isn't that what Spiro Agnew said a few years
ago, before he resigned as Vice President? He attacked nattering nabobs of
negativity. I think he was referring to the liberal press, though."

"I wouldn't compare Yogi Bhakta to Spiro Agnew in any way," said
Will testily. "Yogiji is talking about letting our light shine forth. My work
is part of our effort to show this country a better way than we've been able
to achieve with our usual politics, rat-race greed, and spiritual apathy. The
way of the spirit gives hope."

Another interaction, however, showed me that Will was sometimes
frustrated by his role. In 1977 there was a lot of controversy about deceptive fundraising and solicitations in O' Hare Airport by members of Hare
Krishna, the International Society for Krishna Consciousness. This group
received most of its income from selling books, beads, and knickknacks,
and occasionally from misleading appeals to support "world peace and
prayer." Members sometimes wore a hat and business clothes and did not
reveal the organization for which they were collecting contributions. Hare
Krishna was getting a lot of bad press and Will surmised that, in the minds
of most Americans, Bhakti Dharma was no different.

Will proposed making the Hare Krishna controversy the occasion for
a public relations campaign to distinguish Bhakti Dharma from ISKCON.
Bhakti Dharma, for instance, required its members to work at paying jobs,
and, like the Sikh tradition generally, placed a high value on service to
other people and honest hard work. Sikhs do not require renunciation and
asceticism, but affirm the householder role, participation in the business
world, and economic success. Will asserted that the airport controversy
was the perfect moment to define Bhakti Dharma's distinct identity to
Americans who thought that all Asian traditions were the same.

One day when I called Will at his office he was still stinging from
a rebuke he had been given by his boss, the director of communications,
a man with the Sikh name of Amritsar Singh. I had met Amritsar once,
and found him a very intense person with wide-open, staring eyes behind

old-fashioned granny glasses. He was one of Yogi Bhakta's earliest followers and spoke with the guru by telephone every week.

Will sounded disappointed, even wounded, as he told me in a hushed voice that Amritsar had told him that Yogi Bhakta did not want to associate his movement in any way, even by contrast, with negative publicity about Hare Krishna. As far as Amritsar was concerned, that ended the discussion. When Will wanted to talk more about the issue, hoping to change his mind, Amritsar told him sternly that this was not a matter for debate, but rather for obedience.

Still nursing a raw feeling, Will muttered, "I can't believe he threatened me. It's chilling. Follow orders or I'll turn you in to the KGB. Amritsar told me that Yogi wants to know about any teacher or Bhakti Dharma representative who expresses doubts. Then my boss stared at me with a serious face, not speaking, not revealing anything, until I got up and walked away. While I'm trying to do everything I can to support the movement, he threatens to accuse me of undermining it. He won't allow for an honest disagreement or a few minutes of discussion."

That was not the only time that the Hare Krishna movement had an impact on Bhakti Dharma. Will was angered by the media's lack of interest in Yogi Bhakta's followers. There were no news reports about a movement that by the late 1970s had thousands of people in it, perhaps as many as ISKCON. Yet because of Hare Krishna's greater visibility in public places, and because of numerous scandals and controversies in that movement, there were hundreds of stories about Hare Krishna. Many of them concerned the downfall of most of the eleven gurus who succeeded Swami Prabhubada after his death in 1977. A civil lawsuit by a former devotee and her mother charged several ISKCON branches with kidnapping, false imprisonment, and brainwashing. The income of an ISKCON group in California was linked to drug smugglers and stolen guns. In 1977, Hare Krishna was banned from soliciting at O' Hare airport. There were charges of child abuse in schools run by ISKCON. The media never tired of presenting women in the movement as subservient, exploited, and deluded victims of a misogynist organization. After the mass suicide at Jonestown in 1979, the press often stated or implied that Hare Krishna posed a similar threat, and a spokesperson for ISKCON complained of "post-Jonestown dog-pack journalism." Hare Krishna dominated the media and shaped America's perception of all new religious movements.

Will complained bitterly to me. "People love a scandal. They want to see a guru dragged through the mud. They want to view religious people as kooks or a public menace. But try to get them to read a story about thousands of people getting up before dawn to do yoga, or drug users turning their lives around, or lost souls believing we have found God. Just you try to get a reporter on that story. No one knows we're here. It's to counter that neglect and distortion that we have to put out a positive image of Bhakti Dharma."

Sometimes after these outbursts Will tried to backpedal, as if he had revealed too much to me. Then he would paint a smiling face on everything related to Bhakti Dharma. Yet he also needed a sounding board, a confessional, or an outside perspective as he sorted out his conflicting feelings. If he shared his doubts with others in the ashram, they would be denied or squelched. He must have thought that he couldn't reveal his conflicts to other outsiders without damaging Bhakti Dharma. Yet he apparently trusted me not to pass on what he told me. I was a safety valve to relieve building internal pressure. Maiko's opinions were important to Will, too. A part of him needed a woman's sympathy, and he trusted and confided in her. She provided some insight or point of view that he didn't find in the women of the ashram community.

According to Maiko, Will wanted to report problems developing within Bhakti Dharma, as well as troubling events in the world. In the Communications Office just off Belmont Avenue, he was well aware of what was going on in other ashrams and the national headquarters. He read the Chicago Tribune and the New York Times and kept up with radio and television news reports. This was rather unusual; most members of Bhakti Dharma didn't read newspapers or watch television. That was the world they had left behind. Yogi Bhakta discouraged attention to the news as a time-wasting distraction little better than gambling or sports. Members of Will's ashram were remarkably ill informed about political events in the 1970s. They were puzzled when gasoline prices suddenly shot up, and Will had to explain how events in the Middle East affected them. Most devotees had been liberal Democrats in the past, but now they were apolitical and, as the election of 1980 loomed, they didn't think much of consequence rested on whether Jimmy Carter was re-elected or Ronald Reagan replaced him. Most members of the Chicago ashram found out about Jonestown from family members who phoned to ask whether the devotee thought anything like that could happen in Chicago. Will was troubled by his position as a conduit for news and information. He was on the boundary between the movement and the larger world, making decisions about what they each knew about the other.

"What is my responsibility to tell my brothers and sisters about what is going on in the world?" he asked Maiko. "Sometimes I feel like I want to shake them and tell them to wake up. Yes, we should be happy and positive, but there is a lot wrong with the world that we can't ignore. Is it my job to educate them? Should I force them to look at what they don't want to see, what they have deliberately turned away from?"

Maiko listened sympathetically, and Will seemed relieved to get things off his chest. After one of her rehearsals at an alternative theater, he told her that he knew things about other ashrams that he could not disclose. Maiko explained, "First he said he didn't want to talk about it, and then it spilled out of him in a rush. There are divisive conflicts about the future of Bhakti Dharma. Certain teachers and communities want to stress some idea of Yogi Bhakta's that conflicts with something else he said."

Will told her, "Yogi Bhakta tried to synthesize so many different religious themes and then explain and translate them to an American culture that is incredibly different than India. I don't know if it all hangs together. The movement has grown so rapidly, and perhaps we can't do everything we hoped. I know about arguments at the level of the ashram leaders. They disagree about many things, such as the role of women, whether we have to renounce the world or accommodate to it, and what it means to be committed to a guru. If I'm Sikh can I keep my American name? I have my own views about these things. I'm not sure I'm the right person for this job. I want to be fair and also for my beliefs to prevail. I dread the conflicts I see coming. I'm not supposed to talk about this with other people because it creates doubts. Amritsar and Jeff have warned me that I am a servant of the movement, not the guide. I know that. But lately I've been feeling so much pressure building up. I'm glad I can talk to you, Maiko."

Maiko summed up her own feelings. "I didn't have any advice. He's come so far, out of such a deep hole. I hope he can be positive and stay in the movement. I really care about Will. It's hard to imagine him outside Bhakti Dharma."

"Yes," I agreed. "I would fear for his sanity, even his life, if he had to give it up."

Eight

Soul Sisters

WE WERE AWAKENED AT four fifteen. I was in a sleeping bag on a pallet near Will's bed, our bodies aligned on an east-west axis in accord with Yogi Bhakta's theory about cosmic fields. Will's roommate, Ben, snored softly most of the night. I had received permission to spend one night in the ashram. I wanted to experience the early-morning devotions practiced by residents. I had gone to several evening events and Will, perhaps hoping for a miracle, persuaded the house leader that I might be moved towards a deeper engagement, or at least greater sympathy, if I had a preview of what happened in the inner circle.

I took the prescribed cold shower, put on white, loose-fitting cotton pants and shirt, and sat quietly in a warm, carpeted room with heavy wooden shutters on the inside. The house, one of three owned or rented by the Chicago Bhakti Dharma community, was next to the one where Maiko and I had experienced Will's yoga teaching. It was a rambling Victorian mansion with a spacious downstairs containing an instructional room used for evening gatherings, dining room, kitchen, workroom, and a lot of hallway. You take off your shoes in the entryway and go barefoot or sock footed in the ashram. Upstairs were several bedrooms for members and the yoga room where we now gathered, contemplating a candle in the early morning darkness. A large photograph of beaming Yogi Bhakta watched over us. It was almost completely silent except for an occasional far-off horn, and once a siren. Eleven people lived in this house: Will, Ben, another guy, a married couple, four young women, and Jeff and Susan, the ashram leaders. I had met Priscilla, a good friend of Will's, twice before. She was thin and pale; Will said that she had struggled for several years with food issues, and that one of their bonds was their common focus on eating and fasting as spiritual practices.

Jeff began with a prayer and led us through some strenuous yoga. Several of these exercises ended with a version of "breath of fire" that just about knocked me out. While holding a posture, you do the usual bellows technique, exhaling rapidly in short bursts, the diaphragm forcing the air out about twice a second. After about thirty seconds of this, you take a deep breath and hold it, then let it out slowly. My mind went blank as I held that breath forever, and then, exhaling, relaxed into pleasant languor. This was one of the practices that Will said raises the kundalini to a higher sphere.

After active physical postures, we did breathing exercises, first through alternate nostrils, then slow deep breathing, and chanting "om" during a long out breath of perhaps thirty seconds. Finally we sat and meditated for half an hour while chanting a mantra out loud, then whispering it, saying it silently, whispering again, and aloud.

All of this took about ninety minutes, and then Jeff read us some devotional poetry. We chanted different names of God, sometimes with the syllables reversed. Not knowing these hymns of praise, I listened and watched. The devotees' faces became radiant as their torsos stretched upwards, yearning for contact with the Holy One. In English and Punjabi, they recited God's holy names and praised Yogi Bhakta, the teacher who brings divine knowledge and is himself divine.

Jeff gave a little sermon about service to the community as a way of overcoming pride. Devotion to God, Yogi Bhakta, and the ashram discipline the fat, insatiable ego. After talking for a few minutes, he asked if anyone had personal experiences related to this topic. There was a pause of several seconds, and then Priscilla raised her hand tentatively and spoke.

"We have to overcome our pride, and service is one way to do it. But I'm having a spiritual struggle because I'm becoming proud of my service. You all know I have troubles with food. I hate to be around it, and my job is to work in the kitchen and prepare meals. I'm tempted to eat in secret, and then I have to throw up. I can work with food if I must, but I spend my time hating it and thinking I'm a saint because I can make this sacrifice. Would it be better for me to do a different job? One that doesn't tempt me to be proud of my service?"

Jeff's chest tightened and he clenched his fists. As he spoke he strained to suppress his anger. "This is not the place for a discussion of work arrangements in the ashram. This is the third time lately that you have brought this matter up, and now you do so in front of other people, including a visitor to the ashram. Priscilla, you need to learn to obey. You have stepped out of your place. If you want a gender revolution, you are in the wrong place. This is not a woman's movement, or a twelve-step group for eating disorders. If you think you are too fat, eat less. But you must eat. I put it to you for the last time. Do as you are told or go start a new religion for women. Here we follow the way that Yogi Bhakta has given us."

Priscilla flushed red and covered her face with her hands. She grasped for words, whispering "I . . . I . . . just," and then gave up. The group stayed silent, waiting to see how she would take this reprimand. Priscilla stood up suddenly and looked around the room. She muttered, "I can't do this anymore." She quickly left the meditation room, her yoga clothes making a buzzing sound as she crossed the room.

Jeff looked furious, but maintained his lotus posture. "Let's just breathe for a moment," he said. We went back to meditation, supposedly, but my heart was beating rapidly and I felt an adrenaline surge flood my body with nervous energy. After a minute Jeff said, "I spoke in anger. I lost my temper. Let us return to solid ground, to Yogi's teachings. We were talking about spiritual pride and the ways it can be expressed. We just witnessed one form of it: thinking that you are better suited for some other kind of work than the duties you are assigned. It is time to end our discussion and get ready for today's work." He said a little prayer of gratitude for the morning's devotions, and we filed out.

As Will and I were getting dressed back in our room, I heard clunking noises in the hall. Will opened the door as Priscilla dragged a large suitcase past us toward the stairs. Will offered to help her, but Priscilla said grimly, "I've got it." The front door opened for a few seconds, and then closed decisively.

After a breakfast of rice, fruits, and tea and a few minutes of polite chitchat, I made for the door. Will accompanied me to the front porch. I asked about Priscilla. "So she's been wrestling with her work in the kitchen for a while?"

"Yes," said Will, "and she also has some issues with Bhakti Dharma's understanding of gender roles. The job assignments for men and women reflect a pretty traditional Indian view. Yogi Bhakta thinks that's one of the reasons Americans are so messed up. We don't know what men and women are supposed to be anymore."

"I wonder if she's gone for good."

"She took her suitcase."

I found out a couple of weeks later, when I talked with Will on the telephone, that Priscilla had moved back to her parents' home in Wilmette. She got a job as a waitress in an Evanston restaurant and planned to go back to college in Ohio the next fall.

Against Jeff's instructions, Will saw Priscilla a few times in the months that followed. They walked along Lake Michigan and talked. Then they decided not to see each other any more. Priscilla went back to "the old life," as Will called it. She didn't smoke or do drugs or even drink, but she liked music and dancing and she was thinking about possible careers.

"She wants to be an independent woman," Will said. "I don't wish she was dependent on me or anyone else, but I don't seek a life independent of Yogi Bhakta. And when I talk about how important that is to me, she is quiet or shakes her head. She doesn't try to change my mind, but there is a huge gap between us. She's stirred up and wants to argue but stuffs it. Just once she burst out at me. She said it's easy for a guy to praise dependence on God because guys have plenty of independence. It balances out. But she needs to establish some kind of life for herself first. Maybe, she said, I'll give myself to God one day. But first I've got to find a way to live that is different from my mother's generation. What I'm told to do in the ashram, be obedient to a man, isn't helping me. Things had been building up for a long time before I hit the wall that morning in the ashram."

Will's voice trailed away. I shifted the phone to my other ear and told him, "It must be hard to lose your friend."

"Yeah, it is. She was my best friend in the movement, my soul sister. If we hadn't been so devoted we would have been lovers. We started to kiss one time, but pulled away just when the fires began to burn. Now when I say something to her, it's like throwing a stone into a deep well. It goes down and down, and far away there's a little splash noise. But no water comes back out of the well. She listens to me, and there's a little echo in her of what she used to feel about Yogi Bhakta, the Way, and the joy of losing yourself in yoga. But she won't admit that she knows what I mean. She has hardened her heart. I'm shut out. I don't want to see her again."

"I feel for you, old buddy," I said, "I really do. You sound lonely."

"I don't know if I am or not," Will responded. "I've got what is most important, and that should be everything. But it's not enough, so yes, I'm lonely, damn it. I should get going now. I've got a few chores to do before bed at nine. And I really need more than seven hours of sleep. This early to bed, early to rise schedule makes it hard to stay connected to the rest of the world."

Renunciation

"Okay, hang in there," I said, but the phone was already dead.

I wasn't his kind of lonely but a different kind. Maiko and I weren't doing too well right then. We had been living together for several years. After she finished Macalester, she had traveled in Asia for six months, and then waitressed in Minneapolis, where she also acted in a few small theater roles. When she joined me in Chicago in January 1974, it was a huge decision for her, because it went against her parents' wishes. Dr. and Mrs. Shikoku were Japanese Buddhists who came to the United States in the early 1950s, just after Maiko was born. Her father was an optician in Cincinnati, where Maiko grew up. She was bilingual in Japanese and English, and, she said, "a little schizy" in her attempts to placate her anxious parents while she learned to twirl a hula-hoop, ride a skateboard, and put on lipstick.

Her parents worried about what Maiko would do for work in Chicago, and they frankly disapproved of the two of us living together before marriage. I sensed that getting married might not help things, because I was a Christian and Maiko a Buddhist, at least in the eyes of her parents. She told them that I was very interested in Buddhism.

"Interested?" her mother retorted. "This is not an academic topic. Buddhism is a way of life, a culture, and a bond between partners who understand each other. How can you marry someone who doesn't share that with you?"

"But Mom," Maiko argued, "in Japan you and Dad were Buddhists and you also went to the Shinto temple and practiced Confucian virtues. You had more than one religion there, so why can't Peter be Buddhist and Christian too?"

"Ha!" snorted Mrs. Shikoku, who had a violent way of saying this American laugh-word as if she were giving a karate chop. "That's different. Those three religions harmonize in Japan. But this is America, where Christians want to be the boss. I heard the missionaries in Japan denounce paganism and idol-worship. They pretended to be open-minded to get us in the door of the church. Then they tried to convert me and said I could only have one religion. I warn you, daughter, don't turn my hair white too soon."

I was amazed to hear Maiko's account of these vociferous arguments, for Mrs. Shikoku was very gracious and gentle when we met. I thought Buddhists, as well as Japanese people in general, were tolerant and accepting of other religions and cultures, but there was another side of Mrs. Shikoku that came out in relation to her daughter. I told Maiko that her mother's public behavior fit my stereotype of older Japanese women, but her private actions seemed "out of character."

"Exactly," said Maiko. "You have a stereotype. But my Mom is unique, and so am I."

Maiko's father agreed with his wife about this issue, although he did not seem very involved. During the two weekends we visited them in Cincinnati he spent a lot of time reading the newspaper.

Maiko was disturbed about her disapproving parents, but we believed that love conquers all. We picked up the stuff that she had stored in a friend's basement in St. Paul, drove to Chicago, and she moved into my apartment on Kimbark Avenue. She found a job as a waitress in a restaurant and began auditioning for theatre parts. They were hard to come by, and she was frustrated not to be making more progress toward an acting career. It was difficult to be sure whether her not being Caucasian was a factor. When I was skeptical she retorted, "Yeah, right, the casting director can see me as one of Chekov's three sisters, or as Blanche DuBois. There just aren't any roles for Asian Americans."

On Kimbark Avenue, we had recurring battles about two things. One was who did the housework. We agreed to split everything fifty-fifty, taking turns shopping, doing laundry, cooking, and cleaning. Maiko was determined to do no more than half of the chores, and I was theoretically willing to do half but often lazy or negligent about what needed to be done, and when. So she would nag me until I stomped off to the kitchen or grocery store, grumpily doing my fair share. The fifty-fifty arrangement sometimes led to absurd quarrels, like when she stopped doing my laundry because she said my bigger clothes, including a lot of sweaty athletic gear, took up more than half the load. Once while I was irritably cooking dinner alone and she was reading contentedly, I refused to chop half the carrots for a stew until she joined me in the kitchen.

I didn't understand why we were locked into this repetitive conflict. I admit that it was exactly fifty per cent my fault. But why couldn't she fix her half? One day Maiko told me something revealing. She has a younger brother, Shinji, who she claims is "spoiled rotten." I was skeptical until Maiko and I visited her home in Cincinnati. Mrs. Shikoku waited on him hand and foot and completely changed the dinner menu when he said he didn't want beef teriyaki, but an American dish. Sparks flew between Maiko and Shinji, and the Boy Prince got his way. On the drive back to Chicago, Maiko, still seething, remarked to me, "Now do you see what I mean? The little brat is a tyrant. He goes to college in Cincinnati so he can take his laundry home to Mommy."

"Yes," I said, "he does depend on her and boss her around a lot, for a guy who is twenty. But I guess your Mom must like it that way."

"She likes it, but she has created a little monster. This is one reason I always insist on equality and going fifty-fifty and make you do your share. I see what happens when a wife or mother sacrifices for a man. When a woman gives up so much for him, whether it's her husband or son, he becomes a monster of egotism. I reject self-denial not only because of what it does to women, but because of the effect on guys."

I glanced at her but remained silent as we drove on through Indiana. I thought about my own family. My mom, too, is devoted to her children and would do anything for us. Maybe I'm like Shinji, and so is Will. Are we monsters of egotism? But then why does Will have a burning desire to sacrifice for something beyond himself?

Maiko jolted me out of my reverie. She reached across the car, put her hand on my shoulder, and said firmly, "I won't let you be that way, Peter. I'll slap you around until you grow up."

We laughed and talked of other things. I wish I could always respond to her challenges light-heartedly.

Another issue about which Maiko and I battled was how to spend time together. Half of her waitress shifts were scheduled during the lunch period and half in the evening. On free nights she wanted to see a movie or theatre performance. The cost was not just money but my precious time, because evenings were when I did most of my studying. I could do that six nights a week very contentedly.

Whenever we fought about chores or an evening out, Maiko would assert that she had given up a lot to come to Chicago to be with me. She had suffered strains with her parents, miserable job prospects, and even, she once suggested, the condescension of Christians who treated her as an entertaining native informant. This was on the morning after a party of my fellow graduate students of religion, and I took it personally.

"Does that include me?" I asked incredulously.

"Yes, even you see me as an exotic lotus flower who will teach you what your own religion lacks. Who is getting crucified here?"

"Crucified? What are you talking about? You are being absurd." We had been drinking coffee in the kitchen, but now I was on my feet. Maiko jumped up, too, and tears came into her eyes.

"I've given up a lot for you," she said. "While my friend Sharon is in law school, and everybody else has a job or fellowship, I'm stuck in this shithole apartment with a guy who does nothing but underline books."

"Well, what about what I've given up for you? I wash your laundry and cook better meals than you can come up with. I drop my work and go to stupid plays by hacks who will be forgotten tomorrow. I stand here and argue with you when I should be studying for my exams."

"Well, fuck you, Mr. Never Do Enough! Go read the encyclopedia! I'm leaving!" She grabbed the car keys and stormed out, slamming the door on the way.

After an hour of muttering to myself at my desk, I went to the library and buried myself in the fourth century all day. I had a bowl of chili and studied until midnight. When I got home Maiko was in bed with the light out, and I slept on the couch.

That was one of our few explosive fights, but usually things didn't come to a head like that, or get resolved the next day. Rather, we each bottled our anger and resented the other. In time, I came to recognize this pattern and dubbed it the Bitter Martyr Syndrome.

It seems to have both Christian and Buddhist exemplars, and probably Muslim and Zoroastrian ones as well. Even atheists do it, I'll bet. It's a form of moral one-upmanship that uses self-sacrifice to dominate another person. I would suffer in stoic silence, but, Maiko claimed, very visibly, so that she would know how much onerous labor I was doing for her, or how ridiculous I thought an experimental theatre production was. According to her, my deep sighs were intended to make her feel guilty.

I couldn't admit this. "What sighs?" I asked. "I'm just breathing. It's good for you. You should try it sometime." I really didn't intend my deep breathing as a personal insult to her. When we give up something, even the wish that things could be different, its departure can be audible. It's like releasing the last breath before death.

She could play the game pretty well herself. She would let me know that she did not really want to have sex, but was doing this out of love for me. Or suggest that if I realized what a crappy job she had at McBundy's Lucky Aces, I would make it up to her by driving her to Evanston for an audition.

Reading about early Christian martyrs one day, I learned that a heroic death for Christ was a strategy in the struggle against pagan Rome. The death of a martyr, wrote one apologist, is better than stabbing a persecutor with a sword, for it wounds his conscience. Those who lay down their lives are Christ's army, wrote this hermit in a Syrian desert. Their enemies will be slain by the sword of the rider on the horse. To this image from the Book of Revelation, the author added a lot of vivid thrusting and piercing imagery, portraying a violent death by martyrdom as the best available weapon for defeating the imperial power of Rome. The Syrian hermit compared the sighs and groans of suffering Christians to hymns.

I remembered that the night before, Maiko heaved a heartfelt sigh when I had told her that I couldn't come with her to the North Side for a concert that Sunday evening. It struck me that she didn't sigh when I first got to know her in Minnesota. She must have learned that mannerism from me.

Sophie stayed with Maiko and me for almost a month during the summer of 1978, interviewing women in Bhakti Dharma. After graduating from the University of Minnesota, she had lived for a year in Philadelphia doing an inner-city tutoring project run by the Lutheran Church. Working with teenaged girls, she became interested in how their family situations helped or hindered them in growing up in healthy ways. She decided that she wanted to be a social worker doing family counseling. She returned to the University of Minnesota and enrolled in their social work program. For an independent study she set up in the summer, she researched alternatives to the traditional nuclear family. An ardent feminist, Sophie believed that the patriarchal system oppresses women by making them think that their happiness depends on finding the perfect husband and settling down to raise children. "I'm not supposed to believe in the myth of brainwashing, according to Will," she joked, "but I think girls get brainwashed in their family of origin."

She investigated communal experiments with other ways of raising children and understanding women's roles. She visited two Christian groups that raised their children collectively, and was appalled at how they used biblical injunctions to justify the subservient positions of women. She studied an "ecological farm kibbutz" in Kentucky that tried to make "honoring the earth" its central principle. The kibbutz was in a state of crisis during a leadership transition, and its forty residents were fighting bitterly. It was a bad time to visit, and Sophie didn't find out much about gender roles except that everyone agreed that if you got right with Nature, everything would fall into place. No way is gender an issue for us, they all asserted. That was almost the only thing they did agree on.

Sophie knew from her interactions with Will in Minneapolis that Bhakti Dharma members had definite views about the proper roles of men and women. This new religion offered a striking alternative to the usual American nuclear family, yet it limited women's freedom in ways Sophie didn't like. She was intrigued. Now that Will had moved to Chicago and become a member in good standing with the Bhakti Dharma group there, she enlisted his help in getting access to women in the ashram so as to learn first hand how religion affected their sense of identity. The ashram director, Jeff, gave her permission to interview several women whom he selected. For several weeks during July, Sophie slept on the couch in the apartment Maiko and I shared. Every day she went to the ashram to tape record interviews, and in the evening she returned and told us what she had learned.

This was not a purely academic study for Sophie, but raised troubling questions about her own future. "I don't understand how these women can go back to such a traditional idea of the family," she said. "It combines an outdated American ideal and ancient Indian family structure. Women and men are seen as very different and each gender has a prescribed role. Women are supposed to uphold spiritual values that men forget and to maintain the home and family through strong and gentle care for others. Bhakti Dharma buys into the eternal stereotypes. Women are more emotional and in touch with their bodies, yet somehow more pure and spiritual. The women I met are happy to conform to the views of an aging Indian male and to give up the freedom and sense of possibility that my generation has compared to our mothers."

We were sitting around the kitchen table as a noisy fan relieved the oppressive humidity. Maiko had been twisting her cloth napkin into a knot and untying it. Now she laid it out flat and looked up while she spoke. "You know, as an Asian American, I can see some advantages. I remember talking with a woman in Will's ashram who felt overloaded with expectations and pressures. It simplified everything for her to give up some of them. Her life became manageable and serene. It's not what I would do. The life that was good for my Mom would drive me batty. Yet I can understand why some women choose a life that says you are first of all a spiritual being. As a woman, you have special gifts and potential. Men and women are not the same."

Sophie responded vigorously, "But they are living in a fantasy world! Life is more complicated than that. It doesn't have to be prescribed for us by men. Women can make choices!"

Maiko was still working on the napkin, smoothing out wrinkles with her hands as she gazed at Sophie as if pleading with her. "Yes, that's true, Sophie. I think I agree with you about my own life. But can't Bhakti Dharma women choose a traditional role? I can see some gains and losses each way. You are looking for alternatives for American families, especially situations that might be better for teenagers. Well, here's an alternative. Yogi Bhakta's movement, like the Japanese Buddhist culture from which I come, says that the good of a whole family is more important than an individual woman's goals. From a religious point of view, and that of most Asian societies, putting your own desires first is egotism."

"That's the same line they gave me. A woman named Shanti said she struggles every day to overcome her ego. And the group has deliberate strategies to shatter your pride. Yogi Bhakta sometimes humiliates a person in front of her ashram or a satsang gathering. They say he does this out of love to break down the ego and form a new self that is graceful and serene. But what I see is a technique to enforce conformity. The community's ideas about discipline squelch dissent. Isn't that brainwashing?"

Sophie told a story that illustrated the technique of silencing and reminded me of shunning in early American Christian communities. When a woman was argumentative or stubbornly insistent on her own way, Yogi Bhakta advised her husband to give her the silent treatment until she relented. The same strategy was practiced by the whole ashram when a man or woman did something that violated the community's norms. It was a traumatic experience, reported Sophie's source, because everyone you cared about treated you in a cold, rejecting way, avoiding even eye contact. Few people could withstand this treatment for long, and many broke down in tears, begging to be forgiven and accepted back into the community's esteem. Sophie was horrified by this effective instrument of social control and by the way Shanti expressed her gratitude for it. The experience of isolation made Shanti realize how much she needed affection and affirmation from her husband and the other ashram members. "Silence brought me back to the joy of serving others. By doing that generously I obey God and find my own true nature."

Sophie wanted to argue with her interview subjects, who told her only positive things about Bhakti Dharma. She hoped to unearth some criticisms or at least acknowledgment of difficulty, but none of the women in the ashram were willing to do that. So she sought out the perspectives of women who had left Bhakti Dharma. Although Will was reluctant to give her this information, he eventually gave in, warning Sophie that ex-members were often bitter and unfair. "Take their complaints with many grains of salt," he said grimly. For helping Sophie track down the apostates, Will was later censured by his "two boss-men," as he called them, Jeff and Amritsar.

Sophie contacted two former members of the ashram who had disaffiliated from the group. For one of them, Rebecca, the decision to leave hit her suddenly, "like Paul on the road to Damascus," she said. Yogi Bhakta had told her and her husband that they were spoiling their child and devoting themselves to him at the expense of their duties to the ashram. He said that they should ask another couple in the community to raise the boy for two years, after which he would be returned to his parents. "I knew instantly that this was the end for me," Rebecca recalled. "I could not deny my maternal instincts, even in the name of religious commitment. I loved Yogi Bhakta, I really did, still do. But he wanted me to deny my love as a mother. To live without Siddhartha, my little boy, would have been worse than amputating an arm or a leg. It would have killed my love for Bhakti Dharma. I will always be grateful for what I learned there. I just can't live in an ashram any more or submit to the leaders' authority. I knew this all at once, when Yogi spoke to me in his deep voice and an even stronger voice within me rebelled and screamed a silent No."

Through Rebecca, Sophie found another woman named Maria, who had moved to Indianapolis after leaving the Chicago ashram. Sophie spent two days with her, "talking nonstop" as she put it. Maria's doubts built up slowly and she struggled for a long time to overcome them. She had an arranged marriage with a Bhakti Dharma member from San Francisco, and the couple was sent to Chicago to help build the new community there. Maria had reservations about her marriage from the start. Sophie read from her transcript of the tape-recorded interview.

"I was not attracted to my husband. From our first meeting, I felt that he was bossy and controlling, and that he would sacrifice my happiness for a noble but abstract principle. For a long time I tried to fight feelings of anger and resentment. I told myself what Yogi Bhakta said at our wedding, that the perfect spouse is not perfect, but someone who challenges me to become perfect. It worked, sort of, for a couple of years. I learned a lot about patience and self-sacrifice.

"One day a memory came to me while I was chopping onions in the ashram kitchen. I was brooding about how my husband had told me not to bother him with foolish questions. I was chopping really hard, and then I couldn't see through my tears for a moment. I suddenly remembered a big horse I had ridden when I was a girl at a summer camp. It was so amazing to me to feel the huge bones and muscles of the horse's back, and to be able to control this enormous creature. The horse had blinders, those flaps on the bridle that keep it from seeing what's off to the side. I was crying over the onions. I said to myself, you're blind. You couldn't see to the side, and now you can't see anything at all. You've been so focused on Yogi Bhakta, trying to see only the truth he proclaims, that you don't recognize what else is going on. But something is over there, off to the side. Your intuition knows it's there. I clutched the knife and wanted to stab the cutting board. Then I admitted what I had been avoiding. I didn't love my husband and wanted him to die. Now I understand what it is to really love someone. But then I didn't know and thought it was my fault that I wasn't a good wife."

Sophie stopped reading and said, "Maria had been trying so hard to be the perfect spiritual woman. The blinders gave her focus and direction for a while, but at the cost of awareness. She couldn't admit to herself feelings that would have warned her that something was wrong with her marriage and her life."

"De Nile is a big river," I punned. "When people give things up for religion, they can fool themselves about what is really important."

"That sounds heartless, Peter," Sophie continued. "If you had been there with Maria, you would have admired her courage in recognizing that she was living a lie, and then doing what she had to do in order to leave Bhakti Dharma. She didn't have children, but her friends, job, memories, and lifestyle were all based on her religious community. It's not easy to leave a cult, that's for sure. But she took off her blinders. This woman is my soul sister."

Maiko asked, "What does Maria do now?"

"She moved back in with her parents in Indianapolis and got a minimum wage job in a bookstore. She met a guy at the University who is also into yoga. She doesn't know what comes next. I think she'll be all right. But it sure gives me a different picture of gender roles in Bhakti Dharma to talk with Maria and Rebecca. There's no way I could ever belong to a movement like that, after what I've heard. For me individual choice is the highest value. And coming from my family, I've struggled to be decisive, to cut through the analyzing and the scruples."

Sophie returned to the women in Bhakti Dharma, using a more confrontational style of interviewing. Having studied cognitive dissonance in a social psychology class, she wanted to test how women in the ashram fit together the roles their religion prescribes for them with their understanding of American society. Sophie concluded that Bhakti Dharma women see American women as caught in a deluded and self-destructive pursuit of material things and social standing. They resolve their cognitive dissonance by denying the value of individualism, which they call egoism. Sophie saw some value in Bhakti Dharma as well as things to which she objected. She wasn't sure how much her social scientific approach permitted her to assert her own point of view and evaluate the groups' ideas. She struggled to stay detached in the interviews and not argue with her subjects, even when, she admitted, "I sometimes wanted to shake a woman and tell her to open her eyes."

One morning when she arrived at the ashram, Susan, the senior woman there, met her at the door and spoke with her on the front porch. "We must ask you to stop your interviews," she said. "You are making people uncomfortable and disturbing our harmony."

"I was very angry," said Sophie, "but I also felt embarrassed, as if I had done something wrong. I asked Susan what she was afraid of. I said that letting people tell their stories can't hurt anyone. Then I really blew it, because I accused her of suppressing the truth in a cover up."

"How did Susan react?" asked Maiko.

"She was unflappable, cool as a cucumber. She didn't react in a negative way, but stayed calm even when I lost my temper. She asked me politely to leave at once. I have to admit that she knows how to handle a conflict gracefully and forcefully. I tried to thank her for the group's cooperation up to that point, but I was disturbed and frustrated. I left the ashram feeling angry, but now I'm ashamed of how pushy I was. My agenda was to find out how they handle cognitive dissonance. I was insensitive to what these women are feeling as I probed for what I wanted to find. It was like I was trespassing, being in someone else's space, ripping through their belongings."

"It sounds like you were wrapping things up anyway," I said. "You probably have enough material to write your paper."

"Yes, I can pull my thoughts together. I am frustrated about Will, though. I can't get him to talk about this issue at all. He stonewalls me, puts on a blank face, tells me to ask the women in the ashram what they think. It reminds me of press conferences with Nixon or his generals during the Vietnam War. I think he's hiding something."

"He's a P. R. guy for Bhakti Dharma," said Maiko. "He's gotten in trouble before for deviating from the official line. And gender is a touchy issue now for so many reasons. He's trying to keep out of trouble and wants to leave that whole side of life behind. Come to think of it, I can't get Peter to talk about sex roles most of the time."

I finished my beer and belched. "Here's to traditional male vices," I said, and got them to laugh. "I try to stay out of trouble, too. And by the way, I think something else is going on. I run into this when I talk to Will and bring up some academic point, like when I compare his movement to early Christianity or introduce some scholarly concept. When religious people are being studied, they feel like they are being used or exploited. They think their complex and precious faith is reduced to psychological or social forces. Or that they are being judged, in this case by a feminist perspective. Will once said to me, you see only what you want to see. Yogi Bhakta is a Rorschach test. You think you understand him but you just show your own biases and preconceptions. Yogi Bhakta is a mirror that reveals you to yourself, if you are willing to see."

Sophie said she would have to think about that for a while. Two days later, she went back to Minneapolis. I'm still thinking about the mirror and what I'm willing to see.

Nine

Let's Get Gone

I BECAME AWARE OF increasing conflicts, both in Bhakti Dharma and in Will, when he came down to Hyde Park one Saturday in September 1978, just before the autumn term began. That summer I had buried myself in the library stacks to write a chapter of my dissertation, and I was glad to take an afternoon off. We decided to go to the Point, a chunk of land that juts into Lake Michigan, and take a long hike north along the shore. It was still shorts weather; I had on a Cubs baseball cap and Will wore his turban.

As we walked, Will told me about a meeting of ashram leaders in California from which he had just returned. He and Amritsar had gone as communications personnel who would explain official decisions to the members of Bhakti Dharma. The three-day meeting was held in a hotel in San Francisco near Fisherman's Wharf. There were about a hundred people present, mostly members of the central office staff and ashram leaders, including Jeff from the Chicago community. Yogi Bhakta attended several sessions, observing the discussion. The purpose of the meeting was to address discrepancies among the practices of different ashrams and to propose changes in the movement since its founding a decade earlier. Yogi Bhakta wanted to get a better sense of what the ashram leaders thought. Later "he will lay down the law," said Will. "This is not a democracy. When our guru commands, we obey."

Will's brow furrowed and his voice strained as he explained the situation Although he asserted that whatever Yogi Bhakta decided was best, he was clearly troubled by what he had witnessed at the San Francisco meeting. Economic considerations played a large role in how the movement was evolving. Unlike Hare Krishna, whose income came primarily from solicitations, most of Bhakti Dharma's members held jobs in ordinary society. As more and more devotees adopted the Sikh identity, including its lifestyle and striking appearance, it was sometimes difficult for them to fit in with mainstream American life. Many ashrams established a small independent business such as a restaurant, bakery, yoga studio, natural foods grocery, or landscaping company. These enterprises demanded a lot of time and energy, and sometimes ashram rules had to be relaxed, for instance when bread bakers needed to be at work during morning sadhana. Certain ashram leaders complained about lazy or unproductive members of their community, and even about pious souls who would rather chant or do yoga than wash the dishes necessary for the next meal.

Will stopped at a park bench. He sat down and gazed out at the lake. A brisk north wind was pushing the waves parallel to the shore. He spoke carefully, diplomatically. "I wanted to talk, but there were too many people there, and I'm not an important person. I wished I could defend devotees who care most about a spiritual life. The financial pressures are real and we have to deal with them. But they shouldn't determine the most important decisions. It's a question of priorities. How can they laugh at people who are yearning for God? That's what bhakti is, what we're all about. I could see who the real movers and shakers are. They had spiritual reasons for joining Bhakti Dharma, but it's not those qualities that elevate them to positions of power. No, the guys with the authoritative voice have political savvy and are efficient and ruthless. They are organization men, corporate types who know how to form an alliance and play the power game. I even wonder, sometimes, if they manipulate Yogi Bhakta. Sitting at the back, outside the power vortex, I could tell who makes things happen. There was a lot of ego in that room and a lot of male energy."

I said to Will, "What you are describing sounds like what happened in the early Christian Church. Maybe any religion goes through this. A charismatic founder attracts followers. But if the religion is going to survive, it must become an institution. It has to pay the bills. Leaders must be practical and efficient people who answer the phone and turn reports in on time. These bureaucrats may or may not have charisma. They may discover that spiritual energy is chaotic and makes their work harder."

Will didn't say anything for a minute. A couple of African American teenagers walked by silently, staring at Will's Sikh garb. When they were past us, they both burst out laughing, and one of them put his hands up on his head and swayed as if he were balancing a huge turban.

I turned to Will. "I suppose you get that all the time, huh?"

"I'm used to it. It doesn't bother me." He frowned a little. "Here's what bothers me, Peter. They're talking about disbanding some of the ashrams. The old-timers are now thirty or older. They are getting married and having children. More devotees want to live in their own place instead of a communal house. Families desire privacy and their own record player. They want to own a car, not share one, and to start saving money for their kid's college tuition. One guy in our Chicago community, Kirpal, has a pregnant wife, and he tells me they are both worn out from early morning sadhana, working full time, and then community meetings in the evening. He said to Jeff, 'I love Yogi Bhakta and I want to be a Sikh, but cut me some slack. Be practical and accept the limitations of human nature.' Kirpal's wife was crying one night saying she can't keep up. Keep up! That's what Yogiji shouts when he's pushing us in kundalini yoga. C'mon, you lazy bums, keep up! He's funny and serious at the same time. His commands help us exceed what we thought we were capable of. But now some people can't do it."

"You have a high standard. Can't you also be flexible and accommodating, and even compassionate about those members' struggles?"

"I know, I know. I can see that side of things. But when we make our way of life easier, there is a huge cost. What will happen to the intense commitment and sacrifice that were so important when we got into this? I wanted to destroy my material self in order to liberate my soul. And now I'm supposed to start saving for retirement. Something is changing and it doesn't feel right. We're getting more practical but we have less vitality. We used to think we could change America, and now we mimic its materialism and sloth. A month ago we had a long debate about getting a television in the ashram. And now we argue about the rules for watching it!"

"Will, isn't this partly about growing up? You were, what, about nineteen when you converted, now you're twenty-six, and before you know it you'll be forty. You won't want to sleep on the floor forever. You are single and the monastic ideal appeals to you. But what if you had a wife and kids? You would want time and a place to be together. You would want to take special care of them."

Will muttered softly and quickly, as if talking to himself. "Another thing that's dying is the ideal of being a sanyasin. Jeff has been married for many years, since before he and Susan joined Bhakti Dharma. One evening we were sitting around in the back yard after supper, and he told me that in India the ideal of the sanyasin is for an old man at the end of his life. First comes the student stage and then the householder. He asked me why

I want to skip over those phases of the cycle and be a holy elder while I'm still a young man. Yogi Bhakta encouraged renunciation of the world when people joined his movement, and he let us call ourselves sanyasin. But the wind is shifting. The Sikhs in India have never liked celibacy or poverty or reclusive holy men. They are into hard work and building a stable family. With their work ethic and financial shrewdness, they are like Protestants and Jews. I think what I wanted isn't going to be possible. Jeff asked me if I want to get married. He said it's time. But I'm not ready to commit myself to a woman. My first commitment is to God and Yogi Bhakta. If I make my family my biggest concern, what happens to the ideal of the whole community as a family? Ashram life is beautiful. Arising together, moving through the morning sadhana in silence, smelling and tasting *prashad*, the sweet food served after worship. We shared a common life and devotion to the same ideal. In the old days we were united, brothers and sisters in the family of God. Now we can't agree about what to watch on television. We can't get away from politics, as we had hoped. I'm overwhelmed with sadness when I remember how it used to be."

"Let's keep walking," I said to my brother. "Let's make it an eight-miler." We strode along briskly as far as McCormick Place convention center, stretched for a few minutes, and headed back south, the afternoon sun warming us as the wind cooled our backs. "I guess you really miss the good old days, huh?"

Will looked irritated. "It's not just nostalgia, damn it. Something's happening here, what it is ain't exactly clear, as the song says. And here's the really big thing. I can hardly talk about it. The guru."

"Yogi Bhakta? What about him? A secret scandal? That's what usually destroys these movements. Let me guess. He sleeps with his secretary."

"No, no, no!" Will cried out as he held his hands out toward me, palms spread, pushing me away in disgust. "There is nothing wrong with Yogi Bhakta. Just listen to me, will you? Yogi Bhakta is a spiritual genius. He is as close to God as a man can be, so he shows us God. In India, the guru is one who brings light out of darkness. We worship the light he brings us, and we worship our guru, because you can't have one without the other. But there is tension between people like me, who see Yogi Bhakta as divine, and the other people."

"What other people? His detractors?"

"Not exactly. There are people who see him as a prophet, a pointer to the divine but not divine himself. In Sikh tradition, there were ten living gurus, starting with Nanak. The last one, Guru Gobind Singh, said that after him the voice of God would be found in an eternal guru, a holy book, the Adi Granth. This sacred text of the Sikhs is also called the Guru Granth Sahib. There is a copy of it in our places of worship, and we remove our shoes and bow before it, venerating the living, speaking voice of God. Because the holy book is the guru now, some Sikhs criticize Yogi Bhakta for allowing himself to be worshiped as if he were God."

"Ah, I see. The problem is not some secret sin, but the question of idolatry. It is controversial to worship him, to treat a human being as divine. I can understand that."

"Yes, I remember," said Will, musing for a moment and then going on. "The irony is that Yogi Bhakta's scruples about this matter make him even more worthy of devotion. He comes not to be worshipped, but to be a teacher of yoga and a guide to a better way of life. His humility makes him a true guru."

"Oh, humility! Well, I'm pretty humble. Does that make me a guru?"

I immediately regretted this scoffing remark, but Will didn't take offense. He sighed and said wearily, "Oh Peter, you idiot. Ye of little faith."

"Well, it certainly is going to have an effect on Bhakti Dharma if you don't worship Yogi Bhakta any more. That is what drew you into the movement in the first place, right?"

"Of course. The fervent devotion of bhakti is the highest yoga, the sweetest nectar of God. Jeff tells me that it is still possible to feel that passion without worshiping a guru, but I don't know. Amritsar agrees with me on this one; he's absolutely devoted to Yogi Bhakta. Tensions within our community are building. I miss the oneness we had before everything became a battle. I want to go back, but it's too late. Now every issue gets debated as if we were a democracy. That's a change, too. In the beginning, Yogi Bhakta decided everything. He still does, finally. But some people want greater openness and elections and accountability of leaders, although of course not Yogi Bhakta. They want him to be a spiritual leader and to turn over administrative chores, especially finances, to a governing council. I know this because I receive correspondence reporting on the central committees' deliberations. It's all talk at this point, but a lot of problems are simmering. Are we loyal to our guru or to the rules of parliamentary procedure? What happened to the perfect harmony we had when we just followed Yogiji's commands? Everything is political now. I see what is happening to the community and fear for our future."

Once again I thought about parallels between Bhakti Dharma and the early Christian church. But this time I kept my mouth shut. I remembered

Paul's dismay at the factions and infighting that divided the Corinthian church he had founded. He tried to hold the church together by getting its members to affirm their common faith and to appreciate the many distinct gifts of the spirit. Paul rebuked those who would divide the church and asserted the version of orthodox belief that finally prevailed. The issues were different, but the process of becoming an institution was similar to what Bhakti Dharma would have to go through to survive. Becoming a coherent and stable religion involves sloughing off dissenters, eliminating heretical views, and disciplining those who won't conform. If Yogi Bhakta is like Jesus, a charismatic founder of a new religion, Bhakti Dharma will not survive without its Paul. And a Council of Nicea and a bureaucracy like the Vatican. Accountants and watchdogs like Amritsar. What does a religion have to do to survive, and at what price? When it casts out its demons, does it lose its soul? I didn't share this analogy with Will, knowing how he sometimes winced at my academic interpretations that seemed to reduce his faith to one example of a basic pattern in the history of every religion.

I mentioned Dad's frustration with committee meetings, and his running joke that he was for democracy everywhere except in his own church, where he wished he could lay down the law. Memories of Duluth and being kids bubbled up, and we recalled our secret hiding places in the church. Soon we were at the Point again.

Will stopped, gazed at the waves and bright sun, and grinned. "Hey, how about one more swim? This has got to be our last chance this summer."

It was a little too cool, and the waves and wind a little too strong to be safe. But on the south side of the Point, the land stuck out into the lake just enough to shelter us. We climbed down to the flat rocks and stripped to our underwear. There was something strange about the big cement blocks built along the edge of the water: they were exactly the size of coffins. These human constructions seemed to serve no obvious purpose except to remind swimmers of their mortality.

Will took off his turban and his long hair fell down on his shoulders. He dived into the water before I had my shoes off. He howled when he came up. "This is almost as cold as our morning shower," he laughed. "C'mon in, you academic wimp. I do this every day while you are snoring."

I dangled my feet and calves, reached in to splash some water on my chest, hesitated, and rolled my eyes in disgust at my own cautiousness. I slipped into the water and gasped. Will was thirty yards offshore. I swam out to him and we rolled onto our backs, looking up at the fleeting clouds.

I looked back at the Point, and beyond it at the skyscrapers in the Loop. The Museum of Science and Industry was to our left, just half a mile or so away. No one else was in the water, and a dozen strollers and sitters were watching us. It had been easy swimming here with the wind behind us, but now we were exposed to the wind and waves, and we would have to swim against them to get back. We crawl-stroked a few minutes and didn't make much headway.

"The hell with this," I yelled to Will. "Let's go with the wind. Cut across it at an angle to the Fifty-seventh Street beach." Will agreed, and we covered the distance quickly. We came out of the water and trotted across the sand. Immediately the wind made me shiver, and my teeth chattered. "Let's run," I said. So we did, two guys in their underwear, laughing and dripping, running barefoot along the sidewalk back to the place on the rocks where we had left our clothes. It was like the old days on the beach off Duluth, before politics, before religion.

On November 19, 1978, news reports began to come in describing a mass suicide in the jungle of Guyana. Nine hundred thirteen members of The Peoples Temple had ingested a mix of cyanide and tranquillizers in a fruit punch. Some of these people, and certainly the children, were forced to die, but the vast majority of them went voluntarily to their death, praising and adoring the leader of the Temple, Reverend Jim Jones. Shortly before the mass suicide, Jones had ordered the assassination of visiting Congressman Leo Ryan and several news reporters, as well as members of the Temple who were attempting to leave the remote settlement in the jungle.

That same weekend I was attending for the first time the annual convention of the American Academy of Religion, which met that year in New Orleans. The AAR meeting involves hundreds of academic presentations, book exhibits, and interviews for the job market. It was obvious that religion played a crucial role in the Jonestown events. Yet the several thousand members of the AAR seemed as baffled as the general public by the religious dimensions of the tragedy. I was preoccupied with the "meat market," as we graduate students called it, although I wouldn't be applying for jobs until the following year, when I hoped to be almost finished with my dissertation. I spent a lot of time checking out the interviewing area, the notices of which candidates would be grilled by each hiring committee, and descriptions of jobs. Could I teach early Christian history, and also Islam, Bible, and sociology of religion, as one college asked? I listened to gloomy or anxious fellow students recount horror stories about absurd questions or pompous department chairs. Scraps of conversation about another horror story, the one in Guyana, popped up occasionally. "Did you know that they killed the dogs? And they even poisoned the fish. Why did they do that?"

At a café just off Bourbon Street, my friend Robin and I eavesdropped on a boisterous table of four middle aged professors next to us as they swapped stories about Jones' harangues, beatings, and sexual humiliations of his followers. The language of insanity and perversion dominated their conversation, just as it would in the media reports that poured forth in the next months. Yet clearly there was religious meaning in the Peoples Temple suicides. This event seemed unprecedented, although one speaker at a plenary session, in his opening comment on the importance of studying religion, referred to Masada, the first century suicide of Jews defending their fortress against a Roman army. There could hardly be a more compelling case than Jonestown for the relevance of the academic study of religion, yet I didn't know how to begin to think about it.

After I returned to Chicago, I followed the press's extensive coverage of Jonestown: lurid details about Jones' sexual demands on his congregation, reports on the condition of the corpses, and interviews with a few survivors, Peoples Temple members in California, and ex-members of the group. I talked on the telephone several times with Will, whose reaction to Jonestown was at once intense and subdued. He tried to find words for deep and conflicting feelings, stuttering a few times. He needed to talk about this event, but his fellow Bhakti Dharma members quickly dismissed it. They said both Jonestown and talking about it were bad energy, wasted spirit.

Will was interested in the media reaction partly because of his work in communications and public relations. The sordid press coverage was consistent with what he had seen before. He spoke of a process of "demonization" that made the people of Jonestown out to be either evil or the helpless victims of "that lustful, wrathful madman," Jim Jones.

Will was struck by the fact that every group with which Jones had been associated now tried to distance itself from him. The Peoples Temple had been a congregation of a Protestant denomination, the Disciples of Christ, and now many Protestant groups labeled Jones's ideas a perversion of true Christianity. Billy Graham wrote in a *New York Times* editorial that it would be "a sad mistake to identify the Peoples Temple in any way with Christianity," and that Jones was "a false messiah" and "a slave of a diabolical supernatural power from which he refused to be set free." Most of the residents of Jonestown were African American, and now the black religious community, including many of its leaders who had once support-ed the Peoples Temple, asserted that suicide was inconsistent with black religion and culture. California politicians who had helped the Temple scrambled to denounce it. New religious movements, most strikingly the Unification Church of Reverend Sun Myung Moon, made public state-ments emphasizing their differences from the Peoples Temple. Left-wing thinkers, academics, and politicians asserted that Jones's model of com-munal society was not true socialism.

Will's voice on the phone was indignant. "These claims may all be true. It isn't surprising that groups react this way. But do you see the pat-tern? They all say the folks in Jonestown are utterly different than anybody we know, or good old us. They aren't true Americans, authentic Christians, good socialists, or normal black folks. They aren't even religious; they are an insane cult led by a demonic madman. Those weird fanatics have noth-ing in common with us. The people in the Peoples Temple aren't people."

According to Will, we don't know the truth about Jonestown because the media distorted events and demonized the Peoples Temple. The press coverage confirmed his opinion, born out of frustration with public rela-tions challenges for Bhakti Dharma, that the concept of a cult is a pejora-tive term for other people's religion.

"No wonder Jones was obsessed with the media," he said. "Listen to this news report. It says Jones hated the media and thought they were part of a conspiracy to destroy the Peoples Temple. One of the main reasons he left California was because of negative press coverage. In Guyana, Jones read daily news reports from Radio Moscow over the Jonestown public address system. The guy was insane, yes, but I can actually understand why he went crazy when he dealt with the media. It caters to an American public that wants to think its religion is totally different from that of other people. They only want to have their biases confirmed."

Will sometimes treated me as a handle on Joe Public, even though this conflicted with his claim that I live in an ivory tower. He wanted to know whether I think that most people consider Bhakti Dharma to be similar to the Peoples Temple. In the wake of Jonestown there was a revival of anti-cult hysteria. In an interview in early 1979 in *Playboy* magazine, Ted Patrick, one of the leaders of the anti-cult movement, asserted that Americans should expect further outbreaks of violence inspired by cults.

He predicted that thousands of people would be killed in the United States. A few days later, a man appeared on the doorstep of the Chicago Bhakti Dharma ashram. The father of a twenty-year old woman living there demanded to see his daughter. Carol came out from vacuuming the carpets to meet him, accompanied by Jeff. Her distraught father asked her to prove that the Bhakti Dharma movement did not worship Yogi Bhakta. He pulled out a photograph of the guru and asked Carol to walk on it. He demanded to know whether there were any guns in the ashram, "like the Hare Krishnas have." He wanted Jeff to confirm that celibacy was a requirement for devotees who were not married.

Jeff calmly explained several ways in which Bhakti Dharma is different from the Peoples Temple. We have no apocalyptic beliefs, he said, we are not isolated from contact with other people, and members are free to come and go as they chose. There is no policing, violence, or sexual exploitation. Yogi Bhakta's positive values are totally incompatible with the worldview that led to the tragedy in Guyana. Carol assured her father that she was fine and he shouldn't worry about her. The father calmed down, but departed with a worried look on his face after telling Carol to call him at once if she had the slightest suspicion that something bad was going to happen. He would return at any hour, day or night, he said, bringing "whatever force it takes to rescue you."

"After Jeff told me all this," Will continued, "we discussed whether the Communications Department should issue a public statement explaining how we are different from the Peoples Temple. He said if we hold a press conference, no one would come. We aren't news. Jeff checked with the central office in California. Yogi Bhakta doesn't want to make a public statement. He said that Jonestown is a sign of a sick society, and there is no need to say anything about it. If we talk about our positive vision of life, people will see the difference. Show them a clean glass of water and they will see how dirty their own glass is. I guess that makes sense to me. So much P. R. work is fighting with shadows and wasted effort."

In the months after Jonestown, Will poured out his volatile feelings and thoughts. I didn't have much to say in response. I told him that although I can see a lot of differences between Yogi Bhakta's movement and Jim Jones's church, the American public probably lumps them together as dangerous cults. If Southern Baptists think other Baptists are wrong and Missouri Synod Lutherans believe other Lutherans are going to hell, you can't expect most people to be open-minded about shaven-headed guys chanting in orange robes or a bunch of Sikh hippies doing yoga.

Will's voice came over the phone so loudly that I had to hold the receiver away from my ear. "Why can't they see we're not a cult? Jones invented his own version of a church. We are an ancient tradition with roots that go back to Guru Nanak in the early sixteenth century. Yoga was practiced before there was writing. Yogi Bhakta is different from Jones in a million ways. We are a legitimate religion, not a cult!"

"Hey, you don't have to convince me. I'm just telling you what the average Joe thinks. He doesn't know a Sikh from a Halloween ghost. He thinks that religion is something you can't understand, an irrational act of faith. To Joe, you are all crazy and probably dangerous. You steal America's youth and brainwash them. A cult is what he calls it when he doesn't understand it and doesn't want to."

Will exhaled loudly. "You know, we are really in this together," he went on, subdued now. "The scholars of religion and the media both have a hell of a lot of work to do to educate this country about religion."

I agreed, although I added that our country is no different from any other. There is a part of human nature that doesn't want to understand other religions because it might undermine one's own faith. Seeing the similarities can plant a mustard seed of doubt.

Will followed closely the revival of anti-cult legislation in the aftermath of Jonestown, and he continued to call me up, express his alarm, and ask what I thought. A New York legislator sponsored a bill in 1978 that would have made it a felony for anyone to promote a "pseudo-religion." "What the hell is a pseudo-religion," Will demanded, "and who's going to decide?" In 1980, a bill proposed to alter mental health guidelines so as to grant parents greater powers of conservatorship, which would allow them to deprogram their adult children. Twice the bill passed the New York assembly but was vetoed by the governor. After Jonestown, Senator Robert Dole organized Congressional hearings to investigate whether something should be done to prevent similar tragedies in other new religions. The hearings eventually fizzled out as scholars, civil libertarians, mainline churches, a Utah senator who was a Mormon, and representatives of new religions all opposed legislation that endangered the First Amendment right to freedom of religion.

Yet in 1979 it was not unreasonable to be worried about the influence of the anti-cult movement. Anti-cult bills were introduced in many states, including Minnesota and Illinois, although they were usually defeated while still in the hearing stage. Foundations raised money, formed networks, and hired professional psychologists to testify as expert witnesses in court cases. Several times Will phoned me and read a newspaper clipping about the forces that wanted to destroy new religious movements. He yearned to explain how Bhakti Dharma differed from the Peoples Temple. "They aren't the same!" he would exclaim, and begin what strongly resembled an academic lecture. But once he said, so softly that I could barely hear him, "They aren't another species. Everyone erects a wall, puts them in a zoo. I won't do that. The people in The Peoples Temple were like me. I won't turn my back on them. I could have been there. I might have done that."

"Will, what are you talking about? Hey, man, you are way too preoccupied with this Jonestown business. It's over. Let's go for a long walk or do something fun together. It'll be good for both of us to take a break and lighten up."

We planned to walk along the lake, but it turned out to be a windy, rainy April Saturday, so we met at the Field Museum instead. We shuffled through the Native American exhibits and stuffed animals, had a cup of hot chocolate in the café, and sat down on a bench in the vast exhibition hall, where we contemplated an enormous skeleton of a tyrannosaurus.

Will looked up at the pile of bones and said to it ruefully, "There's no place in this world for you, buddy." He lay back on the bench and stretched, arching his spine backwards, until his head almost touched the floor. He came back up and exhaled. "Aaaargh." His face made a painful grimace. "Where will these bones end up?"

"Do you think you're headed for extinction?"

"I don't know, I'm just venting." He paused for a moment, frowned, and then went on in a rush. "I can't stop thinking about Jonestown. One thing that really hit me is the defectors. Jones was furious at the members of the Peoples Temple who left, especially several who had been part of his inner circle. What triggered the final events was the visit of the Committee of Concerned Relatives and their departing with members who wanted to flee. It was traumatic for Jones to see anyone leave his movement. He ordered the assassination of Congressman Ryan, the news reporters, and the disgruntled people fleeing his utopia. Then he commanded the suicide and murder of the entire Jonestown community. Men, women, children, animals, even fish. All together in life, all together in death. Do you understand the reaction to those who ditched out? They were traitors and apostates from the true faith. It reminds me of something I've seen in Bhakti Dharma: the anger and the feeling of betrayal. We say that those who fall from the faith must have been bad people who were never seriously committed in the first place."

"How does that happen? Is there an official statement?"

"It works like this. There's no room for doubt or questioning while you are in the ashram. That is seen as negative behavior, and it is smothered by cold silence or rehearsing the official line. Because of the pressure to conform, there's no warning when someone leaves. You wake up and they're gone. Then it's a real shock. If someone moves out of the ashram, there's a little ritual to deal with the feelings stirred up. It's not an official event, but there always comes a time, usually during the next community meeting, when the leaders do a post-mortem. They explain why the apostate's faith died or was never real in the first place. She didn't keep up, she lacked trust in Yogi Bhakta, and she was sneaking junk food when she was in the outer world. Other people pitch in, suddenly remembering earlier signs of doubt and vacillation. It's like an exorcism. We are casting away our own dark side, and a lot of anger and grief comes out. The defector is a scapegoat, and our harsh judgment shows our own struggle with weakness or temptation. We denounce the renouncer to pump ourselves up. When I read about Jones's hatred of the followers who left him and the conflict between outsiders and insiders in Jonestown, it seems like a magnified version of what we go through when somebody leaves Bhakti Dharma. Am I making any sense?"

I assured Will that he made a lot of sense. I was very surprised that he was so critical of Bhakti Dharma. He sounded like a detached observer, or even, heaven forbid, a scholar formulating a theory about the sociology and psychology of religion. Will had mined the Jonestown transcripts for insights about that religious group, and it was affecting his view of his own community.

"I'm hungry," I said, "how about a snack?" We went back to the café in the basement. There was a turning rack with bratwurst sizzling on it, and I decided to get one. I usually avoided eating meat when I was around Will, but today I had an irresistible urge to devour a juicy brat with sauerkraut and mustard and, while I was at it, a coke and potato chips. So much talk about religion made me want to pig out. While I wolfed it down, Will looked around uneasily at the other customers, glancing at me occasionally. He was trying to hide his disapproval of my junk food but not doing a very good job. I disapproved, too, but the brat was delicious. Will seemed embarrassed and fidgety. He pulled out a wad of folded-up newspapers from his pocket and started reading it to himself. After I finished my food, he said, "I want to read you this. But let's get out of here, I can't stand the food smells in here." Our tyrannosaurus-viewing bench was now taken, so we found another spot at the other end of the main hall. The rain came down hard now, and people ran into the Museum with their coats pulled over their heads, shaking umbrellas and making puddles on the marble floor.

"Listen to this," Will said," reading from the newspaper. "Its from *The New York Times*, March 15, 1979. This is a transcript of a tape recording of Jones talking at the end of the White Night, the suicide ritual they had rehearsed several times. Listen to the way he talks about their deaths as revolutionary suicide. Killing themselves is an act of revenge against their oppressors. He says, 'They brought this upon us. And they'll pay for that.' But he also asserts that dying is a courageous act that makes a positive statement. He tells his followers as they line up for poison, 'I, with respect, die with the beginning of dignity. Lay down your life with dignity. Don't lay down with tears and agony. It's nothing to die. It's just stepping over to another plane.' Jones says his people are black, proud, and socialist, and they are going together to another place that he calls 'the green scene thing.' Let's get gone, he says, let's get gone."

Will looked up at me, his face somber and pale. "These are his last words. 'We are one thousand people who said, we don't like the way the world is. Take our life from us. We laid it down. We got tired. We didn't commit suicide, we committed an act of revolutionary suicide protesting the conditions of an inhumane world.' Then there is only the sound of organ music."

"It's shocking," I said. "He interprets suicide in heroic terms."

Will did not answer. He sat on the bench staring out at the pounding rain. It was almost too noisy to talk. Will held the newspaper pages open before him, his head tilted forward as if still reading, but his eyebrows were raised. He gazed ahead blankly at the huge doorway entrance to the museum. Children shrieked as their parents tried to get them in or out of raincoats, and custodians mopped up puddles. One toddler didn't want to go into the museum and sobbed in her father's arms. He reassured her, Everything will be all right, honey. We were silent for several minutes. The white noise of the downpour washed away White Night, and we came back to the present moment. Then we were gone again.

"I've read the whole transcript a dozen times. It brings back that terrible summer in Minneapolis. I wanted to get gone. I wanted to be in a better place, a green scene. I even thought I was doing a good thing, because my death would bring the ashram together in grief and celebration of my life. By dying I would commit an act of service."

"Do you mean that the Jonestown tragedy was somehow like what you did? Will, you were really unbalanced then. You were mentally ill."

"I know I was. And so was Jones. But religion was part of the equation. I still don't completely understand what happened to me. Some of the things I did then weren't me. I was hanging on a cliff. There's a line of poetry Mom quotes by Gerard Manley Hopkins that I remember. 'O the mind, mind has mountains, cliffs of fall/Frightful, sheer, no-man fathomed. Hold them cheap/May who ne'er hung there.' You can't judge me or even understand me if you were never hanging over the edge of that mountain. That's where I thought I would be saved. I would fall into the arms of God."

"I'm not judging you, Will. But suicide is wrong, no matter how we explain it."

"Of course, what else is new? I'm not talking about the morality of suicide, but its psychology. Get inside my head for once. Reading the transcripts where Jones is ranting and raving, I wince, because it's a mirror. I didn't like this world, either. I wanted to get gone. I wanted to slough off my bad self like a snake leaves its old skin. By dying I would be purged of the part of me that is worthless and be pure, a good self, the one I long to be. I would merge with Yogi Bhakta and be like him, all light, all love. I was so tired of fighting myself, utterly exhausted. I would gladly lay down my life. In my mind, it wasn't suicide. I would give up what little I had for something better. I let go of the present because I expected a better future. A vision of something beyond made what I had here seem so limited, so pitiful."

"So you tried to get gone."

Will had become agitated as he spoke about that desperate period of his life. The air was thickly humid, and he broke into a sweat. His eyes were wet and a tear skidded down his cheek. He slumped forward, his elbows resting on his knees and head hanging low, his breathing labored and uneven. I felt compassion for Will's pain, but also relieved that he recognized the self-destructiveness of heedless devotion. I put my arm across his back and didn't say anything. We sat that way for a long time. The downpour was letting up. Then I said, "Your search for self-transcendence almost cost you your life. You turned your will against yourself. I'm glad you're still here, buddy."

He sat up quickly and turned towards me. "What is transcendence? It's such an abstract word. What does it really mean?"

"Is it just wanting more? I guess literally it means to rise above or go beyond a limit. To climb above or overcome some obstacle. My professors use that term to talk about human religiousness, which is always dissatisfied with itself, seeking more. It's the spirit fighting against its own past and its own achievements, yearning for what it can't even define. What were we talking about?"

"You said my search for transcendence almost made me kill myself."

"Yes. And I wonder whether trying to get to a religious place, a green scene, has to mean leaving this world behind. Does trying to be a good or pure self always mean denying a bad self, the body, or evil desires? Is religion a disguised self-denial and hatred of the world? Because sometimes it seems really sick and crazy. We are never happy with our best effort. I'm attracted to Buddhism because it tells me to accept whatever is and learn to be here now."

Will looked at me with amusement.

"What?" I asked.

"Aren't you, too, wanting more than you've got? When you try to just be content with whatever is, you're not accepting your yearning for more. But let's get out of here, this place and this head-trip. Religion is not about logic, it's learning to live with paradox. I'm chilled. The rain has let up and I want to walk."

We stood up, stretched, and set out through light drizzle, traversing Grant Park to the Art Institute. By the lions on the front step we said goodbye. Will walked north to catch a bus to the ashram, and I headed south to board the Illinois Central train back to Maiko and home. From the train I looked up at the towering office buildings. I imagined being so high and looking down at all the little people toiling like ants, wanting more. My thoughts turned to Saint Simeon Stylites, a fifth century Syrian ascetic and saint who lived for thirty-nine years on top of a pillar. He wanted to transcend the world, but he demonstrated this in a most conspicuous way. Pilgrims and even a Roman Emperor came to seek his wisdom, climbing up a ladder to converse with him. Simeon Stylites did not truly get gone so long as he was still in this world.

Maiko and I were sitting on the back porch of our apartment one June evening, waiting for the coals to get hot on a small hibachi grill. The smells of lighter fluid and roasting meat from neighbors' grills wafted up to us.

Dozens of apartments with their gray lattices of staircases and porches backed into the fenced yards in the middle of our block. On a summer weekend when everyone was cooking outside, smoke and greasy fumes pervaded every room of the apartment. As a vegetarian, Maiko found the Fourth of July to be a formidable challenge to her equanimity and patriotism. Tonight we counterattacked by grilling marinated tofu, eggplant, peppers, and mushrooms. While the coals took their time, we drank white wine and talked about a Harold Pinter play we had seen. When the doorbell buzzed, we looked at each other in surprise.

It was Will. I brought him and another chair back to the porch. He looked excited and was breathing rapidly, not only from climbing the steps to the second floor but as if he had escaped some danger.

"They locked me out," he announced. "Can you believe it? After all I've given. I've been walking around all day. I had to get away."

"Wait a minute, start at the beginning," Maiko said. "Are you talking about the ashram?"

"No, I can still go there. I'll be given some new assignment, too. But when I got to the office this morning, the locks didn't work. I'm standing there fumbling with my keys, and I think I must be crazy because none of them fit. Amritsar comes to the door to let me in. He has a totally blank look on his face, like this is no big deal. As if there is no reason he should have warned me. He tells me about new policies. The locks are just the tip of the iceberg, but that's what brings home to me that I'm not trusted any more."

Yogi Bhakta had announced a sweeping program of reforms. It was hard at first for me to understand why they were so significant, but to Will it was as if the Pope had announced that Catholic churches would now practice snake handling and speaking in tongues. Over the next two hours, he explained how the changes had come about and what they meant for him.

Some of Yogi Bhakta's reforms simply regulated the practices of ashram life, following up on the discussions Will had heard in San Francisco the previous year. In addition, Yogi Bhakta defined for his followers what it meant to be a Sikh. Individual devotees can no longer adopt various practices, beliefs, and symbols piecemeal or not at all. Members would adopt a Sikh name and use it consistently. There are still significant differences between the practices of American-born converts to Bhakti Dharma and those of Sikhs who emigrated from the Punjab. For instance, Indian Sikhs eat meat and tolerate a wide range of observance or non-observance of traditional Sikh customs such as the five K's, the uncut hair, dagger, steel bracelet, loincloth, and comb. But Yogi Bhakta's movement now follows strict regulations that bring them into partial alignment with historic Sikh practice.

The more conservative Punjabi Sikhs are highly critical of Bhakti Dharma for two reasons. They sometimes openly ridicule the idea that yoga and meditation can be the means to spiritual liberation, because for them the heart of Sikh religion is an act of trust and faith in God. They also criticize the way in which some of his devotees worship Yogi Bhakta as divine. How can he act as a living guru, they ask, when the only true guru is the sacred scripture, the Guru Granth Sahib? On several occasions when Yogi Bhakta was teaching, angry foreign-born Sikhs disrupted the gathering, denouncing him as a pretender and heretic, interrupting and heckling him. Several vociferous protesters were forcibly expelled from one meeting, cursing and threatening divine retribution. Another meeting had to be abruptly disbanded. These conflicts were deeply upsetting to Yogi Bhakta, for he hoped to maintain good relations with fellow Sikhs while crafting a new religious movement suitable for the young Americans who followed him. Doing yoga does not automatically make you one with God, he explained, but it is an essential practice in the way of life I teach and takes you many steps on the path.

Yogi Bhakta split his movement into two parts. One branch would henceforth be called American Khalsa, which means "the pure ones." This religious group would adopt the traditional markers of Sikh identity, the turbans and beards, five Ks, and Sikh scripture and forms of worship. They would continue to practice most of Bhakti Dharma's distinctive religious activities, such as sadhana, the early morning discipline of yoga, chanting, and meditation. Members of American Khalsa would live according to their leader's idiosyncratic views about bodily and psychological health, including vegetarian diet, proper attire, and the roles of men and women. Yogi Bhakta sloughed off some of the practices that resembled Hindu customs, including the role of sanyasin, or ascetic renunciate. This was an upsetting change for Will. There would still be ashrams for single celibate devotees, but they were expected to marry eventually and form an independent household and family.

The second organization created out of Bhakti Dharma would be called the Higher Consciousness Organization. It was essentially a business corporation that would control the increasingly complex and diversified finances, represent the group's public face, and organize outreach activities to American society. You don't need to be a Sikh to do yoga in one of their studios, buy a meal in a natural foods restaurant, or hire their landscaping crew. The spiritual side of HCO is not hidden, but it is expressed in New Age terms that appeal broadly to Americans not eager to don a turban. The way yoga is taught emphasizes empowering the self, not handing the self over to God.

Bhakti Dharma was a syncretistic mix of Sikh, Hindu, and New Age themes that coexisted well in the movement's early days. But tensions among these elements had mounted, and now Yogi Bhakta would eliminate certain elements and distribute the others in two different organizations. There is a good deal of overlap between American Khalsa and the Higher Consciousness Organization, but in theory they are distinct. The name Bhakti Dharma would no longer be used. It was going to take a lot of public relations work to explain all this to various audiences. Time will tell whether Yogi Bhakta's strategy will work on both the spiritual and practical levels.

Maiko asked what all this institutional reform had to do with the locks on the door. Will had nibbled a little at our grilled veggies, but he was too agitated to eat much. He looked away from us, towards a raucous gathering that spilled off a porch into a back yard. About ten people our age, probably grad students, were drinking beer and picnicking on the lawn.

"It's so easy for some people to be together without religion," he said. "Why does it have to be so hard for us? Why do we need locks? Amritsar is evasive and talks about new organizational security procedures. He says it's nothing personal. But I know I've been pushed out because I spoke against some of the changes while they were still proposals. I don't just follow orders. There will be two public relations offices eventually, one for the Higher Consciousness Organization and one for American Khalsa. Amritsar and Jeff—now he's named Jagesh Singh—they know I don't like the reforms. I've argued too much with them and said negative things. My job will be reassigned, and they'll find something else for me to do. I can't believe this is happening. The best parts of me—my devotion, creativity, and critical thinking—are seen as negative. I thought we could be honest about our disagreements. Instead, I'm viewed as a troublemaker. They don't trust me."

I was struck by the paradox of Will's frustration, given his frequent assertions of the need for absolute obedience to a guru. I asked him how that ideal can be squared with the kind of disagreement and political debate he wanted. "Do you want things to be run more democratically? What would happen then to obedience?"

"I am totally committed to Yogi Bhakta! But there has to be room for discussion and various points of view in his organization. Religion is one thing and politics is another."

"There is spiritual leadership and there is the institution. They sure aren't the same. But every religion needs both, right?"

"Yes, of course. But now they are both changing in crucial ways and pulling apart. The organization men who will take over are bureaucrats. In San Francisco I saw how they work. They don't need charisma to do their jobs, which I admit are necessary, but I don't want them to squelch the spirit, either. The new power in the movement is based on file cabinets and accounting and flow charts. On door locks and a chain of command. But I haven't even mentioned yet the really big change. Yogi Bhakta is not going to be a guru any more."

"What? How can he not be a guru?"

Yogi Bhakta's role had always been ambiguous. Sometimes he said, "Don't worship me, but follow my teachings," thereby seeming to disavow his divinity. At the same time, however, the name he chose for his religious movement and himself highlighted bhakti, passionate devotion to a divine figure. He had said, "To know me is to know God, and to know God is to know me." He wanted it both ways. Now he was going to play down the divine side. The term guru would not be used, and there would be recommendations about what expressions of devotion are appropriate. For instance, his photograph will always be lower than the ten gurus of Sikh tradition. Certain prayers and hymns will be rewritten, often substituting God for invocations of Yogi Bhakta.

"Appropriate! Recommendations! As if the overflowing love of a devotee can be measured out by the teaspoon, or calibrated so as not to offend an abstract principle. You can't unguru a guru. I wouldn't have joined Bhakti Dharma if I couldn't be passionate about my gratitude and faith without needing a committee's approval."

"Why are these changes happening now?" Maiko wanted to know. Will's response to that question involved a lot of speculation and conjecture about pressures on Bhakti Dharma. We sat on the back porch as twilight fell, and then darkness. The lights on back stairways came on and Maiko brought out a candle lantern. I wished we could see the stars through the light pollution.

Will had heard several theories about what lay behind the reforms. Amritsar, who was keenly attentive to the nuances of Sikh identity politics, asserted that the reforms were basically a response to criticisms of the American *Gora* (white) Sikhs by Punjabi Sikhs. Yogi Bhakta had decided to make compromises in order to maintain good relations and to assure his movement's historical continuity with ancient Sikh tradition. He had felt the force of criticisms of his followers' veneration of a living guru, and would henceforth portray himself simply as a teacher.

Jeff knew other things. Yogi Bhakta had suffered a serious illness the previous year, an intestinal problem that sent him to the hospital for ten days. A friend of Jeff's who worked in the national office confided that as soon as he came out of the hospital, Yogi Bhakta asserted that his illness was a sign from God. This warning about his mortality meant that he should take steps to organize a smooth transition to new leadership that would carry on his movement when he died. Yogi Bhakta was a lot less egotistical and considerably wiser about his organization than other contemporary gurus, according to Jeff. Yogi Bhakta observed the troubles that quickly divided the Hare Krishna movement when Bhaktivedanta Swami Prabhupada died in 1977 without explaining how his movement's leadership would continue after his death. The eleven senior disciples who took over the role of guru were soon embroiled in conflicts among themselves and with a governing commission responsible for administrative matters. The struggle over how to transmit and organize leadership brought turmoil and schism to the Hare Krishna movement, and thousands of people quit.

In 1976, another popular guru, Maharaj Ji, disbanded his religious movement. He changed the name of the Divine Light Mission to Elan Vital, closed his ashrams, and taught meditation as a practice that could be done by anyone, effectively ending the communal organization of his followers' lives. He radically cut back the movement's administrative structure, saying it was as unnecessary as "lipstick on a cow." He discarded Indian terminology and customs and no longer wished to be worshiped. He would henceforth be known as Prem Rawat, and capitalized letters would no longer be used with pronouns referring to him. "Festivals" became "regional meetings," and his followers no longer devoted their whole lives to propagating his message, as had been the case a few years earlier. Like Guru Maharaj Ji, Yogi Bhakta no longer wished to be treated as divine, but he intended to maintain a strong religious organization and to require his followers to live, worship, and practice together in a community.

Perhaps, too, the fallout from Jonestown and other scandals involving religious leaders made Yogi Bhakta realize the dangers of idealizing or idolizing a fallible human being. Jeff claimed that Yogi Bhakta was a most unusual religious leader, more a prophet than a messiah, who tried to wean his followers from excessive adulation. How often does that happen? Ironically, Yogi Bhakta's very humility, as Will interpreted it, only confirmed for my brother his teacher's worthiness to be revered as a guru.

"So what are you going to do?" I asked. "Are you going to go on worshiping him or see him as a really good yoga teacher?"

Will leaned forward, intently gazing into the courtyard, which was now empty and quiet. "I don't know," he said, sighing deeply. "All day I've felt devastated. I feel like my heart has been torn out of my body. I can't change how I see my guru. I can't turn bhakti on and off as if it comes through a faucet. This reform throws the baby out with the bathwater. I'm upset and disillusioned about Bhakti Dharma. Which is probably good, since it doesn't exist any more."

"What's the baby getting tossed with the bathwater?"

"Bhakti, the passionate love of the incarnate God. I know what God is like. He's a person, not an abstract principle. For him I renounce my own will and declare my obedience to the living Lord who commands me. I feel like the value of my spiritual experiences is denied by this move to downplay the guru and bhakti love. I wonder if I chose the wrong guru."

"You mean you should have shopped around first?" I asked. "Well, there are other gurus out there, I guess. Maybe you can find another. Or maybe—here's another paradox—maybe you will have to give up worshipping your guru as the ultimate act of devotion to Yogi Bhakta."

"Hmmm." Will shot me a suspicious sidelong glance. "I suppose that is theoretically possible, but it sounds cerebral and contrived. Maybe that is what Amritsar will do. He'll support the reforms and nurse his faith in his heart, but not express it. But could I do that? I would give up the outward expression of bhakti while inwardly viewing Yogiji as God, or as close to God as I'm going to get. It seems false, too devious and inward. We couldn't have the free flow of praise and exaltation that comes when a group worships God. When we are laughing and crying and praising and everything is accepted, whatever you have to give, that's when I know what grace is. Or when we are quietly meditating and my heart overflows with gratitude to the man who showed me this path."

"You can still do that, Will," Maiko said. "No one can take that away from you."

"I don't know what I'll do." He yawned. "I'm exhausted. I got up at four. Can I stay here tonight? It's too late to go back and I need some distance anyway."

We put sheets on the couch and turned in around eleven, which was a very late night for Will. When I cracked my eyelids and looked at the alarm clock at five thirty, I could hear him doing yoga. The rapid "breath of fire" exhalations made a nice steady rhythm, reminding me of steam clunking in our radiators in the winter. I smiled, rolled over, and went back to sleep until about seven, when I smelled the coffee Maiko had brewed. Early morning sunlight poured through the window that looked out at the park, and the three of us sat in the front room in peaceful silence, drinking coffee or tea and watching dog walkers, joggers, and early commuters. The birds were chirping, swooping, and eyeing the worm prospects. Will didn't feel like small talk or big talk. He was preoccupied and brooding as he left to catch a bus.

"Thanks for letting me crash and for talking. I'll be in touch when I decide."

I was about to ask him what he was deciding, but he turned abruptly and was gone, walking quickly towards Lake Shore Drive, his silhouette dissolving into the dazzling sun.

Ten

The Starving Buddha

WHILE WILL STRUGGLED WITH his conflicting feelings about Bhakti Dharma, I was trying to get Saint Benedict and Buddha to talk to each other. After three years of coursework in the Divinity School, I spent another year studying for PhD exams and putting together a proposal for the thesis. Starting in 1977, I began writing a dissertation on Christian asceticism. I also worked part time as an editorial assistant for *The Journal of Religion*, which was housed in a windowless office in the basement of Swift Hall, a sterile place of sensory deprivation. By the autumn of 1979, I was almost finished with the first draft, except for the question of whether to compare Christian to Buddhist asceticism, and whatever grand conclusion I came to in the final chapter. But I was stalled.

The dissertation, entitled "Starve the Body, Discipline the Will, and Test the Soul: Asceticism in Early Christian History," explored various forms of self-denial during the first six centuries of Christian history. In the name of religious devotion, just about every conceivable human activity has been curtailed or prohibited: sleep, eating, sex, physical movement, study, owning property, interaction with other people, attending to one's appearance—and the list goes on. Many of these disciplines can be carried to the point that making the body and mind suffer becomes an exquisite art of self-torture. Pious souls have created ingenious forms of mortification such as carrying heavy weights, self-administered stigmata, flagellation, and wearing a haircloth that itches and provides a breeding ground for lice. In the fourth century, Macarius spent six months sitting naked in an Egyptian salt marsh, offering his body in penance to hordes of stinging insects.

I wanted to understand why the early Fathers engaged in these practices, their motivations, justifications, and ways of distinguishing between the right kind of self-denial and abuses or excesses. Some ascetics thought they were punishing their sinful nature, while others competed for glory with rivals in the penitential Olympics. An ascetic may have been expiating his own or another's guilt or trying to ensure a higher status in heaven. Sometimes asceticism was politics, as Christians withdrew to the desert or mountains to protest against corruption in the Church. For certain monks and hermits, self-denial was a way to imitate the martyrs once there were no more persecuting Roman emperors to throw them to the lions. So they practiced "the white martyrdom of virginity" and proved their utter devotion to God by despising the things of this world. Asceticism became popular in the fourth century, just as identifying as a Christian became a safe, even advantageous position in the Roman Empire. In the name of the holy, some ascetics rejected as second best the goods of this world. These guys, like Augustine, were the sane ones; others saw all finite things as evil.

I was trying to synthesize too much material, including theological treatises by Augustine, Tertullian, and Origen and random sayings by the "desert fathers," the *abbas* and hermits of Egypt and Syria. I should have focused on just one type of self-denial such as celibacy or fasting. I could have examined just one person's thought, perhaps John Cassian, a monk who brought the teachings of Egyptian monks to southern France in the early fifth century. I might have zeroed in on "Celibacy in Augustine's Milan" or "Whips, Chains, and Thorns in Sixth Century Syria." But I was stubbornly ambitious. I focused each chapter on a key debate about asceticism. For instance, in a chapter about renouncing sexuality, I discussed a disagreement about the meaning of persistent sexual fantasies and nocturnal emissions in monks sworn to celibacy. This debate was connected with the Pelagian controversy about the freedom of the will and original sin. What are humans capable of? I kept seeing how my topic was connected to many important issues, but I couldn't stay on track. Thompson, my advisor, told me to prune digressions, rein in my speculations, and stick to the topic. "You need to crystallize," he warned. "Less is more. Since you are writing about denial, practice what you preach." He told me to postpone my grandiose ambition to provide the key to the history of Western thought and just write the damn dissertation. "It's a union card," Thompson said, "a meal ticket. Wait a few more years, until you get tenure, to change the world."

It may have been because of my brother's name, as well as his life story, that I saw the ascetic's central struggle as with his own will. One Desert Father asserted that even when a monk has apparently overcome greed and sexual desire, a love for one's own way persists "deep down in the heart, like a snake hidden in the dung." Not the body but the heart, the essential self, is what keeps a Christian from directing his desires toward God. It wasn't the fruit on Eden's tree that Adam and Eve wanted, but their own way. Certain Desert Fathers criticized extreme asceticism because those devoted to it were willful, proud, and contemptuous of other people.

The hero of my tome was Saint Benedict, because he realized the dangers of self-mortification and created a form of monasticism that, while austere by modern standards, was moderate and wise about disciplinary practices. *The Rule of Saint Benedict* tried not to inflict anything "rough or burdensome" on monks and was always concerned about the weaker brothers. In reaction to other monasteries and ascetic regimes that competed to mortify the flesh, Benedict recommended a different kind of self-denial that focuses on disciplining the will. The Benedictine vow of obedience requires submission to an Elder. The vow of stability commits a monk to stay in one place; it disciplines rootless, restless wandering, a symptom of a vagabond heart. What Benedictines call "conversion of life" is a vow to continually conform one's daily life to the principles of the Rule, a never-ending test of patience and humility. Benedict challenged the popular view that a hermit's renunciation of human society is the ideal expression of devotion to God. He expects most monks to remain in community for their whole lives, and he repeatedly points out ways in which living with other people tests and teaches Christian virtues. Benedict knew that the will can never be completely overcome or denied, but it can be disciplined and focused on God in a daily struggle best undertaken in a community of fellow believers.

I could imagine putting all my chapters together and giving them to my advisor and readers. But there was a lingering doubt in my mind. What about Buddhism? I had given up on having Professor Sakorn Premchit as an official reader, although I took a couple of classes from him. Instead, I enlisted a scholar of the late Roman Empire, Jacob Holbrook, a dour elderly sage from the History Department. I told him, Krupat, and Thompson that I still hoped to compare asceticism in Buddhism and in Christianity. Thompson was increasingly skeptical about that idea, asserting that I was already spread too thin over a vast intellectual map. Yet I would not relinquish my desire.

In August 1979, I got a break that freed me from this limbo. The previous spring I had applied for a grant that provided travel funds for students working on their dissertations. Although I had a weak case, both Professors Krupat and Premchit were on the committee that awarded the grants. They must have known that I was out of my depth, but perhaps they hoped that a trip to Southeast Asia might get the Buddhist bug out of my system so I could finish the dissertation before my hair turned gray. Or maybe there weren't many applicants that year. In any case, I received a letter awarding me sufficient funds to travel to Thailand and study Buddhism at Chiang Mai University for two months that autumn. When Premchit called me into his office, he happily explained how his personal connections would facilitate my visit. The monsoon rains would end in October and cooler weather begin in November, so a Westerner would find it a comfortable time to live in Chiang Mai. "What a marvelous opportunity!" he exclaimed. "You can see what Buddhism looks like on the ground and decide how much further you want to take your studies."

Why did I not feel excited about this marvelous opportunity? Rather than elated, I felt anxious and depressed. Maiko was baffled. "You look like your best friend just died. What's the matter?" I told her that the whole trip would be a scam. I couldn't possibly write about Buddhism with authority. I didn't know the languages, history, or culture of modern Thailand or the ancient Buddhist texts. So what was the point?

"Are you nuts?" she asked. "Go, and you will learn a lot."

"But I need more knowledge before I can understand what I see. I don't want to just wander around like a tourist. I need to conceptualize what I see."

Maiko looked at me sadly. "You know, you remind me of someone who followed the Buddha. Ananda, one of Buddha's first disciples, was great in knowledge, but he lacked the ability to experience ecstasy."

I remembered that Ananda was not allowed to go to the first great Buddhist council because other disciples felt he understood *nirvana*—liberation from suffering—only on an intellectual level, but had not felt or experienced any intimation of it. Premchit used Ananda's example to warn us about the limitations of an academic approach. He said we students are like a traveler in a desert who looks down into a deep well and sees delicious water but cannot taste it. When I told Maiko this anecdote, she gently admonished me.

"Peter, go to Thailand. If you don't go, your studious nature and scholarly conscience will become walls cutting you off from life. I see it so often in university people. They erect intellectual defenses to stop them from feeling. Yet they secretly steal energy from what they study. Especially you religion students, who analyze ecstasy but can't experience it yourself. Maybe you study it *because* you can't have it."

"You may be right," I admitted. "I suppose I should go. Two months is a long time, though. I would miss the American Academy of Religion meetings and the job interviews there."

"Are you kidding? You would turn down a free trip to Thailand to go to a bunch of job interviews! Don't worry about it. Maybe you will get a job this year or maybe it will take another year. This is the chance of a lifetime. Do it!"

"Okay," I said, feeling reproached, "I'll think about it." I sighed.

A few days later I saw Will. He had bicycled all the way along Lake Michigan down to Hyde Park on a sunny Sunday morning. Maiko was working the lunch shift at McBundy's. While I made a big batch of French toast, Will gazed out the kitchen window. He was brooding about something and so was I.

"You seem a little low, Peter."

I told him about my travel opportunity and my hesitation in going. "I just don't know if I want to go all that way and spend all that time if I can't get something out of it."

"Get something? How could you not? Who can know before it happens what you will get from anything worth doing? To decide what's important before you go is living backwards."

"I need to have a goal and a plan. I want to finish my dissertation this year and get a teaching job. I've got to have priorities, and one is to be productive." I dropped onto the table a plate of French toast, as if it were a heavy book.

Will raised his eyebrows and shook his head. He forked over four pieces and piled on some yoghurt and maple syrup, then paused thoughtfully.

"What is it?" I asked. "You're thinking of something."

"Well, I was reading the *Bhagavad Gita* the other day because it celebrates bhakti. You know the climactic scene where Krishna appears to Arjuna and tells him to do his duty. Krishna says that Arjuna must act without attachment to the fruits of his actions. Although he can't control the outcome, he must do his duty. This is renunciation *in* action as opposed to renunciation of action. You don't stop acting or give up anything finite, but you act in all things as if the consequences don't matter. I wonder if your Christian monks have a version of this ideal. Peter, there is a message for you in the *Gita*. This sounds preachy, I bet. But I'm going to stand tall in the pulpit and say that Krishna is speaking to you."

"What is Krishna telling me? I don't get it."

"Then you're not listening. A call has come. Go to Thailand. You can't know beforehand what will happen. Maybe it will be a waste of time if your only purpose is to gather material you can put in a footnote. You say you've given up on writing about Buddhism. But so what? Maybe this junket is an academic scam, but God is knocking on your door."

"God?"

"Hell yes. Not Krishna, Jesus, or Yogi Bhakta, but Buddha. God works in a lot of ways, and maybe this is one. So what if you don't deserve this adventure and didn't expect the grant? Take it as grace. Let go of your agenda, get on the airplane, and something will come of this journey that you can't imagine. Like Arjuna, act without attachment to the fruits of your action. Amen."

I put my elbows on the table and my face in my hands. I felt a hot flash and a sinking sensation in my stomach, as if I had just taken off in a plane. I was ashamed of myself for being so cowardly, so anxious about my academic work, and so full of doubts about any decisive action. I wished I could be like Will, always ready for a new experience and flexible enough to change to fit new circumstances. He, spontaneous and mercurial, could be converted, but not me. I study religion, not do it. Damn it! I groaned.

"Are you all right?" Will asked. "It's not the end of the world to receive grace."

I laughed at this ludicrous remark. Then at my ridiculous paralysis. Maybe I could take a baby step, anyway. I took my hands away from my face.

"Okay, I'm going to Chiang Mai. I'm glad you encouraged me." This felt strange, as if our usual roles were reversed. He was acting like a big brother, heartening a younger sibling who needs a gentle nudge. Will seemed much older and wiser in the ways of the world than me. I started thinking about travel plans and forgot to ask him what he was brooding about. I put the Doobie Brothers on the record player in the living room and cranked up the volume. Will washed the dishes, wagging his funky butt a little and pausing to play a riff on an invisible guitar, while I cleaned up the rest of the kitchen mess. He slapped me five, a secular blessing. He said, "Bon Voyage, bro,'" and carried his bike downstairs for the ride home.

Renunciation

Arkoam Chaiariyakul met me at the Chiang Mai airport on October 12. I never learned to pronounce his last name, and he instructed me to call him Ajahn (meaning "teacher") A Comb, making a combing motion through his hair. To address a Thai professor, one combines formality and friendliness, using both the professional status and the personal name. Ajahn Arkoam called me "Professor Peter" for a few days and then, after I protested, simply "Pee-tah." He was a classmate of Professor Premchit during their undergraduate days at Chiang Mai University, had gone to graduate school at the University of Virginia, and now taught early Thai history and architecture. Premchit asked Arkoam to shepherd me around Chiang Mai for a few days and orient me to the city and university. We enjoyed each other's company, and Arkoam went far beyond the call of duty in hosting me for the next two months. He must have liked practicing his English, and he asked me the latest American slang terms for sex, drugs, and rock and roll. He was a little disappointed that I didn't have more to offer, and he reminisced nostalgically about his days in Charlottesville in the late 1960s.

A few days after I arrived, Arkoam picked me up at dawn from the apartment he had found for me just outside the main gate of the university, off Huay Kaew Road. My living quarters were behind a maze of open-air food stalls, and the smell of frying food usually pervaded the air. This morning, however, we were up before most of the vendors had gotten their stalls ready for business. We drove over to a road running through the university, where hundreds of people were already sitting, waiting patiently. Today was Awk Phansa, the end of what Westerners often call "Buddhist Lent," a three-month period when wandering monks settle down during the rainy season. The Rains Retreat is a popular time for a young man to be ordained as a monk. Most Thai men—even the king—become a monk at some stage of their lives for at least a few weeks or months. This temporary period of renunciation is a rite of passage to adulthood.

Ten minutes later, an impressive procession of monks appeared, moving slowly down the street. Awk Phansa is an annual event and ritual that recognizes the important relationship between monks and laypeople. Instead of the usual practice of doing their morning alms gathering alone or in small groups in various neighborhoods, on this day the act of giving (*dana*) is performed in a festive public ritual. After short speeches by a couple of senior abbots, the monks began to work their way down the street, collecting alms from the people lining each side. Thousands of residents of Chiang Mai placed offerings of food, usually a small box or a bottle of juice, in the monks' alms bowls. In their saffron robes, with shaved heads, hundreds of monks of every age made their way along the road, casting their eyes down as they received alms. They did not thank those who gave food; they allowed the act of giving to take place, meditating as they moved slowly along the line of people. When a monk's bowl was full, he returned to a truck and deposited the food. Arkoam had brought several little cereal boxes of what looked like Rice Krispies and Cheerios and some juice bottles with a picture of a mango. We gave them to the monks.

The Thai people showed their deep reverence for the monks, waiting in silence, bowing, and receiving blessing. Arkoam explained his gratitude. "The monk makes it possible for me to be generous. Offering *dana*, I practice selfless giving. This morning I need to make extra merit because yesterday I ate bacon for breakfast."

As we sat on the curb in the sun's early rays, I mused about the paradoxes of giving and getting. Arkoam did not see any contradiction between the ideal of selfless giving and racking up a little extra merit. Both monks and laymen give up something and receive something. Food and respect come to the monk who renounces the ordinary world, while the layman accumulates good karma by putting a box of Rice Krispies in an alms bowl. This choreography of mutual sacrifice honors the monk's separate status and rewards the layman's gesture of support for the *sangha*, the Buddhist monastic community. This ritual of symbolic renunciation is oil that lubricates the Thai social machine.

Arkoam guided me around Chiang Mai, a fairly small city of about a hundred thousand people that would be a mere neighborhood in Bangkok. The old city lay inside a moat and ancient crumbling brick ramparts. I spent most of my time at the university, a mile or so to the northwest, on the edge of town. Arkoam introduced me to several other Ajahns to whom I described my intellectual interests. They liked my story about the Egyptian monk seeking out stinging insects and warned me to be careful not to catch malaria. I was confused for a moment and then said I would be careful. I clarified for them that I was not in Thailand to practice austerities myself, but to study Buddhist renunciation. "Ahh, I see," nodded one of the Ajahns, frowning slightly.

I browsed through the shelves of the university library for the few books in English and found two that I hadn't seen before, collections of sermons about the virtues of compassion and patience. They were deadly dull. On the terrace of a little café that sold iced coffee, I spent many hours

reading my own scholarly books about Theravada Buddhism and, to escape, *Moby Dick*. The sweet Thai students, elegant even in their prescribed
uniforms, shyly checked each other out. I attempted to learn a bit of oral
Thai, but didn't get beyond Please and Thank You, numbers, and food.
Even for those words, I quickly gave up on the five tones, counting on the
Thais' benign forgiveness of an awkward *farang* (foreigner). Several times I
caught a *tuk-tuk*, a motorized three-wheeled taxi, or flagged down a *song-
thaew* (literally "two rows" of benches), the red covered pickup trucks that
carry passengers on fixed routes.

Chiang Mai has more than three hundred Buddhist wats (temples),
as well as shrines, museums, and monasteries interspersed with the commercial areas. Orange robes are everywhere, including being wrapped
around many trees. Scooters zoom by with two or three laughing boy
monks hanging on. Thailand is the most religious place I have ever been,
and it is ninety-eight percent Buddhist, except for three largely Muslim
provinces in the far south. Thai Buddhism is tangled up with ancestor
veneration and placating natural spirits. Each home has a tiny temple on
a pillar in the yard that shelters the ghosts displaced when the house was
constructed.

Walking the streets of the old city, I peered into dark go-go bars from
which came pounding music: Eric Clapton, Led Zeppelin, and Credence
Clearwater Revival tunes performed with impeccable precision by Thai
musicians. During the Vietnam War, soldiers on leave had given a huge
boost to Thailand's sex industry, and some of the bars had all-but-naked
girls dancing on tables, as well as dozens of very friendly young women
wanting to strike up a conversation or frankly offering themselves: "Hey,
honey, you want it?" These places were full of Caucasian men of all ages,
most of them gleaming with sunburn, sweat, and a desperate, pleading
expression. Many of them were loudly, obnoxiously, or fall-down drunk.
Although this was not my scene, Arkoam took me to a joint called "Easy
Street" for a beer the first week I was in Chiang Mai. Before the drinks
were served, two young girls who looked about fourteen had put an arm
around each of us. "Big guy, you like me?"

"Yes, but no thanks," I laughed, embarrassed, and Arkoam informed
them that we weren't interested. The music was too loud for conversation.
I pointed to the door and yelled that I was glad to see this place, but I
would prefer a place we could talk.

We moved on, and a few blocks later found ourselves at the night
bazaar, a huge open-air market selling the embroidered wares of hill

tribe people, pirated tape cassettes, chubby Buddha figurines, fake Rolex watches and knock-off imitations, mass-produced lacquer ware and carved wood, souvenir T-shirts, silk goods, and much more. Tourists from around the world crowded the stalls and street. Raucous laughter filled the air. We took in the carnival mood, standing in a spot sheltered from the flow of pedestrians, tuk-tuks, and motorcycles. Traditional Thai music filled my left ear, while rock and roll was louder in the right one.

"Pretty amazing," I said to Arkoam.

"Thai people know how to have a good time," he nodded. "And they like to make others happy, too."

We went on to a street near Thapae Gate, where a dozen outfitters sold packaged "authentic" encounters with hill tribe peoples. I took one such excursion in November, which involved driving two hours to a Hmong village selling the same handicrafts you could buy in town, a waterfall stop for lunch and a hike, and a Lisu village selling identical souvenirs. Chiang Mai was the take-off point for Westerners who wanted to experience "the real Thailand," whether on a one-day jaunt or a weeklong trek into the mountains near Mae Hong Son or Chiang Rai. Those hills are crawling with backpackers searching for a spiritual utopia that they assume must exist as far from what they know as they can get. They return to Chiang Mai with relief for a hot shower and an expensive hamburger made with Australian beef. They have "done" Thailand.

Hundreds of friendly restaurants offer delicious dishes I had never heard of: Burmese curries with pork, fried fish swimming in sweet orange sauce, chicken stewed in secret sauces based on lime and basil or lemon grass, shrimp and scallops in coconut milk soup, stir-fried noodles with pickled garlic, red chilies, and vegetables. Like Indian food, Thai food tries to tickle every taste bud at once, as sweet, salty, bitter, and sour flavors mingle and, like a jazz combo, take turns as lead or backup. Spicy hot peppers dance fast or slow with sweet coconut milk, pungent herbs, sour lime juice or tamarind, and salty shrimp paste. The colors and aromas are almost as shocking as the red-hot chili peppers. I heard that biting into one of those little devils causes the brain to release pain-suppressing enzymes, so the aftereffect is a bit like that of certain illegal substances that Thailand offers to people seeking oblivion.

Those mind-altering substances aren't hard to find, Arkoam informed me. In the nearby village of Pai, you can support a heroin or opium habit for a dollar a day. Some Westerners settle in for a few days of rest and relaxation and wake up a few years later, sweating, shivering, and vomiting, out of money or in jail. They may have started selling drugs themselves and impinged on local arrangements between suppliers and police.

And the massages! Some of the parlors are fronts for prostitution, but there are plenty of legitimate places where trained professionals will stretch and pound your every joint and muscle into a state of blissful relaxation. They kneaded me into a slack, mellow version of my usual self. The guiding principle of the masseuses was the same as that of the cooks stirring in chili peppers: no pain, no gain. So relax into the pain.

For the druggies, the old guys looking to get laid by a teenager, gourmands caressing their taste buds, and work-driven Westerners like me who, for once, could take a deep breath and relax, Chiang Mai is a place whose allure depends on all that we think we have to deny ourselves back home. She provides countless opportunities for hedonistic pleasure and self-indulgence, offering with a smile to satisfy the cravings denounced by the *farang* conscience. With unfailing courtesy and grace, Thailand is glad to give you what you thought you had to give up.

I followed the usual tourist itinerary in Chiang Mai. I rode an elephant, visited wats, ate myself into a stupor, and climbed Doi Suthep, the majestic peak overlooking the city. At the top is Wat Phrathat Doi Suthep, a fourteenth century monastery and temple, where I circumambulated the central stupa, gazed at golden statues of the Buddha, and enjoyed a fabulous view of the city spread out five thousand feet below me. Along the course of my dazed pilgrimage through the tourist attractions, I had a few moments of insight, the only souvenirs I brought home.

Arkoam and I were accompanied by a former monk named Chayakorn Thiphakorawong, who mercifully asked me to call him Golf. The youngest son of an illiterate farmer from a village north of the city, Golf had been sent to a monastery when he was nine years old. His parents knew that this was the only way that the boy could get a good education. Golf had left his *sangha*, his Buddhist community, at twenty when he was reprimanded for questioning certain teachings. The decisive moment of deconversion came after he fed some of the dogs hanging around the monastery. Temples and monasteries in Thailand are often overrun by skinny street mutts. In my experience they don't bite or bark, and spend their lives sprawled on cool stone steps or in shady patches. Golf had started feeding these pooches regularly, and soon twenty or so of them expected a meal in his canine soup kitchen. The senior abbot decided that too much food was going to the dogs, and their increasing number was inconvenient, perhaps even dangerous. Golf felt strongly about what he was doing and argued that just as *dana* was given to monks, so a monk should be allowed to give generously to any hungry creature. To do so expresses compassion for suffering, and isn't that what Buddhism is all about? One of those dogs may have been his mother or the abbot's father in a previous lifetime. Why, he asked, should he curtail his natural inclination to express compassion to all sentient beings?

The abbot refused to argue with the headstrong novice and commanded him to stop feeding the dogs. Golf persisted on the sly and was caught. He was given one more chance, with the threat of expulsion. Golf described the scene when he confronted the abbot. "I was very upset. I did not have *jai yen*, a cool heart. Thai people hate loud voices and public anger. It shames everyone present and their families, too. It's better not to reveal pain. A cool heart does not lack compassion, but is free from greedy desire. We Thais say *mai pen rai*, which means 'never mind' or 'no problem,' and walk away from entanglement. I made a big mistake with my superior to whom I owe respect. But he could have explained to me why I was wrong about feeding the dogs. Buddha says that his teachings should be questioned and tested. They are not dogma we must accept blindly, but insights we can discover and verify for ourselves. Why did the abbot command me instead of leading me gently to the truth, as Buddha did?"

Golf's departure from the monastery was possible because of his English skills. He was naturally quick with the language, which he first picked up from visiting tourists. The monastery had groomed him to give tours and planned one day to provide instruction to the growing number of Westerners seeking a retreat center for a meditation course. Golf's language skills impressed the University's English Department examiners, and he received a fellowship to support his studies. At present he was a graduate student and low-level instructor in English.

Golf reminded me of Will, who was the same age, twenty-seven. His gentle, detached manner was quite different from my brother's intense and mercurial temperament, and his small stature contrasted with Will's big bones. What struck me was their common situation of disillusionment as they challenged the institutions of religion. Will was wrestling with whether to leave Bhakti Dharma, while Golf had abandoned his monastery. I asked the ex-monk whether he was still a Buddhist.

"Of course," he said, "I will always be a Buddhist. I practice meditation most days and I go to the temple to make merit. But I don't want to
be a monk and submit to authority. Now I can think for myself. I see a lot
of corruption in the temples and monasteries. It is all about money. They
sell charms to the people and will say a prayer for your crops if you give a
donation. How do you say it in English? The dog's tail is wagging?"

Arkoam jumped in. "The tail wags the dog. I remember that funny
expression from Virginia."

"Yes, the tail wags the dog," Golf repeated, chuckling. "Things that
are not so important make the rules. It is different in the forest. There
are two Buddhisms in Thailand, that of the temples and that of the forest
monasteries. The forest is where you must go if you want to meditate and
come closer to enlightenment."

"So why don't you go there?" I asked.

"I'm not going to be enlightened this time," said Golf. "Maybe next
time, when I come back. In this life I make merit so it will be better next
time. For now, I like learning and teaching at the University. I don't want
to be a monk any more. I'm happy as I am. I take care of eight dogs who
depend on me."

Golf had gone through a relatively painless exit from religious life, so
far as I could tell, and was without lingering doubt, turmoil, or ambivalence. I hoped that Will would get to the same point.

I learned a lot about Buddhist asceticism from reading, listening to
Golf and Arkoam, and "monk chat," the discussion sessions at Wat Suan
Dok, a temple and monastery not far from the university. A couple of
young monks held informal meetings there on Wednesday afternoons for
inquiring Westerners. In spite of their limited English, they had an uncan-
ny way of penetrating to the heart of a question and presenting Buddhist
teachings. Although these ideas were familiar to me from my Chicago
coursework, here Buddhist wisdom seemed compelling and profound.
These ingenuous youths spoke with compassion directly to suffering ques-
tioners: an elderly Canadian man with cancer who said he had only a few
months to live; the girl from New Zealand disappointed by a string of boy-
friends; the French businessman worried about an international war over
oil reserves. The Four Noble Truths seemed at once profoundly simple and
incredibly difficult to realize in daily life. It would be easy to live by this
wisdom—if only I were one of these people. If only I were someone else.

I began to meditate every morning for thirty minutes, hoping that
this practice would help Buddhism enter into me and change me. Or that

I would recognize that I am changing all the time. Or that there is no "I," not even the consciousness that realizes this. I remembered Premchit's detective-novel formulation of my task: to solve the case of the vanishing self. Although my sense of a continuous self did sometimes change or disappear, it also kept coming back.

As to my academic interest in asceticism, I came to accept what I already knew. Although the topic is of vital importance in Buddhism, I didn't know enough to make it part of my dissertation. Too bad, I mused, because I was becoming absorbed in this subject. I read everything I could find about it, borrowing several books from a British researcher I met through Arkoam. Buddha rejected ascetic practices when he quit mortifying himself and proposed a middle way between that approach to liberation and the life of luxury and indulgence of his privileged upbringing. There is no point in tormenting the body, for it is the mind that causes suffering and is the source of our problem. Since attachments and desires create our misery, the answer is detachment, letting go of desire, renouncing our hope to cling to what we want or to escape what we fear. I saw Buddha as similar to Saint Benedict in his formulation of a way of life that was restrained, moderate, and wise in steering between hedonism and austere practices of self-denial. Benedict and Buddha would have enjoyed a friendly chat over a nice cup of tea, appreciating the aroma. Just one cup.

To a modern Westerner, of course, Buddhist monastic life involves almost unimaginable hardship. Not eating after the noon meal seems to me as painful as walking on coals. As the rules and regulations for monks evolved over centuries, the written accounts of them, including how each requirement came to be formulated, were collected in the *vinaya* (literally, "taming"). These codes of monastic conduct form one of the three "baskets" of the *tripitaka*, the Buddhist written discourses. A great deal of Buddhist scripture is devoted to resolving debates about how strict and demanding monastic life should be. Does a monk have to beg at every door, or can he pick the houses he knows have tasty food? Should he eat only food obtained by begging, or also meals prepared by or donated to the *sangha*? Is it permissible to go back for a second bowl? May a monk sleep on a bed? How comfortable can a bed be, and how high off the ground? May he talk to or look at a woman? Specific rules prescribe that a monk's cheeks should not bulge when he eats, and he should not open his mouth until the rice reaches his lips. Monks are instructed when a crack in one's food bowl is big enough to justify replacing it and where they can answer nature's call.

Robes are a central symbol of monkhood, and Buddhist traditions have lots of rules, regulations, and debates about how to treat them. How raggedy or luxurious can they be? How many robes can a monk own? How should they be hung to dry after washing? Can a monk wear a robe made from donated new cloth, or only from discarded old cloth?

Defining the middle way between luxury and excessive self-denial is a central preoccupation of monastic life. A dispute about the degree of asceticism required of monks was the cause of a major schism during Buddha's lifetime, when a follower, his cousin Devadatta, advocated a more demanding regimen; for instance, he insisted that monks live only in the forest. Buddha ruled that harsh austerities were an option for some, but not necessary for liberation, thus depriving them of their appeal. The more demanding ascetic practices came to be followed by only the most devoted renunciates living in the forest. These hard-core folks, too, argued among themselves about whether one should stay in one place or wander; dwell at the foot of a tree or in the open air; or sleep in a hut, a tent made from one's robes, or a charnel ground. Can one sleep in any bed that is offered, or should one never lie down to sleep? Thinking about parallels in Christian monastic tradition, I began to see religion as a huge debate about how much to deny the self and why doing so obeys God's will or is the only sure path to nirvana. Every faith distinguishes the right kind of self-restraint from excessive asceticism and from the vices of hedonism, sloth, and sensuality. Religion is the practices that restrain desires and turn them in a new direction, and it is the beliefs that justify this discipline.

In another incarnation I could happily spend a lifetime studying obscure treatises from Sri Lanka and Tibet that prescribe how a Buddhist monk should treat his robe. Maybe next time around the wheel of *samsara* I'll do it, if I come back again as a scholar of religion.

Toward the end of my time in Chiang Mai, during the first week of December, I attempted a short meditation retreat. Arkoam recommended a wat that was in the forest, but conveniently located on the outskirts of the city. Wat Umong was a halfway house between an urban temple wat and a true forest retreat such as the one Ajahn Chah directed in the rural northeast province of Ubon. Several Thai wats had recently begun giving meditation instruction to Westerners in order to spread the dharma and pay the bills. Most retreats were thirty days long, but I didn't have time to fit that in before I left Thailand. Arkoam and Golf arranged for a private seven-day retreat. I would receive instruction the first day and have a daily meeting with an English-speaking monk, but I was basically on my own. I could join the monks in chanting or silent meditation and use a small hut to practice alone during the day. I would eat lunch with the monks and could sneak a snack from my secret stash if I got hungry later. I was assigned a tiny guest bedroom, almost a closet, for sleeping. My kind Thai friends set up this perfect arrangement. They warned me to watch out for cobras and drink only filtered water. I was taking anti-malaria pills, which was lucky because the mosquitoes often joined me for a meal, especially at dusk and dawn.

Beginning on Thursday morning, I was supposed to sit and observe my breath and notice where my mind tried to go instead. This was the same Vipassana (insight) style of meditation that I had learned from the Thai monk who taught a course at Carleton in 1971. It sounds so simple yet is so difficult. If I tried to count ten breaths, simply focusing on the sensations of breathing, my mind was somewhere else before I got to five. I thought about whether the next meal would have a different vegetable in it, had sexual fantasies about Maiko and my eighth-grade girlfriend, wondered how bad an itch had to get before I scratched, remembered the childhood sound of Dad's electric razor in the mornings, and, opening my eyes, contemplated the sun's rays falling on a lizard that crawled across my hut's bamboo floor. I quickly became bored with my thoughts and longed for any kind of diversion. I invented a scale to measure the intensity of smoke, tried to guess what kind of motor endlessly stopped and started, and watched a spider weave a web.

A typical minute: Will the Chicago Bears make the playoffs? Coffee is better than tea. Stomach growling. Remember to renew driver's license. Damn mosquitoes. How long have I been meditating? Breathing deeper now. I'm sleepy. Maybe nap later. *Mai pen rai* means "never mind." Does Golf play golf? Am I meditating now? Does this count? My back is sore.

I tried the slow walking meditation a monk had taught me, but there was so much going on in and around me that I didn't think I was meditating. No credit or a grade of D minus? I was very hungry the first night, and ate two contraband granola bars with the fruit juice that was permitted as "medicine." On the second day, Friday afternoon, I was so glad to talk to the monk that I almost hugged him, which would not have been *jai yen*, a cool heart. When I told him I felt a little bit crazy and my mind was racing, he said I must learn the most important Buddhist virtue, patience. Instead of that, cutting right to the chase, I asked him my big question.

"What is the self?"

Ajahn Sumedho was a middle-aged man, surprisingly plump for a Thai, and wearing glasses. A couple of gold teeth flashed when he spoke. He was a scholar, I'm sure, but undoubtedly more aware than I of the limitations of the rational mind in understanding anything important. It occurred to me, while I waited for Sumedho to respond, that you can make a career out of criticizing intellectual approaches to religion, and I thought of several of Yogi Bhakta's little sermons.

"You want theory? Or practical knowledge? What for you ask about self?"

"I want to understand myself. I want to know what Buddhism says about this person I think I am, and if I have to lose him to be happy."

Sumedho almost always paused for a few seconds before responding. "You want, you want, you want. This smart fellow's attachment, to know answer. Buddha say this not often helpful. All his teaching about suffering and how end it. Not theory, not smart talk. This practical knowledge how to live."

I sat for a moment, formulating my thoughts, and Ajahn Sumedho regarded me gravely, like a doctor informing a patient of a very serious disease. I tried to figure out how to ask a question without sounding like an ivory-tower academic, which I am. This conversation reminded me of talking to Will. I really do want to know how to be happy, content, free of suffering. But my path requires understanding. I posed a logical question that had bothered me for a long time.

"Here is something I don't understand. Buddhists say there is no self, no permanent soul. Everything keeps changing. Yet you also believe in reincarnation, that souls are somehow passed on to other beings when we die. The whole notion of karma depends on this, and merit-making and the moral weight of our deeds. What gets passed on to what, if there is no soul?"

Ajahn Sumedho sighed. "Ahh, this question again. Sounds like a trick. But say you want answer. Okay, I tell you two ways think about it. One, flame on candle. Light second candle with it. Not same flame, but come from first candle. Yes? Second idea is seed. Seed not same as tree, but tree come from seed. Fruit come from tree. One from other, but look different. Now you happy? Suffering go away?"

I laughed. "Yes, for now. I don't know if I understand, but I'll think about your analogy. So I'm happy."

"Watch that this happy not seed for unhappy tomorrow. You dissatisfied when answer too easy. Need new puzzle toy."

I looked at him a long time, taking that in. Remember this, I thought.

Then Ajahn Sumedho said, "Half hour. Enough today. Same time tomorrow."

The third day, Saturday, I could hardly stand to meditate. I tried three times and watched my mind obsess about units of time. I thought about how many minutes I had been sitting there, when I could justify looking at my watch again, and how much longer I would have to sit to call this session a success. I started thinking about quitting the retreat. Not until I have stayed at least three days, I vowed. Monday morning would be four days, more than half the length of the retreat, and I could say I had given it a sincere effort. That was forty-eight hours away, an eternity. I was only halfway there. But I would be asleep for sixteen or so of those hours, a third of the time.

I calculated how many months it would take me to finish my dissertation. I thought about being twenty-nine years old and estimated that, if I lived to be eighty-seven, I had spent one third of my time on this earth. I felt disoriented and opened my eyes many times to recall where I was. I thought about carving notches on the wall of my hut, marking days like a prisoner in jail. I wanted to fix myself precisely in time with these mathematical calculations. I did not really understand the meaning or value of what I was doing during my retreat, but quantifying time was something I could measure. I, I, I, I!

My mind kept racing, anxiously trying to catch up with or run away from something I couldn't identify. Several times that day, without deciding to leave the hut, I found myself exploring the grounds of the monastery. In the big hall, I listened to about forty monks chanting, ringing bells, and reading old texts. It was a relief to be with other people. I sat on a bench for an hour, watching two barefooted monks sweep the winding paths. A troop of saffron-robed monks strolled by, hardly noticing me. By afternoon the heat hung heavy in the air, and I was grateful that the forest canopy allowed only a few shafts of direct sunlight to break through. I hoped that I wouldn't get too hungry tonight. I desperately wished I could read a book, but I had been instructed not to read or write during the retreat. I was killing time until I could see Ajahn Sumedho again. It was a long day.

Finally it was time for our interview. I arrived fifteen minutes early and sat waiting for Sumedho outside the office where we met, which was apparently a place of bookkeeping and administrative records. As in almost every other room in Thailand, a photograph of the King, never smiling, hung on the wall. I noticed, through the open doorway, a pad of paper and a pen lying on a table. I wanted them, with a craving as strong as lust or hunger.

When Ajahn Sumedho arrived I removed my sandals, made a respectful bow with my palms pressed together, and was off like a racehorse, babbling about my difficulties, talking out of control. Relaxing the restraint of "noble silence" that I was supposed to observe on my retreat produced a torrent of chaotic verbiage. This time I asked no questions, but rather confessed the reasons I couldn't meditate. I started to get angry, too. This retreat was more than anyone should have to stand, it was too demanding, there was not enough support for a solo American with little experience. My anger modulated into whining and then a pathetic whimpering plea for pity. I didn't know if I could keep going. I had come to many brilliant insights and would go on thinking about them for a long time somewhere else. Expressing all this pent-up frustration took much of my half-hour. Sumedho listened patiently, smiling kindly several times. I suppose that expressed compassion, but he didn't say he felt sorry for me or encourage me to hang in there. Instead he told me an anecdote.

"Teaching story about Ajahn Chah. He ask disciples how big is a stick. They don't know. He say, depends what you want use it for. If you want big stick, then your stick too small. You want smaller stick, then yours too big. Your stick too big or small because of your desires. This how suffering come into the world. Stick isn't big or small by itself."

"I don't get it. Are you saying I have a stick?"

"Your stick is time. Too long or too short, too fast or slow. You want quit in fifteen minutes, not twenty. Live a century, then want another. But time is what it is, not what you want."

I absorbed this for what felt like a long time. "I see what you mean. You are right. But how can I ever stop?" I felt a wave of sadness, because I could see how I make myself unhappy, but not how to change. It's who I am, I said to myself. I can't help it, it's my self, my sweet, sweet, miserable self.

Ajahn Sumedho nodded. I wondered if our time was up. He nodded again, and snapped his fingers. "Talk time gone. You try one more day. Uproot every attachment, like pull weeds. Maybe tomorrow be easier."

"Okay," I said, feeling drained by my outburst. "I'll try it again."

On Sunday morning I started out with a fairly serene period of solitary meditation in my hut. When I looked at my watch, an hour had passed. I was elated. Maybe I can make it, I thought, I must be a pretty good meditator. But now I'm finished. I can't take it any more, empty out any more. I took a little break and climbed up on to a small man-made plateau with tunnels carved into it that led to relics of venerated abbots. On top of the grassy mound I was confronted by the strangest of the thousands of representations of the Buddha I saw in Thailand. It showed the future Buddha while he was practicing severe austerities. An emaciated Siddhartha carved out of black stone sat in the full lotus position with his hands in his lap. His ribs stood out sharply, his stomach had caved in to a hollow, and his arms were like sticks. His eyes were closed and his gaunt, expressionless face revealed nothing. A few small pots stood in front of the statue, holding smoldering incense sticks. A garland of fading yellow flowers had been placed in his hands some days ago.

No one else was around. I sat down on a low wall and gazed at this statue of the Buddha as a starving ascetic. He had surpassed his teachers, so the legend went, and learned to survive on one grain of rice and one drop of water a day. But while bathing in a river one day, Siddhartha fainted from weakness. He decided then that extreme asceticism was not the way to spiritual freedom. He accepted a dish of rice and yoghurt from a young woman who thought he was a ghost. Abandoned by his five companions, who derided his lapse from their strict regimen, Siddhartha sat down under a tree, determined not to rise until he found the liberation he had sought for so long. He meditated through the night and attained enlightenment, the awakening to the nature of reality that is summarized in the Four Noble Truths. The Buddha's ascetic period was a crucial step on his spiritual path, a necessary experience in his journey to enlightenment. He had to go through the near-death of renunciation in order to awaken to the true nature of things.

After all the gold-plated statues, the fat, happy Buddha figurines sold in the markets, and countless bodhisattvas with *mudras* (postures) demonstrating a particular symbolic hand gesture, this stark, black statue called me. It emanated a powerful yet negative energy. A force like a magnet pulled me into this Buddha's dark hole. The world around me faded away, and all I could see was a point of luminescent black light. For a few moments all sounds ceased except for a loud rushing noise, perhaps coming from inside me. It felt as if invisible waves were pulsing toward the

Buddha, and I was riding them, drawn into a vortex, as into a whirlpool beneath a falls. This suction pulled me into starvation, darkness, and death. Both terrified and exhilarated, I shuddered, unable to endure what would annihilate my sense of self. I hesitated for a last, thrilling moment on the verge of extinction, pausing as if on a threshold. Then I stood up abruptly and tore myself away, hugged myself, squeezed my upper arm muscles, noticed my weight on the ground. The sounds of the world came back: bird calls, a light wind in the treetops, a faraway cry. A trio of adolescent monks walked on the path below me, looking up curiously at the tourist squeezing himself. I must have looked like I was shivering, and perhaps they thought I had a fever. I turned quickly and walked down the hill and back to my hut, where I sat in dappled sunlight for the rest of the morning, dazed.

I tried to understand what this unexpected experience meant. Was it a hallucination or a momentary psychic breakdown? Perhaps my mind produced something in reaction to its disorientation in a foreign culture or the mental emptiness of this period of solitude. Or was it some kind of religious intuition or insight into finitude or the fragility of my sense of self? All of these interpretations made sense to me but left out something that lingered just out of reach. Despite thinking about it for the rest of that day, I was baffled. The starving Buddha seemed to be a wake-up call, a signal trying to reach me. Yet an equally strong response in my deepest being made me move away from the impersonal force field that carried no moral or message but wanted only to swallow me up and pull me under the pulsating waves. My instinct to remain conscious of ordinary existence, my desire to go on living, brought me back to the hot, dull, dusty day. I didn't want to lose it or get gone.

I couldn't wait to talk to Ajahn Sumedho. I felt excited all that long afternoon and didn't try to meditate any more. I strolled around the grounds restlessly, wishing that I had a pen and paper to write about my strange and inconclusive encounter with the emaciated Buddha. When I wrote it down I would understand it, I believed. I would make something of this incident, give it meaning, whether or not that meaning was really there.

Ajahn Sumedho did not seem surprised at what had happened to me. He was interested but said not to make too much of it. "Some people see lightning or think they fly. Some masters meditate all life long, never have funny experience to talk about. Don't hang on to it."

I was amazed. The first mystical experience of my life, if that's what it was, and Sumedho seemed to be dismissing its significance. I protested,

"But surely something important happened. What do you think it might mean?"

"Maybe Buddha call you. Could be karmic opening up. Maybe not sleep enough. Let go for now. Meaning may come later. How go meditation?"

Crestfallen, I told him it wasn't going very well. Today I had been thinking too much about the Buddha statue to concentrate, and yesterday, utterly bored with the contents of my mind, I had been mentally racing to get somewhere else. "I just don't think I can do this any more," I pleaded. "Maybe my turning away from the Buddha statue was telling me to leave this retreat." I wasn't sure that's what my encounter meant, but it seemed like a plausible interpretation. The starving Buddha had to mean something, and I wanted to go home. I thought nostalgically about my little cubbyhole apartment behind the food stalls with the delicious aromas of spicy peanut sauce and sizzling chicken and shrimp.

Ajahn Sumedho sat thinking for a minute. Outside the window, leaves fluttered slightly in the faint breeze. A scratching sound nearby must have been a broom sweeping, endlessly removing leaves from the path.

He spoke slowly, patiently, as if explaining something complicated or obscure, or else teaching a child something very simple. "To practice meditation is continual letting go. This is true renunciation, not give up food or women or money. We farewell what is inessential, distract us, bother us. Anger, fear, memories, plans, judgments. All unnecessary. Return to the breath. Concentrate. Contemplate. This is freedom. Enjoy present moment. Renounce and enjoy."

I think that's what he said. I was too agitated to fully take it in or understand. I wanted his blessing to leave, and he was telling me to begin again. I stood up and said to him decisively, "I have to go. Tomorrow I will say goodbye." I remembered to *wai* respectfully, and he nodded. On my way out, passing through the outer office, I saw the small ream of lined paper on a card table. I casually picked it up, as well as the pen. I went back to my hut and wrote furiously until it was dark, describing the starving Buddha encounter in pretty much the words I've used here. Then I slept soundly and woke up refreshed, glad to be alert and alive.

So I cracked. I couldn't just sit on my butt and watch my breath for a week. On Monday morning, after four days on my retreat, I went back to Sumedho, catching him in between the communal chanting and his regular office duties. I told him that I had decided that my strange encounter with the starving Buddha meant that prolonged meditation was a kind of self-denial that I wasn't capable of. It was not the Middle Way for me. I was grateful for this retreat and would continue to meditate, but I wasn't going to continue any longer and would leave immediately. He didn't argue with me and seemed to have expected this. I put on a cheery, matter-of-fact face, but inwardly I was disappointed with myself, as if I had failed my PhD exams or secretly done something wrong. I remembered the paper and the cheap plastic pen I stole, but I didn't confess to the sins of stealing or writing. As I left I made a deep bow, and Ajahn Sumedho did the same, flashed his gold teeth, and said, "I am glad you are coming along. You have meditation experience. Good, bad, don't judge. Don't reject, don't cling, only enjoy."

"Thank you, Ajahn Sumedho, thank you." I felt relieved, as if I had been forgiven for a lifetime of sins. I gathered my few belongings, stuffed them into my little backpack, and walked out the gate of the wat and along a narrow lane, back to the bustling markets and streets of Chiang Mai. When I arrived on Suthep Road to the south of the university, I found the beginnings of a parade underway, as people milled around the street and a few frantic policemen tried to get them into an orderly procession. Fireworks, cars honking, costumed marching bands, singers and dancers on floats pulled by flower-garlanded trucks, and crowds of well-wishers had already begun to celebrate the King's birthday the next day, December 5.

A week later, on my last night in Chiang Mai, I sat with Arkoam and Golf in a restaurant on the east side of the Ping River, looking at the lights of the city. For the first time I had brought along a light sweater, although it wasn't necessary. For dessert we had my all-time favorite, sticky rice with mango. I smacked my lips after the last bite and said that I was tempted to get another, but that would probably be indulging my craving for sweet pleasure.

Golf laughed. "Finish your beer instead. There's nothing wrong with pleasure. You enjoyed your mango sticky rice. Monks like it, too. It's not pleasure but clinging to it that creates problems. One dessert is the Middle Way. Wanting two is attachment."

"I agree," said Arkoam. "Bottoms up, as the Australians say," and he raised his mug.

"Thank you, guys, for all you did for me and showed me. I saw a lot of Buddhist sites and survived half of a meditation retreat, but it took a mango sticky rice to really bring home the lesson of nonattachment."

At the airport we gave each other American style hugs. I invited them to come to Chicago, where I could show them Wrigley Field, the Museum of Science and Industry, and deep-dish pizza.

On the plane going home I felt peaceful. I looked out the window for a long time, letting things settle. My visit to Thailand had been a failure in two big ways. I had realized that all the work I had put into studying Buddhism was not going to pay off academically. I wouldn't use any of this rich material in my dissertation. And second, my attempt to attain enlightenment in one week had fizzled. I turned away from the starving Buddha, and am still not sure whether or not I understand his message. He triggered some deep aversion in me to the self-denial that prolonged meditation requires. I did not want to give up my monkey mind's freedom to go wherever it wants. I couldn't starve my body or my intellect. I lacked the stamina, motivation, focus, or whatever it takes to just observe with interest what the mind does. I had failed, but it was okay, I could let it all go. It would be good to kiss Maiko and see how Will was doing.

Eleven

Hanging on to a Corpse

A WEEK AFTER I got back to Chicago, Will came over for dinner. The first snow had fallen the day before and the temperature had dropped to single digits. Will took off his parka and embraced Maiko and me at once, a three-way hug. We had a long candlelight dinner, with vegetarian enchiladas and a cinnamon apple crumble. I told Will about my Thailand experience, including the encounter with the starving Buddha and my debatable interpretation of its meaning. He was intrigued, like Maiko, but neither of them had much to say about it. They seemed as puzzled as I was, and as resistant to a fixed interpretation as Ajahn Sumedho. "Maybe you needed to rationalize your failure to finish the retreat," said Will. "Or maybe you saw beyond your own ego. Time will tell."

Will was unusually subdued that evening. He moved slowly and deliberately, as if each motion required a decision and determined effort. Maiko explained her new jobs, working on costumes, set construction, and in the ticket office at the Goodman Theatre. It wasn't acting, but it was the theatre business, so she was medium-happy, she said. Then she asked Will how he was feeling about Bhakti Dharma.

"Not so good. I haven't seen you guys for about three months, but I've been slowly facing things. I've been reassigned at work, and it's a demotion. They don't call it that, but I'm just a secretary now, pushing other people's papers around my desk. I don't have a voice. The movement is changing. They are going to close one of the three Chicago ashrams and have married couples find their own apartments. I feel a lot of tension with Amritsar and Jeff, and even with the ordinary devotees. We make polite empty conversation about trivia. I've been down in the dumps lately, numb and depressed, and it is difficult to function. One evening I went to a bar and had a beer. I took off my turban, put my hair in a ponytail, and put on a Cubs sweatshirt, so I looked like a normal hippy. I didn't want to disgrace Bhakti Dharma, but I wanted to remember what it was like to be in the world. I crossed an invisible boundary."

"What was it like to be in the world?" I asked.

"It was pretty depressing, sitting there alone. One beer in a crowd of rowdy boozers was enough to tell me that's not where I want to go. The next morning I decided to go to India."

"India?" Maiko asked in surprise, her eyebrows at their highest elevation.

"Yes, and I've come to say goodbye. I have a plane ticket next week to Delhi."

"Whoa, whoa, whoa," I said, "slow down. Why India? What will you do?"

"My plans are sketchy. First I'll go to the city of Amritsar to see the Golden Temple, the spiritual center of the Sikh universe. Visiting it may help me decide whether I am truly a Sikh or not. That will determine a lot of things. Until I know that for sure, I'm stuck in limbo. If I don't become a Sikh, I may be open to a new guru." He looked at us seriously, even gravely. Something about his somber and diplomatic manner reminded me of an army lieutenant telling a family that their son and brother has died.

I didn't know what to say. I was shocked. Was he really leaving Yogi Bhakta? Maiko asked him how he felt about his guru now.

"I'm torn apart. It's because I love Yogi Bhakta so much that I can't stand what is happening to Bhakti Dharma. I have felt just about every emotion as I wait at this crossroads. Guilty about leaving and angry at Yogiji for letting this happen. I'm desperate to be free of turmoil but anxious about what to do and who I will be with. Have I wasted eight years? Was it all for nothing? I've been down in a hole of desolation whose bottom kept getting deeper. And then, the day after Thanksgiving, I had a vision, an intense daydream after a morning sadhana practice. Everyone else had left the yoga room but I stayed there, meditating. In a reverie, I saw Yogi Bhakta the first time I encountered him, surrounded by his followers, on a stage in New Mexico with the Sangre de Cristo Mountains behind him. He asked me whether I wanted to be with him, and I said I didn't know. Then he said, At one time you would give up your life for your Lord. You pledged yourself to things you didn't understand because you had faith."

Will stopped and closed his eyes, remembering the details of his vision. "I asked Yogi Bhakta to take me back. I wanted to be with him. I flashed back to the feeling that I would do anything he said to keep having the longing that is itself perfect happiness. I'm still yearning, but now everything is different. The sweet bliss is behind me, not in front, and it is fading, not getting stronger. Then another part of me said, it's gone, this is just the aftertaste, and you can't have the real thing any more. I heard Yogi Bhakta's voice, clear and distinct, and the crowd was completely silent and the whole earth listened. He said, You are no longer with me, but lost. Find your own way. Yogi Bhakta and his followers got smaller and smaller, and they floated up onto one of the mountains. They rose into heaven and I still sat on the ground, alone and afraid. It was utterly quiet, and I was back in the yoga room in Chicago."

Will opened his eyes. "That was a terrifying moment, but it was a turning point, I see now. I didn't have to think about what it meant. Yogi Bhakta told me what I already knew way down deep."

"This must be so hard for you, Will," said Maiko. She reached across the table and put her hand on his. How do you console someone who has lost faith in God? I felt compassion for Will, yet I also wondered whether this was rock bottom and now healing might begin. But in India? After a few moments of silence, I started to raise questions and objections to Will's plan.

"India is a dangerous place, and you shouldn't just wander around in a daze looking for a guru. Aren't you trying to go back to the past? You want to recapture the rush you felt when you first had faith in Yogi Bhakta. But you can't go back. There must be a way to go forward. You have to get to the next stage. It seems as if you are repeating the time in 1971 when you hit the road, running away from pain and disgrace at St. Olaf."

Will frowned and shifted uncomfortably in his chair. "I don't think of it that way," he muttered. "I'm not going back, I'm going on. Perhaps the Sikh religion will become the center of my life; that's what I must find out in India. But I may also search for another guru. I'm not nostalgic, but I know what it means to worship with the passion of bhakti and that's most important to me. Maybe I'll find a guru or maybe I won't. India is full of people who claim to be a guru, and I've learned a lot about true and false ones."

Maiko asked how Will would go about finding a guru. He didn't have a method, he said; he and his guide would recognize each other. "If things don't work out for me in India, maybe I'll go back to Bhakti Dharma, or whatever they call it by that time. Or it may not be in the cards for me to have a guru. I don't have a plan, I don't know what will happen, only what I need to do now."

I voiced another objection. "What about Mom, Dad, and Sophie? Why are you leaving right now, just before Christmas? Come home for a few days to see them, and then say good-bye if you must."

"I don't want to go back to Duluth. I can't stand to explain what I'm going through and have them try to talk me out of it or feel sorry for me. I don't want to justify what I'm doing or go over and over my pain. I talked to the folks on the phone, and they have the same reservations as you. Sophie is more supportive; she said, Do what you have to do to be free. I don't think she understands that I want commitment and trust as much as I want freedom. Anyway, I won't be gone all that long. I have a one-year deadline on my return ticket. I'll be home next Christmas, I'm sure."

I had an unpleasant sense of déjà vu, because this dispute brought up feelings similar to those I had during the first four years of Will's involvement in Bhakti Dharma, before he moved to the Chicago ashram. I resented his putting his own religious search ahead of our family, especially at Christmas. He was free of bonds that tied me to an ideal of family unity linked to that holiday. I made a sarcastic remark. "You can't make a pilgrimage when you don't have a destination. And do gurus advertise themselves in the yellow pages? This road trip is an adolescent fantasy."

Will shook his head slowly. Maiko put her hand on my arm and said "Enough, Peter." She asked whether Will had any contacts in India. He had the phone numbers of a couple of Indian Sikhs who were supporters of Yogi Bhakta, but he planned to travel alone so as to be open to whatever he discovered. He said, "I don't want other people to control my destiny."

Still I argued. "When I went to Thailand, I had several people to show me around. They would have taken me to a hospital or gotten me out of trouble. You have to take precautions and be savvy in Asia. You are acting like a teenaged dropout in the sixties, just grooving along in a fog. Grow up, Will!"

Will gazed at me fixedly without expression. He was not provoked by my outburst. He seemed to discern why I was upset and settled down into himself, steeling himself against my tantrum. "My mind is made up, Peter. I purchased my ticket. I'm sorry that you don't understand. There are other gods besides the family. I will write to you as often as I can. This is going to turn out okay. You will see."

I made a last, desperate attempt to dissuade him. "Will, you don't know what you are doing. This trip is dangerous, even self-destructive.

Your pigheaded stubbornness pisses me off. Why are you giving up what you've got for something that may not exist?"

With a weary shrug, Will answered me. "Yes, I'm letting go of what I had because I believe there is something more. I hope to find it. Even if I am wrong, my journey will justify itself. It frees me and opens me up to a larger vision than I have here and now. Enough of this. Please, let's talk about something else."

Maiko told him news about Sophie, who had begun her first job as a social worker in Milwaukee and was dating a nice guy named Jonathan. I grudgingly explained the remaining steps needed to finish my dissertation by the summer and how the academic job market worked. But I wasn't present. I felt crabby and distracted, and it was an awkward evening. He had borrowed the ashram's van to come to Hyde Park, so he drove himself home. When he left it was clear that we would not see each other again before his departure. As we said goodbye, he put his hands on my shoulders, looked deep into my eyes, smiled, and said, "We'll be together again." He embraced me and turned away.

Will left for India on December 23, flying from Chicago to London to Delhi. Maiko and I visited my parents that Christmas, and, with Sophie there, the usual five dining room chairs were occupied. We were used to Will being gone, but this year he seemed unreachable, on another planet.

In late January, my parents received a long letter from Amritsar postmarked January 18, 1980:

Dear Mom and Dad,

Long flights, I arrived tired and excited. Too eager for Sikh country to stop in Delhi, will see Taj Mahal, etc. on my way out. Straight to train station for eight hour journey to Amritsar. No air con on second class reserved, but a pleasant trip. I could travel even cheaper, but why suffer for no purpose? Sleepy but thrilled. It's the cool season, with a nice breeze flowing through the carriage. Peanut and candy sellers, beggars, chai and coffee vendors, musicians, crying children, all staring at me. The train station was chaotic, with several lines for reservations and too many options to understand, but a Sikh helped me. Lots of them in Delhi and on the train, all of them fascinated to meet an American Sikh. Their turbans are blue or orange, mine white, but we are kin.

On the train, a beggar girl with a hole for a nose and no ears. She held out her hand and said, "Please, uncle, for bread." I gave her my change and a minute later three more children came to me, hands held open. When can I stop giving? The world has a hole, too, right where its heart should be.

Sadhus and devotees everywhere. The whole country is on pilgrimage, seeking God. Out the window, wheat fields like Kansas, but full of people and animals. A row of people squatting on the tracks, their bathroom. From the train window I saw skinny people washing a sacred cow with milk. Rows of families living in cardboard shacks, each with a television flickering, and hundreds of wires hooked in to a huge electric tower.

When I woke from a nap, a grim-faced Sikh told me not to sleep on the train. He stood guard over my backpack. "Many thieves, even on second class reserved," he said. He's from Amritsar, and guided me to a tourist hotel near the train station. I arrived at dusk, nauseous, and collapsed into bed, slept like the dead. For two hours, and then I was wide awake; my body is ready for morning practice in Chicago. Jet lag for more than a week.

Every day I go to the Golden Temple. The Sikhs' spiritual center was built in the late sixteenth century in the middle of a man-made rectangular lake, whose waters are full of the nectar (amrit) that gives immortality and the city's name. A narrow causeway leads to the central shrine. The golden domes gleam, especially in the morning, and still waters mirror them. In the main room is the original copy of the Guru Granth Sahib, our sacred scripture, which is read continuously. Lovely *kirtan* music is performed, people wash in the pool, and Sikh pilgrims from around the world mingle with tourists. An atmosphere of serenity and joy. I love these people.

Away from the Golden Temple, Amritsar is not attractive. Narrow dusty streets with lepers, cripples, bands of children, and bikes and motorcycles coming from every direction. Move too fast or too slow and you're dead. The smells come in waves heated by the sun: burning onions and garlic, urine and feces, sandalwood and incense, the reek of old sweat and vomit, smoldering cow patties and hash. My eyes burn and stomach turns, and then I smell curry and am hungry. Suddenly the sense of sound takes over: growling generators, tingling brass bells, rumbling trucks, whining motor rickshaws, a riff from a distant sitar, quickly swallowed up in a chorus of children's laughter, a priest's chanting, clinking cowbell, blaring loudspeaker, screams, whistles, taunts, and a hysterically piercing boom box.

The city vibrates with hubbub, constant din, the noisy confusion of urban life. And then hearing fades as vision kicks in—but I won't even start on that sensory overload. I'm saturated, reeling, overwhelmed—and then I emerge from a narrow alley and see the cool white walls of the Golden Temple and the soothing waters that wash away impurity.

There is so much about this religion that I love. The early gurus wanted to break down the barriers of caste, so they began a ritual of communal eating, *langar*. At the Golden Temple there is a huge canteen that provides food, free of charge, to everyone regardless of caste, gender, skin color, or religion. It's just chapati and black lentils, but the symbolism of this gigantic common meal is compelling. I think about Dad's concern for social justice and his assertion that to be sustained it must have deep roots in a religious tradition. We need to overcome our tendency to curve inwards on our nearest kin and ourselves. The Golden Temple has four doors, open to all directions, all faiths, and all four traditional Hindu castes. The Sikhs have always affirmed the equality of women. Guru Nanak denounced the Hindu view of women as a cause of ritual pollution, as well as wedding dowries and *sati*, the practice of a widow's suicide on her husband's funeral pyre. Christians could learn a lot about ethics from the Sikh religion. They practice what they preach, so far as I can tell. One old guy told me that you become like the God you worship. He says that for the Sikhs, God is love. Sikh faith is a lot like Christianity, yet so different, too.

I have to admit, though, that I'm realizing that I can't be a Sikh, at least not here. I've been hanging out in restaurants near the Golden Temple and my guesthouse, talking to people who try to understand what I'm doing. American Sikhs always wear white clothes, but here they dress in lots of colors. Saffron turbans and deep blue knee-length tunics are worn by the conservative *nihang* sect. There is no uniform or single Sikh identity, but many ways to be a Sikh, and most are not as strict as Yogi Bhakta.

The desk clerk at my guesthouse is named Gopal. After work he badgers me about my version of being a Sikh. He eats meat, like most Sikhs here. I knew about some of the differences because I was aware of criticisms of Yogi Bhakta. But being here in my state of uncertainty, I am perplexed about what it means for me to be a Sikh. What is truly important and what is just details or optional?

What most disturbs me is not the question of Sikh cultural identity, but what it means to seek and serve God. Gopal and his pals rip into many of Yogi Bhakta's teachings, especially in the old days before the reforms. Gopal hammers on me with verses in scripture like this: "Attempts to subdue the desires through self-torture only wear out the body. The mind is not subdued by fasting and penances. Nothing else is equal to God's name." Gopal says what Jeff told me but I tried to ignore: Sikhs reject the role of sanyasin and practices of renunciation and austerity. They affirm the householder's duties, family life, and the hard work of peasants and craftsmen. All right, so maybe I can't be a sanyasin, I can accept that.

But what about bhakti and the guru? Gopal took me to have chai with some older men, Harnam and Rajinder, a teacher and a high school principal. They are educated men who are trying to define Sikh religion for the next generation. It's a life or death issue for them, because the survival of the Sikh way depends on what they transmit. They don't talk about bhakti because it sounds Hindu, and that threatens their belief that the ten Sikh gurus received a unique revelation. Harnan says that the only true guru today is God. When I said that Yogi Bhakta is my guru, they freaked out. Rajinder banged his fist on the table, knocking over his teacup, and his eyeballs almost popped out of his head. They had heard of this "heretic" and met other American followers who came to Amritsar. The principal said that Yogi Bhakta is not a Sikh if he calls himself, or lets himself be called, a guru. "There are no avatars in Sikh religion, no descents of God to earth! God is timeless and formless!"

A big part of Guru Nanak's message was the renunciation of renunciation—or rather, redefining what should be given up. In the Guru Granth Sahib, he says this in disputing with a yogi: "Make the renunciation of self and attachment be your earrings. Behold the Lord who is all pervading, make him your patched coat and begging bowl and he will ferry you across the world-ocean. Let control of your body be your asana (yoga posture) and mind-control your loin cloth."

Rajinder jabbed his finger at the text and asked me sarcastically, "Do you think you can find salvation by standing on your head? Holding your breath? Changing your semen into kundalini power? If you put your faith in these silly things, you will drown. As the scriptures say, He who utters the Lord's Name swims across." Rajinder says yoga is not harmless but pernicious, because it makes a false promise. I had to excuse myself, because I was trembling and could not respond. Gopal ran after me and tried to comfort me. We walked to the Temple and sat by the water until I calmed down.

Writing helps me clarify my thoughts and sort out my feelings, folks. I'm not sure I would confess my doubts if I was with you, but you are so far away I feel like I'm talking to myself and you overhear me. There are things you can say in writing that you can't speak out loud.

Last week something happened that made me realize I'm not a Sikh. I have been picking up hints about the political situation and trying to understand the factions. There are divisions among different castes, even though in theory Sikhs reject the caste system. The Punjabi Sikhs and Punjabi Hindus feud with each other. And the most explosive issue is the division among Sikhs about whether they should have an independent state, Khalistan. The hard-core extremists want one and will use violence to get it, including assassinations. Many Punjabi Sikhs want to secede peacefully from India. A lot don't. It's confusing because the Congress Party is stirring up trouble here. My friends at the restaurant said that the threat of an independent Sikh nation is being exploited to arouse nationalist feelings among Hindus. India is supposed to be a secular state where all religions are treated equally, but that is not the reality. The Hindu majority is eager to dominate minority groups, including the Sikhs. But in the Punjab, Sikhs are in the majority, so they could rule their own state if they had one.

Now, just this month, Indira Gandhi has come back to power after losing the previous election, and no one knows what will happen next. Negotiations always seem to break down mysteriously or get sabotaged, according to my Sikh friends. A lot of money flows and disappears like water into the ground. The Indian political parties talk peace in public while they secretly try to divide and conquer and appeal to sectarian prejudices. Behind the scenes, someone funds the hard-core Sikhs so that this threat will stir up Hindu fundamentalists and nationalists. Half of this talk is rumor and paranoia. How can I tell what is true? I was at a table of Sikhs, six of them and me, as they got madder and madder at Indira Gandhi, the Muslims, the Hindus, and each other, and I just watched them, feeling as embarrassed as if I witnessed a family quarrel I couldn't understand.

It's more than I want to know about Sikh politics. I care about these people and love their religion. But it's theirs, not mine. It's a complicated and painful political mess that I'm not part of. And for all I admire about the American Sikhs, I don't think that can be my path any more. We never understood where we came from, India. We were playing Indians because we didn't want to be cowboys or Christians.

That's bitterness speaking, getting the better of me. For a while, Yogi Bhakta brought a lot of things together into a beautiful way of life. There was yoga, bhakti, and a guru, giving everything up for God, Sikh traditions, the music, and all of us living together as one community. Now these things are pulling apart, disintegrating. I'm pulling apart, too, and I don't know what to do next. The glory is fading; the incredible thing we had is history. No more singing at dawn, no more eating sweet prasad, no more living with excitement for Yogiji's next visit. It's all a blur now, a cloud dispersing in strong winds. The spirit slowly fades, dissipates. And here I am in a foreign city, looking for another way to serve God. A religion is not a static thing. It grows, changes, and has a lifespan. I have been hanging on to a corpse. There must be new life somewhere else, where my faith can be reborn.

I don't want to worry you with this melodramatic talk. It's just babble, folks, I'll be fine. I'm going south to see the famous cave temples at Ajanta and Ellora, and then to Mumbai, which the English call Bombay. There are many holy men and gurus in the state of Maharashtra, and maybe I will find one or he will find me. I'll stay in Amritsar a few more days. When I leave, I'll cut my hair and take off my turban. I'll keep the beard and go incognito as a harmless American backpacker. I'll write again when I can, and meanwhile, don't worry about me. Give my love to Peter and Sophie, and please share this letter with them.

Much love,

Will

Several weeks later, my parents received another letter from Will, postmarked February 12, 1980 from Aurangabad, a city in the state of Maharashtra.

Dear Mom and Dad,

I'm still reeling from seeing the Buddhist wall paintings in the Ajanta caves and the huge temples carved from rock at Ellora. These are not true caves, but temples hewn by hand out of solid stone. At Ajanta Buddhist monks took shelter during their annual retreat in monsoon season. Ellora has a winding row of thirty-four cave temples cut into the hills by Buddhists, Hindus, and Jains. There are open courtyards, big porches with massive columns, and lots of bas-relief carvings with writhing figures. Shiva, the god of destruction and resurrection, fascinates me more and more. It is strange to be in a place that was once thriving with living devotees and is now a museum. What was a temple has become a tomb. I am surrounded by tourists, and I am one, a voyeur of the fading spirit. Yet I am also a pilgrim, searching still, and I alternate between these roles. What I'm looking for isn't easy to explain, and it's not on a map like Jerusalem or Mecca.

Since I last wrote I took several slow trains to Mumbai and saw the sites: the Gateway to India, Colaba Causeway, museums, Chowpatty Beach, the Jain Temple, etc. I wanted to go to the Towers of Silence, where the Parsis lay out the dead for the birds to eat, but non-Parsis are not allowed. I am obsessed with death lately. I hope it is part of some inner transformation. Because Parsis believe that earth, fire, and water are sacred, they do not bury or cremate their dead. They lay out the bodies on towers where vultures pick them clean and carry human spirits to the heavens. You can't observe any of this except for the birds circling aloft. It gives me a shudder, because an omen of doom hangs over the whole city.

I didn't spend much time in Mumbai—too hot and crowded. I drifted through Maharashtra and Goa for a month, sometimes sleeping on the beach. I visited several ashrams, checking out gurus, swamis, yogis, and miscellaneous saints and sadhus. There is no shortage of holy men here—the problem is choosing one and committing. I'm like a kid in a candy store, except that I don't want any more sugar. Some gurus have thousands, even millions of followers, like Sai Baba. There are wandering sadhus who are utterly alone, having renounced family and caste ties. They sit in train stations, sleep on a piece of newspaper on the sidewalks of Mumbai, or meditate by a holy cow in the shade of a tree. Maybe my true guru is up in the hills with no other followers, alone with the Alone.

As I was leaving the caves at Ajanta, I confronted a sadhu wearing no clothes at all, and his whole body was smeared with ashes, probably from a cremated corpse. His hair was matted, his toothless mouth gaped, his eyes fixed on me. He wasn't begging, but waiting for me with a message I couldn't decipher. These Shaivite (worshippers of Shiva) ascetics shock me, call to me, but what are they saying? They often practice austerities that show they have overcome pain. They walk over coals, hold an arm in the air over their head for years until it atrophies, or lie on nails or glass shards. One sadhu at a temple had his fists clenched, and his fingernails have grown through the back of each fist. Other people feed him and he lives in a corner of the temple.

I am going to visit a guru who has an ashram near here, who they say conquers death through the grace of Shiva. He is buried deep underground for hours and yet remains alive. Perhaps he can slow down his metabolism and breathing, or he may be Shiva's favored one. Shiva is at once the god of yogic asceticism and the god of sexual desire whose erect lingam is worshiped in his temples. He is the unity of opposites, the master of pleasure and pain, the Lord of life and death. Shiva is the power in all things, including what is impure, such as sex, alcohol, ganga (hash), and death. The Tantric practices confront you with what you thought was evil, and you realize that there is no sacred or profane, only Shiva in shifting disguises. From his followers he requires not morality or orthodox belief, but only bhakti, self-forgetting love.

I see that love in his devotees but I don't share it. I envy their longing and I have some, too, but their yearning is fulfilled while mine brings only pain. I can admit this to you now because you know I'll be all right in the end. But I am going through a very hard time as I turn away from Yogi Bhakta and try to find something to take his place. I made the decision to leave, but there remains a lot of uphill climbing. When I'm not distracted by India's noisy fireworks and colorful spectacles, an inner hollowness gnaws at me. I try not to look within, but out at the world. Sometimes I'm just numb, not feeling anything at all. Or I'm like you and Peter were when I got into Bhakti Dharma so long ago, analyzing it coldly. What I had then is similar to this Hindu bhakti and guru adoration. I'm drawn to it but I can't make the switch, convert myself, get to faith on my own. And there is no grace. So I'm like an academic, looking at someone in an ecstatic trance and dissecting his psyche, calculating what makes him tick. Trying to weigh things of the spirit on that clunky bathroom scale we had when I was a kid.

To speak like an academic in his ivory tower, I suppose that the sense of God's presence comes and goes, and lamenting what I've lost shows my love is still alive. To talk like me: I don't think I can take it any more, this anguish and desolation. I left my joy out in the broiling Indian sun and it melted away. The hymns that used to work for me vanished with the morning mists, and I'm left with only these words.

Renunciation

I'm sorry about all this self-pity. Don't take it too seriously, it will pass and I'll be fine. There's funny stuff, too, like the Indian head-boggle. It's not our up-and-down nod that means yes, or the head swinging left to right that in our culture means no. You move your left ear two inches towards left shoulder, then right ear to right shoulder, several times quickly for about a second and a half, while raising your eyebrows in an enigmatic way and pursing your lips. This means not yes, not no, but rather I hear what you desire, and perhaps it will come to pass, although maybe not. I've had several occasions when I asked for something, breakfast served early or for the desk clerk to call a motor-rickshaw at nine the next day, and received this cryptic signal in response. For a long time I was confused, but now I understand that they don't want to say no and offend their honored guest. They also don't want to commit and be held responsible if they don't fulfill your request. They would like to be helpful, but India is difficult to predict, and so much depends on the gods. So they head-bob. I get it. Yesterday the manager of the hotel asked me whether I would be leaving today. I did the head-bob, and he was greatly amused, understood exactly what I meant, and said, "That is fine, admirable sir, most acceptable."

Tomorrow I'm going to leave Aurangabad and go to an ashram devoted to a guru in a lineage worshipping Shiva. His followers call him Swami Tirtha. In Sanskrit, swami means a master of oneself, a person who is free from sensual cravings and masters yogic disciplines. A *tirtha* is a river ford, a place of crossing over, and it has become the Hindu term for both pilgrimage and escape from worldly troubles and the endless cycle of birth, suffering, and death. This swami has many disciples, and we are going there on Mahasivarati, a day of fasting dedicated to Lord Shiva. There will be a procession to the temple, worship, and maybe the swami will be buried alive. I'm going with Dolf Rietveld, a Dutch guy who works as a Christian missionary in Mumbai. We met outside the caves at Ellora and he told me about Swami Tirtha. I can ride in his car.

I don't think Swami Tirtha is my guru calling me. I'm starting to doubt whether I can ever recapture what happened to me with Yogiji when I was nineteen. This burial thing sounds like a circus trick, but I'm going to find out if there's more to it. So much of religion is a deceptive sham, and as much as I try to respect every faith, I also want the truth. If there is falsehood, I must pierce the veil. There is no great virtue in this; even the dog Toto can pull a curtain and uncover the Wizard of Oz.

I'll write again before long. I'll be fine, whatever happens.
Love to all, always,

Will

My parents passed this letter on to me much later, after we found out
what happened to Will. Dad's telephone call woke me up at six. He had
received a call from Ron Jacobs, a staff member at the American consulate in Mumbai. Jacobs reported that the body of Mr. William George had
been found near the Shiva Dharshana ashram, on the Waghora River, near
the Ajanta caves in northern Maharashtra. The body was found on a stony
riverbed, washed up on the outer curve of the riverbank. Will's head had
been smashed, probably by a stone. The police were uncertain whether or
not "the deceased" had an accident while swimming. He was naked but
for his underwear. His other clothes, including wallet and passport, were
upstream in a neat pile, although his shirt was missing. Police were interviewing people who were present at the Mahashivarati festivities. Will
had been involved in an altercation at an audience with Swami Tirtha,
and a detective was investigating different accounts of it. There would be
a full written report, but it was likely to take several months to make its
way to us. What were the family's desires for the treatment of Mr. George's
remains? The staff at the consulate was working with Maharashtra detec-
tives and local police to determine whether a crime had been committed.
Our family had their deepest sympathy, as well as that of Swami Tirtha.

My father's voice was steely in the late winter darkness. As a pastor,
he had informed other families of a tragic loss. His voice turned to gravel
as he described Will's body, and then he recovered and said, "We told them
to cremate Will's body and give the ashes to us. One of us should go to
India and bring them home. I don't think I can leave now. Maybe someday.
Hope is devastated, and I need to be with her. Sophie comes home tomorrow. I can't leave my congregation for the time it would take to go to India.
But if you can go, I will purchase your ticket. I don't know what you can
say or do there, but I wish that one of us could see where Will died and try
to find out what happened to him and what was going on in his soul at the
end. Do you want to go?"

"Yes," I said without hesitation, "I want to go."

A few days later, on March 3, I flew to Mumbai.

Twelve

Crossing Over

Ron Jacobs, an officer at the United States consulate, picked me up at the Strand Hotel in Mumbai. He was a tall, gangly, dark-haired man in his thirties, already sweating through his shirt at eight o'clock. "Damn air conditioner broke," he grinned. "It goes in the shop tomorrow. Feel the heat building? You wouldn't believe it before the rains begin in June; it's a real sauna. Then the monsoon makes it a steam bath for a few months."

At the consulate, Ron was sympathetic and tried to be helpful, but he didn't have much new information. He had been on the telephone yesterday with Sunil Gonda, the detective on the case.

"The investigation is proceeding, that's about all I can get out of him. He hinted to me that the death looks suspicious, but there are no suspects. Try to get anyone in a religious cult to squeal on another member. This Gonda fellow is pretty good. I've seen his work a couple of times, tracking robbers who hit tourists around the caves area. His methods are, what shall I say, unorthodox, but he gets results. We have put a lot of pressure on the police and the ashram, but that sometimes backfires, so we have to be careful. You might be able to learn something by going up there yourself. From Aurangabad, a day trip will get you to the ashram where your brother died."

After a few pleasantries, including his question about how the Cubs would do this year, I thanked Ron and stood up to shake his hand. "Oh, I almost forgot," he said, resuming his funeral face, "I have your brother's ashes." He handed me a metal can weighing a pound or two, wrapped in green paper, with a sticker of a red Christian cross on it and a white ribbon around it. It looked like a Christmas present, perhaps a container of Scottish shortbread. He presented it to me with two hands, slightly bowing in the Indian manner. I took the can in my hands and held it for a few seconds. I shook it gently and heard something solid clink inside. I felt nauseous and my mind went blank. I said thank you and slipped the can carefully into my pack. Ron was at the door, about to walk me out of the consulate, when I stopped him.

"Oh, there's one other thing," I said. "My brother said that he went to the ashram with a Dutch missionary named Dolf who works in Mumbai. Do you know how I can get hold of him?"

"Yes, I took notes as I talked with Gonda." Ron shuffled through a pile of papers on his desk. "Dolf Rietveld operates with an international group of evangelists who stay in the YMCA. It's easy to find, on YMCA Road not far from here. We can get the Y's phone number on our way out."

That evening I met Dolf for a late supper at the hotel restaurant. The air conditioner blasted away like a jet engine, but after walking around the Mumbai sauna all afternoon it was bliss. I had a strong desire for a beer, but the YMCA was dry. We worked our way through some scrawny chicken legs and several puddles of curried vegetables and lentils while he told me about his work. I had expected a very conservative and fundamentalist evangelist, but Dolf was open-minded and keenly interested in understanding Indian religions. He had gone to Swami Tirtha's ashram in order to see the ritual of burial alive.

"Do you see how the Hindus have unknowingly told the stories of Lazarus and the resurrection of our Lord? They are trying to come to God, and we can reach them if we understand their religious needs. The name of my organization is Christian Missions Outreach. We don't reach out in the same way to Muslims, Hindus, Jains, Sikhs, or other groups. We have to accommodate—is that the English word? We make accommodation for everyone in the Lord's house, but in different rooms. I believe that each religion is trying in its own way to come to Jesus Christ."

I asked Dolf to tell me what happened at the ashram, and how he thought Will had died.

"I met your brother at the Ellora caves. We talked about the mysterious energy of the Hindu carvings. He was impressed by Shiva doing a victory dance over a demon, playing chess with his wife Parvati, and lording it over rival deities Brahma and Vishnu. I myself prefer Vishnu, who has more human incarnations, and whose birthday is celebrated much like Christmas. But your brother was drawn to Shiva, who is often linked to death and destruction. The next day we drove for a few hours to the ashram. Thank goodness we had a chauffeur, because only a madman would try to drive in India. It would be suicide. On the road Will and I talked. He followed a guru in the United States, yes? He was interested in Swami Tirtha, but also suspicious. He said that every saint ends up with an organization that puts its own interests first.

"The ashram is on the river Waghora, not far from the Ajanta caves. In the center of the grounds is a big outdoor meeting space, covered by a high roof but without walls so the breeze flows through. A few houses are scattered about, with a blue dormitory for men, a pink one for women. Vendors, a restaurant, and a bus stop. The river lies down below, with a steep hill on the other bank. We got there in the heat of the day, walked around the place, and sat with others in the shade under a huge banyan tree, waiting for the guru to give *darshan*, that is, to offer his presence as a vision of the divine. We didn't know what to expect.

"It turned out, as we hoped, that because it was Mahasivarati, a special day of Shiva worship, the Swami would be buried that afternoon, a rare occasion. We followed the crowd to a clearing in the woods. There must have been several hundred people standing around. Swami Tirtha was led by two of his devotees to a coffin. He's a strong and vigorous man of about sixty, yet his eyesight is not good. He is strangely still, contained within himself. He didn't say anything at all and seemed hardly aware of the crowd. The swami was intent on an inner world and did not react to anything, not noise, his hands being kissed, or a woman who put herself and her baby in his path. He stopped to gaze at the baby, silently held up a hand to bless her, and then his disciples pulled the woman aside.

"They put Swami Tirtha in a coffin and closed it up. Six strong men lowered it into a hole in the ground and threw dirt on top to bury it. We stood there for a long time, perhaps as much as an hour, and sometimes his followers chanted. Then a leader of the group cried out and they dug him up. Tirtha sat up in the coffin and looked around calmly. The crowd was gasping, shrieking, clapping, and laughing. A tremendous wave of noise and movement erupted after our long wait. The swami walked slowly back to the audience hall and received his followers' adoration. He said little, but he received flowers and sweets as offerings and allowed his feet to be washed. As individuals and families came forward, he blessed them by waving a hand and speaking a word or two. There were other tourists there besides Will and me. I heard a French couple speaking and saw three young men, each with a Canadian flag on his backpack. There was a lot of commotion, with cameras flashing, vendors thrusting souvenirs at us, and the music of tabla drums and harmonium. In India, religion is not just religion, but entertainment, sport, art, politics, and business. Not like the church in Utrecht, where I grew up."

"How did Will react to all this?"

"I don't know what he was thinking. I was completely fascinated by the symbolic resurrection. I wondered whether there was enough air in the coffin to breathe, or a secret tube to the surface, or if the Swami can slow his metabolism. I have no evidence, but I have my doubts that God raised him from the dead. Swami Tirtha spoke into a microphone. He talked about conquering fear and about the meaning of his name. He would guide us so that we, too, would cross over to a place without fear. We would leave behind what keeps us suffering on this side of the river.

"The next thing I knew, Will was on his feet. He spoke loudly and appeared angry. Immediately the crowd became quiet. Will said this is not the way of a guru. A true guru would not display his powers to gain followers. He responds to others' needs and shows them their freedom. He gives them back their will, their power. Your brother said something like that. Yes, and that staging a spectacle and performance to demonstrate your own power is not the way to transform another's life."

Dolf paused and pushed his plate away, frowning. I waited for him to continue, as he worked something out in his mind.

"It was a crazy thing to do," he said thoughtfully. "We are guests in a foreign culture, witnessing a religion we don't understand. Shiva is the god of destruction and death, among many other things—of course you know about the lingam—and this burial ritual is connected to an ancient faith. It isn't a magician's trick, I don't think. But there was something about Swami Tirtha that upset and enraged your brother. Will had his hands in the air in front of his face, trembling as if he were pleading with the Swami. I should have tried to stop him, but I was surprised and it all took place so quickly. The crowd started to yell, 'No! No! Who are you? You don't know!' People shook angry fists at him. Will was yelling amid the din, but it was difficult to hear him. He said, 'You have taken the trust of these people. It is a precious gift.' That's all I could understand. Several men stood up and were about to seize Will, but he turned aside and left the audience room. He was jostled and shoved on his way out, and one woman spat upon him. It was very distressing.

"Swami Tirtha held up his hand to quiet the crowd, and they settled down. He said little in response to Will's outburst, only that he does not impose himself on anyone. Shiva gives him powers that help people. Tirtha said the young man is free to come or go, to follow another guru or no guru. We each find our way to Shiva or Shiva finds us. His words were not profound or moving, but his presence has a strange power, and I saw how he captivates people. I sat there for half an hour or so, watching people give him an offering or ask for his blessing. Once he became angry with someone and said, 'When Shiva is angry, the guru will console. But when the guru is angry, only Shiva can save you.' He seems a gentle man, but another side of him flashed out."

"What about Will?" I asked. "Where was he at this time?"

"The darshan, the divine audience, was still going on, but all this time I was wondering where Will went. I left the hall, looked around, and returned to the car. The driver had not seen him. I waited there and started asking anyone passing by whether he or she had seen my friend, the American with a dark beard. No one knew anything, everyone was at the darshan. I became more and more anxious, and then two young boys came running, saying a dead man is in the river. A bell rang the alarm. The crowd rushed to the river, we discovered the body, then noisy babble, the police, and darkness. It was a long evening before I could go to bed. They put me up at the ashram, and the next day I told the detective what I told you."

"Dolf, what do you think happened to Will?"

The Dutch evangelist scrutinized me carefully. I think he was trying to detect any similarities to Will. He decided something and said emphatically, "I think that he was murdered by followers of Swami Tirtha. He had certainly angered them. The Swami is like a god to them. The way Will died is very strange. There is a mystery about what happened to his shirt. His body looked as if he could have slipped, hit his head, and drowned. It could have been an accident. Perhaps he tried to swim in dangerous rapids, and his head struck a rock as he was swept downstream. But even if he did not try to kill himself, the way he confronted the guru was almost suicidal. I remember what Will said in the car as we drove to the ashram. He said life isn't worth living without religious faith, and that he had been disappointed by his American guru, this Yogi Bhakta. He said it in the past tense, like it was a long time ago and he had learned not to trust so much again. But his feelings rose up suddenly and he became angry with Swami Tirtha. I didn't explain this to the detective, because it is just my intuition, a guess. Will risked his life to stand up in a crowd of religious people and speak his truth that was blasphemy to them. To denounce their leader, this is crazy, don't you think?"

"It does sound that way," I agreed. "From what you say, it isn't something Will could have planned ahead of time. He didn't know what he would see or what Swami Tirtha would say. He impulsively stood up and reacted to something that provoked and angered him. I think the Swami reminded him of his own guru, Yogi Bhakta."

"I think so, too," said Dolf, nodding slowly for a long time. I thanked him, told him that I would let him know if I discovered anything, and caught an auto-rickshaw back to my hotel.

The next day I did some sightseeing in Mumbai and tried to get over jet lag before retracing Will's journey inland. I walked slowly through oppressive humid air, pausing in the hanging gardens on Malabar Hill. I visited the Jain temple, a lovely marble house of worship. Jains are committed to *ahimsa*, nonviolence. To avoid harming any living creature, members of one Jain sect carry a broom to sweep aside insects on their path and wear a mask to strain tiny animals they might breathe or drink. Like the Buddha, the founder of the Jain faith, Mahavira, was a prince who threw away his treasures and nearly starved to death. But Jains know no middle way; they try to attain self-perfection by gradually abandoning the material world and living a life of strict discipline. Jains abhor violence and worldly attachments, yet they are savvy businessmen and the wealthiest, most educated group in India. Well, you can't renounce everything, I thought, we all have to pick and choose. Or we convince ourselves that it's all right to abandon the outward forms of self-denial if we cultivate inner detachment. Then, I thought cynically, we can eat our mango sticky rice with a clear conscience.

Late in the afternoon, I entered the Gandhi Museum, Mani Bhavan, a quiet and serene refuge from the dense, hot, anarchic jumble of streets and arcades. Mahatma Gandhi stayed in this building during his visits to Bombay between 1917 and 1934. He was greatly influenced by the Jain concept of *ahimsa*. Here the great-souled one started the nonviolent movement for Indian independence, using the method of *satyagraha*, truth power. I remembered that Gandhi was assassinated by a Hindu fanatic who objected to his attempts at reconciliation with Muslims. He was shot dead as he was about to address a prayer meeting. What a contrast between these two Hindus, the widely admired saint and a fanatic who murdered a fellow believer who got too friendly with Muslims. I stood staring at Gandhi's spinning wheel, which he began to use here to encourage Indian self-reliance rather than depend on cloth produced in England. The wheel seemed to move, and I mused. Spinning, spinning, my mind and feelings are spinning, too, and I need a nap. I had an image of Will at a spinning wheel. He was wide-eyed, grinning, utterly engrossed in this new skill. A loud gunshot jerked me out of this reverie. Startled, I looked around in alarm. The other museum visitors were perfectly calm. I had imagined the shot. Blinking hard several times, I moved away. Thinking of Gandhi and his assassin, I said to myself, religion brings out the best and worst in human nature. It makes good people better and bad people truly evil. And for ordinary people like most of us, longing for God intensifies both the admirable and the dangerous tendencies within our nature.

Two days later, I arrived at Swami Tirtha's ashram with Detective Sunil Gonda. I had taken the train to Aurangabad, spent a night there, and driven in a police car to the ashram. Gonda was a lean, tough fellow about fifty who looked as if he had been dried in the sun. He seemed to doubt or suspect everything, a reassuring trait in a detective. He checked with our driver that the gas tank was full, the tires properly inflated, and the motor running well. I think that he was a Hindu, though he never referred to his own views of religion. He tried to be scrupulously neutral about religion, fair-mindedly skeptical of every claim based on faith.

Gonda had already gone back and forth several times between Aurangabad district police headquarters and the ashram. I was grateful for a ride to the remote location. We sat together in the back seat and he filled me in on his investigation. Unfortunately, there was no material evidence whatsoever, except for Will's clothing, and no obvious suspects.

"Or else we have too many suspects," he said somberly. "There were approximately four to five hundred people in the audience hall at the time of Mr. George's provocation, and all of them were furious at the insult to their guru. Each one of them had a motive to attack your brother. You Americans do not understand the passions that religion stirs up in Indians."

Swami Tirtha's ashram had a large group of permanent residents, including young men fanatically devoted to him and security people. Gonda commented that recent converts are often eager to prove their commitment, even by sacrificing their lives. He suspected that the killer was from one of these groups.

"Killer?" I interrupted. "So you are pretty certain it was a murder?"

"Please do not quote me, but that's what I think. Why is his shirt missing from the pile of clothes? The blow to the head is on the back, as if he were struck from behind. It could be that he slipped and fell backwards on a slippery rock, or that he hit his head while swimming. But would a man go for a swim in such a state of agitation? It is possible, yet I suspect foul play. I interviewed many people at the ashram, as well as visitors such as Mr. Dolf Rietvelt. Everyone seems to have been at Swami Tirtha's darshan at the time when Mr. George died. They bear witness to each other's presence at the crucial moment. I continue to probe for a weak alibi, evidence of guilt, or conflicting accounts, but I am losing hope. It has now been three weeks since the death and we have no more clues than when we started the investigation."

"What about Swami Tirtha? What's his attitude? Can he help?"

Gonda gave me a wan smile and the Indian head-waggle. "Tirtha is a holy man. He is beyond these mundane matters. He expresses sympathy for the deceased person and his family. He says that no follower of his should harm another person. The Swami is as much of an enigma as Shiva himself. At least we know *he* didn't kill anyone. Five hundred witnesses vouch for where he was at five thirty that afternoon."

"He didn't commit a murder, of course not. But is he covering up a crime or protecting his people from investigation? Do you trust him?"

Gonda sighed deeply. "Trust. So much comes down to this, Mr. George, doesn't it? And there is always room for doubt. I don't think he knows more about the death than you or me. I trust his knowledge of esoteric spiritual matters such as Tantric rituals. I don't trust his knowledge of his followers. The realm of the guru is the spirit. He can hardly take seriously the peculiar motivations of an individual. He points to the unchanging Self beyond personal anxieties and troubles. He inspires his followers to have faith in this ultimate truth. Meanwhile, those of us on the earthly plane must use other methods to find the truths we seek." With his right hand, Gonda reached over to his left side and patted it. I could see a bulge under his jacket where his gun butt poked from its holster.

I nodded, wondering how a gun would help us today. We sat in silence as our driver dodged complacent animals, peasants loaded with sticks or bales, and bicyclists. He accelerated rapidly to pass a slow-moving bus, narrowly missing two old men standing near the edge of the road, and veered back into our lane a few yards from an oncoming truck. A dozen times that morning we cheated death, our own or someone else's, by a matter of inches. The driver was perfectly calm, because all things are the will of Shiva, Vishnu, Allah, or Whoever is in charge.

We pulled into Swami Tirtha's compound shortly before noon. The sun was blazing and the ashram appeared deserted. I heard the distant noise of pots and pans and a low hum of voices, and Gonda said that everyone was in the dining hall. A guard told us that we could eat with the community, and we got in line for chapattis, vegetables, and a chickpea stew. Gonda and I ate in silence, the detective's hooded eyes carefully appraising the people around us. A person feeling guilty might have looked fidgety or moved away, but everyone seemed contented and unaware of us. The crowd was mostly Indian, of all ages, both genders, and, I think, many social groups and castes. A few Western devotees or curiosity-seekers were sprinkled around the tables. We sat idly for a few minutes until a fierce-looking man with a large black mustache came and sat down with us. Gonda introduced him as Ramesh Ghurye, the Swami's chief administrative officer. I had noticed him on the edge of the dining area while we were eating. He was heavy-set, with a stern, military bearing, and carried a clipboard that he consulted frequently. He frowned every few seconds and ashram worker bees scurried to and from him, taking orders and carrying out his commands. Ghurye informed Gonda that he had no new information for him. When he found out that I was the brother of "the unfortunate sufferer," he said he believed that Swami Tirtha would be able to find time for a brief audience with me before his regular late afternoon darshan. I replied that I would appreciate a meeting. Ghurye would find me about four o'clock.

Gonda told me that he wanted to talk to the local police chief and several ashram residents. I waited under a huge banyan tree. Enormous roots cascaded to the ground, the older ones thickening into woody trunks. Nothing grew under the tree, and its shade covered an area as large as my father's church. The word "banyan" means merchant, because the comfortable zone under these trees is where traders have sold their goods for millennia.

Feeling restless, I browsed in a small shop that sold beads, incense, snacks, and religious literature. I bought Maiko a picture of a dance performance with rich costumes and stylized gestures. I looked for something written by Swami Tirtha, but he was not the kind of seer who sets his testimony in print. The closest thing I could find was a collection of his devotees' testimonials about his impact on their lives. The swami was quite a wonder-worker, credited with miraculous healings, longed-for pregnancies, sports victories, lottery winnings, and a resurrection from the dead. The book was printed on coarse paper with ink that smeared if you touched it. The shop sold photographs of Swami Tirtha sitting on a stage as he gave darshan. A black and white picture, dated February 1975, showed a crowd milling around an obscure central object. I could just make out the Swami's profile, sitting in the coffin used for the burial ritual.

It was the Indian version of siesta time, when everyone lies low until the sun's most intense rays relent. Small groups sat on rugs under trees or went in and out of the dormitories. I sat down to meditate under the banyan tree. I had hardly practiced at all since returning from Thailand, and it felt good to shut out the swirl of new sights and become aware of what was going on inside me. I tried to concentrate on my breathing. I didn't have much luck and began to feel drowsy, nodding off several times and awakening with a start. Had I heard another gunshot? I roused myself and realized that, now that I had a break from India's sensory overload, I was angry. Examining what I was incensed about, I constructed quite a list. I was angry with Swami Tirtha because his followers had probably killed my brother. I was angry at India because it was so difficult to do or understand anything there, and I feared that I would never find answers to the questions about Will's death. I felt an ancient resentment of Yogi Bhakta stir, because he stole my brother away from me and left him disillusioned and in despair. Finally, I realized that I was furious with Will. What a damn idiot he was, criticizing a guru in the midst of his followers! He should have known better. What a fool, to go looking for a new idol instead of settling for a guruless way of life! A hot wave flushed my face and chest, and I was sweating profusely. I was angry, finally, at God, for not giving my brother a way to love him. Not a dramatic miracle, just a tiny sign, a little help. I wanted to express all this indignation and ire outwardly, and the only outlet I could think of was Swami Tirtha. Was I going to lose my temper, like Will? Not a good idea.

I imagined getting enraged at the swami, confronting him, and challenging him to prove that he was God's incarnation. Maybe that was what Will had been trying to do: force God to reveal himself. That would be insane, because you can't force a revelation, a vision. You only blind yourself to what might be holy around you when you tell God what to do, where and when He should appear if He wants to get through to you.

I told myself that my outrage was crazy. When Will's frustration and fury erupted, he lost control and good judgment. I tried not to feel dangerous emotions. I was back in a familiar place, where my heart told me one thing and my intellect said something else, and I was left paralyzed, unable either to express my feelings or trust my thoughts. I couldn't feel or think my way to a new place, so I just sat, cooling a little as a hot breeze dried my sweat.

Ramesh Ghurye came to take me to Swami Tirtha, who was sitting in a lounge on a couch piled high with pillows. With us were a young woman who occasionally helped him find the English equivalent of a Marathi or Sanskrit word and a large man in a sleeveless undershirt with folded arms and very big biceps, who must have been a bodyguard. The swami was indeed, as Dolf had described him, both subdued and energetic at once, with a coiled power deep within. He had large glasses that magnified his owlish eyes, so that he seemed to gaze deeply into me, yet his vision was obviously weak and he blinked frequently. In contrast to most Indian sadhus and gurus, he had short gray hair and was clean-shaven. He said nothing yet made himself available as if there was nothing else he wanted but to be with me at that moment. I had expected him to be in a dreamy, otherworldly trance, but he was fully present.

He may have expected me to bow or make the Namaste gesture, but I did not feel like acknowledging his authority. My chest was tight, and I feared that I might shout something, although I didn't know what I would say. He waited a long minute and then said, "I know you loved your brother. I can feel your grief at losing him. He was in great pain when he spoke to me. Now he is at peace."

The anger surged again. Yes, he's at peace, I thought, he's dead, damn it. What are you going to do about it? I sat smoldering for a moment, uncertain what I wanted to say, and finally blurted out, "Did one of your followers kill my brother?"

Swami Tirtha nodded. Was he agreeing? If so, he surprised me, for I expected him to deny that anything evil could come from him or his followers. Speaking slowly and fixing his gaze on me, he said, "I do not know what others may do in my name. The guru is not always understood correctly. The guru dispels darkness and mirrors back the disciple's true nature. The light that shines within each of us. Sometimes the darkness in the disciple is strong and will not dissolve. The disciple wants to destroy his own darkness by attacking an enemy outside him."

"Is that it?" I pressed eagerly for an answer, leaning forward. "Do you know what happened?"

Swami Tirtha looked at me intently. He gathered his thoughts and spoke gravely. "I do not know what happened to your brother. I have many disciples, all kinds of people. I don't accept only good ones, and every one of us is a mixture. Darkness overcame your brother, Mr. George. But light and dark, good and evil, are not what we think, they are what they are, and Shiva is in all things. These are all aspects of the Lord everyone serves, will he, nil he."

I was exasperated but could not think what to say. He was not telling me what I wanted to know, nor was he lying or being evasive, so far as I could tell. He told me something I couldn't understand. There must be wisdom in these words, I said to myself, but it is not a wisdom that I can use right now, damn it. It won't solve a murder case. I had a sudden flashback to my daily interviews with the Thai monk, Ajahn Sumedho. I remembered that he had told me things that seemed vitally important at the time, and now I had forgotten them. This, too, seemed like a moment to remember, and I feared that it would slip away. It was already gone. When I write this down later, I thought, I will invent something good but miss another truth. I stared at Swami Tirtha's feet folded under him, tangled in a knot. I was lost in a tumult of memories and emotions. Then something else surfaced.

"What is the meaning of the burial ritual?" I asked. "That seems to have upset my brother. Are you acting like Christ?"

Swami Tirtha turned to his translator and inquired. "This is resurrection, yes?" She nodded. Tirtha's direct gaze swiveled back to me. "I do not preach resurrection of the body. Not everything in the world matches Christianity, or America, or the ideas you have already. What I do is to survive self-destruction. Jesus was executed, yes? I bury myself, as we humans do. Suicide is an English word for this. I show my followers that they may cross over to another state. On this shore they may leave their weakness, darkness, and fear. These are the causes of self-destruction. We must die here so that we can live there. Words cannot express this truth, but actions can show it. Is this correct, Manali?"

The young woman smiled, bowed to her guru, and said, "Yes, Swami." I observed her closely for the first time. She was a small person of perhaps only twenty or so years, animated and graceful like a dancer, with a radiant beauty that lit up her face when she smiled. I felt that much was going on here that I did not understand. The bodyguard shifted his arms, clutching his hands in front of him, and I noticed a small tattoo of a trident on each huge bicep.

Swami lifted a hand as if to bless me. I did not bow to him, or come forward to be touched. I placed my hands together and gazed right at him.

"Namaste," I mumbled, slightly nodding. "Namaste," said Tirtha, "I honor the God within you. I hope that Shiva will help you to cross over."

I nodded my head as if I understood and went outside. Gonda was waiting for me. He asked whether I wanted to stay for the evening darshan. "No," I said, "I've seen enough of the swami. But I would like to see the place where my brother died."

"Of course, I will take you there. It's about a kilometer away, but the sun is low now, and we can walk without discomfort."

We walked down a sandy road along the river. Rushing water cut deeply into the soil. At the ford it widened out and grew shallow. At this time of year the water was only knee deep, so you could safely wade across. Scattered trees and shrubs edged an open gravel beach on each side of the crossing, the *tirtha*. A cow standing in the water looked up, its horns painted pink and yellow, a garland of flowers around its neck. A family—parents with a boy and girl—had just crossed the ford and were walking away up the path that continued on the other side of the river. Leaning against a tree was a staff one could use to balance when crossing.

Gonda showed me some flat rocks on the edge of the water, just below the ford, where the water deepened again as it poured into a narrower funnel and dropped down to the rapids. "This is where we found your brother's clothes and passport."

I stopped and looked down at the packed, cracking earth with a sprinkling of gravel. A few stones of various sizes lay scattered about the clearing.

"We did not find any blood or evidence of struggle," Gonda continued. "If you stand on this large rock here, you can see the spot where the body was found." He pointed downstream about fifty yards, half a football field. The river swept to the right, and on the left side was a sandy bank.

"I want to see the place, if you don't mind," I requested. I took off my sandals, Gonda removed his shoes and socks, and we rolled up our trousers and waded into the stream. The water was lukewarm but refreshing. The pebbles that were a colorless gray on the dry bank gleamed pink, blue, and green under the flowing water. I stopped in midstream to look more closely. The tug of the current clutched my feet, and they slipped a little on the bottom. In the narrower and deeper channel below, the current would be hard to resist. Beyond the flat rock was a fine swimming hole, just dangerous enough that Will would have loved it. You could launch off the rock and get a thrilling little ride through the rapids, then swim to the side and crawl up the riverbank. A path showed where the young men of a nearby village must have done this. There were boulders in the river, some just below the surface, and it would be possible to hit your head on them. But Will was a strong swimmer, and he knew how to ride a rapid, feet first on your back. I remembered frolicking with him in chilly streams and rivers flowing into Lake Superior, as our parents hovered watchfully. Will would have had to choose to hit his head.

We crossed, branched off to the right from the path, and followed the riverbank to the place where Will's body had washed up. There was no sign that anyone had ever been there before. It was the first time in India that no other people were around me, except for Detective Gonda. I asked if I could be alone for a few minutes and meet him at the car in half an hour.

"Certainly, most understandable, Mr. George. I will leave my instructions with the local police chief and see you at the vehicle soon after six p. m."

I sat down on the gravel at the edge of the river. The sun had dropped behind the trees and the light danced and dodged in the leaves and on the ripples. The river babbled and gurgled as it rushed by. On the other side the water was a deep mahogany color, thick with the dusty Indian soil, while the sunlit part near me was white foam and a lighter tan. Here the damp earth smelled as sweet as a Minnesota garden in May. I looked upstream and watched Gonda cross the ford. A child played in the water there, splashing her mother and laughing. They moved on, and I stared at the crossing, where specks of flashing water glinted, gleamed, blinded.

I saw what happened. Will came here, willingly or not, with or without the other men. He stood at the ford. Someone struck him from behind. They removed his clothes and took his bloody shirt, putting the rest of his things on the flat rock. They carried or floated Will's body down to this curve in the river and left it where it might have washed up. The killers covered any tracks and blood, slipped into the trees, and were not seen again. They vouch for each other and believe they serve God. They are in the ashram today or far away. I will never know.

The river blurred and I found myself weeping silently. "The poor bastard," I whispered. "God damn religious fanatics. Will, too, all of them." I put my hands in the sand under me and felt it run through my fingers. "For what, for what? Nothing is ever good enough for them."

The tears stopped and again I surveyed my surroundings. Will had crossed over at this *tirtha*. He had done it in a most unusual way, traveling fifty yards through rough water, instead of the usual safe passage. I speculated about his state of mind at the very end of his pilgrimage, running through possibilities. Then I quit trying to decipher his soul at the instant it departed. My question was swept away with the current racing to the Indian Ocean.

This story is not a murder mystery, but about a mystery of the spirit. I arose, looked around one last time, and headed back upstream.

Epilogue

SINCE RETURNING FROM INDIA, I've spent more than a year writing and looking for a job. No offers in 1980. Early Christian History is not a jazzy field right now, and hiring focuses on areas like Islam and Asian traditions. It's about time, but I want to teach in my field.

I had an on-campus interview last year at a major university. I was sitting at dinner with the Chair and two other professors, and they got to gossiping about people in their department. After a couple of glasses of wine, the Chair said more than he should have. In describing the tenure process, he mentioned someone who was given the boot the previous year. "Well, what did he expect?" the Chair asked. "He didn't have the commitment necessary."

Professor X contributed evidence of slackness. "Did you know that every summer he goes fishing for two weeks?"

The Chair rolled his eyes. "Fishing! Well, we are well rid of him. When have we ever let someone go who amounted to anything? If you want to make it here, you have to give one hundred percent. There's our new young woman, you guys know who I mean. She spends a lot of time playing with her children. I have nothing against kids, I love my own. But for heaven's sake, hire someone to take care of them. Play with them on Sunday. Don't lose those precious years of productivity."

I wished someone would ask me whether I like fishing so I could say no, I despise it, and tell the saga of Leaper. Although bringing this up myself would sound like brown-nosing, it might be helpful if I could disavow this time-wasting diversion from the life of the mind. Alas, no one inquired.

My advisor, Thompson, also had advice about what I should give up. "Nothing else matters but writing," he said. "You'll have time for fun, girl-friends, or saving the world later. You've had your junket in Thailand, and then this messy family business. Now it's time to get to work and crank out some articles. Turn your dissertation into a book. Tell your girlfriend you will see her when you are too tired to think any more. You are going to have to sacrifice some things if you want to survive in this brutal job market. That is what you want, right?"

"Yes," I said, "I have to prioritize and focus." But inwardly something in me rebelled. These guys mean well and want to help, I thought, but they are unbalanced. I want to make a whole-hearted effort at an academic career. But there is something weird about the old guard telling me the price they paid to get where they are, and calling me to make a similar sacrifice. I'm a reluctant Isaac, agreeing in principle with Abraham's commitment, but not wanting to offer my neck. I draw back from the wood on the altar prepared for me.

My tentativeness and ambivalence may have come through in the job interview; in any case the offer went to someone else. That spring and summer I finished revising my dissertation. Following Thompson's directions, I didn't discuss Buddhism. As an act of heroic revolutionary defiance, I put in one long footnote comparing Buddhist monastic codes with *Benedict's Rule,* and no one complained, though they may have rolled their eyes if they noticed it at all. Thompson approved the dissertation with bland praise, saying, "It's got potential. Chop it up for essays and then rewrite it." When I stopped in to thank Professor Krupat, he said, with a twinkle in his eye, "Congratulations. Now your real education begins. You're on your own from here on. Teaching students will change the way you see everything."

Old Professor Holbrook didn't have much to say; I'm not sure he did more than skim the first and last chapters. He once said that most books could be an essay, and most essays should be a footnote; a dissertation must have been for him a tiresome business, although a necessary evil. A busy man, he gave it his stamp of approval and wished me well, cutting short our visit to head for his next meeting. I gave Professor Premchit a copy of the dissertation, even though he had no official responsibility for it. I told him that I hoped to get a job at a place where I could continue studying Buddhism and perhaps teach it at an introductory level.

"Yes, I very much hope so," he said. "By the way, you told me about your trip to Chiang Mai when you returned. But I forgot to ask you something. Did you ever solve the case of the vanishing self?"

I laughed. "I have to admit, Professor, that it remains as mysterious to me as ever. The case is not closed. My self is a constantly changing notion that I construct or invent. Every now and then I can see this. The next day, even the next minute, whatever I want seems a matter of life and death, and the reality of this desiring self is impossible to doubt or deny. Which perception is true?"

Premchit looked very serious. "Both, I suppose, at different moments."

"Yes," I said, considering. "And then there is the question of other people and their moral claims on me. How can I have compassion for them if they aren't real? I don't know if I'll ever sort this out."

"Still, Mr. George, we carry on, eh?" He raised his eyebrows and now seemed light-hearted.

"Yes, we carry on." I was going to miss Premchit. "Thank you for all you taught me about Buddhism. And for setting up my visit to Chiang Mai to see Buddhism as a living culture."

"It was my pleasure, Mr. George. I think that you will be carrying out Buddha's final deathbed directive to his followers: Work diligently to gain your liberation."

"I will," I said, "and I know I'll need assistance from various places."

I spent the past year revising the dissertation for articles and a possible book, applying for teaching jobs, working as editorial assistant for *The Journal of Religion*, and starting another writing project: this memoir about my brother and the religious questions his life raises for me. I probably won't publish this, at least now. I'll stick it in a drawer, and maybe someone will find it when I'm dead. Or I'll pull it out if I ever get tenure and feel liberated to publish something without footnotes. Something in my own voice—although even in these pages my voice speaks mostly about Will and the people who knew him.

In the spring of 1980 I went to two memorial services for my brother. One was at the Chicago ashram of American Khalsa, as it is now called. Members of the Chicago community shared warm memories of the five years that Will lived there. Susan remembered how he had once stood on his head while doing breath of fire and concentrating on the *chakra* points in order to test whether the kundalini rising could sometimes descend. The experiment was inconclusive. Amritsar said that Will brought a literary sensitivity to the production of the newsletter and "elevated the discourse." Jeff (now Jagesh Singh) recalled how Will had vigorously defended celibacy as a spiritual path, while once joking to the gathered group that if there were any single women who had a different worldview, he was "open to persuasion, or even conversion." About fifty people, including three who had come from the Minneapolis ashram, my parents, and Sophie attended the memorial. The mourners sang lovely Sikh hymns in Punjabi and English, and Jeff read from the Guru Granth Sahib. A brief greeting and message of condolence from Yogi Bhakta was read out loud; it affirmed that Will was "a sincere seeker who never stopped striving for God, which is what it means to be a Sikh."

Shortly after I returned from India, Amritsar gave me Will's possessions, which he had stored in the ashram. This was all he owned in the world after twenty-seven years: a duffel bag of sweatshirts and jeans and a box containing a few books, a file of essays he had written for the newsletter, and two envelopes of photographs. I looked with interest at the books he had hung on to as he cast so much aside: *Catch 22*, *Zorba the Greek*, *The Catcher in the Rye*, a collection of Tolstoy's moral tales, and poetry by Kabir, Rumi, and Walt Whitman. The photos he saved were family scenes of his childhood and recent snapshots of Will on the job in the Chicago office, happy cooks in the ashram kitchen, and a photograph I had sent him, taken by Maiko, of we brothers setting off for a bike ride along Lake Michigan one fine summer day. There were no photographs of him between 1970 and 1976.

The memorial service in Duluth was hard to plan because at first Mom and Dad weren't sure how Christian to make it. They decided that the service was primarily for people in Duluth who had known Will, who were mostly Christians. We sang a couple of hymns Will liked, including "Amazing Grace" and "Onward, Christian Soldiers," with its military imagery and cadence that had appealed to a determined and energetic boy. Dad read from Romans about how nothing can separate us from the love of God in Jesus Christ, "neither death, nor life, nor angels, nor rulers, nor things present, nor things to come, nor powers, nor height, nor depth, nor anything else in all creation." Will's old friends from high school and St. Olaf shared memories, and two guys from his college band played a haunting, slow blues number he had liked and the Beatles tune, "Blackbird." I could imagine Will, too, singing in the dead of night: take these sunken eyes and learn to see. Yes, Will, you were only waiting for this moment to be free.

Mom and Dad constructed a collage of photos of Will. The one that stands out for me shows Will at seven or eight years old, riding a bicycle. He's coming at the photographer in the late winter, and a little dirty snow lies in the grass beside the road. Will is wearing a stocking cap and a parka speckled with mud. He's like a pig in mud, he's that happy. His head is tilted back as he looks up into the sky, and his mouth is wide open as he shrieks with joy. His opened jaw and chubby cheeks push his eyes into slits, so he almost can't see where he's going. He wears winter boots but no gloves, and his hands, clutching the handlebars, look raw in the chilly weather. Will has rushed the biking season because he just can't wait to ride again, to fly through muck, down the road, into tantalizing hints of spring.

In the church assembly room I conversed with neighbors, family friends, Will's school chums, Walt the shoe repairman, and stalwart elderly members of the church. They recalled my brother's free spirit, sense of humor, and love of the big lake. "Yes," I agreed, "he was quite a guy." My parents were subdued and dazed, though grateful for reminiscences to store away in memory.

Although Dad is tough and stoical, I sense that part of him will never get over this loss. There is a void in our lives now where Will was. Dad appears to have aged lately, although he's only fifty-eight; his hair is grayer and thinner. It's a good sign that he took some of the kids in the confirmation class up the shore of Lake Superior to stargaze. The first time they relied on the naked eye and binoculars. Then, to celebrate the thirtieth anniversary of his ordination, the church surprised him with a new telescope.

The day after the memorial service, our family drove up the shore of Superior to Split Rock Light House, near where Will had thrown the old telescope into the lake. Standing at the edge of the cliff, we stood silently for a minute, looking out at the vast expanse of flashing whitecaps. Sophie opened the can I had brought back from India and, with a sweeping arc of her arm, released Will's ashes into the wind.

A few days later, I had a conversation with my mother that helped me get to a new place, or at least see it. Mom and I were sitting in the dining room drinking a cup of tea on a rainy afternoon. I told her that I had been wrestling with my responsibility for Will. So often we were disconnected or estranged. I felt a vague sense of guilt about all that came between us and all the times that I didn't reach out to him while he was in Bhakti Dharma. I especially regretted his last week in Chicago after he told me he was going to India. I had argued with him, told him he was a fool to go, and then hadn't tried to reconnect before he left. I never saw or talked to him again after that last quarrel. I told my mother that I wonder what it means to be my brother's keeper. Did I fail to take care of Will?

Mom gazed out the window and inhaled deeply. "I've thought about this question in relation to my own brother and sister, Peter. So much depends on what you mean by keeping. I was the oldest, too, you know. My instinct was to try to keep them on the path I thought was best for them. And sometimes they didn't want to be kept." She shifted her gaze from the dripping pane to me.

"Do you mean I was trying to control Will?"

"I don't know, Peter. It's something to think about. Keeping a brother is letting go of control without relinquishing concern. To keep your brother, in the right sense, means taking responsibility for him, but not taking it away from him. And the brother you want to keep has to welcome what you have to offer. I think that for a long time Will did not want you in his life. He wanted to find his way by himself. And you didn't know how to keep him in the right way. Maybe now there's a different way to do that. Keep what was best about him alive." She reached over and put her hand on mine. She had tears in her eyes. She didn't need to tell me that she was describing how she was trying to deal with her own grief.

"It's pretty difficult for me to understand Will," I said. "In some ways I feel closer to him than anybody I've ever known. Yet there is so much about him that is utterly different than my own nature. For instance, that he could love a guru so much, be so negative about school, and choose to be celibate. That he could do what he did in India. He eludes me; he escapes my mind's ability to stretch around him. How can I keep him if I don't know what I'm keeping? Who was he, finally?" I felt agitated and exasperated with Will, like so many times before.

"These are matters of the heart as well as questions for the mind, Peter. You have a good way to go to be at peace. But you'll get there, I'm sure you will." She gazed at me with quiet confidence, her faith steady and strong.

The sixties ended in 1968 with the assassinations of Martin Luther King, Jr. and Robert Kennedy, the election of Richard Nixon, and the deepening morass of the Vietnam War. The seventies ended six months ago, in January 1981, when Ronald Reagan took office. During the election campaign I listened to the rhetoric from my ivory tower perch, supposedly disconnected from the real world. I thought about the relevance of my dissertation topic, asceticism and renunciation. It seems to me that Reagan's victory means that the United States rejects any restraint or self-denial. We don't need to worry about conserving energy or changing our way of life, but can go on burning up fossil fuels indefinitely. We don't need to address inequality in our country; or, rather, if we reward the rich, good effects will automatically "trickle down" and benefit everyone. America does not have to work co-operatively with other countries or the United Nations, and instead should assert its unbridled will. We can have our way and feel good about it, too. Self-restraint is for wimps and do-gooders like Jimmy Carter.

Sophie's fiancé, Jonathan, didn't agree with my political rant. Maiko and I were with them in Milwaukee at Thanksgiving right after the election. Jonathan is originally from Pittsburgh, and he works as an ER doctor at a Milwaukee hospital. He and Sophie seem happy together. Except that he must have voted for Reagan, Jonathan is a pretty good guy. He's Jewish and wants to raise his kids in that tradition. That brings up an obvious problem. Sophie told me a little parable that explains what she's going to do.

"Peter, Jonathan passed on a story that one of his patients told him. This guy, who was a fighter pilot in Vietnam, described an amazing naval procedure. Sometimes a fighter plane has something wrong with it. Millions of dollars of military hardware are sitting on the deck of an aircraft carrier. Other planes have to land, pronto. So what do they do? They push the plane into the sea."

"Really? Why don't they just fix it?"

Jonathan reached toward the plate of turkey and forked a few slices. "Sometimes there isn't time. Another plane has to land right away or it will run out of fuel. Or bad weather is moving in fast with a dozen jets in the air. So they dump the one on the flight deck. It's worth a fortune, enough to pay for a new wing on a hospital, but you have to clear the deck. It reminds me of triage in medicine. Every life is valuable but sometimes you can't save them all. So you decide, and one man lives and another dies."

"How does this connect?" I asked. "We were talking about Judaism a minute ago, right?"

Sophie sat back in her chair and put her hand on Jonathan's shoulder. "Do you see the analogy? Christianity is the jet on my aircraft carrier. It's not even broken, and it means a lot to me and always will. On the other hand, I've never really been into the whole incarnation thing. Judaism makes sense to me. I want to marry Jonathan, I want us to have kids, and I'm happy to become Jewish so we are all on the same page religiously. Hey, our kids may even join American Khalsa or the Moonies when they are older, but first they're going to have a bar mitzvah!"

Jonathan laughed and said, "Well, we'll see. I'm pleased that Sophie is willing to give up her original faith so that we can worship together."

"Will it be hard in any way for you, Sophie?" Maiko asked.

"Oh, a little at Christmas and when I'm with Mom and Dad. We'll tell them when we visit them next month. But I'm focusing more on what I'm getting than what I'm giving up. It doesn't feel like a huge sacrifice to me."

That conversation made Maiko and me think a lot about our future. We had lived together for a long time, almost seven years, without tying the knot. We hadn't been able to commit to marriage partly because of our religious differences, and mostly because she wasn't sure she wanted to leave Chicago and its theater opportunities to follow me to "any Podunk place that will give you a job," as she once put it on a grumpy day.

In April 1981 our indecisiveness had to be resolved when I finally got a job at St. Olaf College. It is only a one-year sabbatical replacement position, but it is the sole offer I received. Maybe it will lead to a longer stay. Small town Minnesota is a middle of nowhere, backwoods location compared to some places, but it might not be so bad. From sophisticated Carleton we looked down our noses at the naïve Norwegian bumpkins on the other side of town, so pious, simple, and earnest. It feels strange to be going to the place where Will was a student so unsuccessfully. There must be some students at St. Olaf who are a little like Will, and I might make a difference in their lives.

Of the true believers and deeply committed Christians, I will ask, Can you see the dangers of religion, its dark side? I might also help the skeptics and despisers of religion, as well as the merely indifferent, to see how religious faith can empower and enliven people and give them meaning, purpose, and joy. As for the muddled, ambivalent, indecisive searchers like myself at that age and now, maybe I can give them some knowledge and tools that will help them find their way. It seems like a pretty tame and sheltered life, teaching religion—or rather, about religion—in a bucolic hick town surrounded by cornfields. "Cows, Colleges, and Contentment" is Northfield's motto. But, I tell myself, I'll be helping twenty-year olds to think about what is truly ultimate and worthy of commitment. Who better raises this question than the Desert Fathers and Augustine? I feel incredibly lucky and grateful to be able to teach at all in this miserable job market.

I have a Lutheran taproot, I think, as well as some other roots seeking water. I can appreciate that tradition as well as see its limitations as compared to the Desert Fathers, Buddhism, or new religious movements that seek other ways to worship and serve God. My version of Christian faith discerns God at work in other religions. Will's continued spiritual searching and striving, right up to the day that he died, was a form of worship and service. Whatever his final state of mind and soul, his kundalini energy was rising.

In a few weeks I'll leave this Hyde Park apartment and move to Northfield, and Maiko will come with me. It has been a hard decision for her, because she will leave behind Chicago's theater world. "What will I do in that little cow town?" she asked, once with exasperation and anxiety, and once with quiet thoughtfulness. I hope that she finds work in Minnesota that expresses her creative spirit. Maiko is relinquishing a lot of possibilities here so that we can have a life together. Maybe someday I can do something like that for her, and for us.

We will marry in Cincinnati in early August at her parents' home. The wedding and our lives together will be Buddho-Christic or Christo-Buddhist. The label doesn't matter. I don't know how we'll put the pieces together, but I don't want to give up the wisdom I find in each tradition. I need all the help I can get. For all my interest in renunciation, I'm a both/and guy, not a Kierkegaardian either/or type. Or maybe I'm a both/and and/or either/or person, depending when you ask. That must be why I find renunciation so difficult, so fascinating, so appalling—because I want it all. Clinging and attachment will surely bring *dukkha*, suffering, the Buddhists say. But I cling, I hang on, I want it all.

The other day I was telling Maiko what my mother said about keeping and not keeping a brother. I said that I want to keep alive the qualities in Will that I loved: emotion, spontaneity, religious devotion, humor, energy, will. For many years those characteristics were exiled from me because I thought they belonged to Will. Just as he was alienated from some parts of his own nature that he thought were only mine. We each thought we had to choose between head and heart. We needed an alter ego, a road not taken, as we tried to define an adult identity. That's what siblings do, I think, just like religions. We need an other to be different, and then we may lose part of our soul.

Maiko listened carefully and then questioned this hard-won insight. She said, "Peter, what you say makes a lot of sense. But it makes Will just a walk-on with a bit part in your drama. Isn't it narcissistic to see the meaning of his life as those qualities you want to reclaim in yourself?"

"It's just my angle on his life today, Maiko. Isn't that the way it is when you tell a family story? Will was one of the most vivid and real people I've ever known. I honor and love him for who he was. I also know that all our interactions, quarrels, estrangements, reconciliations, and affirmations of each other expressed how each of us was trying to find our own path. We had to assert some things and deny others from the infinite possibilities that were open to us when we were young. At certain moments we needed each other to define what we didn't want."

My siblings are eerily like and unlike me, and I will continue to think about why Will and Sophie and I have wanted to live in such different ways. A brother or sister thinks the same quirky things are funny as you do and remembers what Mom said about opera: "it gives you permission to sing what sounds too silly to say." For you, a crinkled up nose or that familiar shrug or glance is more expressive than a thousand words of explanation. You splashed and howled in Lake Superior together, sneaked downstairs to open presents on Christmas morning, and if you are lucky you will help each other understand your parents and how to keep them, too. Will remains a riddle for me, an enigma of the spirit. But you don't have to understand someone completely to feel your souls are linked. I keep him in my heart.